It Was That Moment When...

This book is dedicated to the friendship between women.

May we always be there to fix each other's crowns.

Love and light

Portia

"But, I did everything right."

Lexie stepped out of her dark blue BMW and took a deep breath. She prayed for a good Tuesday asking the Divine for grace and mercy. She entered the four-story brick building prepping for a good mood. When the elevator arrived on the 2nd floor, Lexie stepped out and her energy was immediately drained. Each day was unpredictable, each scheduled meeting unnerving. Lexie smoothed her pale pink pencil skirt and turned the knob to the pinewood office door. April's soft round pale face was the first smile she saw.

Lexie was the Southeast Recruiting Manager for Grover and Hudson Computer Group, a computer consulting company that brought in programming contractors for project at major companies. Lexie started off as a recruiter 12 years ago after interning at the company. She loved her job and loved the people she worked with, but the last six months have been a test on her sanity. Lately, her job was to tell people she had come to know over the years that their livelihood was being taken away.

"Good morning," Lexie spoke.

"Good morning," April sang back to her.

"I love the French braid," Lexie complimented on the dark brunette girl's hair.

"Thanks! I just put on coffee and Darren brought in bagels from Panera," April announced.

"That sounds good, sweetie. Thank you." Lexie stepped into her office and threw her things on her desk and pulled up her blinds. She sat down in the high back leather chair behind her desk and started checking voicemails. All was the usual until she got to the very last one.

"Hey, it's me, Ana," spoke the German accent. "Don't make any plans for the morning. I should be at the office by 8:30."

Lexie's stomach dropped. This was an unplanned visit from her manager. She was suspicious. She has known Ana for seven years on both a professional and personal level. Ana landed at Jacksonville International Airport last night and did not call Lexie to let her know she was in town. Instead she left an impersonal voicemail at the office. That couldn't mean anything good.

April knocked on the door and Lexie invited her to come in. "Hey, I poured you a cup of coffee."

"Oh, thank you. Hey, have you talked with any of the bosses this morning?" Lexie asked her.

"No, why?" April answered placing the coffee down on her desk.

"Just wondering. Thanks again for the coffee," Lexie said.

April left closing the door behind her. Lexie began to worry. She decided to scroll through her emails to see if there was any kind of hint as to why Ana was dropping in. She told herself, "I'm making something out of nothing," and began to reply to a few emails.

Mark Giordano was 6'4", dark curly hair, dark olive complexion, green eyes and shaped like a guy who spends six days a week at the gym working out. He was also the Sales Manager at Lexie's office and her on again off again boyfriend. Currently, they were off again. He knocked on her door and then leaned in without waiting for her to say come in. His thick black hair was moussed back making his curls less visible and his eyes were brighter reflecting off of his yellow polo shirt.

"Good morning," Lexie spoke as he smiled at her. "Hey, have you heard any chatter lately?"

"No, not yet. Why? Is something going on?" He asked.

"Ana flew in last night but didn't call me. She left a message on my office phone telling me not to make any plans," Lexie explained.

4

"Another round of layoffs?"

"We can't really afford to lose anymore. They are going to have you recruiting your own contractors in a minute," she teased.

"They don't want me doing that. I know my limits," he smiled. "How's Anton?"

Lexie felt guilty when Mark asked about her son. The two were close in the two years they had been dating. Mark was the only father figure Anton had known since her own father passed. She was the reason they were off again. Mark wasn't giving into her demands for him to move in with her and sell his house. As silly as it sounded when she said it out loud, she was still not budging. "He is fine. He woke up this morning asking about you," she finally answered him.

"Is it okay if I pick him up Saturday? If you don't have plans that is," Mark asked.

"No, I don't. That would be fine. Anton would love to hang out with you."

"Great, I'll let you know what time." Mark, who never fully walked into her office turned his attention to the front door and then back to Lexie. "Ana's here."

Lexie took a deep breath, "Thanks. Showtime."

Mark smiled and opened the door a little wider so she could walk through. Lexie wanted to stand on her tiptoe and kiss him, but she held her composure. Before she could step too far Ana was almost at her office door speaking only briefly to Mark. Her eyes were wide and apprehensive, but Lexie didn't say anything about them. Lexie backed up and Ana walked in putting her laptop case on Lexie's desk and sat down in the chair in front of the dark brown stained oak furniture. Mark nodded and walked out.

"Hi," Lexie hesitates making her way to her own chair.

"Hello, how are you today?" Ana asked.

"Confused. A little worried now that you are here. I'm assuming we are laying someone off today," Lexie suggested.

Ana put her hand on her stomach and spoke slowly. "Yes, we are."

Lexie sat back in her chair and asked, "How many this time?"

"Just one today. I have to fly out this afternoon for two others," Ana replied looking at the floor then towards the wall.

Now Lexie's hand was on her stomach when she asked, "Why?"

Ana's eyes were welling up as she got the courage to answer her. "Lexie, this isn't an easy one because you know I consider you more than just a colleague. I'm here to offer you a severance package."

"Excuse me?" Lexie said leaning forward in her chair.

Ana tried to explain, "They are now slimming management. I am being forced to let you go."

"So, you held on to me long enough to do all your dirty work, then come in here and do the same to me?" Lexie pushed up off her chair and learned over her desk, "Are you kidding me?"

"Lexie, you had to see it coming," Ana started as she made eye contact with her. "You and I have been laying people off and we've watched others get laid off. It's not easy but somehow you had to know that you and I were next."

"It should be easy since you are not the one being laid off," Lexie said her voice going up an octave.

"Not fair Lexie. And I'll have you know I went to bat for you. And when I saw I wasn't wining I fought to get you the best severance package I could. You have to know I did not just roll over on this one," Ana defended herself.

Lexie could smell the alcohol coming through Ana's pores as she was beginning to sweat from being nervous. She knew Ana fought for her, but she was still angry at the messenger. "I really just want to throw your narrow white ass out that window, but I can't. Do you realize what you have just done to me?"

"Yes, Lexie, I do. That is why I fought to get your severance extended from three months to six months. I brought the paperwork for you to sign," Ana told her while unzipping her laptop case.

Lexie sat back in her chair again. "I suppose you are going to walk me out of her as if I'm some common criminal?"

"Lexie, I'm going to treat you like a friend. I'm going to treat you the same as you did the employees you had to give this news to. I'm going to treat you like the friend that you are."

Lexie crossed her arms and pouted. She was more angry than hurt. She felt used. She felt they could have let her go six months ago. "I'm sorry to yell at you, I'm just really pissed about this."

"I understand, and whatever you need you know I'm there," Ana assured her.

Lexie was not feeling consulted by her offer. She was humiliated, furious and confused. "So, what now?"

"I know it's a lot to take in. If you want to head out now, you can come clean your office later or tomorrow. Or, if you like, we can go grab a drink," Ana offered.

"You sound like you are doing me a favor," Lexie snapped then rolled her eyes.

"Lexie, I'm trying to be a friend and do what I can here," Ana said standing up. She had a habit of biting her nails when she needed a cigarette but was not in a place she could smoke. Her hands were beginning to shake as she clenched them. She knew this task would be hard, but was not expecting this kind of an attitude from Lexie. Ana laid a manila envelope on Lexie's desk and picked up her bag. "It's been a pleasure working with you all these years. I wish you the best and my offer still stands. If you need anything at all, let me know. You have my number."

Lexie watched as Ana walked out of her office in tears. For the second time this morning, guilt was over taking her. Richard and Carol Simmons did not raise her to be that kind of person. Lexie was just angry and Ana was a convenient target. Lexie logged off her computer and picked up her purse. As she stepped out of her office Ana was standing at April's desk talking to her. Lexie stopped and hugged her and whispered, "I'm sorry and thank you."

Ana squeezed her back, "You know I'm probably next."

Lexie told both ladies good-bye and walked out of Grover and Hudson Computer Group scared and worried. She took the stairs to get out of the building this time. As she got to her car, she just sat there. Minutes were ticking by when she heard the tap on her window. "They let me go," she told Mark as he looked at her through saddened eyes.

"I know. Everything will be okay. You've been here for 12 years and between the two of us, we know this whole town. You'll have another job in no time."

"I gotta go, Mark. I gotta go. I need to leave from here now," Lexie's eyes got watery and she did not want to cry in front of him.

"I know baby. Call me later, or I'll stop and check on you," he told her putting his hand on hers as she was gripping the steering wheel.

"I will," Lexie half promised.

"I love you," he reminded her.

"I know," she told him and put up her window. Lexie started the car and pulled out of the parking lot. She'd be back the next day to clean out her stuff, but today she felt like the house missed the wicked witch and landed on top of her.

Single sistas, single mothers

It was still early in the evening when Lexie arrived at Friday's. It wasn't very crowded on a Tuesday night, yet it was still too early to count. The usual spot for her and her two closes friends was at the bar. Lexie scanned the room upon arrival just to take in the few people that were there. Her pride still had the best of her and she wondered if anyone could look at her and tell she was unemployed. Her eyes stopped on Brie and Phaedra who were laughing about something, or most likely someone. Probably a man. She loved her girls but felt sorry for any man that crossed their paths. Both were beautiful and played the single game to their advantage. Phaedra better than Brie.

Phaedra was a blend of a Puerto Rican Mother and a mixed African-American and Caucasian father. She was 5'10 ½" and usually wore 3" heels to put her just above six feet. Her complexion was darker like her father's and her hair more wavy than curly hanging just past her shoulders. Her eyes were dark brown and deep set, naturally seductive. She used them to not only be the top sales person at her real estate firm, but also to get whatever she needed. Brie was a Bohemian goddess. She stood 5'5" with coffee brown skin and always smelt like sweet vanilla or jasmine. She wore her hair kinky with big curls that usually sat on top of her head pulled up in a band or loose in an afro. Her smile was always wide and her teeth naturally straight and white. She had kind, curious brown eyes which would tend to get her in trouble. Her talent was attracting men, but she fell short at keeping them. Both women were jeweled in their trophies from men of their past, and scouting for more treasures in their futures.

Lexie stood back and admired them both. She knew she could tell them what happened today without judgment. She snuck up behind them asking in a deep voice, "Can I buy you beautiful women a drink?"

"No thank you, sir. You are a little too skinny for my taste," Phaedra answered looking her up and down.

"Whatever! Great things come in skinny packages," Lexie told her while jumping up on the bar stool next to Brie.

"Yeah, like what? Sounds like sex would feel like you're bouncing on a chopstick," Brie laughed.

"I haven't had a complaint, peanut gallery," Lexie rolled her eyes.

The bartender, Eric, was familiar with the trio and already knew that Lexie wanted a vodka cranberry with a splash of orange. He placed it in front of her before she turned around. Lexie smiled at him and said thank you with a wink.

"Is boss lady still around?" Phaedra asked her.

"No, she flew out this afternoon," Lexie told her.

"That was a quick visit. I thought your company was broke and couldn't afford trips like that anymore," Brie pointed out.

"Well, I guess we were both wrong. Turns out they can afford trips like that, just can't afford to keep my black ass around," Lexie explained.

"Wait, what are you saying?" Brie asked concerned.

"I know you aren't saying what I think you are saying," Phaedra added.

"Yes, ladies. I am now one of the statistics in the news when they report on job losses for the quarter. Ana only flew in to lay me off today. That is why it was a surprise visit," Lexie explained to them.

Both women gasped at the news. Brie spoke up first, "Girl, how could they? You've been there since the beginning of time."

"And that is probably why. Between my salary, commission and my bonus, they are going to save a lot of money not having me on their payroll. She did work out a six month severance which is basically my salary and any bonus I would have had coming my way."

Brie jumped off her bar stool and hugged Lexie. "I'm so sorry. You know this too will pass."

"I know, sweetie. Thank you. But tonight is a night of celebrating and laughing," Lexie said looking at Phaedra who had not said anything yet.

Phaedra held up her glass to offer a toast. "You know, sometimes the Universe has to kick you in the ass to get you to do what you were meant to do. So, here is to finding your meaning, your happiness, your discovery to what the world needs you to do next."

The three clinked glasses and Lexie fought with her tears. It was time for her mental escape from her worry so she downed her drink and ordered another one. The ladies ordered an appetizer and found things to laugh about. They were the only ones sitting at the bar as the restaurant was filling up with families coming in for dinner. Lexie was beginning to feel relaxed after her 4th vodka cranberry. Phaedra made her eat before she was totally inebriated. Lexie picked at the vegetable plate, pouting over a piece of cauliflower when someone sat down next to her.

"Hi," Lexie spoke yelling a little too loud.

"Hello," he smiled at her.

"I'm Lexie," she introduced herself.

"Chris. Nice to meet you," he said shaking her hand. "You don't look like you are enjoying that cauliflower."

"I'm not. My friend is making me eat because I have had too much to drink," Lexie explained.

Chris laughed at her because he did pick up on her slurred vocabulary. "It's a good thing you have friends looking out for you."

"Are you going to sit her for a while, because I wouldn't mind watching you?"

Chris wasn't sure if he should laugh or be frightened. He imagined sober Lexie was probably a great person to talk to. Intoxicated, she might be good for a one nighter, depending on how much she had to drink. At this stage, he was just curious. Brie and Phaedra both leaned over to see who Lexie was talking with.

Chris was wearing a Cheshire cat grin while he was talking with Lexie. He was dressed in a red button down shirt with a checkered purple and gray tie and a gray tweed vest. A black jacket was draped over his chair. He had on dark blue jeans and black ankle boots. He was probably larger than his skeletal frame should have to carry, but he was solid. His beard was shaved close and his mustache was trimmed neat.

What Phaedra could see that the other two could not was that his clothes were not off the rack and he was wearing a $10,000 watch on his left arm. She was assuming pro football player because of his size. Brie though he was attractive and wanted to know more about him. Never before had all three of them showed interest in the same guy.

"Good evening," Chris spoke as the two were peering in his direction.

"This is Chris," Lexie introduced. "He is going to have a drink with us."

"Well, I was just getting my food to go," he told her.

"No, no, stay," Brie suggested.

Chris smiled as he onced over Brie's curvy frame in her black dress slacks and emerald green, satin blouse. She was cute and seemed innocent, but he knew better. He imagined she was the good girl of the group. Phaedra looked but didn't speak until he did. Chris couldn't read her as well as he did the other two, but Phaedra's first question was, "What do you do for a living?" turned him off.

Chris took a minute to respond answering her, "I'm a teacher. Physics to be exact."

Phaedra curled her lip because she knew he was lying and went back to her drink. Chris laughed then Brie spoke up, "I like science."

You probably can't spell science," Lexie said her words slurring even worse now.

"I think you are at your limit," Brie huffed pulling the drink out of Lexie's hand.

"No, not yet. Just two more," Lexie begged.

"Sorry," Brie apologized to Chris. "She's had a bad day. She is usually a very nice person."

"Are you going to need help getting her to the car?" He offered.

"We might. Dead weight you know," Brie smiled now standing behind Lexie's chair. She was close enough now to see the few gray hairs coming through his beard. She guessed his age to be late 30's early 40's.

Chris realized the two had locked into a staring contest. He smiled and picked up his water to distract himself. The bar tender had laid his food on the counter in front of him. Chris dug out his credit card and passed it to Eric.

"Brielle Jackson," she finally introduced herself locking eyes again.

"Christopher Hollingsworth," he told her.

"Wow, you guys used full names. I'm Alexia Felecia Simmons," Lexie jumped in.

"No, you are drunk ass Lexie and it is time for you to go home," Phaedra said as she waved goodbye to the guy she was talking to.

"I'm not drunk. I'm happy," Lexie answered sliding slowly off the bar stool. Chris reached out to help her down. Lexie smiled and said thank you to him.

Brie's hair rose on her back as she quickly asked, "Should we call Mark?"

"No, let's not call Mark. We have a Christopher. We don't need a Mark when we have a Christopher," Lexie told her irritated.

"Yeah, but, you might want a Mark when you wake up in the morning with a vodka headache. A Christopher won't be there in the morning," Phaedra advised.

"No Mark!" Lexie demanded.

"We are not usually a group of circus clowns. She is usually the designated driver for us all," Phaedra explained.

"Yes, I know. She's having a bad day," Chris replied with a smile.

"She was laid off today after 12 years with her company," Phaedra further explained.

"Don't tell him that. He'll think I'm broke. I'm not broke. I don't need a man to buy me anything," Lexie protested.

"Lexie, at this moment in time I want you to stop talking. If you open your mouth again, I'm going to shove a napkin into it. Okay?" Phaedra promised her.

Lexie put her index finger to her lip and went, "shhhhhhh," spitting on Phaedra and then laughing.

Chris passed his dinner to Brie and asked her to hold it while he guided Lexie out. He truly wanted to throw her over his shoulders like a sack of potatoes, but that would have been undignified. He walked slowly behind her as she walked with her hand over her mouth fearing the consequences if she said another word. Chris ignored the stares and found the whole thing entertaining. Not what he was expecting when dropping in to grab a quick bite.

Phaedra stayed to settle their tab but Eric informed her Chris had taken care of the bill. Phaedra smiled and told him she would see him next time and added a $50 tip. Phaedra headed for the front door laughing at her drunk friend. In the four years she has known her, this was only the second time Lexie was like this. When she stepped out, Brie was trying to find Lexie's car. Brie did not want to walk them to her car because she did not want Chris to see she had car seats. She feared he would not be interested in a single woman with kids. Phaedra asked what the problem was and Brie explained she did not know where Lexie parked. Phaedra knew Brie well enough to know what she was thinking and gave the woman a smirk. Brie responded with wide eyes which meant don't you dare.

"Ladies, would you like me to just put her in my car and drive her home?" Chris asked them.

"No, stranger danger," Phaedra told him. "I'll drive her home. Wait right here while I pull around."

Chris laughed but indicated that skinny was a handful.

"Good thing you've got big hands," Phaedra smiled and walked away.

"We really appreciate your kindness, Chris. Do you come here often?" Brie asked.

"Not too often. I saw a commercial and thought that I would grab some dinner here tonight before I headed home," he said.

"So, are you coming back? Cause we are coming back. Here, put your number in my phone," Lexie said passing her phone to Chris.

Chris took the phone from her and entered his number. Brie felt a little jealous. "Call me next time you guys come out. It would be interesting to come hang with you."

"We will," Lexie promised with a big smile on her face.

Phaedra pulled up in her silver 2005 Thunderbird. Chris opened the door and helped Lexie in and then turned to ask, "Where are you going to sit Brie?"

Phaedra yelled from her driver's seat, "Brie drove her own car."

Brie cringed and leaned down to give Phaedra an evil look. "Call me when you get home," she said through gritted teeth. Brie turned her attention back to Chris. "The three of us met here. I parked somewhere yonder."

Phaedra yelled back, "I will. Can't wait to talk."

Brie passed Chris his food and told him thank you again. She turned to walk away feeling defeated.

Chris offered, "May I walk you to your car?"

"No, you don't have to," she declined. "You've done so much for us already,"

Chris smiled at her and said, "Sorry I was being polite posing it as a question. You see, my father reared me to not allow a woman to walk to a car by herself, especially at night. I hope you don't mind that I'm going to do it anyways."

"Well, okay then," she said hesitantly happy.

Chris offered his arm and walked with Brie. He knew she didn't want him to and was curious as to why. "I think we parked in the same area."

"I suppose the last thing you expected was to run into three crazy females when all you were trying to do was pick up something to eat," Brie said trying to keep a conversation going with him.

"It made my day more interesting. I am glad I met you all," he told her.

"Where do you teach?" She asked stopping short of her Pontiac G6.

17

"University of North Florida," he answered.

"Oh, you are a professor. I was thinking like middle or high school physics. You are really smart than."

Chris just smiled because he never tells women he just met that he is a professor. There was something about Brie that made him comfortable talking with her. Brie realized that she couldn't continue to stall him. She pulled out her keys and Chris reached for them taking the keys out of her hand. He unlocked the door for her and opened it. Brie slid in wishing her interior light didn't work.

"Boys or girls?" he asked noticing the car seats in the back.

"Two girls, one boy," she sighed.

"I'll see you next time?" he asked.

"Yes, I look forward to it," she said hoping.

Chris closed her door and waved goodbye to Brie. There was something about him that made her want a relationship. As she pulled out, she saw Chris get into his car. It was a candy apple red Alpha Romeo 4c. She knew instantly that he was not a guy with kids and wondered if his question was to see what he would be getting into.

"Damn! I hope I didn't blow this one," she told herself as they both pulled onto Southside Blvd. "Not this time. I don't care. I'll take them both down. Christopher Hollingsworth is mine. Three kids and all. I can always make new friends."

The day after a few too many drinks

The morning had come and the night's mischief were still wreaking havoc on Lexie. Phaedra had walked her up the stairs and helped her out of her clothes and tucked her in bed. That much Lexie remembered. How she ended up on the floor was a mystery. Lexie pushed herself up and slowly walked to her bathroom. She sat for a moment after she peed. The night was one bad dream after another. It hit her. She was unemployed. No matter how she became that way, she was unemployed.

Lexie slumped over her legs and began to cry. She slid down to the floor and lay on the rug. She was scared. The unknown made her anxious. Lexie heard her cell phone ringing, but had no idea where it was. She forced herself up and washed her hands and face. The phone rang a second time. She knew it was either her mother, Mark or one of her friends since they were calling back. She had to pull herself together because she knew whichever one it was would show up on her doorstep if she didn't answer or call them back.

Lexie walked out and found the phone on her nightstand. She smiled knowing Phaedra thought to leave it in a convenient spot. Lexie checked her call log to see it was Mark. He had left her a voice mail both times. Lexie took a deep breath then held it for a moment. Next, Lexie wondered who would find her body if she decided to keep holding her breath. Who would be at the funeral? Would they all be mad at her? She slowly exhaled through her mouth. There was nothing left to distract her, so she called Mark.

"Hey, how are you this morning?" He asked with concern.

"I'm okay. Hangover from hell," she told him.

"So, did drinking help anything?"

"It did. For a night, I didn't have to think about my life sucks," Lexie answered sarcastically.

"Babe, it doesn't suck. It's a setback. We will get through it," Mark started.

"Honey, I know. Don't go getting serious on me. We had fun last night and I drank too much. Phaedra fussed at me for it and then drove me home. And as always, Brie was my little cheerleader all night," Lexie explained.

"Okay, I'm sorry. Well, just to let you know, everyone here is on pins and needles. Even Carl is worried," Mark told her talking about his manager. "When are you heading this way?"

"Tell April I should be there in an hour. I just need to shower and get dressed," she said. Mark kept talking and Lexie tuned him out. Nothing he was saying was making her feel better. "Hey, it's Phaedra on the other line. Let me take it and I'll see you in about an hour."

"You didn't answer my question," he told her.

"Oh, I'm sorry, yes," she said having no idea what she just agreed to.

"Okay, great. We'll talk when you get here. Love you," Mark said with excitement.

Lexie clicked over to catch Phaedra before voicemail. "Hey, what's up?"

"Surprised you are," Phaedra laughed. "How are you feeling? Being positive I hope."

"I guess. I have to go clean out my office today so my positive meter is a little more to the left. Maybe tomorrow," Lexie explained.

"Most companies don't allow you to clean your office the next day, so that is something to be grateful about," Phaedra encouraged her.

"Okay, sunshine," she replied rolling her eyes.

"Look bitch, I'm trying to cheer your drunk ass up. Don't make me write you off," Phaedra told her.

"Okay, okay," Lexie pleaded. "I will be positive. So, was I horrible last night?"

Phaedra started with a slight chuckle. "Girl, you were a hot mess. A complete, but handsome, stranger had to carry you out. I think you tried to take him home with you."

"I remember him. Christopher, the science teacher. I did get his number."

"You go girl. But don't count on anything. Brie was right there reminding you about Mark. I think she liked him also," Phaedra told her.

"Brie will be alright. Speaking of Mark, I gotta go. I told him I'd be at the office in an hour and I still need to shower. I'm nervous about the looks I'll get or what people might say," she confessed.

"And when did we start being concerned about what others think of us. You were laid off Lexie. They know that is going on throughout the company."

"I started being concerned when I fell off the same social status as them," Lexie answered.

"Lexie, I hear what you are saying. Just hear me for a minute. That doesn't make anyone better than you. You are still Lexie and you will survive this because you have all of us in your corner."

"Have you seen the news?" Lexie shouted. "People are losing everything they own and moving in with their parents. Can you imagine if I had to move in with my mother?"

"Calm the hell down. You are not there. You've been smart with your money and you have connections in this city. Come on Lexie, drop the negative hag off your back." Phaedra fussed.

"Ugh! I can't deal with this right now," she continued to yell.

Phaedra knew it was time to bow out. "Call me later. After you leave the office."

"Phae, I'm sorry," Lexie started before she realized that Phaedra had disconnected.

Lexie knew Phaedra was trying to get her to see the bright side. However, she was not ready to deal with the situation. She was blocking it and ready to fight anyone that tried to make her. As far as she was concerned, the company was the bad guy. She felt Ana should have fought harder. Lexie was angry. She told herself over and over that she did everything right. This was not fair. She didn't feel this ever should have happened to her.

"Hey, Mom. I'm just calling to check on my baby boy," Lexie greeted when her mother answered her phone.

"He's fine. I dropped him off at school. I take it you got drunk last night," Carol inquired.

"I just had a couple of drinks with friends then came home and cried. I'm heading to the office to clean off my desk. Can I swing by and pick up Anton's stuff after that?"

"Why don't you come after school? He and I were going to bake cookies. The two of you can join me for dinner if you don't have plans," her mother suggested.

"No, I don't have plans. That would be nice," Lexie agreed.

"I'll see you then. And by the way, have you called and told your sister?"

"No, I haven't. I'll call her later," Lexie said and disconnected the call.

Roni, Lexie's older sister, was a successful attorney living in Miami, Florida. She felt as if grew up in her sister's shadow competing for her mother's attention. She couldn't worry about that right now. Sitting in the parking lot of her, Lexie needed to prepare herself to walk in the office, pack her boxes and officially be unemployed. Thinking about Roni would have to wait.

"I'm so glad to see you," April greeted when Lexie walked through the door. "I worried about you all night. How are you coping?"

"I'm okay," Lexie said looking around at everyone who seemed to be moving at a slow pace. "I hear the foundation is shaking a little more around here."

The two headed for Lexie's office while talking. Mark peeped in to wave and let her know he was stuck on a call. Lexie and April started to pack her things into the two boxes she had.

"I'm sure Mark told you the sales manager in Atlanta and in Charlotte were laid off on his team. Mark is trying not to look worried, but he is despite being number one in the region."

Lexie wasn't interested in the conversation, so she attempted to change it. "Where is Gina? Is she out on site today?"

April's eyes saddened, "No, she was also laid off yesterday. They told her they no longer needed HR managers in each office. Just three for the entire region."

"Are you serious?" Lexie asked surprised. She had hired Gina seven years prior as a contractor and Gina had just transitioned into the HR role three years ago. Lexie felt guilty.

The two finished getting all her stuff together. A few others had come in to say goodbye and wish Lexie well. Lexie hugged each one and wished them the same. Mark tapped on the door and walked in so April politely excused herself giving them their privacy.

"Hey," he said.

"Hey yourself," she smiled stepping closer to him. "What's up?"

"Tension," Mark joked. "Carl sends his love."

Lexie tipped up on her toes and kissed Mark. It had been several weeks, and she was missing him. He squeezed her lightly in his arms. "Thank you," she whispered.

Mark didn't want to let her go but he had to. "Now for news you don't want to hear. Ana on line three for you."

Lexie sighed heavily and dropped her head, "Do I have to take it?"

"If you want her to authorize the paperwork for your severance. Her words, not mine."

"Don't leave yet," Lexie asked him as she walked over to pick up the phone. "Why didn't you just call my cell?"

"I did, you didn't answer. I told you I'm not your enemy," Ana explained.

"I just don't understand why me. I did everything right," Lexie begged.

Ana empathized with Lexie. "It's not just you. Think about all the great people we laid off. Did you forget?"

"Of course not. I cried with most of them," she said of the reminder.

"Our whole industry is failing. There is no place to negotiate a new position. But that is not what I called you for. I just wanted you to know I did get you everything I promised with the exception of them waiving the non-contempt. It has to be for 30 days. But I've signed all the paperwork and it's been sent off."

"That's fine, my severance will hold me. And again, sorry I took it out on you. I hope we are still friends," Lexie said.

"Don't worry about it. I would have been the same way. And when it's my turn, I'll call you so you can cry with me. Don't forget, call me if you need anything at all. Anything!"

"I promise. Good luck, Ana," Lexie told her and then hung up.

She turned back to Mark and he grabbed her in his arms again. "You'll be okay. Remember, you promised you'd let me take care of you."

Lexie didn't say anything. She just kept her head on his chest. Being taken care of was not a comfortable position for her. Silence was safe for her right now. Mark held her until she was ready to take the boxes downstairs closing this chapter of her life.

Now What

The sun rose and Lexie had fallen asleep in her home's office chair. Anton shook her gently awake. On her desk was the empty bottle of sweet wine she had drank the night before. She got up following Anton to the living room and turned on the TV. She told him to give her a minute so she could wash her face and brush her teeth.

Lexie looked in the mirror and realized two nights of excessive drinking had taken a toll on her face. Darkness was developing under her eyes and she was sagging in her cheeks. Lexie tried to wash it away, but it wasn't working. She decided at that moment she would not be leaving the house today.

Lexie came down the stairs and fixed Anton some eggs and toast. She made him turn off the TV and come sit at the table with her to eat. She sipped on her coffee and began to tell him about not having a job anymore. Anton sat back in his chair kicking both of his feet and twirling his favorite curl over his right ear.

"Mommy," the five year old started, "will this be our normal life now?"

"No honey, Mommy will find another job. Don't you worry," she assured him.

"I mean, will you be here to fix me breakfast in the morning and I won't have to go to school?" He clarified.

"Oh, crap!" Lexie jumped to her feet. "You are supposed to be in school."

"But I want to be laid off too. No more school," Anton whined.

"Anton, go get dressed. You are so late," Lexie rushed him out of the kitchen and up to his room. She called the school and explained to the secretary, Ms. Robinson, that she wasn't feeling well but would get Anton to school soon.

Anton's lack of enthusiasm showed as he took a break between each button he did on his shirt. He had already missed an hour of school and it would take her 20 minutes to get there. Summer was only a couple months away, and the kindergartner was ready for it to be over. He was finally dressed, and Lexie combed his hair. Anton had Lexie's brown complexion, but his Mexican father's big curly hair.

"Come on you. We gotta go," Lexie fussed. She looked him up and down one last time to make sure he was neat.

"I already put on lotion and brushed my teeth," he announced anticipating the questions.

"Good job," she said kissing his forehead. "Grab your backpack and head for the car."

Lexie went looking for her purse and keys and pulled her relaxed hair back into a ponytail. Anton was patiently waiting at the driver's side back door as she walked into the garage. She pulled out into traffic and explained to him that she overslept and apologized for not getting him to school on time. She promised she would be super mommy again by the time he got home from school.

Lexie got Anton dropped off and went to find a drive-thru since her breakfast was cut short. She felt guilty for the morning and thought about the night before. That evening after dinner with her mother and before the bottle of wine, Lexie finally picked up the phone to call her big sister. It was two in the morning when she got the courage to talk with Roni. As girls they were close, but as they got older, they both pulled away. Their father's death made them even more distant. They talked at least once a week, but Lexie always felt like it was a lecture instead of just catching up with one another.

Lexie didn't want to say the words again, but deep down she did want her sister's advice, so she dialed her number. "Hey, did I wake you?"

"What else would I be doing at 2 a.m.?" Roni asked her perturbed.

"I could think of a few things," Lexie said trying to make her smile so she would be nice.

"Well, now you know I was not doing anything on your list. I was asleep," she said matter-factly.

Lexie took that queue to mean that the lawyer in Roni wanted her to get to the point and get to it quickly. "I lost my job. The layoff finally caught me also. I was offered a severance package."

"I know, Mom told me. The real question is why you waited until now to tell me?"

"Got tired of saying the words. So, why did Mom keep insisting that I call and tell you if she already did? She kept going on and on about you need to talk to your sister." Lexie told her.

"That you will have to ask your mother. However, my feelings are hurt if I'm the last person you chose to tell." Roni said while sitting up in bed since this conversation was still going.

"I guess I was more nervous telling you than anyone else. I didn't know if I'd be met with criticism or sisterly love," she explained.

"Wow, so you hurt my feelings twice. Not only did you make me last on your list, but you automatically assumed I was going to criticize you instead of showing you empathy." Roni said shaking her head. "Are you okay?"

"Yes, I am. Thank you for asking. And come on Roni, you know sometimes you can be harsh."

"I was not aware of that. And you were laid off, not fired. It's not as if you had any control of it. The real question is what are you going to do now? What plans have you made?"

"Just to call everyone I know and see what is out there," Lexie explained.

"Tell me what you need," Roni responded.

"A job!" Lexie laughed.

"Okay," Roni answered more serious than she did before. "McDonalds and Burger King have great management training. I'm sure you can apply there."

Lexie shook her head feeling the headache coming on strong. "A REAL job."

"Those are real jobs. They get real pay checks that can be deposited into your bank account and have real benefits so you can go to the doctor."

"I can't pay my mortgage with what they pay," Lexie emphasized.

"Then we are back to my original question. What do you need, Lexie?"

Lexie sighed wishing she hadn't called her sister. She wanted to scream, you are not the boss of me, but they weren't teenagers any more. "I need a job in my career field so I can continue to pay my bills and support my lifestyle."

"So, what you are saying is that you don't have any kind of plan," Roni pointed out.

"I do have a plan. I have people in my network I can call. Roni, you have to understand that everyone is downsizing now," Lexie said defending herself.

"That is not a plan Lexie. That's a wish minus a prayer. You went out the night before and got drunk, today you packed your office and then you came home. Now it's time to sit down and put a strategic plan in order. That means you must set some achievable goals. Something that you will be able to measure and a schedule to make yourself accountable. And lay off the alcohol. It's not helping."

"Okay, okay," Lexie interrupted. "I hear you! I need a real plan. I need it now. I got it."

"Then call me tomorrow, before the sun sets, and let's talk about what you've come up with." Roni told her in her big sister voice.

"You don't have to hold my hand through this process you know."

"I don't, but I wouldn't be me if I didn't. You can quit pouting whenever you like."

"Fine," Lexie said rolling her eyes. "Go back to sleep. I'll talk with you later."

"Before the sun sets, please."

"Before sunset. I got it." Lexie laughed and then the two hung up. When she was sure the lines were disconnected, she mumbled, "control freak!".

After hanging up, Lexie's temples were throbbing. She wanted to be overwhelmed, but she knew it would be a mistake. Anton was asleep and Nora Jones was playing on her computer. Her glass of Moscato was still slightly chilled. That's what was going right. That was all she would think about for the moment. Those three things were a safe haven.

Now as the sun rose it was time to concentrate on the other stuff. "I gotta come up with a plan. No, no, a strategic plan," she joked out loud. "I hear you big sis. I honestly do. I can't just put my feet up and hope something happens."

With all joking aside, Lexie didn't know where to begin after step one, update resume. The market was still saturated with the unemployed. She wasn't sure who in her network to call first. She only knew what she had seen on the news. It wasn't good and she was nervous.

"This is too much thinking before a full cup of coffee," she told herself. Lexie had ordered a large coffee and a bagel. She got in her car and turned her cell phone off. She knew her friends and Mark would be calling her. For the morning, she wanted peace and quiet to think. She sat outside the café in the parking lot trying not to worry but to just think what she needed.

Brielle Jackson

Brie had gotten to work early that morning. After what happened to Lexie, she figured she should work a little harder. Brie never wanted to be in that situation again. She had already been laid off three times so far. Brie didn't have the money Lexie had either. She lived paycheck to paycheck and relied on her tax refund at the beginning of the year to pay off bills and take a mini family vacations.

Brie was working as an office administrator for a marketing firm. Business had slowed down but so far everyone was still there. The thought of going back to school again crossed her mind but it seemed too hard a task with three kids ranging from four to 11 and a full-time job. However, her truth was that everyone she knew made way more money than she did. She was not able to pick up the tab and everyone seemed to remind her of that when they went out. She had to do something. Her salary really was not enough. Brie was lost on how to change her situation. So instead, she came in early and worked a little harder at being the best office administrator she could be for Stowett Marketing and Associates. She was doing the job of three people and did any extra they sent her way. Brie was grateful even if there was not a thank you.

When she was at home, she managed her house and did everything she could to make her kids not feel like they were born into failure. Stereotyping had a way of making you feel bad about yourself. Brie carried the labels of single mother, three kids with three different men and food stamp recipient. It always made her feel worse when she met a guy she really liked and she felt she had to explain her story. It was like her kids were nothing more than proof of the men that didn't think she was worth sticking around for. Now she worried that if Chris knew her story, would he be the same way.

Brie idolized the lyrics of Beyonce's songs and tried to be independent and rule her world. Most men stayed around until the sex got boring. In her mind, she used them for the money and they used her for sex. She wanted more. This life was not really surviving. It was more like a slow death. Some days she was ready for it to be over. Other days she'd handle what was dealt.

Lexie and Brie met at a Business Women of Jacksonville meeting three years ago. Brie had been there to assist one of the sales people in her office who had been scheduled to do a presentation. Brie was passing out pamphlets when Lexie stopped her to talk. At the time, the two had exchanged numbers. It wasn't long before the trio was formed and the competition for attention developed between Brie and Phaedra. Brie always knew that Phaedra only tolerated her presence but didn't allow it to get to her. In Brie's mind, it was just pure jealousy. Phaedra was never known to be one that played well with others. To accept her, Phaedra labeled her the ugly girl in the group. Every group had to have an ugly girl she told her. Brie laughed it off and celebrated any time she got a guy's attention that Phaedra wanted.

All the things that made Brie who she was, Phaedra criticized. But that is what made Phaedra who she was and Brie learned to live with it. Phaedra was not her first critic and she would not be her last. Lexie was the anchor in the middle. They drank, they talked about the kids, they talked about the latest man in their beds. They were friends despite what Phaedra felt and Brie loved that. She just hated that she had no way to help Lexie except to be there for her.

Phaedra Escobar

Phaedra got into her office that morning with only two appointments on her calendar. Her third appointment that day would be with RJ. After he detailed her car, then he would detail her. RJ worked for himself since he was 16. Business had finally started to grow and he had enough money to stop with the mobile detail business and buy his own car wash and hire a few people. Phaedra had known him for a year now after bringing her Thunderbird to get cleaned to drive it to a party. She only brought out the platinum silver Thunderbird for special occasions and when she felt like showing off. She watched the care RJ took with the car and hoped he was the same when making love to a woman. She hesitated back then because he was 24 at the time and the age difference made her worry.

She quickly changed her mind when she saw how ripped he was in all the right places. His legs were strong, his quads were all muscle. No fat anywhere. He had a light brown complexion with dark brown eyes. His shoulder length dread locks were Phaedra's favorite thing to hold onto during sex. Those were RJ's physical aspects. The only thing that school taught RJ was how to count a dollar. Then he learned the more dollars you had, the better off you were. Phaedra always tried to push him to go back and get his GED. He insisted he was doing fine without it. His street smarts were getting him further in business then any piece of paper would have.

Phaedra loved RJ, but he was just a temporary fix in between her real goal. George Austin, Mr. CEO and Mr. Multimillionaire. She wasn't holding her breath waiting for him to one day leave his wife and kids for her, but it was a thought that sat in the very back of her mind. They had been dating for three years now. George was selling a dream and Phaedra was in the market to purchase. Phaedra peeped his bank account statement, by no legal means of course, and has been his mistress ever since. He bought her whatever she asked for, paid the mortgage on her house and set up a bank account in her name. Being the other woman and still having the freedom to "date" whomever she wanted was just the life Phaedra wanted.

Phaedra wasn't blind to the fact that business was slowing up and many people were losing their jobs. She, however, was still selling houses. The trend would eventually lead to less qualifying buyers which lead to fewer clients. That would eventually lead to her selling even less which meant less money. Like Lexie, she had plenty in savings to live off of, but did not want it to come to that. Phaedra was a strong believer in the power of the Universe. She wished and it commanded. She respected the power of money and her religion was the Law of Attraction. When others were suffering, she was succeeding. If the clients weren't there, she was confident the money would still show up. Phaedra had been in real estate for 10 years now and was clearing a six figure salary. She saved most and invested some. She spent other people's money on her wants. She lived in a modest house and knew that the market would always fluctuate.

Now she was at her office trying to figure out how to help Lexie. Lexie had Mark, he would offer financial help, but she knew her friend well enough to know that she would turn it down. As far as Phaedra was concerned, Lexie took that independent mess too serious. Then Phaedra though of one of her clients who did the same kind of work as Lexie. She might not take money, but she knew Lexie would not mind working for what she is given.

"Michelle," Phaedra called out to the receptionist in the lobby.

"Yeah?" She answered walking into Phaedra's office.

"Remember the guy that bought the house over by the Jewish Community Center, can't remember the street, but his name was Mark Sperry, Spurrie, Spa-something?" Phaedra asked snapping her fingers as if that would help her recall the memory better.

"Park Sperry!" Michelle called out. "I remember asking if Park was a family name."

"Yes!" Phaedra said turning to her computer to look him up. "Wasn't he some kind of head hunter?"

Michelle looked puzzled at the term. "He was a recruiter of some kind."

Phaedra smiled. "Thanks. I wanted to give him a call about my friend Lexie."

"How is she doing? Poor thing losing her job like that," Michelle said with sympathy.

"She will be fine. She's resilient."

"I'm glad," Michele said then turned around and headed back to her desk.

Phaedra looked up Park Sperry in her client list and emailed him about lunch. She was surprised to get such a quick response from him. But there his reply was. A definite OK and 12:30 would be better. She responded with her own definite OK. This was good Karma. She would do this for Lexie. Her good deed to the Universe.

Back to Friday's

"It's Friday night, you know what the means?" Brie asked Lexie.

"Fridays!" Lexie screamed into the phone. "What time are you getting off tonight?"

"Girl, I will be done by 4:30, shutting it down by 5 o'clock. You should see my happy butt by 5:30."

"Well, it sounds like a date, Momma," Lexie said laughing at Brie running down her schedule for her. "What about the kiddos?"

"Already taken care of. I have spoken with the babysitter. She's got me covered," Brie explained. "Hey, why don't you call Chris and invite him to meet us there?"

"I will call him as soon as I hang up with you. He said he would come if I let him know next time we go up there." Lexie told her.

"The more the merrier," Brie said smiling through her teeth. "So, how is the job hunting going?"

Lexie sighed, she was sick of that question. "It's going, Brie. It's going. So, I will see you tonight. Looking forward to a fun evening, but this time I'm going to stay sober."

Brie felt Lexie ice up after the question even through the phone. She thought by now Lexie would have leveled out, but no. It has only been a week and a half, and Lexie was still easily irritated. Brie was learning to tread lightly with her when it came to the topic.

"I'll hold you that," Brie promised.

Brie still found herself coming in early. She still feared being in Lexie's predicament. She had no one but Lexie and Phaedra to turn to if anything happened to her. There was no packing up and moving in with mom. If her rent was not paid by the 8th of each month, eviction procedures would start. No man was going to step in and save her, no lawyer for a sister and no investments and no savings.

The worst part was there was no do-over button to push. It wasn't stress free but it was her life. Brie held her breath and tried not to think about it. Her position was a support role and she did it well. And she would keep doing it well. Being broke and homeless was not something she wanted to go through, again.

To do: shopping

Phaedra had got the message that it was girl's night out. She was also looking forward to seeing Christopher again. She knew he was not forthcoming about his wealth and her curiosity was peeked. He had introduced himself as a teacher, but later explained to Brie that he was a professor at the university. Still, Phaedra knew he had money by the way he was dressed and wanted to know where he got it from so she decided to Google Christopher Hollingsworth. She found out that he was born into wealth. Chris's father was a chemist who started a company selling organic cleaning supplies before it was popular. Chris was a trust fund baby with his investments in all the money making right places. After the popularity of going green has sky rocketed in the last 20 years, so has his net worth.

As she read on, she found his job is just something he likes to do because physics came natural and he enjoys teaching. This man was worth millions several times over which made Brie a problem. How could he be attracted to what she described as chunky, broke and too many kids with too many men. From what Phaedra researched, Chris had dated models and beautiful women in the science community. Maybe he just saw her as easy. Whatever it was, unlike Mr. Austin, Chris was single.

"Michelle!" Phaedra called out to the assistant.

"Yes, Phaedra?" She answered approaching the door.

"I'm heading out to run a couple of personal errands," she started to explain. "I won't be back in the office today. I'm meeting the girls for drinks, I think around 5:30."

"Does that mean Lexie is getting better?" Michelle inquired.

"She still gets testy when you ask her how she is doing. She just doesn't know what to do with all this extra time on her hands." Phaedra was talking and gathering her stuff up at the same time. "As soon as I can get her to count her blessings each day, she will start to do better."

"It's a scary situation to be in," Michelle said.

"She'll survive. If you need anything, I can be reached on my cell. I'm just doing some shopping. I need an outfit and a mani-pedi," Phaedra told her as she was walking out of her office.

"Have fun. I'll see you tomorrow," Michelle said closing the office door.

That is exactly what Phaedra did, using the American Express card George had given her. If Chris wore tailored clothes and a $10,000 watch, then Phaedra would show him she was on his level. "Got to look like money if you are trying to attract money," she told herself.

George never questioned any of her purchases as long as she looked good when he saw her. It was Friday's so she wasn't dressing up. That would look desperate. Instead, a $600 pair of indigo colored jeans and a brand new pair of cocoa brown leather Giorgio Armani T-strap sandals would do the trick. She had a crisp white button down shirt in her closet that would pull this outfit together. Her next stop would be the nail bar.

Brie not be outdone

When Brie arrived at Friday's, the girls were at the bar on their second drink. Chris was sitting next to Lexie, and Phaedra's back was to both of them. Brie hopped on the bar stool next to Chris and crossed her freshly waxed legs twirling her ankle to bring attention to her Jessica Simpson sandals. Lexie knew Brie was there to divide and conquer. Lexie had to decide if she was in the mood for a fight.

Realizing Lexie's attention was behind him, Chris turned around to see what she was looking at. Brie smiled his way and waived for the bartender. "How are you guys doing?" she spoke.

Chris smiled and answered for everyone telling her they were fine. Phaedra did cock her head back and began to laugh. She knew the game that was about to begin. She elbowed Lexie in the back and when she turned around, Phaedra just smiled. Only Chris was oblivious.

"What took you so long?" Lexie asked facetiously

"I had to run a couple of reports at the last minute before I left. We have a big meeting coming up on Monday," Brie lied. Brie couldn't go shopping like Phaedra was able to, but she did go home and change out of her work clothes.

"The life of an office manager," Lexie stated continuing to decide back and forth if she wanted Chris enough to get into argument with Brie.

Phaedra had now completely turned around to see the show that she bowed out of earlier. It was entertaining to see others quarrel for once, especially if that someone was Lexie since she was not one to put on the boxing gloves when it came to a man. That included Mark. This time, though, Lexie's feathers were ruffled because she did not expect Brie to be competition. Phaedra, who was being an instigator, began to whisper into Lexie's ear, "...and in this corner standing at 5'5" and weighing 150 pounds". Lexie waved Phaedra out of her ear.

"My mother always preached going the extra mile. Hard work pays off was always her advice," Chris commented after Lexie's remark.

"Was she saying that to her personal assistant or the maid staff?" Lexie asked still being facetious. Then she yelled at the bartender, "I need another drink!"

"Can I propose a toast?" Brie stood up and asked, not interested in the tension of the moment.

"What would you like to toast to Brie?" Phaedra asked her.

"To love. May we find it, may it bring us joy and happiness and may we always know that it was worth living for," Brie said holding her glass up then drinking but never clinking glasses with anyone. She didn't need to. Lexie's mouth was putting her out of the competition and Phaedra's distance proved she had already lost.

Lexie drank the rest of her drink and jumped off the barstool. "Brie, let's go to the bathroom."

"I don't have to go. I just got here," Brie protested.

"Yes, you do," Lexie advised her as she headed that direction.

Brie looked over at Phaedra and Phaedra waved her on. Phaedra never jumped off her stool. She just sat there. Chris however, stood up and offered Brie his hand to assist her. He smiled and commented on how nice she looked. She thanked him as she slid off the stool and followed the direction Lexie had taken. Phaedra started humming the 80's hit song *Meeting in the Ladies Room* out loud while stirring her drink. Chris wasn't paying her much attention. He was watching Brie walk.

When Brie entered, Lexie was standing there with her arms crossed and tapping her foot. She knew what this was about so Brie walked pass Lexie and straight to the mirror and dug out her lip gloss. "Say what you need to say so we can move past this point."

Lexie wanted to be angry and offended but couldn't. Brie was way to calm. "Why would you do this to me? This is something you do to Phaedra because it's a game between the two of you. Why Brie? Why?"

"It's not a game, Lexie. I liked him when I first saw him. I was trying to get his attention then your little narrow ass jumped in the way. I'm not letting this one get away."

"How was I supposed to know you liked him? And what if he likes me? You're just gonna jump in, get what you want out of him and dump him on my door step when you're done," Lexie demanded.

"How would you know, you were drunk that whole night." Brie finally turned around and looked at Lexie, "I'm not playing a game. I really like Chris. Broke or rich. That's real talk."

"What? I'm supposed to step aside?" Lexie asked

"No. I don't expect you to do that. I just don't expect you to get mad if I lure him away. Besides, you have Mark. Phae has two or three boyfriends," Brie reminded her. "I'm the only one in this group that should make a move."

Lexie softened, "Mark and I are not together. We are on off again mode right now."

"That's because you are so caught up on being independent. You need to let that shit go. You see Beyonce did. She married Jay-Z and they combined their money. Now they are on their way to being the riches couple."

Lexie laughed at Brie, "Okay okay. Well, again, I'm not going to just lay down. We both saw him and I'm no light competition."

"Fine by me," Brie said sucking her teeth. "Just don't go underestimating me, either."

"Can we please get the hell out of here? It stinks." Lexie asked.

"You the one that called this meeting. We could have gone outside," Brie smiled.

At the bar, Phaedra couldn't help but throw fuel on the fire that was brewing. "So, which one of them invited you to Friday's?"

"Lexie. She said you guys would be here and asked me to come up," he answered still oblivious to the conflict between Brie and Lexie.

"So, you are going home with Lexie tonight?" She asked him.

"What kind of question is that?" Chris asked her cautiously.

"One that you don't want to answer because you aren't sure," she teased.

"I just think that is private. Besides, what do you care?"

"I don't. Just curious where your mind is. Lexie invited you, but your eyes are on Brie," she said letting him know she was watching him.

Chris chuckled, "I'm a man. I notice pretty things. Besides, your friend Lexie treats me more like a big brother than a guy she wants to go home with."

"I see. Well, that is Lexie. She might take you home, hit it one good time then stop answering your calls, but, maybe she wants more from you. Maybe she is trying to be friends first." Phaedra went on to say.

"Somehow, I don't trust advise from you. I'm quite sure you have another agenda."

"Wow Chris, here I was trying to be nice and you have to be a dickless motha fucker towards me. I don't really care what you do. Like I said, I was just trying to see where your mind was. Besides, who knows what your agenda is Mr. I'm a teacher but really a professor."

Chris still did not trust her, but he felt some guilt. He extended his hand her way with an apologetic smile. Phaedra accepted and shook his hand. "I'm just here to hang out. No intentions on my mind."

Phaedra did not believe him but looked up and saw the two girls coming back. Chris, again realizing someone's attention was behind him, turned around. He pulled out both of their stools as they sat down. Lexie cut her eye Phaedra's way. Phaedra sucked her teeth and rolled her eyes. Then she motioned Brie's way and hit her right fist into the other palm. Lexie shook her head letting Phaedra know they did not fight. Phaedra was genuinely disappointed. Lexie laughed.

When Lexie turned back towards Chris he was facing Brie, laughing and sharing an appetizer. They were in their own conversation. Lexie just turned back to Phaedra. "So, is this what it's like to lose a guy to Brie?"

"I wouldn't know," Phaedra answered then snickered.

But baby...please

Sunday was supposed to be a relaxing day. Phaedra's kids were at Disney World with friends, so she had quiet for the day. She turned to a jazz station on one of her apps and connected her tablet to the Bluetooth speaker. RJ had already left before breakfast. Phaedra had showered and was dressed in her favorite sock monkey flannel pajama pants and a white tank.

Phaedra had cooked herself a spinach omelet and was sitting down to eat it when knock rattled on her front door. She despised people who dropped by without calling first. Phaedra wasn't one for surprises. She peeped through the window to see it was George. She walked back to her kitchen and sat back down at the table without opening the door.

George knocked a few more minutes after watching her walk away. He FaceTimed her. "Why you playing?"

"Why are you beating on my door like the police?"

"Come on now Phae, open the door. You got me standing outside looking like a fool," he begged.

"I didn't invite you to my house so you have yourself outside looking like a fool," she told him.

"Phae, quit playing and open this door. Don't I pay the bills here?" He demanded.

Phaedra was not able to sit content with that statement. She put her fork down and placed her hand on her hip. Her head cocked and her neck rolled, "You don't live here, you don't run a damn thing here, you don't even get pussy without permission! You can take that I pay the bills here bullshit to your house! This one ain't the one!"

Phaedra disconnected forcing George to call her back. She didn't answer so he called again. She still didn't answer. He sent her a text, 'Baby, PLEASE'. Phaedra sighed and slammed her hand on her table upset he had ruined her day. She took a deep breath and walked back to the door, this time opening it.

George walked in and slammed the door behind him. Phaedra quickly turned around and stared him down. He apologized and began to tiptoe behind her. She sat on the couch and crossed her legs impatiently shaking the top one. George stood for a few more seconds not sure if he should sit. Phaedra didn't acknowledge him, so he took it upon himself to sit and crossed his leg also.

"What is it that you want?" Phaedra asked after a few minutes of silence.

"We got a problem," he announced.

Phaedra snickered, "We?"

"My wife is snooping. She is getting suspicious. I think she knows we were at the house on American Beach." He began to explain to her.

"So, that leads me back to my original question which is how am I included in this problem? And my second question is why did you bring your problem to my house?"

"Damn, Phae! We been together for 3 years and you consider this my problem? I guess all those I love you's won't nothing but words. No care? No concern?" He said disappointed.

"I meant what I said. I do care about you, but I care about you and me. You and your wife is a separate entity. George, we created our own world. It's a fantasy world. But when we walk away from it, our real lives kick in. The reality is, you are married, we are cheating and the possibility of us getting caught is high. You get busted I can't do anything about that." Phaedra explained.

"But babe, we are still in this together. If it affects me then it affects you." George tried to tell her.

"George, your wife your life. I know my place. I'm just your side chick. I know one day I could lose this, just like that. It doesn't change the way I feel about you. It's just reality. I don't know what you want or need from me. I can't be that friend that tells you to hang in there, it will be alright. I can't tell you to drop that side whoe and work on your marriage. Or even tell you that you are the victim stuck in a bad marriage and you are such a good man and deserve more. I'm not THAT friend George."

"I guess I came to the wrong place for some support," he said leaning back in the chair and shaking his head. "I wanted you to give a damn."

"I do, I just don't know what you want from me. Some sympathy sex?" Phaedra wasn't moved.

"No, I don't need sex. I just wanted to tell you what was going on and expected you to feel something. We probably need to cool it off for a while. At least until she stops suspecting." George shifted his attitude, reflecting Phaedra's calm coolness.

"I understand if we have to lay low for a minute. It's not my intent to ruin your life. But, you know, I'm cautious and I keep secrets. Don't throw me under the bus if you get caught." She warned him.

George smiled. "You know I wouldn't. I'll always protect you. Keep what we got going protected."

"You're not doing too good of a job if your over here scared because you about to get busted." Phaedra pointed out.

George laughed his cocky laugh, "You're right. So, you know, about that sympathy sex?"

"Man, please. Not in my house. You have to set that up elsewhere. I don't need those bad vibes in my place of dwelling," she told him.

"We got different definitions of love," he said standing up.

"I don't judge you, so why are you are judging me?"

"And I was going to do that thing with my tongue you like," he teased.

"Isn't your car parked in my driveway and you worried about your wife following you?" She reminded him.

"No, I'm not crazy enough to drive my car here. I switched cars with a friend of mine. Our story is he borrowed my car to impress a date," George smiled proud of his scheme.

Phaedra laughed at him in her head. To her, him standing there, he looked more like a teenage boy than a man. She wanted to feel for him but couldn't. It wasn't real. He wasn't leaving his wife. She'd replace him if they ever stopped meeting. That was her word for their relationship. Meeting.

As far as Phaedra was concerned, that is what they did. They met at his house on American Beach. They met at nice hotels in Daytona and Orlando. Only once did they boldly meet at The Landing and swung into the hotel there for a quickie after lunch. He didn't talk about his wife and she didn't mention all the other guys. Every now and again he would ask about her two kids or mention something about his. It was about sex. Money was a perk if you made a man feel good. It really was a fantasy world for them. Once inside a room, nothing or no one else mattered.

George and Phaedra met at a networking event for African-American professionals. The sexual tension was obvious when their eyes first met. He took her card lying that he was considering selling his house. She knew better. Phaedra could read men like a book. She had studied his body language and his attempt at swag. She especially paid attention to the way he kept his left hand in his pants pocket not knowing the impression of his wedding band could be seen through the fabric.

George was funny and all over the place. She teased him about having ADHD even though he didn't. Their first date they drove to a little café in Gainesville. George still hadn't confessed he was married and Phaedra didn't mention it. It was a nice evening of talking. Both wanted desperately to hit the closes hotel but they resisted.

Phaedra learned George was owner of a trucking company and worth 7.12 million dollars at the time. She used her ways of finding out a person's net worth. He was business smart but street dumb. He had the finances but still acted like the poor kid that grew up in low income housing fighting for his mom's attention with six other siblings.

She watched him that first night. He was nervous, but this wasn't the first time he cheated on his wife. She wasn't the first woman he brought to this out of town café. George was cautious with his words, careful not to give too much information. Phaedra found him sweet. From experience, she knew sweet meant undercover freak. She could not wait to taste his cocoa brown skin.

His deep set brown eyes held her captive and distracted from his wide nose. He instantly smiled every time he saw her. Phaedra never asked for money. She never had to. George wanted to be her man and he was going to take care of her. First, he started just giving her cash. A few hundred dollars here and there, then he had an American Express issued in her name. After a year and a half, he bought the convertible T-bird for her birthday. They drove it to Savannah and spent the weekend. Phaedra was never concerned with what excuse he gave his family. In her vision of their relationship, it was just the two of them when she wanted to be the only person he loved. This was one that she could put on the shelf when she didn't want to be bothered or wanted to be with someone else, and take it off the shelf when her mind and body was ready.

Now he was standing there in front of her with those deep set brown eyes begging her to allow him to stay. She knew this relationship worked for him also. He could be himself, his escape from his own day to day routine. She didn't ask much from him. He had practically paid off her house, had taken her to Tobago and Italy. Paid for her to take her kids to London and the Bahamas. There he stood, appealing to her soft side. Hoping she loved him enough to ask him to stay.

"You ever pop up here again, I'll call your wife myself and tell her to come pick up your stupid ass," Phaedra threatened. "But, since you are here, we minus well have some sympathy sex, as long as you are going to do that thing with your tongue."

George knows she needs play hard with him, but he liked it that way.

It's time to step back and reflect

It had been a few days since Lexie felt like she lost the attention of Chris to Brie. She had not talked with either since that night, but they both had been on her mind. She wasn't sure if she should be mad at Brie or happy for her. Truthfully, she was hoping Chris hit it and then deleted Brie's phone number. The guilt of her jealousy was making her nauseous. What Lexie should have been doing was focusing on what she wanted to do to make money. She was tired of job hunting and networking. The same people were at the job fairs, at the networking meetings and at the coffee shop. She had had enough. The walls were caving in and the question "how's the job hunting going?" was irritating her last nerve.

She thought about Brie's comment about her having Mark. Their on again off again was more off than on. He tried to be by her side and she refused his comfort. By now, Lexi was pushing everyone away, including her son Anton. Lexie had checked out of her body and was functioning on autopilot.

Her doctor had suggested anti-depressants. Lexie had been on them before when she and Anton's father had split because he didn't want to be a father or want her anymore. Now, six years later, he is married with a child and one on the way. He never calls about Anton or spends money to help. He pushes her away any time she tries to get him to talk to their son. It's hard to accept that a man is a family man, he just didn't want to be that with you. He can be a better man, you just weren't the woman to bring him there. Carlos finally went to work for himself, bought a house and did all the things Lexie tried to get him to do. But this was another thought that was bringing her down and another distraction to avoid the job hunting that was getting her nowhere.

Lexie sat in her office, she hadn't turned on her computer nor did she want to. She thought about visiting her father's grave just to have someone to talk to that would not nag her. She realized that would be even more depressing and would really give her doctor a reason to write that prescription. She had to change the way she was seeing everything. Who better to walk her through that process than Phaedra?

Phaedra immediately answered the phone asking, "You pick your face up yet?"

"I didn't need to," Lexie laughed.

"OK then, you bouncing back from the rich, fat guy with ease. You go girlie," Phaedra joked.

"Stop calling people names. Why can't he just be Chris? Why does he have to be the fat guy?" Lexie lectured.

"Why are you and Brie so sensitive about me calling this guy fat? He is fat. He knows he's fat. But OK, I'll be careful about choosing my adjectives." Phaedra remembered she needed to feel Lexie out before talking. Everyone was still walking on eggshells around her.

"I'm not sensitive about it, but as a mom, I think we should be changing the way we do things. Anyway, believe it or not, I had a Phaedraism this morning so I'm calling you," Lexie told her.

"I'm nervous. What is a Phaedraism? There are so many directions to go with that. I don't know if you are finally sleeping with men for money, found some good karma juju, put Anton out and told him to get a job and stop whining. I'm just saying."

"You know you stupid, right?" Lexie laughed at her. "I realized I need to change the way I see things in order to figure out this job thing. I knew you could guide me."

"It's about damn time!" Phaedra shouted unlocking her car door. She was at the coffee shop getting her daily chai tea fix. "Yes, girl, yes. Change the way you are thinking about the situation and you will see the path so clear."

"How? I know I need to but I just don't know how. I've got cabin fever and need to escape these walls. It's just making me sad. I don't know where to go to think." Lexie explained.

"Then get away. Get away for a week. Find some place you can get still and meditate. No alcohol, no phone, no computer. Don't even think the words job, hunt, resume, I, don't, have." Phaedra told her.

"How am I supposed to get away for a week? I have no income, because unemployment is a joke. Not to mention, I have Anton," Lexie complained.

Phaedra was sitting in her car, she never started it while she was on the phone. "Lesson one on changing how you see things, STOP looking at all the obstacles, bitch!"

"Are spiritual advisors supposed to call you the B word?" Lexie joked but Phaedra did not laugh.

"I'm going to put this car in gear and drive it right through your front door." Phaedra threatened.

"Okay, okay. Get away. I got it. Actually, that is a really good idea. Who couldn't use a time-out?" Lexie agreed.

"I will pick Anton up tonight, have all his little shit packed and you decide on a destination."

"Whoa, wait a minute. You are going to take Anton?" Lexie asked in shock.

"I'm willing, but act fast before I come to my senses," she told her.

"Okay, I'll do it! I'm going to pack a small suit case, get in my car and drive until I feel like I'm where I need to be." Lexie was getting excited about a new scenery to get her head back in the game.

Phaedra was happy to hear excitement in her friend's voice. It had been a while. She hoped this would be a breakthrough for her. Phaedra was glad that something she said had finally permeated Lexie's mind when she needed it most. She just told herself, this will be a good week and Anton will be a good boy who minds his manners. "Just one more thing, the how, that belongs to the Universe. You just worry about the what."

Lexie was excited and scared at the same time. She kept thinking about the finances although Lexie had enough money in savings to survive for the next two years plus her severance package was very generous. Fear had a choke hold on Lexie, and she needed to escape to get rid of it.

She hung up with Phaedra and headed for her bedroom to dig out her carry-on suitcase. She did not know where she was going so wasn't sure what to pack. She grabbed her favorite two pair of jeans and figured she couldn't go wrong with a couple of white shirts. She stood in the large closet debating on dress skirts or just keeping it casual. She decided one dress outfit for just in case.

Lexie packed, closed the suitcase and zipped her overnight bag that she put her shoes into. Now to pack Anton's clothes for the week. She began to smile again at Phaedra offering to babysit. She knew she had been moody with both Phaedra and Brie. She would make it up to them by using this week to get it together.

She needed to call the school to find out what time Anton went to lunch so she could tell him in person she was leaving. Instead, she called Mark. Another person she had been ill with. They hadn't spoken in the last week, because frankly, he was tired of the abuse. She feared he would let it go to voicemail but he answered to her surprise.

"Hi Mark. I'm glad you took my call," she greeted.

"Why wouldn't I?" He asked dryly.

"I've been a real bitch," she answered.

He was glad she admitted it allowing him to lower his guard a little. "Are you doing any better?"

"I will be. I'm going to take a trip to escape these four walls and get out of town for a week, which is why I was calling you," she explained.

"What do you need?" He asked still being cautious with her.

"You," she simply stated.

He began to smile but was trying to contain it. It wasn't working. "What is it you need me to do?"

"Is this 20 questions?" She asked laughing trying to break the tension. "I need you to come with me. I understand if you can't go today, but maybe you can meet me later in the week."

Mark sat back in his seat curious where Lexie was going with this. He had been there as a friend, when she and Carlos broke up. They didn't start a relationship until a year later. It was on a business trip in Atlanta and Lexie was trying to get away from Ana. He scooped her up and they both escaped their managers and went site seeing. At dinner that night she realized those dreamy green eyes were touching her soul. She leaned in and kissed him as they were heading out the door. He didn't kiss her back and she felt rejected. Lexie walked ahead of him.

"I really like you, Lexie," he started before she interrupted him.

"I know, as a friend. Just chalk it up to the wine so I can walk away with dignity."

He laughed at her. "No, more than just friends. I really, really like you. I have for a while. I didn't say anything because you took the break up with Carlos pretty hard. I didn't want to be rebound guy," he explained to her.

"I wish you would have said something. I know all the girls in the office are in love with you and I didn't want to be just another set of googly eyes," she confessed.

Mark had more of a chuckle than a laugh. He loved to smile and told her he was only interested in her and no one else in the office or elsewhere. The relationship lasted for a year before they had a big fight about living together. Lexie did not want to move into his house and he didn't want to move into a townhome. Then her father passed away and Mark was by her side, at least for several months until she began to push him away.

That was how Lexie handled stress. She moved everyone close to her to a comfortable distance. He wanted her to need him, to also let go and trust him to be there for her. He couldn't go through this again with her, no matter how much he loved her.

"Escaping sounds like fun, but what are you escaping? And what role am I playing?" He asked.

"I need to step back and try to figure this out. I don't know what I'm doing. It's like I'm going through all the motions to look for a job but I'm not getting anywhere. I'm over thinking it and all I can say is I did everything right which obviously means nothing. I'm going to go clear my mind," Lexie explained to him.

Mark just listened. She gave all the reasons she needed to get away. He didn't agree with them, and his heart and ego were still on the line. "You do realize that you are your problem and you are taking you with you?"

She knew what he meant and it hurt her, but it was the truth. "Mark, I don't want a lecture right now. I don't want to be talked out of this either. I just want you to be with me."

"Where are you going?" He finally asked.

"I don't know. Where ever my car stops. Where ever it feels right. I packed a few of everything." She answered.

"Call me when you arrive and I'll let you know what day I can get there," he told her. "What about Anton?"

"He is going to stay with Phaedra. She actually volunteered herself."

"You are leaving Anton with Phaedra? You must really need this more than I thought," he said shaking his head.

"She's not as bad a person as she tries to make herself out to be. And yes, I really need to get away," Lexie defended.

"Alright, I'll see if I can get off Wednesday or Thursday and drive your way. Actually...," Mark paused for a moment. "We have a cabin on the lake outside of Atlanta. It might be a perfect place for you. A little less than a six hour drive."

"Who is we?" She asked because she assumed she knew everything about Mark.

"My brother and me. We went camping and fishing last summer and fell in love with the place. Next thing you know we bought a lake house," he explained.

"Oh, I didn't know you went to Georgia last summer with your brother. Is it a timeshare?" She asked.

"No, it's a house. I will warn you, it's not furnished fancy. My brother and I kind of just got some stuff and threw it in there. And I did get that little nudge about not knowing where I was," he smiled. Last summer they were off again.

"I'm just saying," she sucked her teeth.

"I'll tell you what, since you are driving, I'll get a flight out that way and I can drive your car back. Would you like me to bring Anton?" Mark offered.

"No. I want to be selfish. Actually, that's all I have been. At least self-centered. Phae will take care of him. I'll come back and be the mommy he knows and loves." Lexie explained.

"Well, I'm glad you are doing this. Haven't figured out my role, but it sounds like a let it flow thing so I'll just let things happen as they happen."

"It's the role you've always played, Mark. My rock. I'm thankful you never gave up on me, and I'm sorry for pushing you away when you were just doing what come so natural. I know you've had every right to be done with me, but you love me anyways." Lexie wasn't sure where that had come from, but she meant it.

"Why don't I meet you in the next hour to give you the key and address," he told her.

Mark got the apology he had been looking for over a year now. They agreed on a time and Lexie decided to leave early so she would not get caught in Atlanta's rush hour traffic. She was already seeing things in a different light. Getting away gave her a new energy. She had something to look forward to, unlike her usual day of getting up, dropping off Anton and coming home to sit in front of a computer submitting resumes to a blind computer looking for key words.

She called the school and told them she was on her way and just needed to pull him out of class for a moment. Lexie realized she should probably call her mom but wasn't excited about it because she was expecting her to deflate the joy out her plans to leave for a week. But since she was a good daughter, she called. She got her mom's voicemail. She left a message and hoped not to get a call until she was at least two or three hours out.

Everything on her list was completed, her bags were in the car and Phaedra had swung by to pick up Anton's bag. Lexie was ready for her trip. First, she stopped at Anton's school and let them know she was going out of town and Phaedra would be picking up and dropping off her son this week. Next stop was Mark's so she could get the key and the address. When she pulled up the front door was wide open. Lexie walked in calling his name.

"In the kitchen stuffing my face," he advised her.

She stepped down from the foyer into the living room. The room was open and you could see the kitchen and dining room once you stepped down. Mark was standing at the breakfast bar shoveling a ham sandwich into his mouth.

Mark's décor was very masculine. His walls were a light mint color. His mission style sofa and love seat had caramel brown leather seat cushions, and there was a rustic looking printed rug with mahogany, gray and green. The same colors rolled over into his kitchen with mint green and chocolate brown candles and place mats. His bar stools were a grayish green leather he found at a remnant shop. Lexie helped with the accessories including the prints on the walls.

Her signature was everywhere. Both she and Anton would spend weekends at Mark's house. When they broke up, Mark would still pick up Anton and take him to the zoo or park, or just go out to eat. Now walking towards him standing there in his khaki pants and tucked pink collared shirt, she can't remember why she didn't want to move in and put up such a fuss thinking he should give up a house to move into a townhome. His green eyes reflecting off that pink shirt made her wonder why she keeps letting him go.

"Why are you staring at me like you are going to snatch the food out of my mouth?" He asked referring to the grin on her face like a kid in a candy store.

"That sandwich does look tasty," she joked. "I like you in pink. It makes you even sexier."

"I'll have to go get five more of these shirts then," he started before she leaned in and kissed him.

It was more passionate then usual which made him wonder what was going on inside her head. After four months of being frustrated anytime he tried to talk about their relationship, she was now the aggressor. He didn't want to get her in another fury so he let it go and enjoyed the kiss and her body pressing up against his. He pulled her in closer and grabbed the back of her head making up for lost time. Kissing her the way he dreamt of kissing her. He did not want to come out of that moment.

"I'm sorry," Lexie said as they slowed up.

Mark still held her close, still brushing his lips on hers. "Why?"

"Your asking questions have reached its limit for the day," she whispered.

Mark smiled still not releasing her. "Well, I'm not sorry. Can't apologize for something that I wanted."

"I just don't want you to think I'm starting again just to end it again. I'm not sorry for the kiss. Just sorry for not trusting my heart in your hands. You always come through for me and I'm grateful," she told him.

In his heart, he knew he had his woman back, in his head he was still skeptical. "I'll never stop loving you Lexie. I might not keep allowing you to walk all over me and pushing and pulling me away. But I will never stop loving you."

Lexie fought with the tears that wanted to trail down her face. "I know, and I'm going to do better if you give me one last chance."

"We'll see," he said as he let his grip go. "Here's the address and the key, and some cash in case you run into any problems."

Lexie felt her heart stop when he let her go. She accepted the money without argument for once. She thanked Mark, and turned to walk away.

"Lexie, wait," Mark called out to her. He grabbed her arm, "I'll be up there Wednesday. That will give you two days to be alone and think, then we can talk about all of it. By then, my question privileges will be restored."

Lexie smiled and kissed Mark again. She left before they ended up doing anything else.

Coffee or Lunch

Brie and Chris had been talking on the phone all weekend since that night at Friday's. Chris was everything on her list she had created three years prior. In their conversations, he told her his goals and why he got into teaching. The more he talked the more she began to recall the list. She needed to get ready for work but was wrecking her brain trying to find it. "Maybe it wasn't meant to be found," she confessed to herself. She wrote it and forgot it on purpose.

He told her how much he loved to play chess and racquet ball. She grew up playing both but could never find anyone else that liked or knew how to play racquet ball. She brought up her desire drive Route 66 and Highway One so she could see the country. To her surprise, he said it was on his bucket list also. Naturally the subject of kids came up. He told her he liked kids, just didn't want any of his own. She wasn't sure what he meant by that but would make it a point to find out.

They had spoken extensively all weekend but had not gotten together. Brie was hoping he would ask her out soon and they were not on a path to being buddies or friends with benefits. She was interested in Chris but didn't want to come off desperate.

"Mom, what are you looking for?" Ike, Brie's oldest child, asked her as he watched her opening and closing drawers. He stood in her doorway wanting to speak with her.

He was the son of her first love. A relationship she thought would last until the day she died. Ike looked more like Brie than his father which made her happy. He moved cautious and but once friends with you, smiled a lot. He was detailed with his appearance. He only wanted money to keep his hair cut low and his gingerbread complexion moisturized.

"A piece of paper. Are you dressed and ready for school?"

"Yes ma'am. Chonda is putting her books in her backpack and Deena is eating cereal," Ike reported.

"OK. Don't miss your bus. You got your homework?" She asked only half paying him any attention.

"Yes ma'am." He answered her and turned around to leave since she was preoccupied.

"I'm done," Brie told herself. She needed to check on her kids anyways. She also realized she hadn't given Ike any attention or said good morning to him when he walked in her room.

She slipped into her bright orange skirt and tucked the cream, colored blouse in and walked out of her room. Everyone was just as her 11 year old had informed her. Brie grabbed Ike into her arms and squeezed him tight giving him a kiss on his forehead. "Thanks for being the best son a mom could ask for."

Ike, who stood on few inches shorter than his mom, smiled and headed for the kitchen to pack his lunch. He had another 10 minutes before he needed to head out for his bus. Brie walked over to Deena, the youngest, and kissed her cheek and then went looking for Chonda to make sure she was on task. Chonda hated school and found it boring. The work was tedious, and the teachers weren't smart enough. Each morning was a fight for her to get the 3rd grader out the front door.

"Chonda, do you have all your assignments?" Brie asked leaning in the door way of what was both girl's bedroom.

Chonda sucked her teeth, "Yes, I do. But I think I'm coming down with the flu so I probably shouldn't go to school today."

"Thursday, it was tonsillitis and Friday it was your stomach. Funny how Saturday and Sunday you were just fine."

"I wasn't feeling great Saturday and Sunday. I'm obviously coming down with something," Chonda insisted. "I think you should at least take me to the doctor."

"And I think you should find your shoes and tuck your shirt." Brie told her.

"Do I have to die?"Chonda asked sarcastically as she walked towards the closet.

The second oldest and the smartest of Brie's crew was conceived after a night of drinking with a stranger. They tried to make a relationship after but three months in, Brie stopped answering his phone calls. They had nothing in common. He was into MTV and she was into PBS. Once Chonda was born, her farther came around the first few months, but when he realized he was getting no where with Brie, he disappeared. Brie took her son and her caramel drop, as she nicknamed her, baby and moved to Florida hoping for a better life on her own.

"No, you don't. But you do have to go to school, even if you don't want to." She said kissing her daughter on the cheek. "Go ahead and finish getting dressed so I can do your hair."

Chonda sighed and tucked at the same time. "Yes ma'am."

Brie headed back towards the kitchen of her three bedroom apartment to get Ike out the door on time when she heard her cell phone ring. She detoured to her room to grab it. "Hello," she answered recognizing the ring tone.

"Hey Brie, good morning," Chris greeted.

"Good morning, Chris," she said then covered the mouth piece to yell for her son. "Ike, time for you to head out for the bus."

"Sorry, I know you are getting ready this morning," he said now aware he hadn't considered her morning routine with three kids.

"No, not a problem, just give me a minute," she said. She walked out to Ike telling him, "Give me a kiss. You got money for lunch?"

He held up his lunch box reminding her he didn't. "Don't forget I have spelling bee practice today,"

"I won't. I love you. Have a good day," she said as he was heading out the door after hugging his sisters.

"Love you mom!"

"Come on Deena so I can do your hair. Chonda, did you eat?" She was calling out walking through the house. "Sorry Chris. What's up?"

"You sound organized over there," Chris smiled. "I just wanted to see if you had time to meet for coffee this morning."

"I wish I did, but I have that meeting. If it wasn't for that we could," she answered not wanting him to think her family obligations would stifle her dating life as men had felt in the past.

"Maybe tomorrow then. We can meet for coffee or lunch. Whichever you prefer," he suggested.

She was relieved because she was dying to see him again. "Lunch would be nice. That way I have a little bit more time to spend with you."

"Lunch it is. I'll let you finish getting ready. Give me a call later tonight when you get some time."

"I will," she replied with a big grin on her face.

Brie finished up Deena's hair and told her to go put on her shoes. She called out to Chonda so she could fix her hair. She was grinning the whole time and her daughter noticed but didn't say anything. She just enjoyed her mother brushing her thick black curly hair into a puffy pony tail and humming some song she had never heard before.

Prayer isn't easy

Lexie had been just outside of Atlanta when her phone rang. Her Bluetooth announced it was her mother. She was relieved because she was too far to be talked out of her decision. She also felt guilty because it was as if she had snuck out of the house.

"Hey, Ma. How are you?" Lexie answered.

"I'm fine. What is this about you going out of town?"

"I'm getting away for a few days. I just need to think clearer," Lexie explained.

"You couldn't do that at home?" Her mother asked confused.

"No, ma'am, I couldn't. I was getting cabin fever and I keep seeing the same circle of people. I just need a different perspective. That's all."

"You took Anton out of school just to clear your head?"

"Phaedra will be watching him," she said and then held her breath. "I went by the school before I left and he was actually excited about it."

"Okay, I'm going to trust you know what you are doing." She said.

"I do, Mom. I will be better after this. I promise," she assured her. "Love you, Mom."

"I love you also Alexia Felecia. Don't forget to pray," she reminded her.

That was almost too easy, Lexie thought to herself. She did throw in the dreaded middle name to let her know there was a tidbit of disappointment, but then reminded her to pray. It was too much to try and decipher what her mother was thinking. Lexie turned up the jazz music she had on the radio and was glad she was down to her last hour before getting to her destination. She had already called Mark to let him know she was still safe. Lexie had thought of Brie, but was still pouting about the incident with Chris.

Lexie's mind was all over the place. She decided to take her mother's advise and pray. She always feared praying because it always came with so many rules. Was she doing this right? Was she doing that right? Religious people made her feel as if she wasn't worthy. Or she was being punished. Or He was answering, but the answer was no. As a little girl, she could just talk to Him. As an adult, it felt as if He was getting further and further. When her dad passed away, Lexie shut down because she didn't want to hear that her dad was with God now. Why do you have to die to get to God? It didn't make sense to her. But she always felt guilty and apologized to the Heavenly Father and would try again. Before long, another human who knew better than she did, would start rambling off the rules to her.

There were no people around to criticize her.She could talk, but she hesitated. Maybe she should wait until she got to the cabin. Would it be any easier? Probably not, she thought. Lexie took a deep breath in through her nose and pushed all the air out through her mouth.

"Dear Father," she started and that was as far as she could take it. She turned the music up again and started watching her surroundings. It had been a year since she had been in Atlanta. She'd pray once she unpacked and got settled.

Universe, what are you asking of me

"Hey, Sexy, how's your day going?" RJ asked Phaedra when she answered the phone.

"I'm good, yourself?"

"No baby, you are phenomenal," he told her.

Phaedra rolled her eyes and reminded herself he was only 25 and impatiently asked, "What's up?"

"Not much, doll. Had you on my mind. Still thinking about this past weekend," he told her.

Phaedra was also, but not so much her time with RJ. She had George on her mind. She tried not to, but that afternoon on the couch was different. Maybe it was because Phaedra pretended to somewhat care. Maybe because unlike hotels and his house on American Beach, pretending felt more like reality that day. They were two lovers, on a Sunday just hanging on to each other.

George stayed all afternoon catering to her. He cooked lunch for them and they ended up playing a game of scrabble. Afterwards they watched a movie as Phaedra just lay back in his arms on the same couch they made love on earlier. When he left and Phaedra closed the door behind him, she thought she would feel relief that he was finally gone. Instead she missed him. She wasn't sure why, but she did.

"Phaedra! Phaedra!" RJ was calling out. "Are you listening to me?"

"Sorry, no. I was doing something when you called," she lied.

"I'm sorry doll. I know you are a busy woman. I was just asking you about dinner tonight."

"Wish I could. I've got my friend's son all week. I probably won't see you this week. I've got to pick him up from school each afternoon," she explained.

"Ah, babe, that sucks, but I get it. You helping a friend out. Hit me up when you free."

"Okay. I gotta go." She agreed and ended the call.

Phaedra still wasn't thinking of RJ. Her mind was on George. She wanted to call him. She had to get her head straight because the reality of their relationship is that it was fake. She had to keep moving without him on her mind. She tried to start working on her marketing plan for a new house when Lexie crossed her mind. She hadn't talked to her since Lexie got on the road. It was pushing 4 o'clock so she knew Lexie should be close. She decided Lexie would call when she arrived. She wouldn't bother her while she was driving.

Phaedra had planned to leave work at 4:30 to pick up Anton. She had already text her son and daughter to let them know they would have a guest this week. Her daughter, Maya, was excited which for Phaedra meant Maya would be the one watching Anton.

"Phaedra," Michelle called lightly knocking on Phaedra's open office door as she was walking in. "Here are the posters from the sign company. I like the one for the property on Ponte Vedra."

"Ponte Vedra is overrated. I like Amelia Island so much better," Phaedra said taking the packaged from Michelle.

"Well, they are both over priced as far as I'm concerned," she laughed.

"Don't go telling our buyers that," Phaedra smiled trying to join her humor.

"Phaedra?" Michelle started. "Can I ask you something about a personal matter?"

Phaedra wanted to say no. "Sure, what's up?"

Michelle closed Phaedra's door and sat down. "I'm kind of in this situation and I'm in over my head. I hope you don't think ill of me after this."

"I don't judge. Not my assignment," Phaedra told her.

"I cheated on my husband. I feel so guilty and I don't know if I should tell him." Michelle started to cry after saying it out loud.

"If you tell him, what do you think he will do?" Phaedra asked regretting this conversation.

"Hate me. Probably divorce me," Michelle sniffed.

"Michelle, I can't tell you what to do in this situation. The advice I was given, decide the outcome and if you can live with it."

"What would you do?" Michelle asked her.

"It doesn't matter. I'm not the one that has to live with it."

"I just want someone to tell me what to do," Michelle said.

Phaedra realized she needed to do something to make her assistant feel better. She hated having to comfort people, but everyone seemed to need a shoulder to cry on. Phaedra put her hand on the woman's shoulder. "Michelle, we all do. That way when it goes wrong, there is someone else to blame."

"I know you are right. I know you are. I don't want you to be, but I know you are right," Michelle said wiping her tears.

"Why don't you take tomorrow of? I'll cover you here. Get up in the morning as usual, pretend you are going to work and instead just go somewhere to think," Phaedra offered. "Time to yourself, so don't bring anyone else with you. Think clearly. Remember, a decision you can live with."

"I'm so sorry. I try not to bring my problems to work, but it's been eating at me."

"I know that. At some point, we all need to have a breakdown or a mental day to get it back together," Phaedra assured her.

"Thank you, Phaedra," she said hugging her.

Michelle left Phaedra's office and started packing up. "Okay, Universe, what are you asking me? That's two people today. I'm not a psychiatrist, a hugger or babysitter."

Phaedra moved the signs to the side of her desk. She'd look at them in the morning. It was time to leave and pick up Anton and grab something for dinner. She had had enough for one day.

Bad news can be good news. Depends on your perspective.

Brie was getting the office put back together since everyone was finally filing out. The conference room was left a mess for it to have been a meeting with adults. The only bonus was she always ordered extra cookies so there would be some left over to take home to the kids.

Brie's boss walked in to help her straighten up the conference room. Brie had to laugh at herself because she immediately became protective of the dozen or so cookies. Ellie had not paid the cookies any attention. She and her partner solely owned their firm but were working with another firm to do some promotions for a national campaign.

The two worked together for a few minutes before Ellie said anything. "Glad this day is over. Now the real work begins."

"It seems like it went well," Brie said encouraging.

"It did and I so appreciate your help. You always do a wonderful job with setting these things up," Ellie complimented her.

"Thank you. I don't think anyone went away hungry after that lunch."

"No, no. They didn't. A bunch of greedy grown men," Ellie laughed. "Brie, I did want to talk with you."

Brie's stomach dropped. "About what?"

"This campaign is huge for us and will make up for some of the business we have lost." Ellie started. She sat down and grabbed a cookie motioning Brie to sit also. Brie hissed at her boss grabbing a cookie but played it off as she sat. After all, the woman did pay for them.

Ellie continued, "It is no secret that things are tight and I know your review is coming up soon. As much as I know you deserve the highest raise I can offer, at this time, I can't give you one yet."

Brie was relieved but needed clarification. "So, I'm not being laid off."

"Heaven's no! I'm just hoping you will be patient, give me some time and not quit."

"No, I wouldn't quit. I know the economy is crazy so I'm patient," Brie confirmed.

"I know you are doing the work of two people and you still manage to make us look good. I will make it up to you. I will even put it in writing and I will do whatever I can," Ellie assured her.

"More like the work of three people," she mumbled in her head. "Okay Ellie. And thank you. Thank you for looking out for me. I'm confident things will get better." She stood up and shook Ellie's hand and the two gathered the trash cans up.

Ellie came back in and grabbed another cookie and offered the rest to Brie to take home to her kids. Little did she know that was Brie's plan all along. Brie played along and smiled and said thank you. She poured what was left into a plastic baggie she brought up from the break room. Brie headed back to the front because her black stiletto sandals were killing her feet. It was time to sit down at her desk.

Brie checked her phone and realized she had not spoken with either Lexie or Phaedra. She knew Phaedra was about holding grudges, but did not expect it from Lexie. She started getting everything together on her desk before logging off her computer.

Ken, one of the agents in her office, came up from behind her and leaned on the back of her chair. "How's our friend Phaedra?"

Brie jumped startled because she didn't hear "Skinny Kenny" walk up. "Boy! You need to wear a bell!"

"You must not be living right. I'm just sayin'," he joked.

"Phaedra is fine, I guess," Brie answered. "You can call her. You don't need me to be the go betweener for you."

"I know. Just figured you'd seen her."

"I don't know why you are in so love with her. She treated you like crap," Brie pointed out.

"She made me feel good when she treated me like crap," he told her as he reminisced about the month he dated Phaedra a year ago.

"You are stupid," was all Brie could say.

Ken was the only person in the office Brie knew socially. They would meet for drinks every blue moon when he first started working at the company. Phaedra met them once and he bugged Brie every day until Phaedra went out with him. Outside of Ken, Brie kept her business life professional. Only general questions and answers such as how is the family/spouse/kids and did you enjoy your weekend/vacation/event. With her fear of being judged, she didn't allow the people at work to know too much about her.

Brie logged off her computer and grabbed her purse. She checked her cell and no missed calls, but a text. She was hoping it was Lexie. She didn't want to be enemies, but she wasn't willing to give up a chance with Chris either. It was non-negotiable for her.

The text was Chris, an hour ago. It was hard to be happy and disappointed at the same time. He just wrote he was thinking of her and hoped the meeting was going well. She closed it and did not respond. Guilt was kicking in. "What would Phaedra do," she sighed.

"Not give a damn," she answered herself and laughed. Brie headed out locking the door behind her so as to close shop. She would call Lexie when she got home. She'd make sure she still had her friend.

Let's cry this one out

Lexie arrived at the cabin that she was expecting to look like a log cabin. It was a small house. Mark was correct, there wasn't anything that resembled a décor. There was an old couch but it wasn't tattered. A couple of rocking chairs that looked like they should be outside on the porch, and a wobbly table that she is convinced they got off the side of a road.

She carried her bags to the larger bedroom and put them on the bed. She leaned over and pushed on the mattress. To her surprise, it wasn't lumpy or hard. She pulled up the comforter and sheets and was happy to see it was a new mattress. She took credit for Mark not sleeping on a used mattress and keeping his pillows new.

She was glad to not be driving but thought she should have stopped at a grocery store before she got all the way here. She prayed there was something in the cabinets. Lexie started unpacking and laying out her toiletries. She needed to call several people to let them know she made it safely. She would call them all later. She considered a shower, but changed her mind. She was just looking to be distracted. A habit she was perfecting over the last few weeks.

Instead, Lexie decided to check the pantry and see if there was anything that would sustain her through the evening. There were plenty of seasonings and condiments. There was also rice and grits. She continued to open cabinets doors. Fortunately for her, she found a box of crackers and a jar of peanut butter. "Dinner!" she shouted relieved.

Next, Lexie stepped outside to view the grounds. She discovered two plum trees in the backyard and two peach trees. She was happy because that meant breakfast. It was quiet and she started looking around to see how close the neighbors were. She guessed the property was 1 ½ to 2 acres. The lake was a little further up and there was an old golf cart she assumed was how they got to the lake. It was February so it's not like that many people were out. And it was approaching dark with the sun setting so early.

Lexie's hair stood up on her arms and she found herself getting uneasy. She had watched too many scary movies where people die at the cabin in the woods or by the lake. Every scary thought she could conjure up had taken over and Lexie ran for the front door and locked it. She went through the house and started turning on all the lights. She called Mark, and panic was in her voice. Before Mark could say hello, she blurted, "Are there gators in the lake?"

Mark wanted to laugh but he held it in hearing the fear in her voice. "I'm not sure. There might be. Why? Are you going swimming?"

"No! Didn't you see that movie where Orlando Jones was eaten by that giant ass gator that Betty White was keeping as a pet?"

He couldn't no longer hold it in. "Lexie, honey, I promise no alligators are coming up out of the lake to eat you. Unless of course you switched sides and became a Seminole fan since you left here this afternoon."

"Not funny, Mark! And what if some crazy homicidal man is out here who wants a brown skin suit? I'm a woman out here alone," she continued.

"Lexie. Stop. Take a deep breath. Your imagination has just gone into overdrive." Mark heard her breathe deep a couple of times. "Okay, now please know that I would not send you anywhere alone that was dangerous. They have security and cops around and lights down by the lake. People have been swimming there for years and no one has been attacked by an alligator."

Lexie wanted to feel better, but she still wished he was there with her. "You promise its safe?"

"I do. If you get quiet you can hear the bug life," he told her smiling. "Crickets out there are always begging for a female."

She laughed at him. "Now I'm going to be sitting here listening to crickets making out."

"You just hear his mixed tape," Mark joked. "Outside of that, how is everything?"

"Fine. I forgot to go to the store but I did find some stuff in the pantry and some fruit trees."

"That's good. I don't think we left anything in the fridge. At least I hope we didn't, but I'm not positive. My brother was there this past December so I wasn't sure what you could expect."

"It's clean. The room is comfy and at least there are towels and wash cloths," she complimented.

"Yeah, I made sure to have the essentials; towels, dishes, pots, glasses. We figured everything else we would get as we go. Making sure it's just us and we aren't having to rent it out to help pay for it," he explained.

"It's nice. Thank you again. I'll feel better when you get here. But in the meantime, I'm going to do some ugly crying, some journaling and then some planning."

"Good. Sit under the trees. They are always a good place to think. There are a few blankets in the hall closet."

"Okay. Well, I've got the windows and doors locked. I'm going to turn on some music, shower and enjoy my night alone. Love you," she told him.

"Prove it," he said in his head. "Love you too, Lex."

She loved hearing him say that. He never really stopped telling her. She felt like such a fool for not knowing how to love him back all this time, but that would be something to think about later. Lexie peeped out the window once more just to make sure no one was out there. It was quiet, she closed the wood blinds. She looked at her phone to call Phaedra but instead it rang in her hand. It was Brie.

"Hello."

"Hi Lexie, how are you?" Brie greeted.

"I'm good. Tired and ready to hit the shower," she answered.

"Kind of early," Brie pointed out.

"Oh, that's right, I haven't talked to you today. I'm at Lake Lanier, outside of Atlanta. It was a last minute decision this morning. I just got here. I've been driving all day," Lexie explained.

"What are you doing up there?"

"Just needed to get away. Need to think. Mark has a lake house up here."

"Wow! Sounds nice. Is he there also?" Brie questioned.

"No. He'll be here later in the week. I brought a new journal, a bottle of wine and I'm going to work through my issues. I know you guys are sick of my whining and complaining."

"We understand, Lexie. I know you are just scared of the unknown. I know you will bounce back. I have faith," Brie tried to encourage her.

"Thanks, Brie. I really do appreciate it. How was your meeting today?"

"It went well. You know I can plan a party," she laughed.

"I do know. What I don't know is why you don't go into business for yourself."

"Because the market is saturated. Everybody and their momma is a party planner," Brie said.

"But everybody and their momma is not Brielle Jackson," Lexie emphasized.

Brie smiled, "Well, we'll see. Is Anton with your mom?"

"No, Phaedra. I was just ready to call her to check on him and let her know I arrived safely."

Brie felt a little disappointed to find out Phaedra knew Lexie was gone, but she hadn't called her or text her to what was going on. "Well, I'll let you call Phae. Enjoy your time."

"Thanks, I will. And if your phone rings at three in the morning and I sound a hot mess, that's just me sobbing like a big baby."

"I'll be sure to answer," Brie promised.

Lexie felt bad for not asking about Chris. She didn't want Brie to feel as if she couldn't talk about him. She'd be sure to call her later in the week and talk about it then. This was her time to think about herself.

Lexie scrolled through her phone for Phaedra's number. "Hey girle, what's up?"

"About time you called. I was beginning to think you decided to end it all and ran the Beamer into a tree." Phaedra said shaking her head.

"It's not that bad, yet."

"It's never that bad!" Phaedra corrected her.

Lexie laughed. "How's Anton? He's not sad is he?"

Phaedra held the phone up towards the game room. Anton was laughing with Caleb while they were playing fuse ball. "I don't think he's sad. He has Caleb's attention. He told me when I picked him up he was going to have a fun week because he was going to be with Caleb and Maya. So, you don't need to worry. He's fine."

"I'm glad. I didn't want him to think I was abandoning him."

"He doesn't. Grown folks are always under estimating children. Don't go putting issue in his head and telling him he is supposed to be sad when you guys are separated."

"I won't. Let me just say hi," Lexie asked.

"Anton, your mom is on the phone," she announced passing him her phone.

"Hi, Mommy," he greeted.

"Hi, honey, how are you?" She asked as upbeat as she could.

"Caleb and I are playing a game and Maya made chicken fingers for dinner with sweet potato fries, just like you make. It was good. And I'm going to sleep in Caleb's room. He has two beds. And did you know Caleb was a Saints fan?" He rambled.

"I'm glad you and Caleb are having fun and I hope you remembered to tell Maya thank you."

"I will. Are you having fun?" He asked her.

"Yes, honey. But I will be home Sunday and we can tell each other all the exciting things we did this week. I know you are going to have some great stories for me."

"I gotta get back to my game. Love you Mom." He passed the phone back to Phaedra not waiting for her to say I love you back.

"Girl, he is gone," Phaedra informed her. "So, now that you know he is fine go dig around in your soul, get deep down in there, and get yourself together. The answer you seek is in there. You just got to be willing to receive it."

Lexie meditated on what Phaedra told her. She was right. She really did not need to worry about Anton. He was safe. "I'm going to get to work. I thank you, Phaedra."

"Take care of yourself first and everything else will fall into place," Phaedra encouraged her.

"I'll talk to you later then," Lexie said and the two disconnected.

She sat on the edge of the bed and was finally ready to cry. Lexie convinced the tears to hold off for one more moment. She had to talk to Mrs. Simmons and that was not always an easy task as far as Lexie was concerned.

"Hello, Lexie," her mother answered.

"Hi, Mom. Just wanted to let you know I made it safely to Atlanta."

"I'm glad. Lexie, are you going to be okay? I'm worried about you. It's as if you are beating your head against the wall."

Lexie could hear the concern in her mom's voice and felt guilty for being the reason it was there. "Yeah, Mom, I will be. I just felt too close to the situation so I needed to retreat. I guess it just became overwhelming. I don't know what I was expecting."

"Are you moving to Atlanta?"

"No, Mom, I'm not. I'll be home Sunday. And I'll be regrouped." Lexie explained.

Her mom sighed. "Okay, as long as you know what you are doing."

"I promise, Mom," Lexie told her.

"Take care of yourself, and call me in the middle of the week just to let me know everything is okay," her mother requested.

"Yes, ma'am, I will. Bye."

All the people she thought she needed were now gone. It was just her, in that room. She felt a chill, and then she felt empty. Then she lay back in the bed and gave her tears permission to flow.

Can I ask you a question?

The evening was quiet and the kids were watching TV after dinner. Brie was sitting at the dining room table twirling her phone. She knew if she picked it up the kids would immediately want her attention, but it's almost 7:30 and she hadn't talked to Chris all day.

Brie got up and headed for her bedroom softly closing the door behind her. She gave the kids a few minutes to notice she was gone. She waited to see if anyone would knock. She started looking for that list again unsuccessfully, then she finally called him.

"I was beginning to think you forgot about me," he told her answering the phone.

"Of course not. Finished cleaning the kitchen and got the kids settled."

"So how are you doing?"

She was starting to get nervous because she didn't want to scare him off just because she had mom duties. "I'm good. How was your day?"

"Not bad. I only have one class on Mondays and everything else is consultations. Mondays are easy days. I set it up that way on purpose."

"That was smart since everybody always dreads Mondays," she replied.

"Monday does have a bad rep," he laughed at his own joke. "So, listen, there is an Indian restaurant over by your job. I figured we could meet there for lunch."

"Sounds good. I would like that. You weren't busy were you?"

"No, I was reading. Catching up on some articles, so I can get these old magazines out of my house," he told her.

"Do you recycle?"

"Most of the time. These magazines, I will definitely remember to recycle," he answered.

"Can I ask you a question?"

"Usually when you are having a conversation with someone and they ask 'Can I ask you a question' it means the conversation is about to get serious or you've done something wrong."

Brie laughed at the analogy. "Well, maybe just a little serious. I never bothered to ask if you and Lexie had something going on. I was attracted to you and didn't realize the two of you were talking when I sat down."

"No, there was nothing going on between us. The only time I talked to her on the phone was when she called to invite me to come have a drink with all of you," he explained.

"I see," Brie said now wondering why Lexie made a big deal out of it. "Like I said, I was just wondering."

"Did she say something to you?" Chris asked now curious if he had a chance with Lexie also.

"No. It's more because she didn't say anything. I'm just over thinking it. She is going through it right now with having no job. She left town this morning to get herself together."

"I can only imagine it must be hard."

"For sure. My boss came in to tell me she can't afford to give me a raise but at least I'm keeping my job. Too bad my rent and groceries won't be sympathetic to that," she said trying to joke but was serious.

"Are you going to look for something else?" He asked concerned.

"No. I can be patient. Just need to tighten my belt," she explained. "Okay, we did get too serious. Let's lighten this back up."

Chris smiled. "Yeah, let's do that. So, tell me, what are you wearing?"

Brie laughed with him. She worried if she should have told him about not getting a raise. She didn't want Chris to see her as a struggling single mom. She just wanted him to see her as a woman.

Black, single mother, and unemployed

When Lexie woke up she fumbled for her phone to see what time it was. She couldn't find it so she headed for the bathroom. By her fourth step, she found her phone when she stepped on it. She picked it up but never checked the time. Instead, she turned on the bathroom light and looked in the mirror. Her eyes were puffy and her hair was standing straight up on the left side of her head. She had dried drool and tears on her face.

"If I said Candy Man three times, Tony Todd would show up in this mirror and he would be the one screaming." Lexie told herself.

When she sat on the toilet, she finally looked at her phone. It was 3:12 in the morning. Lexie had a text from Phaedra. A picture of Anton asleep with text across the picture reading, "Goodnight Mommy, Love you". She was grateful Phaedra did that. She decided no more guilt about leaving.

Lexie washed her hands and headed for the kitchen. She grabbed the peanut butter, the crackers, a spoon and a bottle of water and went back to the bedroom. She unloaded her arms onto the bed and dug out a pen and the new journal she purchased and sat Indian style in the middle of the bed. She thought again about a shower and remembered her hair was standing up on her head. She closed her eyes and realized again she was just looking for distractions. Lexie took a few deep breaths. It was time to chase her demons away. She was tired of being sick and tired.

"Dear Heavenly Father, forgive me for taking so long to come to you. I'm ready to be guided," she prayed in silence then opened her eyes and then the jar of peanut butter.

Lexie sat there reading one of the three self-help books she brought. She started crying again when the author told her to be open to change. Lexie hated when things changed. She grew up in the same house, the same neighborhood with the same friends. They went on vacation to the same three spots every summer. On the 4th of July she knew without fail she would be at her uncle's house, except once, but she couldn't remember why. Then Roni went off to college in Tallahassee. She thought that would be exciting but she missed her bossy sister. Then her mom and dad sold the house after she graduated from college and her father retired and they moved into a condo. Lexie was distraught over never visiting her childhood home ever again. Then her father died and her whole world came to a standstill. She could never figure out if she was more upset about him dying or for him leaving her alone with her mother and sister.

Change had always been around her. Friends had come and gone. Roni moved to Miami. Jacksonville was growing. The world was moving and Lexie was holding on to only God knew what. She didn't want to change jobs, her style, or her mindset. But the author told her she needed to be open to it. She could feel her heart tighten and an uneasiness come over her.

Lexie needed a cigarette, but she quit smoking years ago. By now she stopped putting peanut butter on the crackers and was shoveling it into her mouth straight from the spoon. This feeling was making her want to hide from the world. The thought of things not going on as normal made her feel noxious.

"I'm acting like a two year old," she told herself.

Again, she took a deep breath. She picked up her pen again and began to write in her journal. She started to cry again but she kept writing. She had sobbed and wrote 10 pages of her story. She wrote about growing up in the house and always being happy when her dad got home. She wrote about blaming herself for being raped when she was in college and being scared as to tell anyone. She wrote about not making the drill team and lying about it to her family telling them she chose to drop off the team. She hid from them that she failed micro-economics twice and signed up for additional financial aid to pay for it so they wouldn't know.

Lexie started to realize how often she hid her imperfections. This was the story the author was pushing her to tell. Ten more pages in her journal and she told how she was upset about living with Carlos. She was embarrassed they were just living together and not married. She would order catalogs with her first name and his last name just so people wouldn't think otherwise. They had dated for a year, moved in together then six months later she was pregnant with Anton. She was 33 years old and hated being single and a mom. She didn't want that stereotype. It made her feel as if she had lost an imaginary battle that only she was fighting. She was black, female, single and had a child. She remembered the disappointment from her parents. It negated all the hard work of getting good grades, getting scholarships, going to college, having a professional job and being successful. What she saw in the mirror was not Lexie, but all the labels.

Lexie dropped the pen and held her breath. Now there was another label to add...unemployed.

She cried.

Still got you on my mind

The sun wasn't up yet but Phaedra was. She was unrolling her yoga mat in her Florida room so she could sit and meditate. Her mind had been all over the place before she went to bed. It had been on George and RJ, then on Lexie and Brie, and everything else in between. She put on some flute music and sat in lotus position. Phaedra closed her eyes and began to breathe.

"What if I got serious with RJ and dumped George and everyone else," she thought to herself. Surprised by the thought, Phaedra quickly dismissed it.

"What if I just got rid of all of them? Shit! I need to clear my mind," she told herself.

Phaedra tried again to concentrate on breathing. It still wasn't working. Phaedra just turned off the music and pulled up her yoga app. Maybe someone in the room talking would get her mind off men. She stretched and breathed for the next 45 minutes concentrating better on the task and not the men in her life. She felt better with a clear mind to plan her day.

Phaedra got up and headed for the kitchen to fix herself some hot tea. She chose plain green tea from her variety of 10 different boxes. While she waited for the tea kettle, she checked her phone. Now she had George on her mind. Not being able to have him made her miss him. How could she be mad at his wife for being the type of woman that knows her man? But Phaedra couldn't figure out why the woman would care now. She has to know her husband has been cheating for years.

Phaedra was speaking from her own experience. Ron, her ex-husband, could never hide when he started stepping out. They got married young, both sophomores in college. The first five years were happy. Phaedra was a little antsy being tied down to one man, but she put forth her best to stay committed. Caleb was still in diapers when Ron received his first of many promotions and they had just moved into their first house. There had been dinner parties and vacations. It was a picture book life, which for Phaedra meant boring.

No matter, she was a good wife. She started her real estate career and started meeting new people. She became friends with a client who was a practicing Buddhist. She found herself asking a lot of questions. Debbie had invited Phaedra to a meeting. Phaedra liked the information and began to read books on both Buddhism and Taoism. That lead to her studying all the religions and beliefs of the world.

Caleb was 2 ½, she was pregnant, and Ron was disappearing. It took a year for Phaedra to start putting pieces together. Sitting at the dinner table one night talking, Ron kept checking his watch. She finally asked him if he had somewhere to be. He told her no. Her curious nature made her watch him. She watched him all night. He was uncomfortable. He barley played with Caleb. She asked him again if something was on his mind. Again, he answered no.

Ron had been short with answers that night and pretended to sleep once she got in bed. Phaedra pretended too. At 2:30 that morning, Ron slowly got out of the bed and eased to the kitchen to use the phone. Phaedra followed him unnoticed.

"I'm sorry, this was the only time I could call," he was whispering.

Phaedra assumed there was an argument to the fact that he woke up others in the house.

"We have to meet tomorrow. I can't accept your decision…I know…I know…I know," he kept repeating. His head was low, his fist was shaking. Ron was pacing as far as the phone cord would allow him.

At this point Phaedra had deciphered he was talking to a woman, but she wasn't prepared for what he said next.

"You have to get an abortion. You just have to. I can't do this. Meet me tomorrow damn it...do it any ways...I have a say in this too...damn you!"

Phaedra froze as she heard him slam the phone down. Ron sat at the table while Phaedra sat in a chair in the dark living room. She didn't breathe. She didn't think. After 10 minutes, Ron walked through unaware of her presence until she spoke.

"How far along is she?"

Ron jumped, startled, "What? What the hell are you doing sitting in the dark?"

"How far along is she?" Phaedra asked again a little more irritated.

Ron took a deep breath. He was caught. "Three months."

"How long have you been sleeping with her?"

"About a year and a half," he confessed.

Phaedra was stunned and Ron was scared. She immediately thought of her grandmother who raised her own husband's child from another woman.

"Why would you be so careless and irresponsible?" was her next question. Not why would you cheat. Ron didn't answer because Phaedra got up, walked to the bedroom slamming and locking the door.

Phaedra did not divorce Ron after that. She accepted she had two kids and her husband had three. She made sure he paid child support, but she did not add her input when it came down to him building a relationship with his other son. That was his choice and his only.

It took another six years before they divorced. Ron did cheat again, but Phaedra wasn't concerned. She had her own entertainment. Ron had too much freedom and told Phaedra he felt she didn't care. Phaedra had been hearing this her whole life. She just believed people should be able to be themselves. She never wanted to be responsible for anyone else.

She wasn't leaving without everything she wanted. She arrived at the court house with pictures. This was the day she put her wall up. She would never give too much of her heart again.

George's wife could be feeling the same way. Maybe his wife has found other interest and was ready for her freedom and just needed evidence. She saw that this temporary separation was a good thing. She did not need her face showing up on any private eye's pictures in a court room. That still didn't stop her from missing him. Those kinds of feelings were dangerous. Fortunately, for her, Anton walked in the kitchen and distracted her from having to think about it any longer.

The journey within

"How is it possible to hate yourself?" Lexie asked herself still staring in the full-length mirror behind the door. She had found the source of her anger. She had developed this image of herself and was not living up to that image.

Lexie stood there in the mirror and had come to realize that as much as she looked in mirrors, she never looked at herself. She looked at her clothes, her make-up, her teeth She looked at parts of her. Never did she really look at her whole-self. She was now 38 years old, her hair had a few more strands of gray. She was still in shape. She stared at the woman in the mirror. The one she had become.

On the inside, she was lost and confused. Educated, successful, beautiful, a mother, a daughter, a sister and a friend. At times, funny. She thought how much she used to love to laugh. She stopped when she and Carlos were no longer going to make it. That's a long time to be unhappy.

Lexie stared a little longer. Why would Carlos not want her? Mark wanted her. Mark gave her his shoulder, then he gave her his heart. Mark loved her and let her know how much each chance he got. He proved she was lovable.She just didn't feel worthy.

Lexie stared a little longer. She repeated the infamous statement, "I did everything right," to herself. Then she walked away from the mirror. Lexie sat on the edge of the bed. The sun was starting to come up. She wanted to quit going down this path, but she knew better. She had come too far and it would be foolish to turn around now. However, she did need a break. Lexie went to the closet to get a towel and a wash cloth, and headed for the shower.

First date

Brie was in morning mode, calling out the same questions she called out every morning. This morning was different though. This morning she woke up with anticipation. She couldn't wait to see Chris for lunch. She would get to touch him again. He gave nice hugs. She would be sure to hug him as long as he would allow her. Maybe a little tighter this time.

Brie hadn't realized how wide her smile was while she was thinking of hugging Chris, until Ike asked her what she was so happy about. Brie laughed harder than normal and told him she was just in a good mood. Then she rushed him out before he missed his bus.

She got to work that morning early as usual. She looked over her to do list. One of the sales guys was already there also. He was also concerned about losing his job. Brie spoke and offered him coffee, but he declined. She went about getting the office prepared for the day. There was an extra pep in her step.

When Ellie arrived, she saw the smile on Brie's face and like Ike, asked what she was so happy about. Brie told her she had a date for lunch, a first date. She was looking forward to it. Ellie joked that it was obvious. A few minutes later Kenny walked into the office. He leaned over her desk and smiled at her.

"Did you get laid last night?" Kenny whispered.

"Boy! What? No. Why do you ask?" She asked him blushing. This would be the 3rd person to point out how happy she was.

"Cause girl, you grinning like a stripper at a party full of rappers," he told her.

"You know you stupid right?"

"I'm only at half a cup of coffee. That was my best for this moment. So, seriously, what are you so excited about?" He asked her again.

"I have a lunch date today. His name is Chris," She explained. "Am I really smiling that much?"

"Yes girl. Like an old G at a fried chicken shack."

"Please stop. For real. Stop," Brie begged and laughed.

Kenny laughed and headed for his office in the back. Brie pulled out her mirror and saw for herself. She needed to tone it down before 11:30. She didn't want to look desperate. She felt like any minute now she was going to burst. Brie thought about what would Phaedra do. Phaedra would be nonchalant about the whole thing. She needed a happy medium. What would Lexie do she thought next. Lexie didn't know anything about relationships. There was one piece of advice they both had given her before that she could use for this moment. Take a deep breath, then breathe slowly. And that is what Brie did until 11:00.

Brie received a text from Chris letting her know he was looking forward to lunch. Then he sent another later on to let her know he was heading her way. He would pick her up at her building at 11:30. Her nerves were rattled again. She was smiling and now sweaty. She went into Kenny's office and closed the door and stood next to him.

"Do I stink?" She asked him anxiously.

Kenny laughed, "Hold on Lou, let me take you off speaker phone."

Brie was embarrassed when she heard the person on his phone laugh also. "I'm sorry. I'm sorry. I didn't realize you were on the phone."

"No problem," Kenny said putting the handset to his ear. He explained to the client his friend was going on a first date and was a little nervous. They spoke a few more minutes and Lou wished Brie well.

"That was embarrassing, and again I am so sorry," she said pleading to Kenny.

"Lou is good people. And no, you don't stink, but what is that wet stain under your arm?"

Brie jumped looking at the under arm area of her dress. She was wearing a pale gray sheath that was knee length, black platforms and a black and white polka dot scarf. Brie's natural curls were big and fluffed up in the back held by hair clips.

Kenny laughed again, "I'm kidding. You look fine and you smell good."

Brie hit him in the shoulder for messing with her. "I need to just breathe. For heaven sakes, it's just lunch."

"You keep telling yourself that," Kenny told her.

"I like him, Kenny. I really like him. I can see a real relationship with this one."

Kenny saw the hope in her eyes. The longing. He smiled at her. "You are a beautiful woman Brie but let him be the one that's nervous and sweating. Don't go in too vulnerable. He deserves you and don't forget that."

She hugged Kenny and thanked him. Brie heard Ellie calling her name and headed back up front. Ellie was coming down the hall and others had peeped out to see the commotion.

"Brie, there you are!" Her boss said relieved. "It's 11:20. We have to check your make-up, your breath, your hair. You know, all the important stuff." Ellie went dragging Brie by the hand to her office.

Brie touched up her make-up, looked over her dress, fluffed her hair, sucked on a mint Ellie had given her. It was 11:28. Brie headed down the elevator to the 1st floor. There was Chris, jumping out of his car to open the passenger door for her. He was smiling huge too.

Call me back please

Phaedra hadn't heard from Brie since Friday night. That was typical Brie. If she found a guy that would pay her some attention then she put Phaedra and Lexie on the back burner. Phaedra made a mental note to call Brie later and tell her about herself.

Her work day had been moving along well despite doing hers and Michelle's job. She was heading out to an appointment when her office phone rang. Phaedra made a run for it, not wanting her clients to have to go to voicemail if she could help it. The fourth ring was just starting when she grabbed it.

"Phaedra Escobar, how may I help you?" She greeted to the unknown phone number.

"Well, hello beautiful," a familiar voice said. She recognized it immediately to be Bernie. He was an older gentleman that enjoyed paying for Phaedra's company.

The most she would ever give Bernie was her time and a kiss on the cheek. She had been his date to a few parties he had to attend and of course lunch here and dinner there. It had been a while since Phaedra spoke to Bernie. He wasn't at the top of her list, so Phaedra didn't know if he finally found a woman to settle down with or if he had just fallen off the face of the earth.

"Well, hello Bernie," she spoke.

"How is my favorite person doing?" He asked her.

"I'm well. On my way to meet a potential home buyer," she informed more so to cut the call short.

"Still busy working I see. I just wanted to say hello. It has been a while. I was hoping maybe we could have dinner this week."

"Yes, it has been a while. Unfortunately, this week is bad. I'm watching a friend's kid," she was explaining while gathering her things.

"Always helping someone out. Saint Phaedra. Well, like I said, it has been a while since I seent 'cha. Just was hoping we could get together, for old time sakes."

"Why has it been so long, Bernie?" Phaedra asked.

"Well," he paused deciding if he should lie or tell the truth. "See, I kinda sorta done got married. I've been trying to be truthful, but, well, Phaedra girl, I just missed 'cha. You was always fun to talk wit."

Phaedra chuckled. "Well Bernie, I'm glad I crossed your mind. But, you go be true with your wife. She's got a good man. I don't need no woman running up on me trying to cut me over you."

"Awe, Phae, she ain't like that," he said laughing.

"Yes, she is. You just haven't seen that part of her. Any woman would be willing to fight to hold onto you. Well, like I said, I've got to run. Heading to Ponte Vedra. You take care, okay?" She said wanting to end it so he would never call back.

"You too, Phaedra. You always will be my favorite person," he told her and then said good-bye.

"Old Bernie done got married," she laughed to herself. Phaedra grabbed everything up including her purse and went out the front door. When she got to her car she decided to call RJ.

"What is up sexy?" RJ answered.

"Hey, sorry, you called me yesterday and I was busy and didn't call you back."

RJ had never heard Phaedra give an apology and was surprised. He wasn't sure how to respond so he went with aggressive. "And you should be. I mean, here I am trying to build my empire and you putting a brother on the back burner as if he don't have options."

Phaedra was silent because she knew RJ was trying hard. "So anyway, what did you want?"

RJ realized aggressive didn't work, but he already knew that. Next time he would start with assertive. "You dammit. I just want you. Was hoping we could get some dinner and then I could have you for desert."

"Bad week. I'm watching Lexie's kid, remember?"

"Then, I could pick up dinner, bring it to the house..."

"Oh no, that won't work," she said

"Damn, Phae, we've been together for a long time. When we taking this to the next level?"

"Stop talking like a bitch. We just..."

"Whoa!" He cut her off. "What you just call me?"

"RJ, honey..."

"Honey hell! I'll tell you what Phae, why don't we just talk another time. You have made it perfectly clear I'm just yo' fuck nigga. Call RJ for a good time." Then he ended the call.

"Aaauuuggghhh," she screamed in her car. "Send text."

"Who do you want to text?" Her phone asked.

"RJ," she answered.

"Contact found. What do you want to text?"

"Baby, I'm sorry. Call me back, please," she told it.

"Do you want to send this text?" The phone asked.

Her head was telling her no, but her heart was telling her yes. She was never one to really follow her heart when it came to relationships. She let George have his time out, she was helping Lexie and Michelle, and now she was apologizing to RJ.

"Yes," she answered with regret.

Within a few minutes her phone was ringing.

"Are you dying?" RJ asked her.

Phaedra laughed, "No, just, well, I don't know. Maybe I am. Or maybe I wasn't done cussing your ass out."

RJ believed the latter reason. "Phae, I just want something different. You still treat me like I'm just some little kid. I might be younger, but damn, I can do better than that rich nigga can."

"RJ, this past weekend was great. The kids were gone, it was just you and me. I'm not ready for this relationship to go to that place where I'm introducing you to my kids as my boyfriend. I'm not there yet. Truth be told, I probably won't be there until my youngest has been dropped off at college."

"That's a long time from now," he pointed out.

"Yes, it is. I'm okay with that. It is my choice. I'll raise my kids, make sure they have what they need and keep my love life separate from them."

"So, when I'ma see you again?"

"Probably next week," as she told him before.

"Okay, doll. Next week. I'll be counting the seconds. But, hey, Phae, I get your reason for not bringing me around your kids, but why haven't you introduced me to your friends?"

This conversation has reached its limit and was now on her last nerve. She decided to breathe and just answer the question since she is the one that begged him to call her back. "Because when the girls and I go out, it's usually just girls. They don't bring dates either."

"Okay," he said satisfied with her answer.

"I gotta get off this phone so I have my mind together when I get to this house."

"Go do your thing. I'll holla at you a later time."

"Bye RJ," she said and ended the call.

Phaedra hated catering to other people's feelings. Why was RJ wanting more and what made him think he could give her anything close to what George could? RJ couldn't as far as she was concerned. Or could he?

She had to be better

After a nice long shower and a brush through her hair, Lexie was feeling better. She jumped in her car and headed for the close's grocery store. While out she looked around the small town by the lake. It seemed like a nice place to retire, but of course this wasn't tourist season. She was sure it was way different when crowded.

Lexie only stayed out for a couple of hours. She would save touring the city when Mark arrived. After she got back to the cabin and put everything away, she grabbed her journal and pen and headed for the lake. The whole reason she was here was to be outside and for a different scenery.

Lexie sat down at the end of the dock and laid her journal down next to her. The lake was beautiful with the February sky reflecting on it. She pulled out her phone to take pictures. This would be the day she was reborn.

Lexie saw a few people down by the lake. She was still cautious. She didn't want to be too close; just in case. She closed her eyes and just listened to her surroundings. A few bugs, the wind, the faint sound of chatter from the people by the water. A thought of her dad appeared but she didn't dwell on it. The wind continued to blow on her face. She sat there for 15 minutes trying to concentrate on her breath in between different thoughts popping up and her dismissing all of them.

She opened her eyes and felt calm. She flipped to a blank page in her journal and began writing again. She started telling the story of the girls she met at drill camp during middle school. They picked at her and called her white girl. It was the first time Lexie had heard of welfare and food stamps. The instructor told her not to pay them any mind. Lexie hated drill camp that summer.

Lexie hated people not liking her. Why would these girls not like her? She asked herself that question for the six weeks and then she finally asked Roni. Her sister told her it was because she thought she was better than everyone else. Her father told her she was and he never lied. Lexie laughed when she started remembering that conversation with Roni. Lexie walked away still believing she was the best. She was even better than Roni. Her dad told her so.

She had to be better. She was told that black people had to work twice as hard to prove themselves. She made the grades she needed to get into the University of Florida. She worked hard, but didn't make the top 20 of her graduating class. As disappointing as that was, she was still happy her degree had University of Florida written across the top of it. It was only a matter of time her mother would remind her that Roni graduated in the top 10 at Florida State. After that, graduating from anywhere was no longer a big deal. Her degree became a piece of paper she pulled out of the frame and tucked away in a drawer somewhere. University of Florida just became a blurb on her resume.

Lexie wanted to cry again feeling angry, but she was outside. She couldn't remember what drawer she stuck her degree in. She hadn't looked at it in years. She had been dreaming of being a Gator and wearing orange and blue since she was nine years old. It made her wonder why her mother felt the need to crush her happiness? Why did her mother not love her as much as her dad loved her? This was deeper than she wanted to go. This was her stopping point.

Lexie put the journal down and stood up. She left it on the dock and ventured down to the lake. She always loved being near water. It was mighty and powerful at the same time it was peaceful and patient. Nothing on earth could beat water. It held treasures of the past and monsters of the present. She respected water. Her family used to go boating and jet skiing. The summer months were hers and her father's favorite season. He worked all year to save up for the summer. She missed him.

She was missing Mark also. She was glad he would be here tomorrow. That gave her today to get through her past so she could get to her future. She was back to wanting to be angry but remembered the author told her to take responsibility and not blame anyone else. It was her story, and she needed to see how she processed situations and reacted to them. Her reactions were hers and hers alone. Lexie was forced to accept that she chose to hinder change, to speak up for herself in the locker room that summer and to hold onto the shame for not being smarter than everybody that graduated with a higher GPA than her, including her sister.

"I did everything right," she said out loud one more time. She walked back to the dock to finish writing.

Lunch

Chris was wearing black cotton khakis with a deep purple, cotton, button down shirt, no tie and Dolce and Gabbana cologne with a fresh haircut. Brie was excited he took time to look nice for her. It was a first. Usually she was the one that spent time and money for what ended up being a waste of both. She was glad she went out of her way to knock Lexie out to get his attention. Time was short since it was her lunch hour, so they were pleased the waitress arrived so quickly. Once their drink orders were taken, they got up and headed for the buffet before they started any real conversation.

Brie reached for a plate but Chris picked up one for each. He suggested she grab the silverware. He asked her what she wanted and she chose Eggplant curry and Dalchini pulao, which is a cinnamon fried rice, and okra, which she regretted later, and what looked like a potato fritter. Chris allowed her to pick what she wanted but he chose the portion size since he was fixing both of their plates. He waited to see if she would be offended or if she was okay with his choice to tell her how much she could eat. Brie said nothing but thank you. He put her plate on the table and then pulled her chair out. Brie sipped her water and smiled at Chris as he sat down. After he picked up his fork and started eating, she picked up hers.

What Chris hadn't yet learned about Brie was that she was raised by a Southern grandmother who insisted on holding onto some of the old ways. A man does not come in the kitchen, does not fix his own plate, and he gets the biggest piece of chicken. Her grandmother, nor any of the kids or grandkids ate before her grandfather. She was raised that it was disrespectful.

"I thought lunch or coffee would make a perfect first date but now that I see you, I wish I had more time," he started.

Brie blushed," I'm glad you called. Lunch is perfect. I get to see you in the daylight."

"Proof I'm not a zombie or vampire?" He joked.

Brie giggled so her laugh wouldn't sound fake. "Something like that. But it's nice to see you."

"You also. So, I've been curious, who is your son named after? Ike is such an old name."

"My grandmother named him. My guess is because she loved herself some Rev. Ike," Brie explained.

Chris laughed, "And Brielle? Where is that from?"

"It's from Gabrielle. My mom thought the shortened version was different and prettier. I don't think she realized it would be shortened even more to Brie. She hates when people call me Brie."

"It suits you. Are you going to Friday's again this weekend?"

"Probably not. Lexie is out of town. Why, were you?"

"No," he said a little harshly. "You did tell me she left. Is she okay?"

"Lexie? Yes. She is fine." Not a subject Brie wanted to discuss on their date.

"That's good. You and Phaedra don't go without Lexie?"

"Phaedra and I don't do much of anything unless we have Lexie. Phae and I aren't that close until we have had a few shots. That's only because at that point Lexie is no longer keeping up with us."

"So, you and Phaedra are just drinking partners?" He asked sounding more like he was interviewing.

Brie sat up a little straighter and crossed her legs. Chris had not let the eye contact go. "I guess you could say that is the extent of our relationship. We do talk on the phone every now and again."

"Oh," was all he said and then looked down at his plate.

"What do you and your boys do for fun?"

"Golf, hiking, skiing, throw some food on the grill, watch a game, fishing, camping, a game of tennis." Chris sputtered off then filled his mouth the chicken on his fork.

Brie felt belittled but did not want to show it. Her only response was the same, "Oh."

"I was asking because I was hoping this weekend we could get together for dinner and then on Sunday afternoon sit around the house and play some chess."

Brie perked back up. "That sounds like a plan."

Chris was grateful for her submissiveness. He enjoyed the rest of his lunch listening to Brie talk about chess and other things before taking her back to work.

Distractions necessary

Phaedra finished lunch and was arriving at the new house going on the market. She was working on her check list when she remembered she hadn't called Brie. It was well after one, so Brie's lunch should be over. She found herself checking to see if George called or text. Disappointed he had not, she called Brie because the distraction was necessary.

"Hey, Phaedra! What's up?" Brie answered.

"Not much. Just hadn't heard from you since you got a whiff of Chris," she teased.

"I know. I'm sorry. We had our first date today. He picked me up and took me to lunch at that Indian restaurant on Baymeadows."

"Oh, really? That was nice. When are you seeing him again?"

Those were usually Lexie's questions, not Phaedra questions. "This weekend. He invited me to dinner."

"Now that he really knows what you look like sober," Phaedra laughed.

There was that bitch personality Brie was familiar with. "He liked what he saw, so there."

Phaedra just laughed again. "Well, I'm glad you and he are getting along."

"We are. It was kind of weird though. He fixed my plate as I told him what I wanted. I've never had a guy do that before."

"That is weird. Sounds like a control freak."

"Or a complete gentleman. I don't think he is a control freak," Brie sung.

"He is so a control freak."

"Well, I still thought it was nice. I wouldn't mind a control freak. I'm tired of making all the decisions."

"You say that now. That shit gets old quick," Phaedra warned her.

Phaedra was giving relationship advise. It was time to switch subjects. "So how is Lexie? Have you talked to her since she left?"

"Briefly. She is working on herself so I'm not calling her. Mark should be heading her way tomorrow. Then she will be working on them. I know she took a journal and some self healing books. She just needs to get it all out of her system. I tell you, I'm tired of walking on eggshells around her."

"Me too! Still, I hope it works out for her," Brie agreed. "Why are you out of breath? What the hell are you doing?"

"Dragging this for sale sign from my car. Doing a walk through and making a list for Michelle."

"Well, I'll let you get to what you are doing."

"Okay," Phaedra said a little disappointed because Brie was her distraction. "I suppose I will talk to you another time. And hey, don't forget to call your friends. Just because you are getting a little dick does not mean you have to drop Lexie and I."

"Did Lexie mention anything to you about the incident from Friday?"

"The incident? Oh, you mean when you came in and claimed and conquered Chris. No. Like I said, she has other things on her mind. But that shit was fucking hilarious."

Brie gave a slight chuckle, "Okay. I didn't know if she was mad at me. I don't want a guy to come between us."

"It didn't. Mark will be joining her tomorrow and Chris will be a distant memory," Phaedra assured her.

"I hope she and Mark get it together. He loves her. Any other man would have run by now."

"That is very true. Her stuff must be made of gold to make a man act like Mark does," Phaedra joked.

"Or maybe it's true what they say about once you go black. Mark probably looks at white girls like 'meh."

"Nah, I believe her stuff is made of gold. He has dated others and keeps coming back to that crazy child."

"Okay, we will go with her stuff is made of gold," Brie laughed.

"I'll talk with you later. Let me get done with this house. I have one other appointment before I pick up Anton."

"How is he doing?"

"Fine. I'm sure he will miss his mom a little more by the end of the week. Right now, he is enjoying playing with Caleb."

"That is good. Alright, I'm gonna let you go for real this time. Bye Phaedra."

Phaedra smiled, "bye Brielle."

Phaedra was happy for the company, even if it was only for 10 minutes. Now to not think about George.

Forgiveness

Lexie found every happy and sad life changing moment she could come up with. Now the true question was what did she learn? Lexie loved her job because she was introducing two sets of people with a need and solving both of their problems. She enjoyed a finished product that also helped with someone's livelihood. She felt accomplished, she was well liked by her colleagues, her staff and her clients. Lexie was a closer.

Lexie saw a break in the system. The human part had been replaced by job boards because the need was so much greater. Now back in the cabin, Lexie sat on the edge of the bed and made one more entry in her journal.

Dear Lexie, you are an imperfect human being capable of extraordinary mistakes. Embrace it. Love and forgive yourself and keep it moving.

Lexie stood in her mirror and read the note to herself. She laughed because she felt stupid, but the author asked her how much she wanted to get to the next level. Lexie really wanted to move past this stage. She read the note to herself again. Then she took off her clothes, turned on some music and danced in her underwear like her favorite TV character would do.

Lexie jumped around to the music like a teenager. She blasted the music since there were no neighbors near. She grabbed the gelato she bought and a spoon and she danced while eating. Lexie danced and danced. The music kept playing and she danced some more. She was sweaty but didn't care. She picked up her journal and a lighter and danced towards the bathroom. One last time, she skimmed through the journal reading briefly on a few pages.

Lexie bowed her head, "I forgive myself for the hurt and pain on these pages. Father, I ask you to forgive me also. I surrender my pain to you. I thank you for blessing me and I will be more grateful for all you have shown me and given me. Thank you, Father. Amen."

Lexie began pulling each page out one by one and setting them on fire over the toilet. When she finally got to the last page, she cried one last time.

Kids are gonna be kids

That evening Brie got dinner ready, kids bathed, and homework checked faster than normal. She couldn't wait to talk to Chris again. They had text a few times since lunch but that was it. She was still smiling. Ike asked her why she was so happy. Again, she told him it was for no particular reason. Brie stepped into her closet to plan what she was going to wear Friday when they go out.

"Each time I see Chris he is dressed nice, and he drives that fancy car," she thought to herself. "I'm sure he's going to want to go somewhere expensive. I'm sure I need something extra nice."

"Mommy?" Chonda said standing next to her.

Brie was startled and holding her heart. She hadn't heard Chonda come in. "Yes, sweet pea?"

"Do you have a new boyfriend?"

"Brie smiled, "Did you pull the short straw?"

"What short straw?" The little girl asked confused.

"I have a date on Friday night. I'm excited about it. You can report that to your brother and sister," Brie answered her rushing her out.

"Are you going to have a baby with him?"

"What?!" Brie was taken aback with the question. "Girl get out of my face with that nonsense. Hell no, I'm not having a baby."

Chonda left her mom's room laughing to report back to her brother and sister as her mother told her. Brie just shook her head and became startled again when her cell phone rang. It was Chris so she closed her bedroom door and headed back for her closet as she answered her phone.

"Hey, how are doing?" Chris greeted.

"I'm good. In the closet hiding from my kids," she told him.

"Hope that is the only thing you are in the closet about," he joked.

"I've got my fair share of skeletons, but THAT is not one of them," she laughed.

"I'm just teasing you. Kids getting on your nerves?"

"No, they just being silly. What are you up to?"

"Still in my office. Making some changes to a quiz so my assistant can get it taken care of. Then I have to meet with a student. Then I get to go home."

"Mommy!" The shouts came in unison from her bedroom door. Chonda and Deena both were standing in her room.

"What is it girls?"

Chonda spoke up first, "Deena is trying to take the last strawberry yogurt. It's mine."

"She won't share!" Deena pouted and then cried.

Brie cringed and wished her girls were not showing themselves with Chris on the phone. She feared it would run him off. "Girls, isn't there more yogurt in the fridge?"

"Yes, but I wanna that kind. I wanna berry kind," Deena cried harder with tears running down the outer corner of her eyes.

"I had it first, Mommy!" Chonda demanded.

"Okay, stop yelling, stop crying," she told them both. "The two of you have to figure this out. If I figure this out nobody is getting strawberry yogurt. So, either get two spoons and share or I'ma eat the yogurt."

The two girls stared at her for a minute not liking either option. Deena sniffed and dried her tears. "Mommy, can we get some granola and that way we both can have some?"

Chonda sucked her teeth but agreed. The two walked out. Brie was nervous lifting the phone back to her ear. "Sorry about that."

Chris smiled, "What are you apologizing for?"

"The girls fighting. They really are good kids."

"Brie, they are kids. They are supposed to argue about the last strawberry yogurt."

Brie was relieved. "I know, but sometimes people that don't have kids think that kids should be seen and not heard."

"Suppression leads to depression. You shouldn't stop kids from being kids," he told her.

Brie liked that thought. "They are making parfaits now. Deena is putting blueberries in their bowls."

"They worked it out. A negotiating skill they will need as adults," he complimented. "I've got grown children in my classes that can't solve problems amongst themselves that well."

"I don't want them too independent but if I'm not around I want them to be able to handle themselves," she said feeling more at ease. "Well, does this mean you are stuck eating dinner at the office?"

"Yes, but I already ate. I had Samantha pick me up a chicken strip salad. When I get home, it will be to relax. Maybe read or work on this speech I have to give at the faculty banquet next month."

"Sounds like you stay busy," Brie said only to keep the conversation going. Brie's mind immediately went to the faculty banquet he would be attending and what she would be wearing. Would he introduce her as his woman or just a date? Would they wear similar colors? She was monologuing in her head and still speaking with Chris.

Brie was willing to change to be the woman Chris wanted, even though she kept telling herself not to change for anyone. But it was a banquet, he was giving a speech and she wanted the experience of being the woman of an important, respected and professional man in his field.

"God, please let this work," she prayed before she went to bed.

"Phaedra...this is Roni."

The kids were tucked in bed and the house was quiet. Phaedra had received a text from Michelle letting her know things were better and she would be at work tomorrow. Phaedra was glad to she worked things out. Now she needed to fix herself. It was only Tuesday and her body was craving attention. She couldn't really leave since she had Anton and self-love did not interest her. It wasn't just a quick fix she needed. She could call RJ for that. However, he was back on his I want to be your only man tantrum. Phaedra didn't understand why she was missing George. She just saw him two days ago. There were times she would go a week or two without him.

"I need a new guy. This George thing is getting out of hand. It's time to go hunting," she told herself.

Hunting for Phaedra meant new lingerie and new shoes. She made a note on her calendar to call for a hair appointment. Again, George would be the financier for her new look. Just as she was making notes on her phone, it rang.

Phaedra didn't recognize the number. "Hello?"

"Hi Phaedra, this is Lexie's sister, Roni. I hope it's okay that my mom gave me your number. I just wanted to check on Anton."

"Oh, yeah, that's fine. Anton is good. He is already asleep though."

"Well, I figured that, it is after 9," she said. "If he is a bother you can take him to my mother. It is not that we would not watch Anton so that Lexie could go figure out what she is doing."

"Oh, no, it's nothing like that. I offered. I didn't want her to change her mind. She needed this," Phaedra advised her.

As a lawyer, Roni was used to being interrupted. "Well, then okay. I'm just saying, he has family."

"Okay, but he's fine. If your mom wants to visit with him, I can bring him over."

"She is going to the school tomorrow to have lunch with him. She didn't want him to think she abandoned him. And I'm heading that way this weekend."

"Cool. I'm sure he does not feel abandoned. I've heard a lot about you. I look forward to finally meeting you."

"The same here," Roni said.

"Well, like I said, if Mrs. Simmons wants to spend time with her grandson, I will bring him by. I know how much she hates to drive."

"I'll be sure to let her know, Phaedra. Thank you for your time. Have a good night."

"You too, Roni. Bye," Phaedra disconnected the call and thought to herself, how weird. "Why didn't she come out and say we want our family with us. It's not like I kidnapped him."

Phaedra shook her head, hooked her phone to the charger, and called it a night.

Mark arrives

"I picked up some Sangria White wine. For a $5 bottle, it was surprisingly good. Oh, and I grabbed some chicken while I was at the farmers market. I figured we could have that for lunch or dinner. Whichever you feel like," Lexie was telling Mark on the drive from the Atlanta Airport.

"We'll decide later. You know me, I'm happy with a sandwich and a glass of cold milk."

"Yes, you are," she said laughing at him. "But I was hoping to pull out the grill."

"That is fine. Does this mean you are over the gators?" He teased.

"Well, let's just say they haven't bothered me so far. Doesn't mean I'm not cautious when I'm out. I like it out here though. I see why you and your brother fell in love with it. I'm glad you brought me here."

"I'm glad too. So, did you accomplish what you came to do? Or do you need more time?"

"No, I'm good. I've been thinking about a few things. I have a business idea and I placed sticky notes all over the closet door," she told him.

"What's the business idea?" Mark asked.

"I'm not sure how to articulate it yet. Maybe you can help me with that part."

"I would be honored to assist. You seem like you are in a much better mood."

"Does that mean you are going to give me some tonight?"

Mark blushed, "Well, um, err..."

Lexie laughed at him. "I'll let you get settled in first."

"Thanks. I might need a minute to get myself together, put my lip gloss on and freshen up," he told her.

"And cook for me. Don't forget that."

Mark's smile got a little bigger. "It's nice to see you laughing. I missed that. I missed you."

"I missed me also. It just became overwhelming. I couldn't fix it."

"It's because you try to control the Earth's rotation," he said in a teasing tone but was serious.

"My name is Alexia Simmons and I am the center of the solar system," she said still laughing.

"And of the 12 steps, which one are you on?"

"I was on two, but I messed up, so I am back down to step one."

"I believe that," Mark said shaking his head.

They pulled into the cabin and Mark turned off the car but had not gotten out yet. Lexie wasn't sure why he was just sitting there looking at the steering wheel and fumbling with the key in his hand. She began to get a little nervous. She wasn't sure if this was his opportunity to tell her about herself or if he was going to call it quits for good. The silence was terrifying her.

Lexie reached over and put her hand on his arm. "I'm sorry."

"You don't have to say you are sorry. Look Lex, I know it's hard. Well, I can imagine. I just want to be there for you, but you won't allow me to be."

"I know, I know. I didn't know what I needed so I didn't know what to ask for. Or what help to accept."

"Come on, let's go inside," he said opening the car door, but Lexie squeezed him arm a little tighter to stop him.

"I thought I had to be perfect. To live up to an image. When it fell apart I didn't know who I was any more," she explained.

"But, that's just it. I never asked you to be perfect. I only asked you to let me be the one to take care of you."

"I don't want to be in a position where I need someone to take care of me," she huffed.

Mark sighed and got out. He grabbed his bag off the back seat and headed for the front door. Lexie was still sitting in the car. If she could take it back she would, but she had put it out there. Her independence was going to keep Mark at arm's length or run him off.

After five minutes of sitting there, Lexie finally got out of the car. When she walked in, Mark was putting his stuff away. Lexie sat down on the edge of the bed and watched him for a minute. He didn't say anything and again his silence terrified her.

"Mark," she started.

"It's okay Lexie. I already know. It's not that big of a deal."

"What's not a big deal?"

"Whatever you are going to say."

"Mark, please don't. You always talk, but you never listen. Our relationship is flipped."

Mark stopped and turned to face her. "Okay, I'm listening."

Lexie started biting her on her thumbnail as Mark stood full attention toward her. "I'm afraid."

He waited for her to tell him of what but she had put her nail back in her mouth. Mark was confused, "Of what?"

"I'm afraid of someone taking care of me. I'm afraid to let someone take care of me."

Mark sat down next to her. "Lexie, you have to trust that I would never hurt you."

"Mark, you are asking me to be vulnerable and it scares the hell out of me," she confessed.

"But Lex," was all he got out before she put her finger over his lips.

"I didn't say I wasn't willing to try. I said I was afraid. I'm willing if you would give me a chance. You see, I'm more afraid of you not being in my life than I am of me learning to let go of my need to be independent."

He smiled looking into her teary eyes. Mark pulled Lexie into his arms. He was relieved that she was willing to curve her need to be in control. He could work with that.

He whispered I love you into her ear and continued to hold her. They were on again.

Relationship advise

"She called you three days ago and didn't want to come pick up Anton? What was the point of the interrogation?" Brie was asking Phaedra after Phaedra told her about the phone call.

"I didn't get it. I called Mrs.Simmons and asked her if she wanted me to bring Anton by. She said no."

"Maybe Lexie told them to leave Anton alone. Have you talked to her?"

"Yes, she called about Anton on yesterday. Well, called to talk to him. She just said everything was going well and she was ready to come home."

"When do they come back?"

"Sunday, but Roni will be here tomorrow. It will be interesting to meet her."

"Yeah, I guess so. Anyways, my date with Chris is tonight," Brie said ready to talk about her instead of Lexie.

"Are you going to his place after dinner?"

"No, I'm going to his house Sunday."

"Oh, wow. Date tonight and you see him again Sunday. Sounds like a girlfriend/boyfriend thing is brewing."

"We'll see. Technically I'm too old for girlfriend/boyfriend, but I am hoping this turns into a full fledge relationship."

"Are you going to let him order for you?" Phaedra asked trying to be funny.

"No, I can order for myself. I told you, he was being a gentleman."

"Yeah, okay. We'll see."

"Oh, that's Chris. I gotta go. See ya!" Brie said hanging up on Phaedra switching over to Chris. "Hey, you, how's it going?"

"I'm well, yourself?" He answered.

"Very good," she said enthusiastically.

"Were you busy?"

"No, just talking to Phaedra."

"How is she doing?" Chris asked.

"She's fine. So, is everything still good for tonight?"

"Yes. We have reservations at 7pm. I'm looking forward to it. I hope you are also."

"Yes, I am. I just have to run in, shower, change clothes and I'm out the door."

"Can I pick you up about 6:30? I'm hoping traffic won't be too bad about that time."

"Yes, I will be ready by then," she promised.

"Text me your address when we get off this call. It should only take us15 minutes to get downtown."

"Okay, I'll do that. So, I feel stupid for asking this, but are there any rules for tonight?"

"Rules?" Chris didn't get what she was asking.

"You know, expectations, what am I allowed to order, etc," she explained.

Chris chuckled, "none that I thought I needed. You can order whatever you want. There are no expectation if you order the most expensive thing on the menu."

"I'm sorry, like I said it probably sounded stupid. I just didn't want any surprises or to be embarrassed."

"No, don't feel like it is a stupid question. Better to ask and know then to not ask and then not enjoy yourself," he told her. "I have nothing but respect for you Brie."

Brie smiled and felt relieved. She had plenty of relationships that ended after a couple of dates. "Thank you, Chris. I'm glad you are understanding."

Brie usually made it a point to order cheap and then still sleep with the guy, then never hear from him again. It became her pattern. A meal, sex, unreturned phone call, repeat. She was putting forth the effort to be different this time.

"So, 6:30?" He asked.

"Yes, 6:30. I'll be ready," she agreed.

Brie hung up with Chris and bee lined for Kenny's office. His door was open and he was leaning over his draft table working. "Busy?" Brie asked.

"Always, but what's up?" He answered never looking up.

"Relationship advise. I hope I didn't just make a fool of myself or scare Chris off," Brie said wringing her hands nervously.

Kenny finally looked over at Brie and saw how uncomfortable she was. "Brie, would you like to know a secret about men?"

"Sure."

"We don't really care about all that stuff that women are nervous about," he confessed going back to his work.

"Kenny, I asked him if he has any rules about what I could order or any expectation. Did I sound stupid asking that?"

"Do you think you did?"

"I don't know, that's why I'm asking you," she answered frustrated.

Kenny laughed at Brie standing there looking like she was going to jump out of her skin. "Brie, I would have laughed if a woman asked me that. To myself of course. And of course he has expectations. He's a man. Doesn't mean that he is not going to buy you a nice dinner."

Brie laughed at herself and relaxed. "He did a light laugh, himself. I'm just scared of messing this up."

"Then you will run him off. If you try too hard, we lose interest. Go out, have a good time. Order the most expensive thing on the menu and then only kiss him goodnight on the cheek. Boldly!"

"That only works for women like Phaedra," she said disappointed.

"It would work for all if they tried," he disagreed. "You won't mess up if you just be yourself."

Brie smiled and thanked Kenny and headed back for her desk. If Chris didn't cancel the date, she should be okay.

Professor Hollingsworth

Kenny was partly right, Chris did laugh at Brie's questions. Yet he was still curious about why she asked. He was hoping she was smarter than to think a joke Eddie Murphy made over a decade ago was a true statement. Chris shrugged it off and kept moving. He needed to get ready for a meeting with his boss that would be happening in five minutes. At 230 pounds, Chris still moved quickly. He gathered up notes and his cell phone and headed for the Dean's office.

Instead of thinking about his meeting, his mind wondered back to Brie. "Expectations? Well, of course" he told himself. She wore that short tight dress and had those thick, meaty thighs. "I hope she isn't one of those 30 day women. It would be nice to keep her around a little longer," he continued to think. Chris had already envisioned them her thighs wrapped around his neck. He had a list of other things he wanted to try also. She was the perfect size. Petite but not skinny.

"Dean Harper, how are you today?" Chris greeted approaching his boss.

The man stood slightly taller than Chris. His hair was dirty blonde and gray and his skin tan and freckled. He wore his black rimmed round glasses on the tip of his nose. Chris had worked for Dean Harper for seven years now. Both men had great respect for each other. Chris was moving up in his career after publishing his first study on the probability of hell freezing over.

"Professor Hollingsworth, I'm well and yourself?" He replied extending his hand to shake Chris'.

"Very good, thank you for asking. I emailed you a copy of my speech as you requested. Did you get a chance to go over it?"

"I scanned it. I'm confident in your speech writing. I'm more curious about you bringing a date. You usually arrive alone and leave with a waitress. I was hoping you'd come with and leave with an actual date." Dean Harper motioned for Chris to sit down in the hunter green, leather, high back chairs near the windows of his office.

Chris first laughed, but then realized the Dean was serious. "Oh…well…yes, I can do that. I can bring a date."

"Good. I'm glad. That will stop the office pool of which waitress you will take home. And the look my wife gives me as I secretly cheer you on."

"I did not realize that there was an office pool. I apologize, sir." Chris was laughing on the inside. He was not aware that his fellow professors paid any attention to his game. He really did not have any intention of brining a date. As usual, he went to these dinners, mingled, flirted with the waitresses that brought him drinks, and at the end took one home for the weekend while she bored him with her hopes and dreams. He hated these dinners and that was the only way he stayed entertained.

"I hate to say this, but I think this is one of those careers that goes better with a wife and family, Chris. Doesn't mean you have to stop your extracurricular activities. It is all about an image," Dean Harper explained.

"Well, why don't I start with a date first. Not sure if I'm ready to settle down yet."

"Of course, by all means. And Chris, I'm making an observation," he said winking.

"I understand," Chris confirmed still finding humor in this conversation but not showing it.

Chris' fantasy went from imaging Brie's thighs to imaging her at a dinner party. She was beautiful, funny and spoke educated enough to keep up with this crowd. He knew she was relationship material, the real question was is he ready for a relationship which would require him introducing someone to family, colleagues, and friends.

Why do you never plan?

Mark was outside cleaning the grill. He had picked up some deer at the processing plant and stopped at the grocery store to pick up a few other things Lexie had forgotten. She had been watching him from the kitchen window. For a pretty boy, he was comfortable outside. Lexie was getting a salad done after she washed potatoes and covered them in sea salt then wrapping them in foil. As nice as this moment was, she was missing Anton. He would have completed this picture. Still, it was good to have the alone time.

The two had talked more about Lexie's need to be independent. Mark assured her he was not trying to control her. Lexie didn't understand what it meant to work as a couple and Mark was becoming aware of that. He joked with her about being relationship challenged. But he truly loved her, and was willing to try because she was willing to try.

She still felt awkward because she wasn't bringing anything financially to the table. She did tell Mark about her business plan to start a job counseling business. Mark thought it would be a great idea. He called it the missing link of job searching. He was open to helping her get it going and set up. Lexie didn't really want help, but said okay. After all Mark was a better sales and marketing person then her.

Mark turned around to see Lexie in the window. He mouthed to her asking if the potatoes were ready for the grill. She hunched her shoulders and indicated with her fingers opening and closing as if she had a puppet over them that she had no idea what he was saying. Mark laughed and headed for the back door.

Just as he walked in Lexie received a text message. She grabbed her phone to see it was her sister. "Oh, great. What the hell does she want?"

"Who?" Mark asked putting the potatoes on a tray to take with him.

"Roni sent me a text." Lexie opened the message and read it to Mark. "What time will you be home Sunday? I don't know. Whatever time we get up and get out."

"Maybe we should come up with a time. You know how your sister is," Mark offered.

"I'm not giving her a specific time. She is not running things. I'm tired of her trying to control everything." Lexie sent her sister a text back reading, 'No specific time. When I get up.'

"Okay, then. Well, I'm going to just take these potatoes and head back to the grill before the war starts."

Lexie laughed at Mark and called him a chicken. Then her phone rang. It was Roni.

Mark laughed looking at the uncertainty look on her face. "Who's the chicken now?"

Lexie sucked her teeth and waved him off, then inhaled for courage and answered her phone.

"Why do you never plan? Why is everything just carefree for you?" Roni complained.

"Because I don't feel the need to be controlled by time," Lexie answered bravely.

"Didn't know the unemployed took vacations," Roni said snidely.

"It was a productive trip. I now have a plan and I'm not depressed anymore," Lexie tried to explain even though she knew her sister did not care.

"I'm happy for you. I'm leaving for Jacksonville tonight. Was hoping to see you Sunday. Do you think you and Mark can hit the road early so I'm not driving late at night?"

Lexie felt a little guilty now, but wouldn't have if she had just told her. "Sure, we can hit the road early. Mark won't have a problem with that."

"I appreciate that. Just send me a text so I know what time to expect you. Anton will be at Mom's house," Roni requested.

"Wait, why? He's with Phaedra and having fun. Mark and I will pick him up when we get there."

"I'm not allowed to spend time with my nephew? I was going to pick him up on Saturday so he and I could hang out and then he could just spend the night with me at Mom's house."

Lexie sighed because she hated feeling like Roni was in control instead of her. She felt she had no choice but to cave. "Okay, I'll let Phaedra to know."

"I talked to her already," Roni announced.

"Well, I still feel it is appropriate that I call her. That way she is confident that I'm okay with it," Lexie said agitated.

"If it makes you feel better."

"It does," Lexie now even more agitated.

"Then I'll see you Sunday. Enjoy the rest of your vacation," Roni said getting in the last word then hanging up.

Lexie let out a scream of annoyance. Mark heard her but didn't budge. He was used to conversations between the two that ended with Lexie screaming at or cussing out the phone after Roni has hung up. Mark continued grilling and allowed Lexie her moment.

Forgive yourself and keep moving forward

Phaedra was on her way out the door to pick up Anton from school. She promised if he had a good report she would take him to Chuck E. Cheese. She regretted that promise. Phaedra was not exactly excited about being surrounded by other people's children. Especially if they were running, screaming and unruly. She was going to pick up Maya so her daughter could keep Anton entertained. Phaedra laughed to herself as she wondered about what the staff would say if she was sitting at the table with a glass of wine she pulled out of her purse.

Just as soon as the thought to call Lexie crossed her mind, her phone rang. It was Lexie calling her. "Hello."

"Hey, how's it going?" Lexie asked sounding defeated.

"Wait a minute. You were feeling better, happy. What the hell happened?" Phaedra asked truly concerned.

"My sister happened."

"Oh, why do you let her get to you?"

"There is a reason she is a high priced lawyer. She is intimidating as hell, argumentative and just plain bitchy," Lexie complained.

Phaedra shook her head disappointed. "You have got to stop allowing others to dictate your feelings. You put in all that work and with one phone call you revert back to where you were Monday."

Lexie knew Phaedra was right, but it didn't feel good to admit just yet. "It's Roni, Phae. She's coming to get Anton tomorrow when she arrives in Jax. It's okay to let him go with her."

"I texted you about that early this week and you said not to. Why the change of heart?"

"Like I said, she's bossy. It's her way of making sure I come visit her while she's in town," Lexie told her. "I'm just frustrated and I know I shouldn't be. She just gets under my skin."

"Then forgive yourself and keep moving forward. Allow yourself to feel frustrated for five minutes, accept your decision, then move on. Just don't let it ruin your day," Phaedra advised. "If I can go to Chuck E. damn Cheese with your son, then you can keep it moving toward a positive light."

Lexie appreciated the advise and was smiling again. "I've got to call Brie. I need her at Chuck E. Cheese with a video camera. Hell, the news crew. I'm gonna need blackmail material."

"Don't count on Brie. She's got a date tonight. Chris is her new boo. They had lunch earlier this week, dinner tonight and then she is hanging out at his house on Sunday," Phaedra informed her.

"Really? Wow. I feel so bad because I haven't talked to her except once this week. I'll have to call her."

"She probably just thinks you are jealous," Phaedra laughed.

"You see how you build up then tear down?"

"Whatever, it's just Brie."

"She's still your sister," Lexie teased.

"Anyways, I've got to go pick up Anton. Later!"

"Bye, Ms. I don't want to talk about this so I'm going to exit stage left."

"That's a long last name. It's going to take me a while to get my signature down," Phaedra said rolling her eyes. "Besides, I have been nicer to Brie. I've talked to her several times this week. How do you think I know her plans for this weekend?"

"Then I will let you off the hook. Go get my baby and you guys have fun tonight. Thanks for everything Phaedra. I really do appreciate your encouragement."

"I'm glad you are doing better. See you this weekend, or next week, or whenever."

Stop teasing her

Brie looked at the clock and it was approaching four. As far as she was concerned the day was moving slow. She was ready for 6:30 to get here. She had been walking through the office making sure everything was neat. She had completed all her work, with the exception of answering the phones which wasn't really ringing, and was now just clock watching. She couldn't stand it anymore. Brie was ready to see Chris.

"You look like you are about to burst open," Thomas, Ellie's partner, told her.

"No, not really. It's Friday. Just ready for the weekend," Brie told him.

"She's lying, Tom," Ellie said walking up joining the conversation. "She got a hot date tonight with the professor."

The corners of Brie's mouth spread widely across her face. "Okay, I'm just a little excited."

"A little!" Tom yelled. "I think we need a fire extinguisher near so when you combust we can put out the flames."

"Stop teasing her. He seems like a nice guy and I'm happy for her," Ellie said smiling as if Brie were her 16 year old daughter going on her first date.

"Why don't you take off for the rest of the day. We can cover the phones," Tom suggested looking Ellie's way for approval.

"Yes, go! This way you are not rushing. We've got the phones covered," Ellie agreed.

"Really? You are okay with that? Thank you so much," Brie said hugging both of them. She gathered her things and shot out before anyone changed their minds.

As Brie was jumping into her gray car, she felt her phone vibrating in her purse. She quickly dug it out praying it wasn't the babysitter or Chris cancelling. She just missed the call but saw it was Lexie. She was relieved but would call her back once she got in traffic. Brie was excited that good things were happening to her. She had a date with a man that was intelligent and not broke. It has been a long time since she had been on a real date, and this week she will have been on two. Brie had to laugh at herself because she was still smiling like Jack Nicholson's Joker. Her cheeks were sore but she didn't care.

Ten minutes into her drive she finally called Lexie. She was still cautious because she wasn't sure where Lexie was coming from. Did she want Chris? Was she upset that Brie had him? Friends should never allow a man to come between them, but statistically, Brie had a better chance of finding another friend than another man like Chris.

"Hey Brie, how are you?" Lexie answered upbeat.

"I'm great. You sound like you are feeling better. Are you?"

"I am. A lot better. Thanks. I've got a business plan started and Mark and I are on again, and this has just been a good trip."

Brie felt a sense of relief that Lexie and Mark were on again. She dropped her defense and was more comfortable with the call. "I'm so happy for your Lexie. What kind of business?"

"Helping people who are out of work by showing them how to navigate and understand job board keywords, helping them update their resume and having several copies, brushing up on interview skills and so forth. There is no real help out there. That is one thing I've learned. I'm hoping to fill the gap," Lexie explained.

"That would be perfect for you. Are you going to do job placement also?"

"No, don't want to. I just want to deal with the job seekers, not the employers."

"You go girl! You found your niche," Brie cheered.

"Thank you. And hey, I hear you and Chris have a date tonight. Where are you guys going?"

"Steakhouse at The Landing. Chris picked the place," she told her.

"You should be more excited. You went after this man, snagged him, going out with him not once but twice this week, and seeing him again Sunday. Yes, Phae caught me up. I need you to be shouting from a roof top."

Brie laughed and smiled because she knew she still had her friend. "You are right. I really like him, Lexie. We've been on the phone all week. He is funny, sweet, smart, understanding, everything I want."

Lexie was genuinely happy for Brie. "I'm so glad to hear that. He sounds like he makes you happy. You're not at work?"

"No, Ellie told me to go home early so I could get ready. She has been extra nice since informing me that she can't afford to give me my yearly raise."

"Are you serious? When did this happen?"

"Monday, after the meeting," Brie told her.

"Well, at least she is not letting you go or closing shop. I'm sorry to hear no raise. Are you going to be okay?"

"Yes, I'll be fine. Maybe now I'll think more about Brie's party planning. I'm gonna have to get some kind of side hustle going."

"We will work it out. And we've got Mark the great marketing machine."

Brie laughed at Lexie's enthusiasm. "At least I know you got my back. When are you and Mark coming back this way?"

"Sunday. My sister is heading up to Jax and I'm meeting her Sunday afternoon or evening. Whenever we get there."

"Phaedra told me she called her. Is she coming up here to drill you?"

"Girl, who knows. I'll find out Sunday. Well, I'll let you get ready for Mr. Man. I will probably call you Sunday on the way down to get all the juicy details. Write stuff down if you think you will forget. Or record it on your phone. Whichever is easiest," Lexie joked.

"You know you are silly, right?" Brie told her laughing. "I will be sure to keep notes just for you."

"Have fun tonight, Brie. Love ya!" Lexie told her.

"I will, and you and Mark enjoy the rest of your weekend. See you when you get back. Love you too."

The ladies hung up and Brie was pulling into her apartment complex. She was glad to be home early to see her kids and have time to make sure she looked perfect. After she parked, she sent Chris a text to let him know she got off early and was home already. Before she got to the door he had text her back that he would pick her up at 6:15 instead of 6:30.

"Well, damn, so much for extra time," she complained. She text him back a simple O.K.

Let me tell you about my mother and sister

Mark was asleep and Lexie was sitting up in bed writing in her journal. She was dreading Sunday and it was still Friday night. Phaedra was right, she was giving Roni her power. Lexie recalled a story she heard Les Brown tell about a dog lying on a nail. When the pain got uncomfortable, the dog would finally get up, but as long as he wasn't uncomfortable, he would lie there in agony.

Roni had run things since they were kids. She was tired of her bossy big sister, but Lexie wasn't uncomfortable. The two sisters had a good relationship. They talked several times a week. Lexie respected her sister's opinions, just not the way she delivered them. Like most sisters, they laughed and played, loved and hated, fought and moved on. But with the burden of being unemployed, Lexie just couldn't bring herself to put up with Roni's delivery. For once, she needed Roni to be the patient caring one.

Roni was only bossy when she felt that decisions needed to be made. There were times Lexie appreciated this, like when her father died. Roni took care of the funeral arrangements, the insurance and the people. Lexie took care of their mom. That was Lexie's role, a care taker, a giver, a referee in an argument and the one you called when you needed someone to just listen. With Roni, you gave her a problem, she solved it.

Carol was not surprised when Roni went to law school. Just the same, Lexie studying Human Resources was no surprise. Lexie wanted to help everyone and be everyone's friend. Lexie made it a point not to see herself through her mother's eyes. It always confused her. She moved cautiously and tried to make everything perfect. This is when she missed her dad. She was more like him. Richard Simmons worked the same job for 35 years and was content. In his eyes, Lexie was already perfect.

Now her family included Anton and Mark. She felt guilty about her son's father never calling or visiting him. She tried to make up for it with extra hugs and attention. She didn't want him to feel unwanted, but everything she read said he would. She wanted to be more for Anton. He was watching her and she was drinking through her problems. She needed to show him a better way.

Fear of vulnerability, the nail, was easier than just being vulnerable. For the last couple of days, she tried with little things. She assumed a couple of them were test. She asked Mark to look over her business plan and to offer suggestions. She had not completed it. She listened to his suggestions and made the changes. This was easing off the nail.

The biggest test for her was asking him to look at her budget. She did not want to touch her 401k and feared her savings shrinking. She had a few investments but they weren't doing great. He promised when they got home he would sit down with her and go over it. She was okay with that. Lexie was still going to need a few days to accept the idea of, showing Mark her money. However, if this relationship did move forward, this would be a good thing. They would have the money part out of the way already.

Too much, too soon," she told herself feeling the nail sticking in her side. "Baby steps."

Morning chores

Roni had text Phaedra that she would be there by 2 p.m. Phaedra told Anton and he was excited to see his Aunt. She was glad because she was ready to get back to her life, and from what she could tell, so were the kids.

Phaedra got up and got breakfast started after her morning meditation. Since it was Anton's last day, she decided blueberry pancakes, eggs and bacon would be a good send-off breakfast. The smell of the bacon woke the kids up. All three came running down the stairs. She sent all three back up to wash their faces and brush their teeth.

After breakfast, she made her kids do their chores and Anton get his stuff together. Phaedra checked her phone to see that George still had not called or text, but RJ did. She threw the phone on the dark plum comforter and headed for her closet. It had already felt like a long day and it was still early.

Phaedra never returned RJ's text. Instead she got on the phone with Brie to find out how her date went. Brie wasn't coming up for air as she told Phaedra everything. Phaedra finally put her phone on speaker and treated Brie as if she was background noise. Phaedra wanted to be happy for her, but George was still on her mind. Anton interrupted the conversation when he came in the room.

"Aunt Phaedra, I have all my stuff ready," he reported.

"Okay honey. We still have a few hours before your Aunt Roni gets here. Do you want to watch TV?"

"No ma'am," he answered. "I want to play a game."

"Okay, I'll have Caleb set it up for you. I'm not sure how to work the game system," Phaedra told him.

"I can show you!"

"No, honey, that's okay. I'll meet you in the game room," she declined. "Hey, Brie, let me get back with you later. Let me get this little boy settled."

"Okay. I'll be around today, but you know tomorrow I get to go to his house," Brie reminded her.

"That's right. If I don't get back with you today, have fun," Phaedra told her and disconnected.

Phaedra headed for the game room calling for Caleb to come help Anton. Just then her phone was ringing, it was RJ. She wished he would stop calling. She has told him several times this week she could not hook up with him. She let the call go to voicemail. Once she got Anton settled, she sent a text to Lexie to let her know her sister would be picking up her son around two. Then she got a text from RJ. 'Just thinking of you, doll' it read. She did not answer him back again. However, Lexie did text her an okay."

Lunch with Chris

The babysitter had been a little late, but Brie tried to pretend it wasn't that big of a deal. Chris had told her to come casual so Brie threw on her jeans with a green hooded t-shirt and her green suede booties. Brie had debated on her dark tight jeans because of her thighs. She wasn't aware that those were her best assets as far as Chris was concerned.

Brie drove down Chris' street in wonderment. There were mansions, luxury cars, and professionally kept yards. She parked in front of his three car garage. The house was painted a light grey color and the wooden garage doors and window panels were a slate gray. Her silver car seemed to blend right in. She immediately fell in love with the magnolia tree in the middle of his yard. It was surrounded by three rows of yellow, orange and red mix of tulips and mums with a brick border.

The walkway also had the same brick border leading up to the steps to the front door. There were begonias on each side of it. She rang the doorbell to the arched mahogany with a stained glass half circle design on each side of the hanging door knobs. Chris didn't leave her waiting long. He had been outside flipping burgers on the grill. "Come in, come in," he greeted her.

Brie stepped into the foyer and looked to the left to see the mahogany table and circular mirror where he kept his keys and dropped off his mail. A silver umbrella holder was right next to it with a large blue and white umbrella sticking out of it. She followed him through the house passing the living room and only getting a glimpse of a navy colored couch and two high back white chairs. No kids had been around here with white chairs. There was a coral short shag rug that extended from the couch to the chairs under the navy ottoman coffee table. She imagined herself sitting on the couch sipping tea with Lexie and Phaedra.

They walked through the kitchen and she imagined herself cooking at the professional stove which was about the size of two regular stoves. There was a grill in the middle with six burners and a large wood, panel hood the same cherry wood as the floor that carried throughout the whole bottom floor. The island had a gray marble top and she counted six barstools around it. Chris was walking quickly so she didn't get to take it all in.

She stepped into the Florida room, which was about the size of her apartment. At least that is what it felt like. He had a heated pool, wicker patio furniture with bright, yellow cushions and a pool table. There was a full bar in the corner with a neon sign that read Chris's Bar.

Chris was back at the grill but had only said a good three sentences to her, including "take a seat here". Brie had not sat. She was taking the room in piece by piece. She settled at the 75 inch television next to the bar. The room was decorated for a man who had his boys over to watch the game. A real man's cave. That was the picture in her mind as she looked around. Just him and his guy friends.

Brie finally walked out of the room and onto the patio where Chris was grilling. She stood next to him taking in the backyard. His grass looked like a plush green carpet. There were a couple of trees and flowers were planted along the back fence. The same red, yellow and orange colors.

Chris grabbed her by the waist and pulled her close to kiss her. "Sorry, I didn't want the burgers to burn. Didn't mean to be rude."

Brie found herself smiling again. "I wouldn't want you to burn those either. Your house is beautiful."

"More beautiful now that you are here," he told her.

Brie blushed, "Anything I can help you with?"

"I have potato salad in the fridge and baked beans and greens on the stove. The only thing left is the meat."

"Sounds like you have it all taken care of," she acknowledged.

"Well, I could use a beer out of the fridge behind the bar," he suggested just so he could watch her walk away.

"I can do that," she said happily and headed back into the Florida room.

Chris watched her until she got inside. He admired her walk, especially how tight her jeans were. He realized he needed to stop admiring because the growth in his pants was telling on him. He went back to the grill and paid more attention to the hamburgers and ribs until he got himself adjusted.

Brie found her way behind the bar and saw it was as fully stocked as a bar at a restaurant. She wished she knew how to mix drinks, especially since he only had top shelf liquor. Besides, she needed something to help her ease her own nerves. She opened the door to what was a small dorm like refrigerator. There were several types of beers but he never gave her a specific choice. She grabbed a Heineken because it was familiar from the commercials.

She looked up and saw Grey Goose vodka and remembered cranberry juice in the small refrigerator. She figured easy enough, two ingredients and it's what Lexie always drinks. Brie mixed it in a glass and then threw an orange slice in it like Eric does. She carried the two drinks out to the patio and passed Chris his beer. He was glad she knew to take the cap off but wished he would have told her to put it in one of the chilled glasses. He drank it from the bottle. Chris was done cooking and put the ribs and burgers on a tray and lead the way to the kitchen.

She took a sip of her drink and made a sour face expression having put more vodka than she could handle. Chris put the food down and asked Brie to get the plates and silverware. He directed her to where the placemats and the dishes were. He left her to set the table while he walked back to his bar to get a glass for his beer. She did just so, including putting the condiments on the island between the food.

"Hope you don't mind, I went into the pantry looking for ketchup but discovered it was in the fridge," she told him while folding the napkin on his plate.

"Isn't the ketchup supposed to be refrigerated after opening?" Chris asked her.

"I know it says that on the bottle, but I hate putting cold ketchup on the hot food," she explained. "I've been doing it for years and I haven't got sick or killed over."

Chris smiled at her justification. "I understand your perspective, but why not follow the manufacturer's directions?"

"Because I don't want cold ketchup on my hot food," she said more in the form of a question.

"Rules don't apply if they don't make you happy?" He teased her.

"Not always, but when it comes to my hot food, then yes."

"Then I will be sure to put a bottle in the pantry just for you," he smiled.

Brie's interpretation, she would be invited back.

I'm going to learn my lesson

Lexie and Mark were taking it easy on their last day before leaving Lake Lanier. They returned from doing some shopping in the surrounding cities and decided to take a walk around the lake. Lexie was content. She felt like she could even deal with being ganged up on by her mom and sister. She couldn't wait to see Anton again. She was missing him.

Mark offered for her to stay with him if she still felt like the walls of her townhome were caving in on her. Lexie promised to keep it in mind. The negative voice in her head was screaming, "too much too soon!" Lexie was trying to quiet the voice. She reminded herself baby steps.

Mark was looking through the fridge to see what they needed to take and what they needed to throw out. Half of his body was in the refrigerator when Lexie walked up and slapped him on the behind causing him to bump his head on the freezer door.

Lexie grabbed his head and started kissing the top of it and laughing. "I'm sorry, I'm sorry!"

They both laughed and Mark picked her up and threw her on the couch. What started off as wrestling turned into passionate kissing. Lexie wasn't comfortable on the used couch, so Mark grabbed her hand and led her to the bedroom.

"This just doesn't seem like a proper punishment for making me hit my head," he teased.

"Oh, I'm going to learn my lesson," she said smiling.

Mark laughed, "You will, because I'm going to just lay back and watch."

Lexie pulled Mark's jeans off and threw them across the room onto the floor. She straddled across him and pulled her shirt over her head then sling shot it across the room also. Mark laughed at her. She laughed also.

He was glad to see her smile again. A real smile. Something he had not seen in several months.

Already bored of the show

Roni called Phaedra to let her know her plane was delayed. Caleb had taken Anton to the park in their subdivision to play basketball with the big boys. Phaedra reminded her son to keep an eye on Anton. She had felt stuck in the house all day. A Saturday at home was not a good for a Real Estate agent. But the house was clean, there was a box for charity and she finally threw out the old coupons in the junk drawer.

Phaedra was not dressed to impress. Her silky black hair was pulled up in a ponytail with gold hoops in her ear and a gold heart in heart pendant on an 18" chain around her neck. The only make-up she wore was a glossy, burgundy lipstick. She had on loose fitting gray sweatpants with a lycra pink sports halter. The doorbell was ringing while she was moving laundry from the washer to the dryer. She grabbed her phone to send Caleb a text to bring Anton home as she headed for the door.

"Just a minute," she yelled to prevent a second push of the button. Phaedra opened the door and invited Roni in. She felt her heart beat a little faster and her palms were sweaty.

Roni was 5'10 ½" and chocolate brown. A tad darker than Lexie. Her hair short, relaxed and hot curled on the top, tapered in the back. Her makeup simple, just foundation and a shimmering beige and brown eye shadow. A clear gloss on her lips. She was dressed in black slacks with a button-down, caramel python print shirt that was tucked. She wore brown crocodile-stamped leather Christian Louboutin ankle boots. Phaedra found herself staring. She saw some resemblance of Lexie but not much.

Roni's hand was extended so she could introduce herself. Phaedra wiped her hands on her pants which is when she realized how underdressed she was for this meeting.

"It's nice to meet you, Phaedra. I can put a face with a name,," Roni said.

"Yes, likewise. My son and Anton went to play basketball. I just sent a text to him. They should be on their way back." Phaedra explained feeling the juice between her legs stir as she directed Roni to sit in the living room. "Can I get you something to drink?"

"No, thank you. I have water in the car. If you like, I can go ahead and take Anton's bags."

"Oh, yes, let me get those. He left them by the stairs." Phaedra was trying to keep her composure. She knew men but she had never been attracted to a woman before.

Roni was used to straight women fumbling over themselves around her. It no longer phased her. If anything, it was humorous. She imagined at this point Phaedra was questioning her sexuality. She assumed Phaedra was not this nervous being around people she just met. She did know a little about her from Lexie. If anything, she was over confident. Phaedra walked briskly towards the stairs. Roni stood up hoping Anton would walk through door soon. She was already bored of the show in front of her.

Phaedra sat the two bags in front of Roni. "Here you go. Oh, let me check the bathroom to make sure he got his tooth brush and tooth paste."

Roni watched as Phaedra this time ran up the stairs two at a time. Roni looked around the house and saw how immaculate it was which made Phaedra's fumbling funnier. Phaedra was organized and put together, but right now she was ditzy and clueless.

Before Phaedra had come back down the front door swung open. Anton and Caleb were running through it, Anton screaming "I won". He high fived Caleb and then saw his Aunt Roni and ran towards her.

"Hi, Aunt Roni. Are you going to take me to Grandma's?"

"Yes, I am. You and I are going to spend the night with her and your mom and Mark should be there tomorrow," she explained kneeling down to be eye level with him.

"Hi, I'm Caleb," the teenager introduced himself shaking Roni's hand.

"Nice to meet you Caleb," she said. "I hear that you have been Anton's best friend this week."

"He's a cool little kid," Caleb acknowledged. His phone rang and he saw it was his mother calling. At the same time, she was coming down the stairs. Caleb answered.

"Where are you guys?" She asked then looked up and saw them both.

Caleb gave Anton another high five and told him to take care. Caleb headed toward the kitchen. Anton turned around to hug Phaedra and thanked her for "the best week of his life." Phaedra smiled at him and gave him a big kiss on his cheek.

"Thank you again, Phaedra. My mother and I appreciated your hospitality," Roni said.

It was the first time Phaedra noticed Roni's brown eyes. "It was a pleasure. He is definitely a cool kid."

Roni grabbed one of his bags and extended her hand for the toothbrush and tooth paste that Phaedra was unaware that she was still holding onto. Embarrassed, she passed it over touching Roni's hand again while looking in her eyes. Again, her insides fluttered.

I might not win next time

Chris tried not to beat Brie at chess, but it didn't work out that way. He considered her a challenging player, he was just better. "Maybe next time we should play strip chess," he said containing his grin.

"Says the winner because he won't be the one naked in the chair."

Chris had to laugh at her, "I might not win next time."

Brie was setting the game back up. She had not agreed or disagreed to strip chess. Chris had asked her if she wanted another drink, but she declined. She was still coming down from the first drink she made. Chris grabbed another beer and another chilled glass.

"You know what would be nice?" Brie started. "A tour of your house. Not that I'm not enjoying this room, but if it is not inappropriate to ask, I would love to see it."

"Then I would love to show it to you," he told her. "This is my favorite room and where I spend most of my time."

"I can see why. If I would have known you had a pool, I would have brought my bathing suit," she said flirtatious.

"I might have a t-shirt you can borrow," Chris suggested grinning from ear to ear.

Brie just smiled. She debated in her head wanting the same thing Chris' thoughts were leading to. "Maybe next time, you know, if I get invited back," she said giving her own test.

"Why wouldn't you?" He asked grabbing her hand leading her back towards the kitchen.

Brie walked with him through the living room. She was wrong, the pillows on the couch were solid white and yellow. One of each color on each chair. The high back chair had a large white pillow with a coral hibiscus flower print on it. He showed her his office. She concluded Chris really liked mahogany wood. His desk was large and had a high back light brown leather chair with gold nails along the stitching. There were bookcases along one wall that were filled. She walked along the wall recognizing names like Isaac Newton, Albert Einstein and Neil deGrasse Tyson. His office was orderly, but that didn't surprise her.

Chris sat down in his chair and motioned Brie to sit in his lap. She was nervous but she obliged. He pulled open a drawer and took out a remote. He turned on his Bluetooth speakers and then his iPad and started playing Coltrane. Brie leaned back into Chris' arms uncomfortably. Not only because of the awkward way they were sitting, but because she was in a fight with herself not to sleep with him. Chris felt how tense she was and tried to make her a little more comfortable.

"This is where I end up spending the other part of my awake time when I'm home. I get stuck in here before I get to relax," Chris told her leaning back further in the chairs pulling playfully on her braids.

"My grandmother always said a man that works hard needs to play hard."

"Maybe. I'm sure that's what vacations are for," he said nonchalantly.

"So, why do you work so hard? Especially since you don't need the money."

"Because the key to happiness is finding something you love so much, you'd do it for free," Chris explained. "I love learning and I love teaching. I love the expression on a student's face when they get it."

"That is a good philosophy on life. Phaedra always says something similar. Maybe I'm still looking for my bliss."

"You don't enjoy your job?" He asked.

"I do. My favorite part is when I'm responsible for planning events. I'm always trying to outdo the previous one. Lexie says I should go into business as an event planner. I told her that there are way too many of them already in Jacksonville." It was the first time she was vulnerable with him about her own hopes and dreams. Usually when she talked about herself she would cut it short because she still feared running him off.

"Then you have to come up with what sets you apart. Speaking of parties, I did want to invite you to one."

"Really? When and where?" She asked turning around to look at him.

"I told you about the speech I have been working on. Well, our department has a recognition dinner each year. It's in a week. I would love for you to be my date."

Brie did remember because she had been planning what to wear and how she would style her hair. She was excited as he expected her to be. "Of course, I would. Is it formal? Just need to know what I'm going shopping for. And will there be dancing?"

"Yes, well, semi-formal. I don't have to wear a tux, just a black suit. And yes, there will be dancing. It usually starts with dinner, then speeches are given, a few accolades and then mingling and dancing."

"Sounds like fun to me," she said grinning then leaning in to kiss him.

"They are okay. Maybe I will enjoy it this year since I'll have you as a date and I won't be trying to dodge out of there early."

"Are they that boring?"

"Just not my favorite part of the job. I don't need an award. I'm not interested in giving speeches to my colleagues. It's more of a see me, I'm important, and this is why event. You will be the first date I bring to one of these things."

"Really? Wow, I now I feel important and better than all the others," she smiled.

Chris was feeling like he just scored a few brownie points. "I haven't been in a serious relationship in a long while."

Brie interpreted that to mean they were officially in a relationship. She leaned in to kiss him again, this time with more passion. "So, are you going to show me the rest of the house?"

"The only thing left is the bedroom," he whispered.

"Then let's go see it," she suggested standing up and pulling him by the arm.

Chris followed her giving directions. He would no longer have to imagine what her big thighs would feel like around his neck. His dream was about to come true.

Family Gatherings

The drive home was not as long as the drive up. That could be because Lexie was not looking forward to her reunion. "I feel like a fish and Anton is the big juicy worm on the hook."

"You do realize that all the bad things in your head are just your imagination? You are going to stress yourself out over something you can't control," Mark told her.

"I know my sister. She is going to lecture me. She is going to rant and rave and try to make me feel bad."

They turned into her Mom's subdivision and Mark pulled over to the side. He threw the car in park and turned toward Lexie. "Baby, you have to stop. You have got to put on your big girl panties and be you. You don't owe anyone anything. If she wants to rant and rave, let her. But don't soak that shit up. You aren't a sponge."

Lexie was grateful Mark was with her. He was right. She did not have to succumb to anything her mom and sister said. It was her choice and she needed to make her own decision.

Mark kissed her, put the car back in drive and drove on to Mrs. Simmons house. When they arrived, Lexie took a deep breath. Mark squeezed her hand and they got out of the car. Lexie put a smile on her face and rang the doorbell.

Roni opened the door not expecting to see Mark. She smiled a little wider and welcomed them both in giving her little sister a hug. Anton came running to his mother excited to see her. She squeezed him until he said "uncle".

Carol was happy to see Mark and gave him her own big squeeze. After everyone hugged, she invited them to sit in the den. Anton was telling his mom and Mark all the things he had done that week. He was excited about hanging out with Caleb and asked if he could have big brother for Christmas.

Roni sat across from the three of them watching as Anton spoke non-stop. She was never crazy about Mark but did not have a particular reason to not like him. He was the only father Anton really knew. He was attentive and patient with her sister.

"Mrs. Simmons, what smells so good?" Mark asked her.

Lexie's mother had just pulled a ham out of the oven just before they got there. "That is the smell of Sunday dinner. I cooked yams, green beans, dinner rolls and a ham."

"I hope I'm not intruding," Mark asked realizing that he didn't know if he was actually invited.

"Heavens no, Mark. You are always welcome," she assured him.

"Thank you. We figured it would be easier to stop here first then Lexie could take me home."

"Well, I'm happy you are going to stay a while," Carol said.

"Mom, do you need any help in the kitchen?" Lexie asked her.

"No, Roni is going to set the table for us and Anton has volunteered to say grace, so if everyone wants to wash up, we can eat," her mother informed her.

They all stood up, Roni went towards the kitchen to wash her hands and Lexie, Mark and Anton towards the guest bathroom to wash theirs.

"So far so good," Mark whispered.

"Calm before the storm," Lexie suggested.

"Negative Nancy," he joked.

"Mark, are you staying at our house?" Anton asked.

"No, I have to go home. Your mom has been away for a week and is looking forward to having you all to herself."

"Ahhh, I wish we were a family," Anton sighed.

Both Lexie and Mark just looked at each other, Lexie genuinely surprised, Mark not so much. Mark leaned into Lexie's ear and whispered, "Ball dropped," and he and Anton headed for the dining room.

Lexie stood there looking in the mirror at herself. She felt uncomfortable in her own skin. Her life was shifting, she felt like she was holding tight to the bar on a roller coaster ride. "Too much too soon," the voice in her head said. Lexie hated that thought. She has said it one too many times now. She placed it in the same category as "I did everything right".

She told herself, "Enjoy the ride girl. Enjoy it!"

Lexie headed for the dining room when she heard her name being called.

Im not in a funk, or bored

Phaedra had already spoken to Lexie and she filled her in on how her week went. Phaedra told Lexie she would come by after work because Lexie was on information overload. For once, the only person Phaedra wanted to talk to was Brie. She couldn't tell Lexie what was on her mind. She had left Brie alone since she had plans with Chris. She knew when she got hold of Brie, she'd want to talk about Chris. Phaedra did not want to hear about Chris. She sent a Brie a text to inform her she had something to tell her hoping that would give her an opportunity to speak first.

Phaedra was walking out of her morning meeting when she checked her phone. She laughed because Brie was so easy to bait. Brie had called her three times. Then she had to laugh at herself because she would have done the same.

"Hey Brie, are you busy?" Phaedra asked returning the call.

"No, what's up? What happened?" Brie asked walking quickly to the break room.

"Have you ever met Lexie's sister?"

"No, just seen pictures of her. Lexie doesn't bring her around when she's in town," Brie answered.

"So, she picked up Anton yesterday, wait, I have to swear you to secrecy," Phaedra paused.

"What? Are you serious?" Brie said feeling as if they were in high school.

"Yes, ma'am. You can't repeat this to Lexie. I would be so embarrassed," Phaedra explained.

Now she really had Brie's attention. "Okay, I promise. Pinky promise."

"So, this has me a little perplexed, but, I have to tell you, Lexie's sister is fine. I got all tingly and wet and was tripping over myself around her. I know I'm not gay, or even curious. It was just something about her."

Brie wasn't sure how to respond. "Wait, you met Roni and you got horny?"

"Not just horny, interested. I mean, she's masculine and feminine at the same time. Her aura just vibed with mine. I spent the whole damn day thinking about her."

"Maybe she just seems like a new challenge for you. Maybe you are just in a funk and looking for something different." Brie was trying her hardest to diagnose the situation.

"Brie, you don't hear me. It's something about her. I'm not in a funk, or bored, or anything else. It's just something about her," she tried to clarify.

"Well, now you've got me looking forward to meeting this woman."

"I think she headed back already," Phaedra said a little sad. She went on to describe Roni to Brie the best she could. She found herself having to say several times that she was not attracted to women, just Roni. Phaedra gave up and asked about Chris.

"It was so fantastic. We ate lunch, we played chess we went out to the movies, we made love," Brie said trying to mumble the last part.

"Wait, you made love? You little whore. I thought you were going to wait?"

"I was but then he mentioned serious relationship and invited me to a work thing. I figured he is going nowhere," Brie pleaded her case.

Phaedra was teasing and not judging, but she could tell Brie was questioning her choice. "Then it should work out Brie. Stop being so wishy-washy and second guessing everything you say and do and just have fun. Was big boy even any good in the sack?"

Brie sucked her teeth at the big boy description, "Yes he is. And I don't want to hear your dumb joke when I tell you this, but he was better at eating it than fucking it. Seem to be his favorite part."

Phaedra fell back laughing, not even trying to hold it in. "I'm sorry, I don't mean to laugh, but come on, you set that one up."

Brie laughed also, "Okay, I did. But still, be nice."

"Fine. Anyways, I was heading to Lexie's after work. Do you want to go?"

"Sure. I miss Lexie. The real Lexie. I hope she's either a version of her old self, or new and improved version of her old self." Brie said.

"I think she is back to her old self, but we will see. She says she has a plan."

"Well, then, I'll see you tonight. I gotta get back to my desk."

"Alright, later," Phaedra ended the call. She really wished she had someone else to talk to about Roni. Lexie was her only other friend. She would just have to hold this one in.

Reminiscing without a spare pair of panties

Brie had been typing a proposal when she looked up to see her phone's indicator light flashing that she had received a text. It was Chris, just said 'thinking of you'. Brie smiled and blushed thinking about Saturday. His bed was a California King size and in Brie's mind they had made love on every inch of it. He was a passionate lover which she was not expecting from a wealthy man. The ones from her past were self-fish.

He sat on the edge of the bed and Brie stood in front of him starting with just kissing. She still had not made up her mind but at this point there really was no turning around. After all, she did initiate this. Trying to hesitate she stepped back and gave him the strip show he hinted at earlier after they played chess. She only got down to her panties and the t-shirt she was wearing under her hoodie.

Chris enjoyed what he saw and pulled Brie close to him. He was the one to pull down her panties. Brie's whole body was shaking as he rubbed up her legs and between them taking his time to learn her. Brie could not stand up any longer. Chris laid her down on the bed. Brie pulled off her shirt and sat up so he could unhook her bra. Brie realized she was naked and Chris was fully dressed. Before she could get uncomfortable, Chris' tongue was deep inside of her. Brie moaned heavy because it was unexpected.

She wanted to grab his hair but he was out of reach. Instead she grabbed a fist full of comforter. Chris ate like a man on death row enjoying his last meal. He savored every morsel. He didn't need to come up for air. He concentrated on her body movements, the vibrations of her moans to know when to keep going and when to move elsewhere. Several times she squeezed his head with her thighs.

When Brie started pushing herself away from him, he knew she had reached that point where she couldn't take it anymore. Chris quickly removed his clothes and asked her to turn over on her stomach. He entered her from behind holding her by her hips. Brie was expecting him to be quick and be done.

That was not the case. Chris made love to her slowly, again learning every part of her. Asking her how she liked it and what she preferred. He flipped her several directions going back and forth from sliding in and out of her to eating her. Before he came he asked permission. By then she was ready for a nap. No man had ever made her climax like that. Brie was ready to drop to one knee and propose. Instead she smiled, kissed him and they both went to sleep before going to the movies.

Reminiscing left Brie all wet and it was still morning. She texted him back, 'Looking forward to seeing you again'.

I'm not five years old

Anton didn't want to go to school that morning so Lexie promised to come eat lunch with him for his cooperation. His teacher bragged to her about how well behaved Anton was while she was away. Anton wanted his mom to stay but she let him know she had work to do. He pouted for a minute, just enough to give his mom a guilt trip, then went off to play with his friends. Lexie checked her phone after she got to her car. She had a text from Phaedra letting her know Brie was coming also. There was also a call from Roni that was missed. She thought about calling her later but decided why put it off.

"Hey, what's up?" Lexie asked after Roni's greeting.

"I was hoping you could come by here or I come your direction," Roni requested.

"I thought you were getting on a plane and heading home," Lexie said disappointed.

"You sick of me already?"

"Only because you are in mom mode. You feel the need to be my parent instead of my sister. You have all these expectations and you keep looking down on me. It's like a rod has been run straight up your ass," Lexie released.

"You are up here being irresponsible. What do you expect me to do?" Roni told her.

"Just because I don't do it your way does not make it irresponsible. You know what, I'm on my way home. Come by if you want."

"I will meet you there," Roni promised.

Lexie rolled her eyes and sighed. "Roni, I'm not five years old, you know."

Lexie looked at her phone. Her sister had already disconnected the call. Breathe deep, she told herself, started her car and headed to her house.

A little flirting won't hurt

Phaedra had been debating with herself whether or not to text Roni. She was interested and decided to test the water. She didn't have a problem with traveling to Miami. It was a place that kept your secrets. She'd have nothing to worry about. She had not been able to read Roni to know if she would even respond. Phaedra wasn't one to shy away from going after what she wants, but this was uncharted waters. Phaedra didn't want to back down.

'It was nice to finally meet you. Have a safe flight home," read the text message. Simple but enough to get attention.

Phaedra called on her favorite restaurants to order appetizers and a bottle of Merlot to take to Lexie's tonight. She ordered Greek meatballs, marinated roasted peppers and capers, mozzarella and olive salad on butter lettuce leaves. After her order she checked her phone to see if Roni responded. She did.

'Still in town, but thanks,' was the reply.

Phaedra smiled because she saw an opportunity. Once again, she has asked and the Universe was delivering. She replied, 'Great. You should join us for drinks and light appetizers at your sisters tonight.'

'We'll see. I'm at my sister's now.'

Phaedra did not want to sound needy. She replied, 'I hope you consider it. Take care.'

Phaedra put the phone down and went to work on other things. She heard the text alert sound on her phone. She decided to keep working. She'd look later.

Invest it in some sexy ass lingerie

Brie and Kenny had gone to lunch together because Kenny wanted to hear everything and Brie wanted to make sure she did not blow it.

"So, big man had a plan?" Kenny asked.

"He had a plan. We did lunch and a movie. Played a game of chess," she explained.

"Sounds boring," he said faking a yawn.

"Whatever boy. It was nice. His house is really nice."

Kenny laughed at her. "Let me guess, you imagined yourself living there didn't you?"

Brie laughed because she did. That made Kenny laugh even more. "It's a woman thing. But seriously, it was a nice day. He invited me to a formal dinner at his job."

"I know you are excited, but don't go reading too heavily into it. I know you." Kenny encouraged.

"I'm not. It's an awards dinner. And you know what else, that means I'm going to be meeting his coworkers and his boss. That has to mean something," she begged.

Kenny didn't want to burst her bubble. He knew how desperately she wanted this to work and how excited she was about it. "Brie, I'm just saying, don't go to this dinner acting like a wife. Go acting like a date. Make him work for wife. You'd be surprised how much a man is willing to do for a woman that is wife material."

Brie meditated on what Kenny said. "Do you think I blew it sleeping with him on Saturday?"

"I doubt it. If his agenda is to see what you are about, then it won't matter if you do it on the 3rd date or in 30 days. His mind was made up the first day he met you. Brie, just be yourself. Loosen up. Stop worrying about every little thing. When you worry, you start nagging him or you'll start catering to him. Then he loses interest. Then we gotta hear about men are dogs when it was really you and your insecurities."

Brie knew she was insecure. She felt Chris was out of her league because of his wealth. Her history told her men did not stick around. Kenny saw the look of concern on her face. He grabbed her hand and smiled.

"I know, I'm reading too much into it. I'm going to take your advice. I'm going to relax and release. So, what about the hot blonde? You still seeing her?"

"Off and on. She is making a brother work hard for the cookies. I'm not used to that. I didn't see no purity ring on her finger when I asked her out," Kenny complained.

Brie shook her head at him. "Obviously she is worth it. You are still chasing the cookie."

"And that damn cookie better be so tight I can't get my middle finder in it," Kenny leaned over to whisper.

Brie laughed, "You are damn crazy. Maybe she is thinking like I do. She has a successful guy that could take care of her and she read all those books on dating and thinks if she holds out you will stay longer."

"Would you like my advice on dating books?"

"No!" She told him.

"You are going to get it any ways. Take that same money, invest it in some sexy ass lingerie, and I'm talking strings, crotch less, and something that makes your boobs sit up under your neck. Invest in that. That's how you keep a man's attention."

Brie laughed at him, but she also made a mental note.

I'm not here to make you happy

Lexie saw her sister pull up in the drive way and opened the door. She was ready to get this conversation over with. Looking through new eyes, she didn't understand what her sister was making a big deal about.

"Hey," Roni greeted as she walked in. "Your back passenger tire looks low. You might want to have that checked."

"I'll let Mark know," Lexie said while building her defensive wall up.

"I guess Mark takes care of everything now," she asked.

"Yes, he does," Lexie said smiling and raising her eyebrows. Then she got serious. "So, what is you want to lecture me about?"

"You left Mom alone and your son with a friend to go on vacation. I don't understand your logic," Roni started.

"Did it ever occur to you that maybe you don't need to understand the logic? And it was not a vacation, it was a retreat. Nobody I'm related to seems to give a damn that I was having a mental breakdown."

"It's been all about you lately, Lexie. We are trying to be understanding and patient. I've asked you a hundred times what you need. And what about your mother?" Roni demanded.

"A retreat is what I needed. And, Mom is not feeble. She does not need looking after. You are using her as an excuse," Lexie pointed out.

"I'm just saying something could have happened to her while you were away."

"She has her church family, friends, and Mrs. Watts and Mom talk every day and meet for lunch or dinner. I was the same distance from Mom that you are. The girl that moved to Miami so she wouldn't have to deal with

Mom's disappointed looks because her beautiful perfect daughter is gay," Lexie said that last part in her 5 year old voice.

"Feel better now that you've got that off your chest?" Roni asked with arms crossed and eyes narrow.

"No, I've got about 10 more years of crap to get off my chest," Lexie answered snotty.

"I'm sure we can Google some therapist right here in Jacksonville that you can visit," Roni suggested.

"Roni, what are you really upset about? I don't see how me going away for a week is really that big of a deal. So, come on, tell me what's really up?"

"You've been unemployed for a while now and I don't see any progress. I know you don't think it is my business, but it is. I'm the one that is going to have to pick up the slack. Your taking off for a week is why I'm upset," Roni confessed.

"Roni, my time at the lake allowed me to come up with a business plan that will make me some income. You don't have to worry about me. I did enough of that for the both of us. I would appreciate your opinion, so come look at my business plan instead of fussing at me. Mark helped out with the marketing. It's still a work in progress."

"Sure. I know it needs my help if you put it together," Roni said feeling somewhat relieved. "You are still irresponsible."

Lexie laughed at her sister who always has to have the last word. "This is going to come as a shock to you, but I'm not here to make you happy. I left, I'm back, and everyone survived."

"Humph," Roni snarled. "Go get the business plan so I can look at it. I'm going to get me something to drink. Not only are you irresponsible but you have bad manners too. Didn't offer me anything when I walked into the house."

Lexie let her have that one. If she didn't the conversation would never end. Roni was a great lawyer for a reason. She doesn't stop until she felt she has won. Lexie smiled and headed to her office to grab her laptop.

Catching up

It was the first time the three of them had gotten together since their night at Friday's. Mark had come by to get the car and he and Anton were going out for guy's night. Brie had arrived before Phaedra which made her happy. There were times Phaedra could be an attention hog.

Lexie gave Brie a tight hug. Then Brie insisted they take a selfie. She was glad they would have time for her to talk about Chris, which she did. Lexie smiled and was genuinely happy for her. Just as she was getting ready to tell her about Mark, Phaedra called to say she was outside and needed help bringing in the food. Both got up to help her.

"I could have cooked something," Lexie began and Phaedra shot her a look. "But I am so grateful you did this."

They set everything down on the counter and Brie retrieved the wine glasses. The conversation picked up with Lexie finally getting a chance to talk about Mark and the promises she made. She told them about the trip. Then she told them about her business plan. They caught up on the week and each other's lives. In between came the text messages from Chris, Mark and RJ. Brie told Chris she was hanging out with her girlfriends and would call him later. Mark just wanted Lexie to know he was swinging by home to get clothes for tomorrow and would be spending the night at her house. Phaedra, again, told RJ she was busy.

This was getting back to normal, or at least a version of it. Lexie had her confidence back, a direction, and a new acceptance of the word change. Her sister and mom might not approve the way she is handling things, but she had her friends who had her back, and that was all that counted.

Girlfriend

Brie had spent the week getting prepared for tonight. She had gone to the salon to have her eyebrows threaded and get a mani-pedi. Then there was the dreaded waxing. The torture chair, as she called it. She had asked Janey, her babysitter, to spend the night. She figured it was going to be a late evening. More like she was hoping he would just ask her to stay over.

Chris had taken her shopping for a new dress and shoes. She enjoyed modeling everything for him. He picked his favorite of the dresses she tried on. A burnt orange, floor length dress that was strapless and form fitting. She picked out a scarf that she could wrap around her shoulders. Her shoes were 3", just enough to bring her closer to his height. Chris had a black suit and a white shirt. He decided to allow Brie to pick out a tie and handkerchief and was relieved she did not try and match them. His tie was a plaid design with slate blue, olive green and a dark burgundy. The handkerchief was solid olive green.

"Is it okay if I introduce you as Brielle instead of Brie?" He asked her as he parked the car.

"Of course," she said pulling down the mirror to check her makeup and hair.

"You look beautiful," he told her as he watched.

She smiled closing the mirror and leaning over to kiss him. "Thank you. And may I add how handsome you are tonight."

Brie got nervous as they entered the banquet hall. It wasn't as many people as she was expecting. Maybe 20 or so. She would have been able to handle a bigger crowd. It would have been less intimidating. She held onto Chris' arm as he looked for his table.

Chris stopped along the way and shook hands with several people and introduced her. As nervous as she was, she still caught site of the surprised look on their faces. A few even emphasized the word girlfriend with a question mark. When they got to the table, Chris pulled out her chair. There were two other couples seated. Again, he introduced her Brielle to his colleagues and their spouses. Brie smiled as she said hello and in her head said, "Yeap, girlfriend."

A waitress had come to the table to take their order. "Good evening Chris," she spoke. "What can I get for you tonight?"

"How about a dry martini, extra olives," he answered to the smiling woman he took home last time. Then he turned to Brie, "And honey, what would you like?"

Brie had been watching the woman the whole time and the couples at the table had been watching her. She knew the grin on the woman's face all too well. She had been walking around with the same one since the first night she and Chris made love. "I don't want anything right now. Maybe later."

"One dry martini coming up," the waitress said, no longer smiling and walked off in a huff.

Brie shot him a look of disdain then excused herself. Chris assumed she was just going to the bathroom and continued conversing with the people at the table. Instead, Brie walked to the bar and ordered her drink from a male bartender. As she walked back to the table the waitress was just walking away but made a point to look Brie up and down. Once eye contact was established they both rolled their eyes. Chris stood up as he saw Brie approaching with a drink in her hand. He picked up his drink and excused himself from the table meeting her before reached the table.

"What are you doing? I offered to order you a drink with the waitress."

"I didn't want anyone spitting in my drink," she told him.

He knew why, but he asked anyways. "And why would she spit in your drink?"

"She is either your ex or you slept with her. After the way she looked at me, I didn't want her handling anything I am going to have to consume. There are obviously still feelings or some kind of expectations. And I don't blame her, but I want to enjoy my evening without worrying about what's in my drink."

He felt like drama was starting, but it was his fault. He honored what she had to say. She handled herself better than he expected, but he did not need his women cutting up at this banquet. "I apologize. Yes, she is a person from my past. I wasn't expecting to see her. If it would make you more comfortable, I can ask to move to a different section."

"No, we don't have to do all of that," she told him.

Dean Harper walked up to the two of them in the middle of their conversation. "Professor Hollingsworth, good evening."

"Good evening, Dean Harper. I'd like you meet my date, Ms. Brielle Jackson. Brielle, this is the head of our department, Dean Jackson Harper."

She was disappointed because to his boss she was introduced as his date and not his girlfriend. She quickly conjured up a fake smile and shook his hand and greeted him. There was some small talk between the two, but Brie was concentrating on the word date. First the waitress and now the demotion. So far, the evening wasn't as great as she wanted it to be.

I don't want to interrupt

Roni was still in town a week later. The last text she sent Phaedra was 'Thank you and I'm sure I will see you again'. But Phaedra had not seen her. She also had not seen George, but she knew where he was and that's where she was heading.

Phaedra laid out a cream colored jumpsuit that V'd down the back. It wasn't tight fitting, but instead flowed. She slipped into a pair of gold shoes, gold jewelry and then her Thunderbird. If she was wrong for making herself seen, she no longer cared. Phaedra felt she could only be ignored but for so long.

The restaurant was busy but there was space by the bar. Phaedra leaned in to order a bloody Mary. After the bartender gave her the drink, Phaedra took a stroll. She spotted the table with three couples sitting at it. George was probably telling one of his jokes because everyone at the table was laughing.

Phaedra approached greeting, "Mr. Austin, what a pleasure to see you again, sir."

George looked up and his heart fell to his stomach, 'Yes, you as well." He extended his hand and shook hers.

"Oh, you don't remember me do you?" Phaedra played if off giving an Oscar winning performance. She pulled a business card out of her purse and passed it to him. "Phaedra Escobar, Real Estate. We've met a couple of times. I apologize, I saw you and wanted to come say hi. I didn't mean to interrupt your time with your friends. Forgive me."

"Oh, that is okay. Phaedra, is it?" George's wife asked.

"Yes," she said leaning in to shake her hand.

"I hope George isn't putting our house up for sale without my knowledge," she said in a joking manner but was serious.

"No ma'am. I also deal in commercial real estate. Our firm has had a couple of meetings." Phaedra explained giving George's wife her full attention.

His wife also gave Phaedra her attention. She was a fit $400 a week for a personal trainer thin. She was wearing a knee length black dress with spaghetti straps. A mauve silk wrap draped just below her shoulders. She wore several diamond tennis bracelets on her right wrist ranging from three to five carats. Her skin was a vibrant brown and her straight bob hair cut bounced with each movement of her head. Her pink stained lips smiled, but her brown eyes were suspicious.

The curved booth was occupied by George, his wife and two other couples. His wife could not see his face. He was restricted to not show the tension and anger he was feeling. "Yes, Ms. Escobar, I do remember you. I apologize I have not gotten back with your company. I'll tell you what, if you allow me to get back to my wife and friends, I'll have my secretary contact you on Monday and we can schedule you an appointment during business hours."

"George! Don't be rude," his wife insisted.

"No, Mrs. Austin, he is correct. You know sales people. We are always trying when we see an opportunity. Again, I just wanted to hi," she told them getting ready to walk off.

"Are you dining here tonight?" George's wife asked before Phaedra walked away.

"No, well, I was but, my partner in crime got a phone call that there was an emergency. I was just going to finish my drink and head home."

"I'm sorry to hear that. I hope everything is okay," the woman said with concern. "Why don't you sit down and have that drink with us?"

"Oh, thank you Mrs. Austin, but I couldn't. I don't want to intrude," Phaedra lied.

"Please Phaedra. Join us," she said and they all scooted to the right putting her right next to George, and George in between his wife and his mistress. "And it's Diane."

The two women became chatty with questions about kids, Jacksonville and the housing market. George made eye contact with one of his friends across the table but he was no help. Phaedra saw how he purposely would not look her direction. The others took it as his disappointment for a sales person barging her way into their circle.

When Diane finally stopped leaning over George, Phaedra moved her hand under the table cloth. She rubbed it up his leg. His thigh tightened. He tried to stop her, but she persisted until she found his zipper. George was trying to hold a straight face and kept looking straight. They both laughed at the joke being told by one of the other guys. Phaedra's hand finally made it inside of his pants. George erected. Phaedra massaged it. George did not want to enjoy it but he missed her touch. Phaedra finished her drink, removed her hand thanked Diane for her kindness.

"Goodnight," Phaedra said to the all at the table and she walked away slowly. She knew all six were watching her. She knew she was just that good. She had accomplished what she needed to accomplish. George's attention. This would break them or make them. She saw someone she knew and stopped to talk with them still in George's view. She stood just long enough to finally feel his tension on her back. Then she left.

Anton and I have been waiting on you

Lexie had been at Mark's for three days. She was slowly feeling out the whole moving in thing. Anton, however, was excited. He had his own room at Mark's also, plus he liked the bigger backyard and his friends he already knew in the neighborhood. Mark had been debating on putting a playset back there. He was still waiting on Lexie.

They had just gotten home from a movie and Anton was fast asleep. Mark carried him to his room while Lexie headed for the living room to take off her boots. She laid back on the couch then noticed the remote was out of arms reach. "Damn," she said to herself.

Lexie was feeling awkward trying to figure out what to do with herself. Even though she had been here a thousand times, her stuff was not here. She sat back up and crossed her legs. She smiled when Mark came up the hall after putting Anton down.

"Little man is tucked and hopefully will stay that way through the night," he informed her as he sat down next to her.

"Thank you for putting him to bed. I'm sure he will be down all night leaving you to have to entertain only me."

"Or I can use you to entertain myself," he said laying back on her lap.

Lexie played in his hair for a minute before she finally said anything. "I think we've moved beyond moving in together. Are we really going to spend another year or two dating and living together?"

"Playing house," he simplified.

"Whatever you want to call it, answer my question," she demanded.

"Don't get hostile little lady," he said smiling at her as she was about to push him off her lap. "No, that is not how I see us over the next year or two. But, Lexie, you have to remember, Anton and I have been waiting on you."

"You and Anton, huh?" She rolled her eyes at him. "Too bad I wasn't included in that conversation."

"You have been, you just weren't listening," he told her and got up. Mark headed towards the bedroom.

Lexie wasn't sure if she was supposed to follow or not. She got up anyway and followed him down the hall. He was digging in his bottom drawer and came up with a box that had tattered wrapping paper around it. Mark ripped the paper off and opened the box. Lexie was holding onto both his wrist leaning in to look at the box.

"I bought it two years ago, right before your dad passed away. I actually had this speech ready, then he had his heart attack so I put it away."

Lexie was still holding onto Mark's wrist. She was holding her breath. It was a 2 ½ carat Emerald cut diamond on a wide gold band. He had paid attention when she mentioned that emerald cut was her favorite. Mark lifted Lexie's chin up so she would look at him. She almost lost her balance when she released his wrist as he moved his arm. His eyes were watery. The room seemed bright than normal. His smile was soft. His face softened.

"See, I always knew it was you. We just had to work out the kinks first," he told her.

"So, why did you never ask since then?"

"We kept breaking up since your father died. Timing was wrong," he explained.

"And now?"

"Now? I think we are better now than we've ever been. I think now we can make it to forever. I want you, I want Anton, I want us to have kids, maybe two, I want us to buy a house, a home. I stole that part from a song," they both laughed and he wiped the tears streaming down his face.

"I love you, Mark. I really, really love you. And I love the way you love Anton. And I can't wait to have a bunch of little Leonardi's running around."

Mark slid the ring on her finger, "So, this means you'll marry me?"

She kissed him tenderly and both were now crying. "Yes, a thousand times yes."

Mark picked Lexie up in his arms and carried her to the bed. That night making love to her was like making love for the first time. The beginning of their forever.

Are we good

Brie got comfortable and began to work the small crowd. Chris was able to leave her alone at time talking with others. There were a couple of times he looked up to witness her watching him talking with the waitress. Her look cut them both.

"Everyone was so nice," she told him as they were leaving out of the parking lot.

"I'm glad you enjoyed yourself," he said dryly.

"I did. And you?" She asked.

"It was a nice evening. We do it twice a year. I suppose I really don't get a kick out of them," he answered looking straight ahead because he could feel Brie staring at him.

Brie began to feel that same feeling from all the other guys she's been out with previously. She asked herself if this is all she was worth; a few dates, a good roll around in the bed and then dumped. Chris was different she reminded herself. She was ready to lose her closes friend for him, so she had to ask herself why she was bowing out to the waitress.

They had driven a couple of miles in silence, Chris still staring straight ahead. He knew the silence was killing her, but he did not want to fight. He did not want to talk about Krista, the waitress that meant nothing to him. But Brie was a woman and as far as Chris knew, woman wanted to talk about it.

"Chris, I asked the babysitter to spend the night. Maybe I was being presumptuous, unless of course you had other plans," she told him feeling a little timid. The voice in her head was screaming fight for this man, but Brie didn't know how to do that.

"And here it is," he said in a huff. Chris slowed the car down and pulled over into a parking lot.

Every bad scenario that Brie could conjure ran through her head. "What are you doing?" She asked scared.

Chris didn't answer her immediately. He put the car in park and finally looked her direction. Brie was reaching for her seat belt. "It was a weekend thing, probably six or seven months ago. I haven't seen or talked to her since then."

Brie saw how calm he was and stopped being scared. She spoke up for herself. "I suppose I should stop assuming we are exclusive. And even if we aren't, when we are together, you talking to your old fling is disrespectful."

"I understand that, but she was our waitress and I did not want to make a scene," he defended himself.

"It made me feel like a 3rd wheel," she said folding her arms across her chest.

"That was not my intent. If you felt that way, I'm sorry. She asked why I never called her again and I said I got busy. That was our conversation outside of drink orders. What I don't need is you watching me from across the room as if you don't trust me,"

"What was I supposed to think?"

"How many black people did you see at the party, Brie?" His calmness was shrinking.

"Not many, but what..."

He interrupted her, "Exactly, there aren't many of us. Five to be exact. I just didn't want drama on a night like this. And as far as Krista, she is old news. I told you that."

Brie put her head down and that familiar feeling was coming back. She couldn't call Kenny, Lexie or Phaedra for advice on what to say next. She needed to decide for herself. If she apologized it meant she did something wrong. Her heart told her not to do it but head was still afraid to lose him.

Brie looked up into Chris' eyes. He looked angry with her. She didn't want him to be but she didn't want to be a fool either. She'd been one for too long. "I'm just asking for respect here Chris. It was a great evening, I had a lot of fun. I wish we weren't arguing right now but instead ending this evening on a high note. If you say she is old news, then I believe you. It's no big deal, I guess."

Brie was not sure how to articulate what she was trying to say because she only knew how to apologize. She wasn't even sure if what she said made any sense. Chris finally softened his face and leaned for her to kiss him. She did, but felt like she lost the fight. Like maybe her babbling was an apology and she didn't realize it.

"You are exclusive," he finally told her. "There is no one else. Your assumption was correct. I'm glad you enjoyed your evening."

Brie was happy to hear that she was his only one. She wished there was more room in the little red sports car, she would have jumped into his lap. "So, we're good?"

"Am I taking you home or to my place?"

Brie smiled, "Your place."

Chris chuckled, "Then we are good."

What the hell am I doing

Phaedra drove to Lexie's and was just sitting in the drive way replaying the scent from earlier. She knew George was mad and probably wished she was a dude so he could beat her. She broke the rules. She broke her own rules. She took something fake and tried to make it real.

She joked with herself that her AmEx would be cancelled by tomorrow. "I should probably call RJ but I need a drink."

She was breaking another one of her rules. She was showing up without calling. Lexie had been up under Mark since they had come back from Atlanta. She figured he wouldn't care. If he did, she didn't care.

Phaedra leaned into the doorbell pressing it a few times. Another rule she broke. She heard Lexie yell hold up. She yelled back to hurry the hell up. She heard the locks being removed impatiently and the door came open fast and angrily. Roni stood in front of her in a robe and a mean look.

"Roni? I'm sorry. I thought Lexie was here," Phaedra fumbled.

Roni walked away from the door leaving it opened. Phaedra assumed that meant come in. She stepped over the threshold cautiously and closed the door. Roni turned around and looked at her with a "what the hell do you want?" expression.

"Is your sister here?" Phaedra asked biting her bottom lip.

"Obviously not if I'm the one that hurried the hell up to answer the door."

Phaedra laughed, especially since Roni was so serious. "Come on now, I thought you were Lexie when I said that."

Roni was still just staring at Phaedra. Phaedra headed for the dining room and made herself a drink. She offered Roni one and Roni was just looking with the same impatient expression. Phaedra wasn't fazed.

"Were you heading for bed?" Phaedra asked letting Roni know she was not intimidated.

"I was getting into the shower," Roni told her.

"Are you expecting company?" Phaedra asked curious why Roni was still annoyed.

"She already left," Roni said in a matter of fact tone.

Phaedra dribbled her drink which made Roni laugh. Realizing Phaedra was not going anywhere, Roni fixed herself a drink and sat down crossing her leg in the short robe.

Phaedra stared at Roni's leg for a minute, admiring her skin tone. She was slightly lighter than RJ. They were strong and muscular. Roni was a runner. Phaedra had to snap out of it.

"So, what were you up to tonight?" Roni asked helping bring Phaedra back to reality.

"Just hanging out with a couple of people I know. I got bored and needed to talk to your sister," Phaedra lied.

"She's been at Mark's for the last few days," Roni advised.

Oh, I guess I should not be surprised. She left you the house?"

Roni didn't answer her. She never liked answering obvious questions. "Well, I'm going to go shower now. You are welcome to sit there all night if you want."

"I see you get bored easily also," Phaedra responded.

"I'm not a chit-chatter. You seem like you don't want to go home and don't have anyone else to hang out with."

"I do, I just don't want to hang out with them. I supposed a movie is out of the question?" She asked stalling while trying to get her nerve up.

"It is," Roni said and then headed up the stairs.

Phaedra sat back on the couch and sipped on her drink. She heard the shower come on. "What the hell am I doing?" She asked herself. She drank the rest of her gin and tonic and grabbed her purse and headed for the front door.

This wasn't her. Phaedra always got what she wanted and what she wanted was upstairs in the shower because what she had was at dinner with his wife and friends.

"What the hell," she said and kicked off her shoes and dropped her purse. Phaedra headed up the stairs. She took a deep breath. She put her hand on the bathroom door knob. "No turning back once you are on the other side of this door." She bit her bottom lip and opened the door.

"You took longer than I thought," Roni said dropping her robe.

I'm gonna burst if I don't tell somebody

Lexie woke up and looked at the clock. It was 3:17. Mark was still asleep and Lexie wanted to call someone so bad and tell them her exciting news. She knew Brie was with Chris and figured Phaedra was with someone. She grabbed one of Mark's t-shirts and slipped her panties back on and made her way to the kitchen.

She jumped on the bar stool and stared at her ring. She held her hand up high and then down low. She pretended she was talking to people and held her hand up to show off her ring to the imaginary audience. She wanted to wake up Anton but knew he would not be as excited as her. Waking up her mom was definitely out of the question. After 15 minutes of talking to herself, she decided to call Brie. She would be the one that would be most excited and not upset about being woken up. It took three rings but Brie picked up in a sleepy voice.

"Hey hon. I'm sorry. I know you were asleep," Lexie said.

"It's okay. Took me a minute to get from under Chris," Brie explained.

"Well, that is a lot of man. I can see why it took some minutes," Lexie laughed at her own joke.

"Whatever girl," Brie laughed with her. "Is everything okay? What's the matter?"

"Well, remember that time I said I would call at 3 in the morning because I needed you to cry with me?"

Brie sat up concerned now. "Oh, honey, what happened?"

"Mark asked me to marry him!" She yelled in a whisper.

"Brie covered her mouth with her hand and jumped out of bed when she saw she had woke Chris. "When? How? Oh my goodness!."

"He asked earlier when we got back from the movies. He was sweet, Brie. He told how much he loved me, how he wanted kids, and how much he loves Anton," she carried on.

"Girl, I am so excited. I'm even more excited because I get to plan a wedding!" Brie was jumping up and down in the living room.

"Yes, I will be using Brielle Jackson's party planning services," Lexie said getting louder.

"We've got a lot to do. Did you set a date?"

"No. He asked, we cried, then we made love, then we went to sleep," Lexie answered.

"That sounds so perfect. Girl, I'm just so excited. I can't wait to see you later," Brie told her.

"We have to because I want to jump up and down and scream with someone. So, how did your evening go?"

Brie looked around to make sure Chris wasn't near. "It was really nice, had some BS moments mixed in with it. I'll have to tell you about that later. However, it ended on a good note. He did confirm I'm the only person he is seeing."

"You got what you wanted. I'm happy for you Brie. Now we just need to work on your girl Phaedra," Lexie joked.

Brie let out a loud laugh and then tried to contain it. "Girl, that is going to take more than a week at the lake."

Lexie laughed also. "I know, but I gotta keep holding on to hope. Call me later so we can get together."

"I will. Congratulations again. Tell Mark the same for me."

"I will. Love you," Lexie told her.

"Love ya too, girlie." Brie said disconnecting.

Lexie felt better now that she got to tell someone. She decided to send Phaedra a text. 'Mark asked me to marry him!' followed by smiley faces.

You have a talent. Don't hide it.

Brie tried to slide back into bed quietly, but Chris was already awake. "Sorry I woke you."

"Not a problem," he said. "Who was that?"

"Lexie. Mark asked her to marry him," Brie explained.

"I thought they broke up?"

"She and Mark have broken up, gotten back together, broken up, gotten back together. I take it this means they will stay together."

"Congratulations to her."

"And the best part, I'm planning her wedding," Brie said excited.

"Have you planned a wedding before?" The question was more to find out if she has planned her own.

"Just for one of my cousins. Everything else has been just parties."

"Brie, do people pay you when you plan parties for them?" Chris sat up in the bed.

"A few I charged. My cousin did because she had me running up and down the road for her. But that really was just to cover gas."

"So, why don't you start your own service business? You can even start it as a side hustle in the beginning," he suggested.

"I don't know. With a full-time job, three kids, and trying to get a business off the ground. It's over whelming. I tried to go to college, that didn't work." She was feeling inadequate.

"But it would be temporary. If you sacrifice for a short period of time, then in the long run you will be where you want. Depends if you want it or not."

Brie had been hearing this for a while. She just wasn't ready to step out on her own and she wasn't comfortable telling him that. But look at what opening up did for Lexie. Brie wanted to bury her head under the covers, but Chris was looking at her, so she sat up.

"That is true, I supposed it is more fear than anything. I love to do it, but attach the word professional and it makes me nervous," she confessed.

He smiled because he appreciated her being honest. "I get that. I have my moments when I fear that I'm not going to know as much as others in my field. Or worse, one of my students. I know I don't have to know everything, but my ego, he is so much bigger."

Brie laughed at how wide he held out his arms. "Ego does have a tendency to make us hide so nobody finds out we are not perfect."

"You have a talent, don't hide it. And that is my philosophy lesson for the day, because I don't know much more about it."

"It's not like science where you can prove everything," she commented.

"Yes. I like evidence. Like it's a scientific fact that if I touch you here," Chris pressed his thumb into Brie's inner thigh. "You will moan."

She did moan as he pressed his thumb in her thigh, then she laughed, then he moved his hand further up her thigh fingering along the freshly waxed skin. Brie had taken Kenny's suggestion and bought a sexy busier and lacy g string. Chris didn't want her to take off last night, but now, he was asking her to remove it.

Brie smiled and whispered, "Round 2."

My car is parked in my driveway

Phaedra hadn't long been home when she heard the text alert from Lexie. She smiled and was happy to hear the good news. "I wonder what she would say if my response was 'I've got great news too. I fucked your sister'.

Phaedra didn't respond that way. She didn't respond at all. She connected her phone to the charger and headed for the shower. Just as soon as the water hit her face she started grinning. She could still feel Roni pressed up against her with the water splashing on them. It wasn't anything she expected. Truthfully, she didn't know what to expect. She broke another rule; Roni like to leave marks. Roni's aggressive demeanor rolled over to her bedroom manners. Roni had left dark circular-like shapes on her inner left thigh, the back of her neck and bite marks on her right butt check that she was trying to scrub off unsuccessfully.

Roni worked her and Phaedra came over and over. She was still throbbing between her legs. The hot water was relaxing but the tingling sensation was increasing. She sat down in the tub letting the water from above just fall on her. She imagined Roni's hands gripping her thighs, as she held them down and had Phaedra wide open. Phaedra had no control and just allowed Roni to do whatever she wanted.

They had gone from the shower to the bed in the guest room. Phaedra had stepped into the shower fully dressed. She immediately kissed her before she lost her nerve. Phaedra was lost at what to do or where to touch, Roni took over. When she did relax, she thought of all the places she liked being touched and touched Roni in those places. Roni wasn't climaxing like Phaedra was, but she was proud that she got a few moans out of her.

The water was starting to get tepid and Phaedra, although satisfied by Roni, wanted more. She jumped out of the shower and decided she would call RJ. She had only seen him once in the last couple of weeks. She threw a pair jeans on her still wet body and grabbed a t-shirt out the drawer. She'd call him from the car.

Phaedra quickly ran up the stairs to check on the kids. Both were sound asleep and she didn't see any unauthorized persons in their rooms. She headed back down and grabbed her phone off the charger. Phaedra pushed the button to open the garage door. While waiting she pulled her up in a ponytail. The door got halfway up, Phaedra was blinded by bright lights from her driveway. She saw a figure dunk under the garage door. Phaedra grabbed her mace and double checked her doors were locked.

George hit her window hard. "Get your narrow ass out of the car!"

Phaedra knew she had to take whatever punishment was coming. She turned off the car, put down the mace and opened the door. He walked back to his car and turned off his lights. Phaedra didn't dare move from her spot. George walked back in the garage and hit the button on the wall and closed it.

"Where the hell you going this time in the morning?" Was his first question as he looked at her breast showing through the wet t-shirt.

"To the store, I wanted some ice cream," she lied and he knew it.

Phaedra was leaning against her car and George stood an inch in front of her. "Are you fucking out of your mind?"

"Yes, I am. That's what happens when I get ignored. I lose my mind," Phaedra said sarcastically. "You didn't call, text, send flowers, nothing. What was I supposed to think?"

George grabbed her by the throat just enough to make a point. "Weren't the bills getting paid? If I had cut you off you would have known it. Phaedra, I swear, you promised that you wouldn't be that woman. I can't afford for you to act like one of those crazy bitches. I've got too much at stake."

"I'm sorry," she said with water forming in the corner of her eyes. She was holding his arm just in case he decided to grip tighter.

"I'm sorry doesn't cut it. Baby, I love you, but I promise God if you pull a stunt like that again this hold will be tighter. I will watch you take your last fucking breath and no one will find your body," he told her leaning in even closer talking through his teeth.

Phaedra knew George was capable of hiding her dead body. He had the means and the property. He released her neck and stepped back. Phaedra didn't look at him. She allowed herself to feel guilty for once.

George was now pacing in front of her. "One minute you acting like you don't give a damn, the next minute you showing up playing me for a fool in front of my wife and friends. Find a fuckin' median."

"I can do that," she said in a whisper because her throat hurt.

"Where the hell were you going? And the truth this time!" He yelled.

"To the store I told you," she answered now in her normal voice but still rubbing her throat.

"Why are you wet?"

"I just jumped out the shower," she told him attempting to push past him but he grabbed her arm and put her back against the car.

"Why you showering at four in the fucking morning?" He demanded.

"What's with the questions? It's my business why I'm showering at four in the morning. I'm at my house."

George put his hands on his hip and smiled at her. "Like hell! You took this to a different level, sweetheart. It's not your house or your business. It's not even your body anymore. All this belongs to me."

George walked towards the door to the house and opened it. He held it open for her to go through first. She stepped in looking behind to see what he was going to do. He walked behind her so she headed for the kitchen. He grabbed her arm and redirected her towards the bedroom. Phaedra wanted to protest but her kids were upstairs and she did not want to wake them.

"You are going to finish what you started," he told her.

Phaedra folded her arms and stood in front of her dresser. Maybe she went too far. The look in his eyes were different. Phaedra wasn't backing down. "So, you think you are running things now?"

George sat on the bed and bent over to take his shoes off. Phaedra didn't budge. He stood up and pulled his shirt over his head still not saying anything to her.

"Um, don't you have to get home to your wife? Your car is parked in my driveway," she reminded him.

"My car is parked in my driveway," he reminded her."

"Oh, no George. We aren't doing this. I was wrong. I'm sorry, it won't happen again, but you don't own a damn thing here," she told him getting her fight back.

"Take off your clothes," he told her standing there in only his jeans.

"I'm talking to you." Phaedra got closer to him and put her hands on her hips mirroring his stance.

George knocked one of her arms down. "Take off your clothes."

Phaedra huffed, then she submitted and sat down on her bed to get undressed. "This motha fucker here come up acting like his dick grew six inches."

George laughed as he walked over to lock the bedroom door. He pulled her up from her seated position and turned her around, that's when

Phaedra remembered the marks on her. She leaned to get out of his view so she could turn off the lights but George pulled her back.

"What motha fucker did all of this?"

Phaedra didn't say anything.

"I'm getting tired of repeating myself tonight."

"Since when do you care about my extracurricular activities?

"Since tonight. I better not catch another nigga up in here, no one else touching you, looking at you, calling you or any damn thing else. Whomever you just left and whomever you were on your way to see, you cutting that shit off. And anybody else," were his new rules for her.

George had backed her up until she fell on the bed, lowering himself on her. Phaedra bit her bottom lip the tingling sensation returned. She said nothing about his demands.

"Why don't you see if that sarcastic mouth can make my dick grow another six inches?"

Phaedra laughed at him and then did as he said.

Why are you acting brand new

Mark and Lexie told Anton that they were going to be a family. Anton was more excited than they were. It was Sunday, so Mark suggested they invite Roni and her mother for an early dinner after she got out of church. Lexie agreed and went shopping.

Phaedra never text her back so she sent another one to her. Lexie had gathered everything she needed for Italian wedding soup. They would start with that, she would give the news and then everybody would jump up and down and be happy. That's if Lexie could wait that long. She finally heard from Phaedra and headed her way before going back to Marks.

"Late night?" Lexie asked when Phaedra opened the door half asleep. She was holding her left hand out as she had done earlier with her imaginary friends.

Phaedra smiled at her and hugged her tight. "I'm so happy for you. Tell Mark I said about damn time."

"According to him and Anton, I was the hold up. So, what's going on with you?" Lexie asked more interested in why Phaedra was still sleep in the afternoon.

"I only slept for a few hours," Phaedra explained. "So, have you told your family?"

The ladies headed for the kitchen where Phaedra had been sitting at the table. She was sipping tea and reading a magazine when Lexie had called her.

"No, unless Anton counts. Brie is the only person I talked to so far, and now you. Why did you only get a few hours of sleep?"

"I was whoeing last night," she joked.

"RJ?"

"No, but I was on my way his place and when I went to pull out of my garage George was in my driveway blocking."

"George showed up at your house? When did he grow a pair?" Lexie laughed.

"When my dumb ass showed up at the restaurant where he, his wife and their friends were enjoying a nice evening and sat my bold self down," Phaedra told her.

Lexie's mouth opened wide and she covered it. Her eyes were just as big. "Are you fucking crazy?"

"Funny. I think those were George's exact words. I don't know. I'm off my game lately. I felt like I was being denied so all my decisions haven't been very smart. He comes over and lets me know this relationship is now on a new level. He will show up here when he wants and I better not sleep with, go off with or look at another man."

Lexie reached across for Phaedra's hand. "Honey, what are you going to do?"

"Play along until he gets over himself," Phaedra told her with confidence. "It is my fault, though."

"Phae, you are going to get yourself killed." Lexie had a worried expression across her face.

"I'm beginning to think you were in the garage last night. He told me he would hide my body if I pulled some shit like that again," Phaedra told her slightly laughing.

"That is not funny. You are messing with his livelihood. I just don't understand why you don't dump him and make nice with RJ."

"That's an easy answer. RJ can't pay my mortgage. He makes a decent amount of money, he is really good in the sack and he makes me smile. If I were 25 and not 42, that would be romantic. Perfect boyfriend material."

Lexie leaned back in her chair. "And George is married and so therefore no real future with him. It's not like you can grow old with him. Besides, you can pay your own mortgage."

This time Phaedra leaned towards Lexie and grabbed her hand. "I'm excited you and Mark are getting married, but, it's not for me."

Lexie got aggravated, "But what about his wife's feelings?"

"Keep your moral standards and your zero balance checking accounts. Not me. I like my house and my cars. I especially like what's in my accounts. Him cheating on his wife is his wife's problem. If she is smart, she is using him the same way I am. If we work together, we will both come out of this rich," Phaedra explained defending herself.

"Do you hear yourself?" Lexie asked fed up. "You sound like an evil bitch instead of the caring person I know you to be."

Phaedra rolled her eyes, "Why are you acting brand new?"

"I'm just saying you sound like you don't even care. I don't get that. Not even from you." Lexie was beginning to feel exhausted from the conversation.

"I'll tell you what," Phaedra said getting up from the table to put her cup in the sink. "I'll be me and you be you and we will all get along."

"Then you go ahead and be you. I just hope you don't get it back as bad as you dish it out." Lexie stood up and picked up her purse and keys. "I gotta go Phae. I'm just worried about you."

"Lexie, I just make it a habit to not deal with other people's feelings. It goes against what I believe. It's too daunting a task. It is what it is." Phaedra walked her to the door.

Lexie turned around to say something to Phaedra, but Phaedra had closed the door on her. Lexie didn't always agree with Phaedra's ways, but they are what made her Phaedra. Lexie didn't know George that well, and no matter what Phaedra said, the look in her eyes said she was taking his threat seriously. That's what had her worried.

You didn't have other plans do you?

Brie was getting her things together so Chris could drive her home. She was looking around the room wishing she had a fast forward button so she'd be at the place on the timeline where she and the kids were living in this house. It was large enough that Deena could ride her bike around it and not run into anything. The kids would be able to swim in the pool and play in the backyard.

Brie wanted the husband, the nice car, the big house; all that she grew up being told was a fairytale. Even standing in his room it wasn't real to her, just a nice thing to put on a wish list. She walked in the closet that was the size of a small bedroom. Chris had one wall lined with suits, the other with khakis and jeans, shirts above them and the third wall with shoes. She imagined her own clothes in the closet. She imagined the closet double the size to fit all the shoes and purses she could buy.

"What are you looking for?" Chris asked bringing Brie out of her trans.

"Nothing, just admiring," she said embarrassed to have been caught.

"My mother told me I have too many clothes for a guy. I don't think so."

"No, you don't. No such thing as too many clothes." She smiled and squeezed pass him.

"Were you ready?"

"Yes, I've got everything." Brie answered somewhat sad. She threw her bag on her shoulder and headed out the room. Chris always opened doors for her, so she was in the habit of walking behind him or one or two steps in front of him. This time she led the way and stood in front of the passenger door of the two seater sports car while he was locking the door to the house.

"I'm actually driving the gas hog today," he said point at his red SUV.

"Oh, okay. You know you have that backwards. The sports car is for the weekend, the SUV is for going to work," she told him as she picked her bag up and walked towards the other vehicle.

"True, but I only drive this one when I need space. I've had it for two years and it doesn't even have 10,000 miles on it yet," he explained.

"Are you running errands today?"

"No. I was going to ask if maybe, well," Chris took a breath in between stuttering which was unusual for him. "I was going to ask if you and your kids would like to go to the zoo."

Brie was surprised at his nervousness and happy with his question. He always asked about her kids but never made any motion as far as meeting them. "Yeah, that sounds fun. They love the zoo."

Chris wasn't sure if he should feel excited or just relieved to get the question out. "You didn't have other plans did you?"

"No, not really. Just to go to the grocery store, and probably take the kids to the park just to get out the house."

"Good. I know I probably should have said something earlier, but, I don't know. I guess it was last minute thinking. I enjoy my time with you, but I know you have to go home and spend time with your children, so I just figured we should make a day of it," he carried on. "They get your attention and I get your attention."

Brie smiled at his explanation. "Let me call Janae and ask her to make sure everyone is dressed," Brie said pulling her cell phone out of her purse.

Chris had dated women with kids before, and he had been around kids. But meeting Brie's kids made him nervous. He could hear them in the back ground on occasion when the two were on the phone. They seemed well behaved. With the way he felt about Brie made it a little scarier than usual.

When they arrived at her apartment, Chris was looking forward to seeing it. He wanted to see if she was as organized as he thought, if she had taste in décor, and if she was living beyond her means. When Brie walked in Deena ran towards her screaming mommy, but quickly paused when Chris stepped in behind Brie. She just stood until her mom came to her, then she just hugged her leg.

Ike also looked curiously and cautiously. "Hi Mom," he said peeking from the couch.

Brie went to step towards him but Deena was still on her leg. She just picked the little girl up so she could hug her son. Brie called for Chonda and then introduced her little gang to Chris. Ike and Deena spoke quietly while Chonda walked up, shook his hand and said hello giggling.

Janae was getting her stuff together and Brie was grabbing her purse to pay her. Chris pulled out his wallet and gave the sitter $150. Brie looked at him, she offered Janae $30. The babysitter gladly accepted and left quickly before Brie asked for any of it back.

After running through her usual Sunday questions of did you bathe, brush your teeth, wash your face, eat and did you put on clean underwear, she finally announced they were going to the zoo. Chonda was the only one to show excitement. Ike and Deena whispered thank you to Chris.

The kids put their few things away and put on their shoes. Brie went in her room to switch from heeled boots to flat boots. Chris sat down on the dark red couch. It was slightly worn but it was clean. Ike looked at him and he looked at Ike. He realized the young boy was the man in this house and he respected it.

"What game are you playing?" Chris asked trying to break the nervousness.

"Minecraft," Ike simply answered.

"That's a popular game. I always hear my students talking about it," Chris said to the uninterested listener.

"You are a teacher? What grade do you teach?" Chonda asked ready with shoes and backpack.

"I teach at the University," he answered glad one of them liked him.

"I hate school," she announced proudly.

"You don't enjoy learning new thing?"

"I like learning. I just don't like school. It's boring, all of my teachers are not that smart. I'm not allowed to call anyone dumb so I have to say not smart. School is just a complete waste of my time."

Chris was impressed to hear someone so young express herself so well. He could tell this was the one that had Brie's personality.

"Chonda, come here. Let me fix that ponytail," Brie called out to her.

Chonda did as she was told waving bye to Chris. Deena was still standing close to her mother, now with her thumb in her mouth. Ike was starting at the TV hoping Chris didn't say anything else to him.

"Okay, is everyone ready? Deena, tie your shoes, please. Ike, turn off your game, please," Brie demanded as she called out her orders and her children obeyed.

Brie checked each child as they filed out the door. Deena was holding Brie's hand as Chris took the keys from her and locked her front door. He followed her to her car so she could get Deena and Chonda's car seats out the back of it. It had been a few years since a guy had taken both Brie and her kids out. She told herself no to read too much into it. It was just the zoo. She still couldn't help but feel some excitement. He was, after all, different.

I'm not happy

December had come and was halfway gone. Phaedra hadn't spoken with Lexie or Brie for almost a month. George gave her more attention than she felt necessary. RJ got tired of hearing no and quit calling. She was feeling trapped only able to go between work and home. She wanted a lover, not a parole officer. Phaedra's stunt broke them. She moved from mistress to what felt like a second wife. Not a role she wanted to take on.

Phaedra had internalized all the pain she had been going through. She had been sitting and meditating when she heard the doorbell. It was six in the morning. "If this is that man, I swear I'm going to kill him," she told herself as she headed for the front door.

To her surprise it was Lexie and Brie standing there with coffee and a chai latte.

"If you didn't come bearing gifts, I would have cussed both of you out," she told them inviting them in.

"You don't call, you don't text and if we try to come by the kids say you are not here. We were desperate," Lexie told her as they hugged.

"You know I hate touching people. I hate being emotional," Phaedra said holding Lexie longer.

Caleb had come down the stairs but his mom let him know it was okay. It was just Lexie and Brie. She hugged Brie also, and the three sat at the kitchen table.

"What's been going on sweetie?" Lexie asked her. "It's normal for you to cut people off, but you usually only do that for a week or two."

"I went to prison for that restaurant scene," she said jokingly.

"What did George do?" Brie asked her.

"Laid down the law," Phaedra said being vague with them.

"I'm sorry I fussed at you and called you a whoe," Lexie told her.

"Wait, you didn't call me a whoe."

"I didn't?" Lexie said confused. "Maybe not out loud."

The three laughed but the silence was back. Phaedra didn't want to talk about it and they respected that. "How are the wedding plans?"

"Great. I just need my other bride's maid," Lexie told her. "Brie is planning everything. I'm her first client."

Brie smiled at the title. "I'm helping. I like doing this kind of stuff."

"And are you still with Chris?" Phaedra asked her.

"Yes, we are still hanging in there. The kids have finally loosened up around him."

"He's met your kids?" Phaedra asked surprised.

"Yes, it's been a couple of months now. We usually go to eat and he's taken them to the zoo, the museum, and that place with all the trampolines," Brie told her.

"Brie, what happened to the six month rule?" Phaedra was upset she broke one of their dating rules.

"Chris is different," Brie whined.

"You always say that. Brie, be careful, okay. You can't bring strangers around the kids." Phaedra reminded her. "But I'm glad to hear that you guys are still going strong."

"Well, now that we have all the formalities out of the way, Phae, what is going on?" Brie demanded when it got silent again.

"Nothing. I told you, I'm a prisoner. As far as George is concerned, I'm his and his only. What is the point of going out if I can't flirt or hook up," she said trying not to show any emotion. "I'm just giving it to the end of the year. Just long enough for him to get over this."

"Do you really think he is going to get over this? He has you and you are not fighting back," Lexie protested.

"He can't control two women, Lexie. That's not what he wants. He wanted a wife and then someone he could see when he needed to release some stress. He will get tired of this. He can't run my house and his," she was trying to convince her friend's and herself.

"Then, let me ask you what you always ask me. Are you happy? The Phaedra I know doesn't do anything that doesn't make her happy. Is being George's woman making you happy?" Lexie asked her.

Phaedra walked to the refrigerator and pulled out a bowl of cut up fruit.

"Well, I guess that answers the question," Brie commented.

"And what would you know Brie?" Phaedra snapped.

"No, no, no. We don't get ugly with each other. Phae, we both are concerned about you. You cut us off, you look sad and we just want to help. Not argue. Isn't that what friends are for?" Lexie was begging Phaedra to let them in.

Brie spoke up again. "I know a lot Phaedra. You've been a good teacher. I might not show that I imitate you, but I do. You are actually a good role model."

Phaedra lightly tossed the bowl of fruit on the table and then put small bowls and plates on the table for them. "So, Lexie, how is the business planning going?"

Lexie saw Phaedra was going to put up her shield and not discuss it, so Lexie told her about the business planning, the wedding plans and any other question she asked. Brie told her about the New Year's Eve party she was planning for Chris and that she was invited.

After a couple of hours of talking about everything but herself, the two left. Phaedra went to her room and sat on the edge of her bed. She thought about Lexie's question. No, she wasn't happy. Being stuck was draining her. She sent George a text message.

'I'm not happy.'

His reply was, 'I don't have time this morning.'

'Then I'm going elsewhere. Tired of sitting in this house playing girlfriend.'

'Then I'll be forced to kill you and your little dread head boyfriend.'

Phaedra smirked and rolled her eyes. 'What if it's a woman?'

'Then take some videos so I can watch,' he replied being funny.

Phaedra sent a smiley face, 'You are stupid. Seriously, I'm not happy in this relationship and I'm getting out of this house today. You are going to just have to be mad.'

Then her phone rang.

I promise

"So, how did the intervention go?" Mark asked Lexie as she was fixing lunch.

"She didn't want to talk about it, but she will be my bride's maid," Lexie informed him.

"Did you tell her we were looking for a house?"

"I thought we were waiting for the beginning of the year?" This was a conversation Lexie wanted to avoid. With her not working, she was still feeling like she had nothing to contribute financially. A thought process she had yet to overcome.

Mark smiled because he knew it was her way of procrastinating any kind of change. He let it go. "So, Anton and I were going to go play some basketball at the gym."

"Do you think I'm pushy?" Lexie blurted.

"You can be," he answered cautiously.

"It's like she is not taking her own advice," Lexie started up.

"Give her time Lex. It took you some time before you would take any advice and open up," Mark suggested.

"I know, honey. I'm just worried about her."

Mark kissed her on the forehead. "She will be fine. But we still need a house and you need to stop avoiding the conversation."

Mark grabbed his sandwich and headed for the den. Lexie followed behind him trying to figure out how to defend herself. They had come so far. She didn't want to go backwards.

"I'll talk to her. We just haven't come up with what area. Trying to plan a wedding, start a business and still continue with day to day life, I'm just saying, that's why I was thinking next month."

"Lexie, its fine. We can wait until next month. We can wait until after the wedding if that would make you happy," he told her.

"Mark, we have not discussed what we want. Are we getting four bedrooms, do you want a separate offices. Again, what area and how about 2-story or 1-story."

"Whoa, wait. We did. You mention you liked 2-stories, I said that would work as long as we have an office since you will start off working from home. We had this conversation," he reminded her.

"We were just calling out stuff. I didn't realize that that was the conversation."

"Okay, Lexie. I'll tell you what, let's sit down and come up with a wish list. When would you like to do this?" Mark was having to make himself keep calm.

"We can do it tonight, after dinner," she said.

"After dinner," he agreed. "Don't make any other plans or allow Brie or Phaedra to talk you into anything else.

"I promise," she said inhaling deeply.

Mark turned on the TV, "I'm checking the scores. Want to see how your Jaguars are doing."

"Okay, I'm going to call Brie." Lexie took the hint and left the room. She didn't really call Brie but instead went to the office to revise her pitch.

Lexie decided that instead of going to the job network as a job hunter, she would be a speaker as a job coach. Her business cards had come in the mail so now she could hire a web designer to set her up online. She wanted to blog on her website with information on how to have the right mind set for job hunting and talk about job searching trends.

As a coach, Lexie would offer resume writing skills to teach others how to have the correct key words so a computer would pick it up. She would help with interview skills and offer assistance with changing careers. She went over her pitch and was pleased with herself. She was excited about getting this project off the ground. Then her thoughts switched to her independence. How it's going to feel making money. Guilt struck over the thought.

Things were getting better. They, as a family, put the Christmas tree up. Most of hers' and Anton's stuff was in the house by now. Anton was comfortable, excited, and content. So was she. She just couldn't shake the idea of being independent. It was a self-fish thought, she told herself.

Lexie had never really paid attention to the pictures on Mark's desk. There was a professional one of her and Anton in a silver frame she bought him a year ago. There was another one in a wooden frame that was taken with his digital camera at Disney World with all three of them. She picked up his digital frame and started to watch the pictures as they scrolled. There were more of Anton than them. Out of curiosity, she leaned up and minimized her program. As often as she sat in front of the computer she never noticed the desktop picture of the three of them at the go-cart racetrack.

Lexie just realized she and her son were Mark's world. "Why in the hell would I not want to spend the rest of my life with this man?"

Lexie walked back to the den. She picked up his plate. "Do you need anything else?"

Mark looked up and smiled. "Well, I could use one of those big wet sloppy kisses you like to give."

"My kisses are not sloppy, thank you very much," she laughed and gave him what he asked for. "Oh, and, I know we said tonight, but think about San Marco and Five Points area."

"You don't want to live closer to the beach?" He asked.

"It's crowed down that way. Maybe if we were going up A1A between Ponte Vedra and St. Augustine."

"That would be a long drive to work," he complained.

"Finish watching your sports. We'll figure it out," she smiled and headed for the kitchen.

"Independent can't kiss like that," she reminded herself. "Come to think of, independent doesn't fuck as good either."

It's an emergency

Brie was just getting home and trying to unlock her door when Chris called. She didn't have time to fish out her phone. She got through the door and asked Ike to help her get the groceries out of the car. Before she finished her sentence, Chris was calling again.

"Hi, honey," Brie answered.

"What are you doing?" He wasn't pleased that she didn't pick up the first time.

"I'm bringing in groceries to the house," she explained. "Why, what's up?"

"My mother will be landing in the next two hours and wants to meet you," he announced.

"Are you serious?" Brie had only met mothers after it was confirmed that the men were the fathers.

"Yes. I apologize its last minute. I have to come up with a dinner idea and get the guest room together," he was telling her in a calm panic.

Brie sighed putting the phone down by her hip so he would not be able to hear her. She had already gotten up early to go to Phaedra's with Lexie, she needed to get her house together and get ready for the week. He was supposed to be on the golf course today so she could do what she needed.

"Why don't we just go out to eat," Brie suggested.

"She would like a more intimate atmosphere so she can get to know you. Can you pull a dinner off in the next couple of hours?"

Brie didn't want to disappoint him. "Yes, I will come up with something. What does she like?"

"Something light. Chicken. More vegetables than meat. In season. I've got to get back, I'm almost done. We are on the 13th hole. If you stop by the club I will leave the house key at the front desk. Is it too late to call Janae?"

"No, it's not. I just have to find something to wear," she said frustrated and nervous at the same time.

"Okay, I'll talk with you a little later,"he said disconnecting to get back to his game.

"You're welcome!" She yelled into the phone.

"Mommy, what's wrong?" Chonda asked putting the food away.

"Chris has an emergency he needs my help with. I've got to leave for a few hours."

"Again?" Chonda whined.

"I know, sweetie. I'm sorry. It's one of those days. I've got grown up things to take care of, but I promise to make it up to you," Brie said hugging her daughter and patting Ike on the head. She went to her room to find something to change into.

Brie called Janae and the young woman agreed and would be on her way. Next she called the deli and ordered one lemon pepper and one rosemary rotisserie chicken. She chose her olive slacks with a deep purple button down blouse. She looked in the mirror and hated it. She kept the slacks and went for a red shirt. She hated it.

Brie looked in her closet and hated all of her clothes. How could he give her less than two hours to get dressed, come up with a meal, run all over Jacksonville to get everything and be in the correct frame of mind. She knew this was one of those moments she needed to think for herself, but Brie felt like this was uncharted territory. She needed direction.

"Hey, sweetie," Lexie answered.

"His mother will be here in less than two hours. He expects me to get dressed, drive to the golf course and get his key and come up with a dinner fit for queen, and get a baby sitter," Brie blurted out in one breath.

Lexie got most of what she said. "Wait, Chris is just now telling you his mom is coming?"

"He said she just called him. I don't know what to wear and I should have been out the house 10 minutes ago to even pull this off. What am I supposed to do?" Brie begged her.

"Well, first thing is you need to tell him to get his happy ass off the golf course and help you. Why can't he just take you guys out to eat?"

"I asked. She doesn't want to go out. I've never met a mom of this caliber before. I can't believe he even told her about me. I don't want her first impression of me to be a hurried look."

Lexie understood. "Take a deep breath, Brie. It's gonna be alright."

"No it's not. I have nothing to wear!" Brie was beginning to panic.

"Yes you do. That navy blue dress you bought when we went to Dillard's last weekend. The belt was tortes shell brown. Wear your Steve Maddens that are the same color," Lexie suggested.

"Good call. I forgot about that dress. Gold or silver jewelry?"

"Neither. I would go with the turquoise necklace, or the olive green wooden one. You know, with the big beads. And seriously, call Chris and tell him to get his ass off the golf course," she told her again.

"I hate telling him no," Brie admitted.

"You can't be like that or he will use you up. You can't pull all of this off in the time he is giving you by yourself. If his mom wants to eat at his house, then he better be there in time to turn on the stove. Remind him, this is important to you, and you are not trying to be half put together," Lexie coached her.

"Okay, let me call him while I'm pumped. What if he breaks up with me?" She asked because it was still her biggest fear.

"Brie, are you serious? If he break up with you over this, then he is a sorry selfish son of a bitch and we will burn his house down with him in it."

"Damn, Lexie! That might a little bit extreme," Brie said taking Lexie serious.

"You telling him to step up is not extreme. Go handle yourself, Brie," she demanded.

"Alright, I hear you," Brie said.

The two hung up and Brie pulled out her dress and shoes. Her hair was pulled up in an afro puff on top of her head. She decided to leave it that way. Chonda and Deena had come into her room to sit on her bed while she got dressed. She took another deep breath and did as Lexie told her. She called Chris.

"Hey, are you at the front desk?" He asked.

"No, I am not at the front desk. Nor will I be at the front desk. Chris, this is your mother's first time meeting me and I'm not meeting her half-baked with some thrown together last minute meal or me thrown together looking half minute. You need to get off the golf course and get to the grocery store. I will text you what I need. I'm picking up the chickens from the deli," she told him.

"I've got four more holes to go. And why are you feeding my mother chicken from a deli?" He pouted.

"Number one, don't care about your four holes and your second question because I don't have time to roast them myself. Meeting your mom is important to me and I would like to make a good impression. I'm not blowing this just so you can play golf." Brie was making her case while putting on her makeup as her girls sat and watched their mom.

Chris was quiet for a moment because he also had an audience. His friends were patiently waiting for him. "But, Brie, I can't just leave in the middle of a game."

"You can if you don't want me to roll up at your front door with two large pizzas," she warned him.

"I'm leaving," he said still pouting. "How long does it take you to get pretty?"

She knew from raising three kids that was just a dig because he was not getting his way. "I'm already pretty. It will take me about 30 more minutes to get dressed."

"Call me after you pick up the chicken."

"Chris," she said slowly. "You have to leave the golf course now. I'll call you when I pick them up but I expect you to have finished at the grocery store by then."

"Alright, text me my list," he complied. "I Love you."

Brie almost dropped the phone. "I love you too."

Brie stood up and started jumping up and down after double checking the phone had disconnected. "He told me he loved me!" She grabbed both of her girls and started jumping up and down with them also. All three started screaming.

Janae and Ike came running in to see what the commotion was. Brie told them her news. Ike said oh and left. Janae jumped up and down with her, then reminded her she needed to hurry. Brie finished getting dressed adding her belt, jewelry and lipstick. She walked out into the living room and asked everyone how she looked. They all agreed she was beautiful.

She walked over to Ike to kiss him. Brie knelt down to his eye level. "You know you will always be my first love."

"I know. I just worry that you will get your heart broken," he told her.

Brie smiled. "I'll be careful."

You liked my free spirit

Phaedra hesitated but answered the phone, "Hey."

"Why are you acting up? I told you I'm busy. I've got family stuff I have to do," George said.

"George, I'm serious. This has gone on long enough. You made your point," she told him.

"I wasn't making a point. I just decided not to put up with the extra shit anymore."

"And you and I both know it was working better the other way. For three years we were both happy. Now, it is work and that takes the fun out of it. You don't need this extra stress." Phaedra expressed trying to convince him that it would be better for him.

"So, what you are trying to tell me is that I'm not enough," his voice was going up.

Phaedra matched his tone. "I'm lonely. You have a wife to go home to. I go to bed to my two pillows and have to sit around and wait for you to be available. So not interested in this life."

George had to find a place to hide. "You knew that when we got together."

"I know George, but I wasn't a prisoner. You have to know that things are different now," she pleaded. "You liked my free spirit."

"Actually, I didn't. I tolerated it. I figured if I wanted to be with you I was going to have to accept it. After three years, I don't think I should anymore."

"Then we need to figure this out. You can't keep me locked in the house and you can't keep threatening to kill me. I am the woman that puts your dick in her mouth, full of teeth."

George laughed. "We need to get away which is hard because it is the holidays. Just give me a minute. I have something to take care of with my family. I'll be over tonight."

"Okay. I'll sit still for a little bit longer," she promised.

"Why don't you take the kids out to do something? I'm sure there is something somewhere they would like to go or do." George advised since he had to go out with his family.

"Just text me when you are free."

"I will. I gotta go. My name is being called," he told her.

"Bye," she said and hung up. I love you's didn't get said when on the rare occasion they talked when he was at home.

Phaedra knew the only way to gain her freedom was to breakup this relationship. It was no longer a relationship she could put on the shelf. Her feelings were in it. She did as George requested. She gathered both kids up and they headed for St. Augustine to go shopping, eat out and take a carriage ride. The kids were excited about seeing all the decorations.

Phaedra sent Lexie a quick text. 'Thank you.'

Lexie answered back. 'You know I'm here for you.'

Breakfast dinner

Lexie had to chase down her phone when she heard it ring. It was Brie's ringtone. She was worried Brie had gone too far with standing up for herself. "Hey, what's up?"

"He said I love you!" Brie screamed in a high pitch voice.

"Wait, what?" Lexie asked thinking there was no way she heard correctly.

"He told me I love you. Chris said I love you." Brie repeated not screaming, as loud, this time.

"Are you serious?"

"I told him he needed to get off the golf course and go to the store and not expect me to do all of this and his response was I love you," Brie explained.

"See girl, I told you. Don't let him walk all over you," she said knowing she was not expecting it to turn out like this.

"I'm on my way to pick up a couple of chickens and some garnishment to put around it so it don't look store bought," she explained. "I'm wearing the blue dress and the heels you suggested. I hope he likes it."

"He will. Wow, and I love you and meeting his mom all the same day. You've been doing something right," Lexie teased.

"Whatever it is I need to figure it out and do more of it."

"Well, get off the phone so you can drive. Have fun, sweetie," Lexie told her.

"I will, thanks. Talk to you later," Brie said and disconnected.

This is all Brie has been talking about so Lexie was happy for her. Lexie stuck her phone in her back pocket and went back to the bedroom where she was flipping through bride magazines. Mark and Anton where at the basketball court. The house was quiet except for Boney James in the background.

She had found two dresses she liked but was still looking. She and her mother had an appointment on Tuesday for a fitting. Lexie settled on yellow and white as her colors since they set the date for March. For the rest of the country it would be end of winter coming into spring, but for Jacksonville, it would be spring temperatures going into summer. The first dress was sleeveless and had a sheer, white shawl to go around her shoulders. That was just in case the temperature did not cooperate this year. The other dress was strapless and had pearls sewn in a paisley design. Her mother was not crazy about that one. She put the pictures to the side so she could show Mark during their conversation about where they would live.

Brie had given her some good ideas as far as decorating, what flowers would be in bloom, a list of bakers, best florist and caterers. She had also given her a list of honeymoon destinations and gotten her started on her guest list. "It's the holiday season Brie, this can wait," Lexie had told her when they were getting the planning started. Brie had let her know that it would not wait. She had less than six months to pull off a wedding and that was not enough time. As Lexie thought of that, she decided maybe it was time to go through Brie's emails and get more serious.

Lexie was impressed at how organized Brie was. She had all the information in a database where the only thing Lexie had to do was click on a link and it pulled up the menu. She looked through Brie's suggested menu items. There were three for each caterer titled according to budget range. Brie simplified everything for her. Lexie's only job was to choose.

She heard Mark and Anton coming through the door. Lexie got up to greet them. Anton was excited because he slammed dunked a guy who was over 6' tall. Lexie of course was mystified but high fived him. When she looked up at Mark he was motioning that Anton had been on his shoulders. They both laughed. Anton was proud and she was proud with him.

"Hey, look at this," she told Mark passing her tablet to him. Lexie then turned around to get both of them cold bottles of water out of the refrigerator.

"These are the caterers you are going to try?" Mark asked her looking over the list as he clicked through the links.

"Brie put this together. I didn't know Brie knew anything about programming databases. This is what she created," Lexie said proud of Brie.

"It is impressive. Why is she wasting her time as an office admin. She could be making so much more money."

"That is my question. I can't wait to ask her," Lexie said taking her tablet back.

Mark grabbed her from behind and hugged her. She turned her head to kiss him. "I'm going to go shower. What's for dinner?"

"Oops, I forgot about dinner. I was looking at wedding stuff," she answered.

"Can we have breakfast for dinner? Waffles, bacon, eggs, orange juice," Anton asked listing his wishes.

"Mmm, that sounds good. Let's pull out the waffle iron," Mark sided with him.

"Okay, then you two get cleaned up and I will make breakfast dinner," Lexie smiled rushing the two out of the kitchen.

Lexie didn't immediately start cooking. She pulled up the other emails that Brie sent her. She was equally impressed with what she saw. She made a note on her tablet to call Brie in the morning and talk about her skills.

You think I'm smart

Brie had the chicken and the garnish and picked up a few things to make a center piece. Chris was already home and in the kitchen scrubbing potatoes as he was told to do. He had left the front door unlocked for her. She entered calling out his name to announce she was coming through the door.

"Do you need any help?" He asked her.

"Yes, I have a few bags in the car," she told him.

Chris put the scrubber down and took the bags out of her hand. He sat them down on the counter and then grabbed Brie by her shoulders and looked her up and down. He smiled and said, "I don't think you are capable of looking half done. I think you are beautiful even when you wake up in the morning."

Brie smiled and kissed him on the cheek. "You aren't getting off that easy. Please go get the bags. I have a miracle to pull off."

Chris did just that and Brie grabbed the apron the hung inside of the pantry door. She went to work first pulling the chickens out of their boxes and placing them in pans then the oven on warm. She finished the potatoes Chris had started, seasoning them and placing them in the oven. Then Brie started on the fresh green beans.

Chris brought her a glass of wine and attempted to get a real kiss. She thanked him and offered her cheek. Chris left the kitchen. Brie checked the food and then started fussing with the center piece. Chris walked in again looking for attention.

"That looks nice," he told her.

"Thank you. I bought extra flowers for the guest bedroom. You can put them in a vase and place them on night stand. What time are you picking her up?"

"She scheduled a car to pick her up from the airport." Chris grabbed Brie's arm and pulled her into his. This time she gave him a real kiss.

"I'm nervous," she confessed.

"You don't have to be. She's a little up tight but she has a heart," he told her.

"What did you tell her about me?"

"Just stuff. I told her how smart you are, what a great mother you are, and of course how well you take care of me."

"You think I'm smart?" Brie was surprised because he was the one with the PHD and she saw herself as just an admin.

"Of course I do. You just never give yourself credit," he said letting her go and heading for the kitchen from the dining room.

Brie followed him. She knew he was right, but she was not going to admit it to him. "I'm just excited to hear someone with your credentials saying it."

"What credentials are those?" He asked sitting down at the island.

"Professor."

"Oh, I see. My professional credentials," he said laughing.

"It doesn't bother her that I have kids?"

"Not at all. She even knows their names and ages."

"How did the subject of me come up?"

"She asked me what was new in my life and I told her you." Chris was trying to make it sound as if it was not the big deal Brie was making it.

"I'll be a little nervous, but I'll try not to show it," she promised. Brie checked on the food again. "Let me wipe the lipstick off your face."

"I'll get the lipstick," he said stopping her from wiping his face with the napkin. "Besides, my mother is pulling up now. Put your shoes on and remove the apron for now."

Now Chris was the nervous one.

Divine Creator, what in the hell are you trying to teach me?

Phaedra pulled into her cul-de-sac and saw a car sitting in her driveway. It didn't look familiar and George had not sent her a text.

"Mom, who is that?" Caleb asked her.

"I have no idea. I don't recognize the car," she told him debating if she should turn around and head back out to call the police.

"Pull in, I'll see who this is," Caleb told her with his chest puffed.

"No you won't. Nobody is getting out of this car." She did a slow turn on the street and was about to head back to the street when her phone rang. She didn't know the phone number. "Hello?"

"Why are you doing a drive-by. You've got me scared. I'm not sure if I should duck or run," the caller told her.

She recognized the voice and passed her phone to her daughter confusing the teenager. "Hello?" Maya said.

"Hi baby girl, how are you?" Her father asked.

"Daddy!" Maya yelled sharing in his excitement. Caleb turned around immediately after hearing the name called.

The two kids were now lit up with excitement and Phaedra opened her garage door. Caleb and Maya jumped out of the SUV while the garage was still rolling up. They jumped in their dad's arms and drug him inside. Phaedra parked but did not get out of the car.

"Divine Creator, what the hell are you trying to teach me? Lately everything has been out of control and people are pushing me places I don't want to go. I'm not a feeler or a healer, but I'm finding myself in these situations. Now I've got my ex-husband at my house and that crazy fool is on his way. Whatever lesson I'm learning, please show it to me so I can move on. I'm ready. Thank you, thank you, thank you."

Phaedra finished her prayer but she did not immediately open her eyes. Instead she sat there and meditated. She wanted her calm life back. Then Ron knocked on the passenger side window for her to open the door.

"Why are you here, Ron?" She asked. Just as she did a text came from Caleb asking, 'Mom, please be nice.' "It was a 12 hour drive from Miami and not once did you think to call?"

"I did, think to call that is. I just figured that with you, it might be easier to ask for forgiveness than for permission."

Phaedra shifted to look his direction. "Ron, what do you want?"

"I'm moving to Jacksonville and I'm going to need a house. I want more time with you and the kids." Her expression sharpened which made him readjust. "Mostly the kids."

"Why are you moving to Jacksonville?" She asked frustrated.

"I just told you, to spend more time with my kids."

"No, that does not even sound like you. Did you do something illegal, or did you piss somebody off and you are hiding? What is the real reason? And know that if you lie, I will find the truth," Phaedra demanded.

"None of the above. I promise. Look, I had a tumor, it was removed, then they found another one. The doctors did another biopsy. The surgery sucked. The fear of dying sucked even more. But dying alone was the worst thought. It made me rethink my life," he explained.

"Is that why Caleb is asking me to be nice?"

"I didn't tell them about being sick. I'm in remission so I don't want them to know. They don't need to worry."

"So, where are you staying while you look for a house?"

"I'll check into a hotel, since I know you are not going to set me up in your spare room," he said trying to get her ruffled because it always makes him laugh.

"First you don't call, then you think you can stay here. You haven't changed. I'm giving you one night with your kids here. One! I don't care what they say. One!" Phaedra told him to both of their surprise.

"One. I got it," he grinned since he was only joking about her putting him up. "I'll get my bags out of the car."

Ron jumped out of the car and headed for his. Phaedra shook her head and asked herself what was she thinking. "My life is turning into a horrible soap opera" she said rubbing her temples.

Ron walked up to her window and tapped, "Where do you want me to put these?"

Phaedra gave him a big grin because of the thought that went through her head. "The spare room upstairs. Caleb can show you."

"You wanted to say up my ass, didn't you?" He laughed.

"So, I'm not the mature adult I should be," she laughed with him.

"I'm sure I deserved it." Ron smiled and then made his way indoors.

Phaedra smiled watching him walk in. He was still attractive. His hairline was receding at the temples but still all black. He finally got rid of, what she called, that ridiculous mustache. However, she did like the salt and pepper beard on just his chin. Ron was still in shape but his olive skin tone wasn't as tan as it usually is, but that could be from being sick.

Maya had stepped out into the garage and Phaedra put the window down again. "Mom, are you going to get out of the car?"

"No, I was considering turning on the engine, rolling windows down and sitting here until I fall asleep."

"Mom!" Maya yelled at her.

"I'm kidding. You know I'm too pretty not to grace this earth with my presence," she said half joking. "I'll be there in a minute. I just need to make a call."

"Okay. This has been the best day of my life. Better than the day I got to start wearing makeup. Better than the day I got my iPhone and iPad. Thank you, Mom!" Maya reached through the window to hug her mother.

Phaedra smiled and kept her opinions to herself. Her daughter was happy and there was no reason to ruin that. Her phone rang and it was George. "Hey you."

"Hey. Whose car is this in my driveway?"

Phaedra opened the garage door and got out of her SUV. "My ex-husbands. He showed up without calling first."

Phaedra slid into his car and sat straight up in the seat like a kid in trouble. If he was going to act a fool about this, she did not want to watch him do it.

"I thought he lived in Miami," George questioned.

"He does, well, did. He was sitting in the driveway when we got home. He announced he is moving to Jacksonville to be closer to the kids," she explained.

George didn't act up because George didn't feel threatened. "So, why are you feeling lonely?"

"I don't know. Just want something different I guess."

"You tired of me after all these years?" He asked playing in her hair.

She always liked him in her hair. He liked to tug at it gently and rub his hand through it when they were just talking. "No, lately I just haven't been getting anything that I want. Feeling lost."

"You know I try to give you everything," he begged.

"But you can't, because what I want can't be bought," she said pulling her hair away from him.

"You didn't know what want," he huffed and sat back.

"True. I just know it can't be bought. I want to feel like part of something," she tried to explain.

"What do you call us? Come on Phaedra, why are you trying to change this relationship into something I can't do?" George was frustrated.

"I'm not the one. You did. Maybe I contributed."

"I can't divorce my wife. It was never my intent to divorce my wife. Not even after the kids are grown and gone," he reminded her.

"I never asked you to," she scolded. "What? Are we going to do this for the next 20 years?"

George got impatient. He knew where this conversation was going and had tried to procrastinate the inevitable. "What if you got away, or we got away, or something. Don't let those words come out of your mouth."

Phaedra caved into George's pleas. "Then tell me what you want."

"I want us to go away after the holidays. Somewhere that we don't have to pretend. If you are looking for me to give you permission to fuck around, it's not happening."

"Then stop hounding me about what I'm doing and where I'm going," she told him realizing they were both too chicken to move on.

"Do I have anything to worry about?" He asked leaning into her ear.

"No. Just hanging out with friends," she said still not looking his way.

"Female?" This time grabbing the back of her neck.

"I just said stop hounding me. You can't run two houses. You run the one labeled Austin." She rolled her eyes and moved his hand.

"What if we meet downtown this week for lunch?" George began to play in her hair again.

Phaedra made a deep sigh sound. "You know that is dangerous. Gainesville or Daytona."

"We always go there. How about Brunswick?" He suggested.

"That's fine," she agreed with no enthusiasm. Phaedra opened the car door to get out. "You know as well as I do this isn't going to last."

George ignored her and pulled her back in for a kiss. "I told you, just give me some time."

Phaedra kissed him goodnight and headed back to her door. Phaedra had locked herself out by closing the garage door so she had to ring the doorbell.

Ron opened the door, quick to ask, "Who was that?"

"No one," Phaedra answered.

"Can you and no one hurry up and get married. Alimony is kicking my butt," he said trying to make her laugh.

Phaedra didn't respond and got her purse and keys out of her vehicle.

"Hey, it was a joke. I'm sorry. I hope whatever it is it gets better. And thanks again for allowing me to stay."

"I'm just frustrated right now. I'll see you in the morning," she told him and headed for bed.

A girls gotta do what a girls gotta do

Lexie put Anton to bed while Mark cleaned the kitchen. She had gotten comfortable with their nightly routines. Everything seemed to flow in harmony. She had quieted the voice in her head. She could do this for the rest of her life she told herself.

Lexie checked her phone to see if Brie called or text. She couldn't wait to hear about the evening. She wondered about Phaedra, also. No text since earlier. She sent up a quick prayer hoping Phaedra was okay.

Mark walked in and crawled over her knocking her over as she was sitting on the bed. "What are you doing?"

"Just checking for messages, nothing though. We aren't single anymore so it's like we don't talk much," Lexie answered.

"Everybody has new best friends," Mark said.

"Yeah, I guess that is one way to look at it. Still, we are long overdue for a girl's night out. Even if we only get to do it once or twice a month, we need to do it."

"I will agree with you there. It's a little harder now that Brie is dating Chris, and then there are five kids between the three of you, and you have work, home and family."

"We, sir, are women. We can do and have it all. Didn't you know that?" Lexie said smiling into his bright green eyes.

"If you say so," Mark laughed. "While you are doing and having it all, can we decide from what part of Jacksonville you are going to do and have it from?" Mark rolled off of her and sat up on his side of the bed.

"How about the Intercoastal area? Close enough to the beach yet still far enough away," she suggested.

"It's crowded over there," Mark complained. "How about San Marco like you said earlier. Or even Julington Creek."

"Talk about over crowded," she huffed.

"Okay, let's agree on one thing. Jacksonville is crowded," he said and they both laughed.

"Okay, okay. We'll check both of those out. But can we still look over in the Intercoastal area?" Lexie asked sitting up on her knees and pulling her shirt over her head.

"See, foul on the play. You are cheating!" Mark said before he got a mouth full of breast.

Lexie thought in her head, "a girls gotta do what a girls gotta do." She pulled him in close grabbing the back of his head, then straddled his lap. "Do you think five bedrooms is too much?"

Mark shook his head no but Lexie wasn't sure if he was just playing with her breast or answering her. He stopped long enough to give her a definite no and pull his shirt off too. She leaned in and kissed him, pecking and asking other questions about the house. "Square footage? What price range? Are we going to pre-qualify at your bank or mine?"

Mark answered each question as he moved his kissed down to her neck while he fussed with his zipper. "Maybe we should find a place to build new."

Lexie was sliding out of her sweats, "Is there any land left to build new?"

They both were naked now and Mark was kissing down her torso. "There is always land. If not, they will start knocking stuff down."

Lexie reached for his erection and began to massage it up and down causing Mark to bite down a little harder on the nipple he now had put back in his mouth.

"I'll ask Phae for a list. And something else I should probably ask but I can't think right now," she said as he slid inside of her.

"Oh, I'm sorry. I forgot we were supposed to be deciding on a house. You want me to stop?" He teased.

"Do you want to die?" She threatened then smiled.

Mark laughed and went back to moving his hips back and forth watching Lexie's facial expressions with each thrust. He had put her on her back and felt her walls tighten around him which made him thrust even harder, faster. He saw her eyes roll up which made him slow down. After two years it had become a dance. Not a routine where they did the same thing each time. Lexie was always showing him a magazine article or a position in the Kama Sutra she wanted to try. But tonight, Mark was in the mood for missionary. He could be in control. He lifted her legs to his shoulders and went deeper until she grabbed a pillow under her head, breathed heavier and made her loud moaning noises. Then he flipped her over.

You really need to work on that credit score

When Chris's mother walked into the room her presence commanded attention. At 5'10", she wore a tailored black suit with genuine pearl buttons and Versace black heels. She wore a ruby tear drop pendant on a gold necklace and a five carat diamond on her left ring finger. She kept if simple because she could. There was no one for her to impress. Brie wanted to hide.

"How was your flight?" Chris asked as she walked in.

"It was delightful. The turbulence was just awful, but it always is. And how are you Christopher?" She asked hugging him and looking him up and down.

"I'm well, thank you. Mother, this is Ms. Brielle Jackson. Brielle, this is my mother, Gwendolyn Hollingsworth," he introduced the two.

Brie extended her hand to greet the woman. "Mrs. Hollingsworth, it is a pleasure to meet you."

"You as well, dear." Gwendolyn looked around the room for a minute. "Where are the children?"

"Um, they are at home," Brie stuttered confused.

Chris jumped in quickly, "I asked Brielle to get a babysitter. I hoped we could just talk with no distractions."

Just then the chauffeur stepped in holding a gift bag and three boxes that were wrapped. "You said they were well behaved so how could they be a distraction? Well, just tell William where to put the gifts."

Chris directed the chauffeur to Brie's car and his mother directed Brie to sit down on the couch. She mimicked the way Mrs. Hollingsworth sat with back straight, hands crossed on her lap. It was uncomfortable but Brie sat still.

"It has been a while since Christopher dated anyone. He did not bring you home for Thanksgiving so I decided to come see for myself," she explained.

"Well, I'm glad you came," was all Brie could think to say. She was wishing Chris would hurry up and come back before she made a fool of herself.

"Christopher says you are an office manager for Stowett Marketing and Associates.I understand they just got the account with the Organic Bread Company. That should help their bottom line, but I don't see them closing this year out in the black. Too many missed opportunities earlier this year."

Brie first thought, "what the fuck?" How did she know so much about the company she worked for? "You follow business news I see."

"Of course not. I had my people run a full inquiry on you. I follow who my son is dating news. By the way, you really need to work on that credit score," she said matter-factly. "I'm sure a tighter budget would help."

Chris had walked in not hearing any of the conversation. Brie was staring with a stunned look on her face, but Chris hadn't noticed that either. "Mom, can I get you something to drink?"

"Yes, I would appreciate a glass of wine. I think Brielle could use one also," she requested. She turned her attention back to Brie when Chris walked out again. "Oh, honey, don't look so perplexed. I'm rich. It's what I do when I want to know something about someone. My son really likes you and as his mother, I needed to know that he hadn't picked up a gold digger. He's my only child and I will protect him and his money until I die."

Brie wanted to hit her one good time, but she played along and tried to pretend to be understanding instead of irked. "I love your son and you are right, financially he could take care of me. But, ma'am, that is not why I left my three kids at home with a babysitter on a day I could be with them. I did it because he is worth making happy, no matter what he has in the bank.

"Then I suppose we should put our claws away since we both want what is best for Christopher. And since you don't know what it is you do to make him happy, maybe you should ask. He'd tell you." She smiled but her claws were not retracted.

"What make me happy about what?" Chris asked catching the last sentence. Chris gave both women their glasses and stood back waiting for an answer from either one of them.

Brie wanted to gulp the entire glass down at once but instead she properly sipped. Mrs. Hollingsworth looked at Brie to answer his question. "Oh, I was just saying that I don't know what I do that makes you happy."

Chris smiled then tried to hide it since his mother was looking at him. He cleared his throat and told them both, "That's easy. Brie is very intelligent so I enjoy our conversations. She is organized and capable of pulling off a grand dinner with less than a two hour notice. She is a great mother. Her kids are very likable. We get along really good and have a lot in common."

"It does smell wonderful, Brielle. What are we having?" She asked giving Brie a wink.

"I have a Tuscany rosemary and a lemon-pepper chickens in the oven right now. To go with it we will be having roasted red potatoes and green beans with garlic toast. For desert, I picked up a pint of gelato. Chris mentioned before it was one of your favorites," Brie told her as she was standing up. "I do need to check on everything so please excuse me."

"Sounds delicious and thank you for remembering. I am going to go wash up. Christopher, please place my glass on the dining room table," his mother requested passing it to him.

Brie headed to the kitchen gulping the rest of her wine down. She put her apron back on and started pulling things out of the oven. Chris walked in and hugged her from behind and kissed on her neck.

"Breathe Brie," he whispered. "She is human just like us. Capable of mistakes. Don't tell her that."

"I don't think she likes me," Brie announced while placing the chickens on a silver serving tray.

Chris turned her around to face him. "But I do. I have fallen madly in love with you. My mother has to be that way. That is who she is. You'll see when Ike starts liking girls."

"I know. Oh, by the way, thank you. It's nice to know you are on my side. This is new for me."

"Always," Chris promised sealing it with a kiss.

Get out of bed Phaedra

Phaedra's alarm clock was calling her for a second time that morning. She hit snooze again. She needed to get up and do her yoga but she wasn't in the mood. She considered not getting out of bed for the rest of the week. Phaedra pulled the covers over her head and then heard a knock. It could only be one person. "Come in Ron."

"Good morning," he entered cheerful. "I thought you are usually up this time of morning."

"Not in the mood to live today," she said from under the covers.

Ron sat on the edge of the bed. "That's when you are supposed to push harder. You taught me that."

"Why is everybody telling me what I taught them, lately? I'm glad my advice is working for all of you," Phaedra whined.

Ron stood up and pulled her covers off. "Get up, Phae! Do something with that raggedy ponytail, brush your teeth and throw on your exercise clothes. We are going running."

Phaedra tried to give him an evil look but it wasn't working. He didn't budge and just matched her stare. She sat up and as he said. Ron waited in the living room giving her a 20 minute time limit. Phaedra came out with a pouty look on her face but didn't say anything. She obliged and headed out the door with him.

The two ran six miles not saying anything to each other. She was grateful for his presence. Over the years they stayed cordial. He took the kids for the summer and flew them down for weekends every now and again. They learned how to co-parent. As long as her alimony and child support came on time, they never had anything to argue about.

The cool morning air and the run made her feel better. They were greeted with the smells of sizzling bacon and toasting bread as they walked inside the house. The kids decided to fix breakfast for their parents. The two were unusually all smiles so early on a Monday morning. Phaedra wasn't surprised. They loved their dad.

"Hey, I'm going to go take a quick shower and how about I drive you guys to school today?" Ron asked.

The two agreed and continued preparing breakfast.. Phaedra remembered another lesson as she noticed the happier atmosphere in her house. She was aware she was going through a shift. Her wants were changing. She thought of her prayers and what she'd been asking. She knew in her heart that when you are ready to learn, the teacher shows up.

Phaedra sat down at the kitchen table and watched Caleb and Maya. She was grateful they were not arguing and not blocking out the world with their headphones. Was Ron her teacher. She would wait and see. She was still curious if there was more to his story. Still, having the four of them together was nice.

Caleb set the table and kissed his mom on the cheek. Maya put the food in serving dishes. The tea kettle was whistling and Ron was coming down the stairs. He was wearing faded boot-cut, blue jeans with a black pair of Timberlands and a long sleeve black and white gingham button down shirt. He didn't look anywhere close to his age. You'd only make an educated guess by the few grays in his beard.

Phaedra watched Ron, Maya watched Phaedra and Ron smiled at both. "Smells great. Let's eat!" He said.

Now, I am a business woman

Lexie was leaving the meeting with at least 50 of her business cards passed out and a handful of cards from web designers. It felt good to feel employed even if she didn't have her first client yet. That part would come. She was positive it would. She had visualized it a hundred times. She was close to Phaedra's office so she sent her a text to see if she was available for her to stop by. It would be for business and personal. Phaedra told her to come on.

Lexie called Mark first to tell him how well things had gone. He, naturally, was excited for her. Next, she called Roni to tell her how great things went for her. Roni was happy for her and let her know how proud she was of her. She wanted to call Brie but didn't have time. She had talked to her sister until she got to Phaedra's office.

"You look like a giddy school girl," Phaedra told her as Lexie was walking in.

"I feel like a school girl. Everything is going great. I'm soaking it all in," Lexie told her grinning wide.

"I'm glad to hear. And I take full credit." Phaedra reached out and hugged Lexie. Lexie still was not used to her hugging.

"And how are you doing?" Lexie asked now concerned.

"Sit down please. You are going to need to for this one." Phaedra advised as they both sat in the chairs in front of Phaedra's desk. "Ron showed up at my house last night. He is moving up here and he stayed over."

Lexie's mouth gaped. "You slept with Ron?"

"Girl, no! He slept in the spare room upstairs. An ex is an ex for a reason." Phaedra told her.

Lexie laughed. "Okay, but it would have been priceless. Maybe even get you to move on from George."

"I do need to move on. I just can't figure out why I won't. Well, I kinda sorta know why," Phaedra started.

"Why? And if you say for the money, I'm going to reach over there and punch you."

"No, well maybe that plays a small part. But it's not the main reason. Truth is Lexie, I love him. It's been three years. He makes me happy. It's the relationship that doesn't anymore. The sneaking around is no longer fun. I told him that I wanted to be part of something real, which doesn't make any sense because I'm not really into the whole committed relationship thing." This was Phaedra's first time having the courage to open up about it and admit, not just to Lexie but to herself also, that she was ready for something different.

"But Phae, you always say that if we don't make room for blessings then they won't come," Lexie reminded her.

Phaedra hit the butt of her palm to her forehead. "Why is everybody giving me my own advice. Do none of you have your own material? I should have charged your asses for wisdom."

"You taught all of us well, now it's your turn for us to teach it back to you," Lexie said with a big smile on her face.

"The kids are happy to see their dad. He made me get out of bed and go running this morning," Phaedra continued.

Lexie noticed Phaedra's face lit up as she said that last statement. "Why is he moving?"

"Cancer. He's in remission, but you know when you are faced with the reality of your own mortality you start rethinking your priorities. He looks good though. A little pale."

"You know what I think?" Lexie asked her.

"I'm not sure I want to know," Phaedra told her smacking her lips.

"Well, I'm going to tell you anyways." Lexie sat up straight to make she sure was heard. "I think you are finding that your house is almost paid off so that goal is close to completion. And, despite the economy you are still prospering so you don't really need his money, so that desire is not necessary. The material things are no longer completing you because you have leveled up. However, despite all of this, you are fighting what you already know for reasons that you are not sure. I know you are aware of this. It just a matter of facing the unknown."

Phaedra leaned back in her chair and meditated on what Lexie said. "I hate saying these words, but, you are right. It's hard to walk away from a man whose net worth is over $7 million. What fool hearted woman would do something so stupid?" Phaedra stood up frustrated waving her arms as she talked. "Come on Lexie!"

"A woman who is in a position to make her own millions. A woman that the Universe is trying to take to the next dimension on every level. A woman who is smarter and capable," Lexie answered still sitting up straight.

People always talk about confirmation when they ask for something or thought of something and told no one and then out of the blue, another person says it. Phaedra knew Lexie said what she needed to hear. She didn't want to let go because it was comfortable. Lexie was right in saying that it was time to level up. Phaedra turned around not sure what she should say next. Instead, she asked, "Why do you always put up air quotation marks when you say Universe?"

"Don't be changing the subject when I'm right," Lexie teased.

"You are right. I've become complacent and stopped with my own goals because financially I was being taken care of. And remind me one more time why I would want to give that up?"

"Because it's going to make you insane," Lexie replied.

"Another lesson I taught you I take it?" Phaedra smiled her direction. "The student has become the teacher."

"Sometimes a teacher needs a lesson also. I am proud that I was the one with the words of wisdom this time. Just wish I had recorded it so I would have proof that you said I was right." She teased again.

Lexie talked Phaedra into one more hug and then the two sat down to look at houses. This time Phaedra sat on her side of the desk. Lexie gave Phaedra her wish list of what she and Mark wanted and the two went to work.

Kenny, let me tell you what happened

Brie received a text from Lexie asking which would be easier, getting together for lunch or after work. Neither, was her thought. She had a few things to catch up on and was going to work through lunch. After going to Chris' yesterday, she wanted time with her kids.

She opted for lunch and would just stay an extra hour after work. She did want to tell Lexie about meeting Chris' mother. Lexie let her know that Phaedra was coming also. She envied them both because they were not tethered to an office. They both had their freedom to take a long lunch, run errands, and schedule their work around their family. With all that, they both also made more money than she did.

Brie missed hanging out with them. Her weekends consisted of getting together with Chris and doing stuff with the kids. She had met a few of his friends, gone to a dinner party and now met his mother. Brie was knee deep in a relationship. Something she always wanted. This was her audition for the role of wife. However, it was starting to feel overwhelming. She was juggling a lot of balls that she was not used to juggling. It was time to figure out how to balance them. If she was ever going to fill role of wife, she was also going to have to be mother, friend and worker too.

"What evil deed are you contemplating?" Kenny asked walking up on her.

"Just trying to figure out how to do everything I have to do. Feeling like I'm in what my grandma used to call a chaos storm," she told him.

"You need help with anything?" He offered.

"Not really. Hey, did I tell you I met the Mom?" Brie asked turning towards him.

"Wow! Really? How did that go?" Kenny sat down on the edge of her desk to get the full story.

"So, you know I was nervous and sister girl was a little intimidating. She was dressed sharp though, looking like money. She came off mean in the beginning, but she walked in with gifts for the kids," Brie started.

"She came baring gifts for her son's girlfriend's kids. That's different." Kenny said through his nose.

Brie continued, "I know right! I was stunned. She had those American Dolls for the girls including a wardrobe full of doll clothes. Then for Ike she had an Xbox with games to go along with it and some comic books."

"I guess the kids liked her after that."

"They didn't meet her, but when I told them who they were from, yes, they loved her. They can't wait to get home from school today so they can play with their new stuff. Christmas came early for them," Brie said proudly.

"And how about you? Do you like her?"

"I do, in a way. I mean, she is a little much, but I see it from her point of view. Their family is rich and she is making sure I'm not a gold digger. But Kenny, check this out. She ran a credit check on me," Brie said in her I'm offended voice.

"Wait, what? How she get your social?" Kenny asked choking on his laugh.

"Probably the same way Phaedra can. Whatever it is, it's not legal," Brie answered.

Worry came across Kenny's face. "Wait, Phaedra can run a credit report on someone that didn't fill out an application?"

"Yes. She has someone somewhere that could tell her your GPA in the 3rd grade if she wanted to know it," Brie told him making him uncomfortable.

"Wow, Phaedra is fierce. I wonder what dirt she has on the person that gave her the password to that system," Kenny said shaking his head. "So, moms ran your report and you and Chris are still dating. What's the problem?"

"She snooped in my personal business. That's not fair! What if I want to see her credit report? What if I show up and drop a tit-for-tat bomb on her?" Brie argued.

Kenny put his hands on her shoulder. "And what would that accomplish? Usually tit-for-tat leads to war and I'm not sure you want to risk your relationship with a man you have worked hard to get over a power trip."

Brie sighed. "No, I don't. But still, it's the principle."

Kenny laughed at her. "Okay, principle. I'll tell you what, see if you can curl up on a Saturday night with your principles."

"Ugh," she groaned. "I hate it. Plus, Chris said not to worry about it because he loved me no matter what. Oh, wait, I forgot to tell you. He told me he loved me!"

Kenny mockingly jumped up and down with her. "You go girl. Chris got the bug."

"Whatever Kenny," she said pushing on him. "I suppose I'm doing something correct."

"You know what? I hope I'm there to be a witness, in the front seat, on the day you stop doubting yourself." Kenny smiled at her and kissed her on the forehead and then walked back to his office.

Letting go

Phaedra had taken Ron around Jacksonville to show him the different areas. He chose a subdivision close to hers so that the kids wouldn't have to travel far to get to him. Phaedra accepted his excuse and started looking for a three bedroom house. For her it was urgent because he was still at her house. She didn't really see a point in making him stay at a hotel. The kid's attitudes were better and they were coming home excited. Phaedra knew it would wear off but she was going to enjoy it while it lasted.

Again, it was that feeling like her reality was fake. A fantasy. Her real life would show up soon. She wasn't sure if it was what she wanted because the fantasy seemed to have all the things she felt like she needed.

It was Wednesday morning and she was supposed to meet George for lunch as they planned. She found herself asking what was the point. She felt guilty because of the restaurant scene. She felt guilty because it had been three years into this relationship. Phaedra realized the root of her problem was she was feeling. She wasn't supposed to feel. It was an affair with a married man. No feelings should have been involved.

"Good morning, beautiful," George answered when she called.

"I'm not meeting you today," Phaedra told him straight out.

George huffed and muffled the phone to clear someone out of his office. "So, we are doing this?"

"What is THIS?" She asked.

"You are really walking away from this relationship because I asked you for some loyalty?"

"No, that is not why. I'm walking away because I've come to realize that we have reached a plateau. We can't go backwards or forwards. I made a mistake falling in love with you, and once I did that...I ruined us," Phaedra explained.

"I thought you agreed to give me some time," George reminded her.

"Time for what? I've already proven that I can't be away from you. We can't do anything else from this point. I don't want to leave town just to go on a date anymore."

George was silent for a moment. Phaedra could only hear him breathing and feel him thinking. She knew George would get silent when he got angry or upset. That's why she was trying to do this over the phone. She would have caved in person.

"You have to say something. You can't ignore this until you think I will give up. You have to talk to me George. I need you to say something," she said as she began to tear up. She wanted to fight it but no longer could hold them back. Her feelings were getting in the way. Again. She was in love. She hated that this had to end. Living in the moment was painful. She had to feel the pain now or feel the pain later. Either way, there would be pain.

"I've given you everything you wanted. This is how you show gratitude?" George was also fighting tears. He wanted to be angry, but he knew. He was expecting this since she had needs he could not supply. He knew for three years Phaedra was more than one man could handle. He wasn't surprised that trying to tame her would break her.

"And I've given you everything that you wanted. I've made you happy. I've been there when you called. And for a couple of months, I've tried to be what you wanted and sacrificed my own happiness. I am grateful. You know I've been grateful. And losing you is the hardest thing in the world. But we can't go anywhere from here. Loving you...," she paused for a moment to try and pull it together. "I fell in love with you and I shouldn't have. I...I shouldn't have." Phaedra wanted to lay the phone down so she could sob. "I gotta go George. I can't..."

"No, wait!" George stopped her from hanging up. "All I'm saying is give me until the next month, Phaedra."

"What will be different next month?"

"I don't know. What if I moved you and the kids to a different city? I could be there part-time. When I'm there we would be free to do what we want," he suggested.

"No. That is not freedom. I'm not going to keep sitting around waiting for my turn. It's time to let go," she whispered that last statement. They were the hardest to get out.

"I'll agree to this, for now. I'll figure out a way to win you back. Is it because of that nappy headed little dreadlock boy? Or is it because of your ex-husband?"

"How do you know about dreadlock?" She finally asked.

"I make it my business to know everything about you," he told her.

"It's not anyone else. It's about you and me. You have to say you will let this go," she pleaded.

"I don't have to say anything," he yelled and then corrected himself. "I'm sorry. I don't have to say anything. Do you realize what you are asking me? I will call you next month. I will have a plan."

"I won't answer. If you love me the way I love you, you won't call," Phaedra told him. "I love you. Good-bye George."

Phaedra disconnected before he could say anything else. She couldn't drag it on any longer. She would stay true to her word. She wouldn't answer if he called.

Blackmail

Lexie was shuffling through her closet still trying to figure out what to wear to Chris' Christmas party. Red, green and black were the obvious choices. Gold and silver dresses would also be everywhere. That didn't really leave her much more to choose from which lead to an excuse to go shopping.

Just as Lexie was gathering up her purse and shoes, she could hear her cell phone. She went through her usual process of looking for it and catching the call on the 4th ring. "Hey Roni," she answered.

"Hello. Why does it always take you so long to get to the phone?" Her sister asked complaining.

"Because I don't keep it attached to my hip like everybody else."

"You are an entrepreneur now. I could have been a client," Roni advised her.

"It's Saturday. Mine is a Monday through Friday job," Lexie told her.

"Then you are going to fail. No one every gained success working Monday through Friday," Roni pointed out.

"So...anyways, what's up?" Lexie wasn't in the mood for unsolicited advice.

"I changed my plans. I'll be up tonight. Can I crash at your townhouse since you don't use it?"

"Yeah, not a problem. Does Mom know you are coming up a day early?"

"No. I would appreciate it if you did not tell her. I will see her Monday." Roni requested.

"Hmmm, let me think. What would my silence cost you?" Lexie started thinking about what she could get out of Roni.

Roni quickly ended any expectations of blackmail. "How about I not tell Mom that Carlos was married at the time you were living with him and pregnant with Anton?"

"You do know you are an evil bitch that will rot in hell for eternity, right?" Lexie sucked her teeth pouting because she never wins when it comes to her sister.

Roni laughed because she enjoyed having the upper hand. "Yes, I do. Although, I am convinced I will move up in the ranks quickly and eventually take over."

"Keep dreaming. I'm sure you and all the other type A's think that," Lexie said shaking her head and rolling her eyes. "What time will you be here?"

"I land at 8:30."

"I'll be at a party. I'll leave the key under the mat. I'll get the one from Mom's house," she said jokingly.

"No need. I had a key made the last time I was there," Roni said smiling because again she had the upper hand.

"What!" Lexie wasn't that surprised. "Whatever. I'll see you at dinner Monday."

"Okay. Enjoy your night," Roni told her.

"You do the same," Lexie said grinning and then disconnecting the call.

Lexie threw her phone in her purse and called for Anton. He met her at the door unhappy because he hated going shopping. He was ready to be dropped off at Phaedra's house. Maya agreed to babysit for both Lexie and Brie. Lexie bribed him with a new toy if he put up with her for a couple of hours. Anton sighed, but agreed as he bucked himself into the car.

The Invitation

Brie was glad this day had finally come. She had gone through her list a few times and everything was where it was supposed to be. She had only run into a couple of hiccups which she felt fortunate about. Chris was getting dressed and she had been fussing over her hair. He walked up and hugged her from behind as he always liked to do when he saw her standing anywhere.

"Do we have time to get undressed and do the nasty?" He asked kissing the back of her neck.

"Do the nasty?" Brie laughed. "I don't think anyone has used that phrase since 1988."

"That doesn't answer my question," he told her pulling down on the side zipper of her dress.

"Chris, stop!" Brie pushed him off her with her butt. "I have caterers in the kitchen and the DJ will be here soon."

Chris laughed and went to his side on the double sink counter. "I was thinking," he started.

"About what?"

"The kids are out of school, Christmas is in a couple of days, both of us are off, so why don't you and the kids just stay here for the week? We can bring all the gifts here and do the whole Christmas thing."

Brie stopped breathing for what felt like minutes but was only seconds. "Yeah...I mean...so it wouldn't bother...yeah, yeah, that would great."

"I'm not sure if that was a yes or a no, but I'm going to guess it was a yes," he said smiling at her.

Brie blushed at her stuttering. "Yes. It was a yes."

"Okay," he agreed and then left the bathroom slapping her on the butt as he walked by.

Brie watched until he was out of view and then silently screamed jumping up and down. A week at his house with the kids she thought and then smiled to herself. She again reminded herself to breathe. She was on stage. This was the try before you buy moment. Her chance to prove herself as wife material was her intention. Brie stepped back to look at herself in the mirror. It had taken her a half hour to get her natural curls twisted up and then in a bun on the top. She was wearing the dress Chris had picked out. It was a satin red, floor length with thigh high slits on each side.

The Christmas party had been a lot to plan. Chris invited a few faculty members from his department and several friends. He said he wanted simple but simple kept getting bigger. The list grew to 20 people. It was no longer just a dinner party. She had to hire a wait staff, bar tender and a DJ.

Brie had rearranged the furniture in the Florida room so there would be room for dancing. She hired a DJ that would be set up by the bar. From there the music could be heard inside and outside. She also hired a bartender to mix the drinks so neither one of them would be stuck behind the bar. Brie chose heavy appetizers and set it up as a buffet in the kitchen. There would be plenty of room for socializing between the kitchen and the Florida room.

The nine foot Christmas tree in the living room was decorated with red, green and silver ornaments with a lit star at the top. Brie carried a "Northern Star" theme throughout the house. A six foot tree was in the Florida room with silver stars and white lights. The last tree was four feet and on the patio with colorful lights wrapped around it. Everything had been professionally done, however, Brie was crossing her fingers that next year she and the kids would be there to do the decorating themselves as a family.

This wasn't as nerve racking as meeting his mother, but she still had butterflies swimming around in her stomach. She double checked herself one more time in the main mirror after she slipped on her red Jimmy Choo's, also compliments of Chris. She was complete and now it was time to head to the kitchen to see what the caterers had done. As she reached the living room Chris informed her that the DJ was setting up and he was heading for his office. Brie walked in and everything was good with the caterers. She said a silent prayer of gratitude that everything was going well. Next, she went out to greet the DJ.

"DJ Killawatt, how are you?" She asked extending her hand to meet him.

"I'm good girl, how you doing," he said grabbing her hand and kissing it. "So, you and I getting together after this party?"

Brie blushed and giggled at the same time. "Um, I don't think so. The person paying you wouldn't like that."

"Girl, I already got my check," he smiled patting his back pocket. "You need to tell money bags he needs to put someone as fine as you on lock down if he doesn't want a Mexican like me trying to get you on my team."

Again, Brie was blushing and giggling. "I'll be sure to let him know. Did you get my music request?"

"I sure did. Would you like to step back here with me?" He smiled directing her behind the booth.

Brie smiled back shaking her head no. "I'm scared to go back there. I better stay on this side so we both don't get put out of the party."

He winked then pulled up the list she sent. He offered additional suggestions. Just as she got ready to walk away Chris walked up eyeing both of them.

"You guys didn't discuss music beforehand?" He asked suspicious.

"We did. I just wanted to make sure my specific request were in," she said taking a guilty step back.

"Umph," was Chris' only comment. He then went behind the bar to fix himself a drink.

"Would you like a drink?" Brie asked the DJ walking towards the other side of the bar.

"Nah, I've got one," he smiled holding his beer up. "The bartender already got me started."

"Great. Well, since I'm not needed here, I'm heading for the kitchen," Brie announced and left the room.

Chris followed her eyeing back at DJ Killawatt. Chris grabbed her by the hand and led her to the living room. Yelling at the housekeeper, he told her to leave the room which she did quickly.

"You don't get to flirt with other men in my house, especially on a night like tonight which is important to me," he said standing an inch from her face.

Brie hadn't seen Chris mad in a while. "I wasn't…"

"Shut up! Before you deny anything, I was behind you during your little conversation."

"Chris, I was only asking about the music. Nothing else. I brushed off anything else he said. I promise to never disrespect you," she told him. The doorbell rang and Brie was relieved it did.

"You better not," he said and went to answer the door.

Brie pulled a smile on her face. It was his closes friend, Jay and Jay's girlfriend. Brie played the perfect hostess taking their coats and giving them holiday wishes and compliments. When Brie returned, she sat next to Chris on the couch and he pulled her closer to him while the four of them talked for a minute in the living room. She finally got the courage to look at him but he hadn't softened yet. She played it off and continued talking wishing Lexie and Mark would get there.

They all stood up and headed for the Florida room so Jay and Debra could get a drink. The two walked ahead and Chris grabbed Brie's arm and pulled her back. "Don't make a fool of me Brie. It's the one thing I can't forgive."

She stood on her tiptoes and kissed him softly. "I promise I would never."

You, love birds, come on," Jay called from the kitchen. "You had time for that before we got here," he laughed.

"I tried man. I was turned down," Chris said laughing as if it was a joke and not true. He grabbed her hand a little gentler this time and followed his friend to the bar.

Together

"That's a lot of kids," Phaedra said to Maya as she stood in the doorway of the game room.

"It's just four kids, Mom," Maya sang.

"Four is a lot of kids," she reiterated walking out. "Ron, are you even close to ready?"

"Yes, close. I just can't find my socks," he said walking towards the dryer.

Phaedra shook her head at him as he walked barefoot in the black suit through the house. It had been a couple of weeks of Ron being at her house. The kids talked her into allowing him through the holidays. She was reluctant, because she herself was feeling vulnerable.

"You look nice Mom. I like you in black better than the gold. Gold drowned you out," Maya told her.

"Thank you," Phaedra smiled. "Haven't been able to breathe much since I put it on."

"It looks good to me," Ron chimed in sitting down to put on his socks.

"You both look nice," Maya said grinning at both. She added, "Together."

Phaedra looked at Maya and sent her out of the room. Ron was just sitting and smiling as he put on his shoes. "Don't you start," she told him.

"What, I'm just sitting here," he laughed then stood up.

"It looks good to me," she mocked him in a high pitch childish voice.

Ron laughed. "Well you do. It's not as if it's a secret. And that slit up the back is working."

She smiled then rolled her eyes. "I don't mind being fashionably late, but that doesn't mean I want to miss everything."

"Let me grab my wallet," he told her realizing he was not going to get anywhere. He had been trying since he'd been there, just to get shut down each time.

Ron never made it a secret that he was still in love with Phaedra. He was just not the faithful type, and he regretted that. He was enjoying them being a family again. It was nice to be there when the kids arrived home from school and sitting down to eat dinner together. Phaedra had to admit it was nice when they sat around the night before playing Scrabble. However, Phaedra was back on her game and fake was fake. Mommy and Daddy were not getting back together.

George had text her a couple of times. Once to say he loved her and always would and the other to inform her he left her a gift in the garage. It was an engagement ring. Three carets. She put it back in the box and stuck it in the glove compartment of the T-Bird.

"Are we taking your car or mine?" Ron asked.

"You really have to ask?" Phaedra asked walking out the front door towards his car.

Ron ran out after her so he could open her door for her. She smirked and slid in. "Is this a date or I'm just a friend?"

"Ron, let's get this convo over with," she said smoothing her dress so she can turn to him even though he wasn't looking her way because he was backing out. "We are just friends. Friends who used to be married. Friends who have two kids together. Friends going to a party together. That is the definition of our relationship."

Ron smiled and did finally look her way as he stopped at the stop sign. "I got it. Friends. Allow me to rephrase my question. When I go in here and meet your other friends, am I your, 'Oh, this is my ex-husband the date', or am I, 'Oh, this is my ex-husband but we are still just friends'."

Phaedra stared at his lying eyes for a minute," You are Ron, my ex-husband whom I'm hanging out with tonight."

Ron smiled. "See, not so hard. I don't know why you keep complicating things."

Phaedra didn't stop staring at him, but it was not a look of admiration. More of frustration. He smiled and leaned over and pecked her on her lips. Then he pulled off from the stop sign.

Phaedra sat back in her seat. She wanted to laugh, but contained it. "You make me sick," she told him folding her arms.

Ron laughed for her. "I don't mean to. I just like to see you smile. So, why do you never drive the Thunderbird?"

"I do, for special occasions or when I just want to drive."

"Maybe we can take a drive up A1A this weekend with the top down," he suggested.

"This isn't Miami. It is 60 something degrees. That's not top down weather," she told him.

"We don't have to ride with the top down." Ron was fishing for information about George. Phaedra hadn't been forthcoming but he knew something was wrong.

"Why don't we just drive up in your car that way we can take the kids?"

"Caleb has plans this weekend, but I'm sure Maya would love it" he told her.

"You know, you don't have to include me. Maya would enjoy the time alone with you," Phaedra offered.

"I know, but it's nice to have you also, unless you have plans. I understand."

"I agree, the family thing has been nice. I really have been comfortable these past few weeks. In another week, you will be moving into your house and everybody's life goes back to normal," she reminded him.

"You've always been a realist. Have you ever considered just trying to see how things would work out?" He asked.

"I have, it didn't work, so I became a realist," she snapped.

Ron finally got bold enough to ask, "Is that why you and the guy you were seeing broke up?"

"Yes, it is," she said bluntly.

"But, Phaedra, honey, at what point do you stop being a realist and start being a romantic. Let it just happen. It has to be worth fighting for," Ron suggested.

Phaedra didn't say anything to him. She didn't want to tell Ron that George was married. That she got out of the relationship because she felt like she made a fool of herself. She didn't want Ron to know that love was hard for her and distance was comfortable. She didn't want him to know that part of her secretly wished he could stay and they could be real.

I'm a wreck

When Lexie and Mark arrived at the house, Lexie suggested they look in this neighborhood for a house. Mark agreed and told her that as soon as he got the contract with the NFL, they could afford to live out here. There were only four other couples there so far and Brie was relieved when she saw her.

"This place is beautiful," Lexie told her as she hugged her hello. "And you look fabulous!"

Brie returned the compliment, "Mark, welcome. I will find Chris so I can introduce you."

"You did a fantastic job. I love it," Mark told her giving her a hug.

Brie direct them both to the kitchen and point to the bar which she herself had been avoiding so she wouldn't have to say anything to the DJ. She spotted Chris outside and bee lined her way towards him. Lexie watched her but wasn't sure why she was in such a hurry to introduce Mark to Chris.

Lexie and Mark headed towards the bar. There was another couple sitting at the bar. The introduced themselves and Mark ordered him and Lexie a drink and dropped a five in the tip jar. Brie walked up with Chris on her arm not looking towards the DJ. Lexie could see tension on Brie's face.

"Mark, this is Chris, Chris, Lexie's fiancée Mark," Brie introduced the two.

"Nice to finally meet you. I hear your name all the time when these two are talking," Mark joked.

"All good I hope," Chris smiles shaking Mark's hand. "And nice to see you again stranger. Congratulations to both of you on the engagement."

"Thank you," Lexie replied hugging him. "Brie did a beautiful job. Now I'm even more excited about her putting my wedding together."

"Yes, my girlfriend is very talented. I'm beyond impressed," Chris agreed kissing Brie on the cheek.

"Thank you both. Hey, Lexie, we need a bathroom break," Brie said reaching for Lexie's hand.

Lexie and Brie excused themselves leaving Chris' co-worker's wife as the only woman in the group at the bar. Brie led Lexie to the bedroom and closed the door. She was still leaning on it and took a deep breath and exhaled even longer.

"What is wrong, sweetie?" Lexie asked hugging her tight.

"I am so nervous. I'm not sure where to stand, what to say, who to talk to the longest. I'm a wreck," Brie told her.

Lexie stood back and left her hands on Brie's shoulders. "Sweetie, everything is going great. People are laughing, the food looks good, the music is pumping, and most of all you look beautiful. Plus, Chris is happy."

"He was mad at me earlier," she whispered as if the room was bugged. "The DJ was flirting with me and he overheard and hit the roof. He's never been that mad at me before."

"Brie, you are fuckin' drop dead gorgeous. He should know men are going to look your direction and should be proud. Remind him you can be trusted and know who you belong to," Lexie advised her. "And by the way, couples fight. That's how you know its love. Look at Mark and me. We have broken up, got back together, broke up and so on. We made it. So just know this is the first of many."

Brie smiled and felt a little more relieved. "He invited the kids and I to stay here for the week, of course that was before he got angry at me."

"I'm positive he has not changed his mind. Chris is beaming out there. This party is going to be great. I can't wait to taste the food. He's proud of you, and I am too. And I was serious when I told you that the database you developed is better than a lot that I've seen. We need to get you from behind that phone," Lexie told her.

"I'm so glad you are here. I'm so glad we are friends." Brie hugged her again. "I'd be a hot mess if it weren't for you."

A soft knock came from the door and Chris poked his head in. "Sorry to interrupt ladies. Your friend Kenny is here."

"Oh, great. I'm coming," she said wiping her eyes.

Chris stepped in and Lexie took the queue from him and stepped out. She found Mark still by the bar and Kenny and his date with him.

"Phaedra is not here yet?" She asked anyone.

"Phaedra's coming?" Kenny asked.

Lexie snickered at him, "Yes, she should have been here by now. Kenny, are you going to introduce me to your date?"

Kenny tried to contain his grin. "Lexie, meet Michelle."

The two shook hands and Kenny made his way to the kitchen to fix a plate. Mark followed. The girls stood and talked and introduced themselves to others. DJ Killawatt threw on a song that got a few more people dancing, including Lexie and Michelle.

Our guests are going to have fun without us.

"Is everything okay?" Chris asked Brie closing the door after Lexie walked out.

"Yes," she told him walking over to the mirror to dry her eyes.

"Then why are you crying?" He asked standing next to her in the dresser mirror.

Brie got the water off her face then fixed her make up. "Happy tears, Chris. I'm proud of what I accomplished here, and to share it with Lexie just made me cry."

"I'm proud of you also," he reminded her.

"I know. I would have felt silly crying with you. It's probably a girl thing," she joked. "But thank you for not only the opportunity, but for tonight. I feel like the queen. I really enjoy being your girlfriend." Brie smiled and kissed him, then wiped her lipstick off his lips.

Chris pulled her hand down and kissed her again, gazing into her eyes. "We better get back to the party. Our guests are going to have too much fun without us."

She agreed and led the way. As they passed the front door, the door bell rang. Chris opened it and there stood Phaedra and Ron. He stepped to the side and invited them both in. Phaedra did a quick introduction to the two of them.

"About time," Brie told her as she handed Phae's coat to the maid.

"Ron couldn't find something. I don't remember. I just know I was stuck waiting for him," Phaedra complained.

"Hi Ron, I'm Brie. Nice to finally meet you."

"Like wise. Lovely home," he told them both.

"Sounds like the fun is that way," Phaedra pointed towards the back of the house.

"Yes, it is.. Follow me," Brie said dancing as she put her arm through Chris' and led the pack.

When they walked in the kitchen, Brie was glad to see people were finally eating. As they entered the Florida room, she saw people were dancing. People that had been outside were now inside. It looked like the parties she had imagined as a teenager but her grandmother forbade her to have or to go to. It was hard to contain her enthusiasm. She spotted Kenny and ran to give him a hug. She was excited to meet Michelle but even more excited to introduce Chris. Afterwards, she led Chris to the dance floor.

Chris was pleased that Brie made him look good in front of his colleagues. He was pleased with how beautiful she was and the nods from the other males in the room. With Chris pleased, Brie was happy.

Tonight, she is the butterfly

"Kenney! How have you been?" Phaedra asked hugging him.

"Well, and yourself?" He greeted back happy that she hugged him.

"Very good," she smiled.

"Yes, I can tell, but you always look good," he told her wanting badly to drop to his knees and beg for another chance.

"Well, thank you," she said, smirked and walked away.

Kenny watched in agony.

"Who is that?" Ron asked.

"Kenny. You met him like 1 minute ago," she said giving him a 'what the hell' look.

"He's drooling so I was merely asking how you know him," Ron explained.

Phaedra laughed, but didn't turn around to look. "He was a short-term fuck friend."

Ron wasn't surprised. "I see."

"Good for you," she said patting his shoulder. "I'm going to dance. Care to join me or would you prefer to stay and have a staring contest with Kenny?"

"Yes, I'll join you. No point in two guys you used to kick it with but have no intent of kicking it with again challenge each other for a prize neither are going to get."

"A simple yes would have sufficed," she said as she walked towards Lexie and Mark on the dance floor.

Ron followed grinning towards Kenny's way. He couldn't help himself. Phaedra and Lexie danced leaving Ron and Mark more as by-standards. Lexie started to pull Brie over to their group but Phaedra told Lexie no. Brie was getting to know Chris' people and it was okay.

"Tonight, she's the butterfly. Let her have her fun. She'll be the ugly caterpillar tomorrow and we will welcome her back with open arms."

"Every time I think you are growing up, you open your mouth and prove me wrong," Lexie said laughing.

"You shouldn't put expectations on other people. You are the one the ends up disappointed and hurt." Phaedra smiled and then turned around to dance with her ex.

Brie worked the whole crowd, sometimes with Chris; sometimes without. The three did slip away and Brie was able to tell Phaedra about staying with Chris for the week. She didn't hide her excitement so Phaedra tried to be happy for her. While the three hid away in the bedroom talking Lexie mentioned her sister was in town. Phaedra's ears perked with interest. Only Brie paid attention to the plotting on Phaedra's face. When she realized she was being watched, Phaedra changed the subject.

On the way home, Phaedra sent Roni a text.

'Heard you were in town. Feel like company?'

She waited patiently for her text alert to sound the response. She and Ron talked about the people, the house and how much fun they had. He noticed she kept looking at her phone but didn't mention it.

When they got home, Phaedra checked the game room. Everyone was asleep. All four kids and Maya were on the couch. With shoes in hand, she headed across the burlap carpet to her room. She paused when she heard her phone chime and she quickly read the answer.

'Not tonight. Already have company.'

Phaedra was disappointed.

Ron was paying attention. "You know, if you get bored or don't get a response, you can come upstairs and sit on my face," he said raising his eyebrows at her.

Phaedra walked towards where Ron stood. She turned her back to him and asked, "Will you unzip my dress for me?" She knew she could reach it but what fun would that be.

Ron smiled, "I would be glad to help you out of this dress." Ron unhooked the eye out of the loop and then slid the zipper down.

Phaedra stepped out of her dress and turned towards him with her exposed breast and silk, black thong. At 42, her body was toned and her breast were still perky. Phaedra knelt down in front of him stopping her face in front the growth in his pants. She gathered up her dress in the same hand she was holding her shoes and slowly stood back up. She lightly grabbed him cuddling the hardness. "Ron," she whispered. "Don't go blind tonight." Phaedra winked and walked away to her room closing and locking the door.

Ron stood there at the bottom of the stairs. He smiled. He was rock hard and nowhere to put it. Ron headed up the stairs to shower.

We can start on the patio

Since Anton was staying at Phaedra's, Mark and Lexie headed straight home.

"We should consider doing something like that next year," Lexie told Mark. "That was so much fun."

"It was," Mark agreed. "So, Ron is still at Phaedra's?"

"Yeah. His closing date is December30th. He will be moving after that. Why?"

"Just curious. He seemed to watch Phaedra like a lioness stalking her prey. But, if I think about it, so were the wives and girlfriends anytime one of the guys smiled at her," Mark joked.

"Well, she broke up with George, so she will need a new financier," Lexie began to gossip then stopped herself. "Oh, come Mark, she is a beautiful woman. I'm sure Ron regrets losing her. It has to be hard being under the same roof but not able to touch."

"Phaedra is very beautiful. Kenny looked like he would sell his soul if she asked him to," he said laughing.

Lexie laughed also. She couldn't help herself. "You need to leave my friend alone. Tell the truth. If you and I weren't together, would you make a move for her?"

"That is hard to answer because I know Phaedra too well. I don't make enough money for Phaedra's taste. However, I do respect that she does not play games. She will tell you upfront it is about the money," he explained.

Lexie debated his answer. "I beg to differ. RJ is not rich."

Mark laughed, "RJ is 25 years old and probably hanging like Dexter."

Lexie cracked up at his Eddie Murphy reference. "I'm done with you. Phaedra could have anyone she wants and Ron is just not the one."

"Well, you can't fault a man for trying," Mark told her.

"So, if I were more like Phaedra would we still be together?"

Mark looked at Lexie from the corner of his eye. "No, we wouldn't. Phaedra is not the committed type. I want someone to raise a family with and grow old together. If you were like Phaedra, you wouldn't want that."

"I don't think there is anything wrong with her being like that. She's having fun and she is not hurting anyone. And she doesn't involve her kids. Maybe by the time they are gone, she will be ready to settle down. Who knows, she may even take old Ron back."

"Why so much talk about Phaedra?" Mark asked.

"Um, hello, you brought her up," she reminded him. "So, I was thinking no Anton tonight. We have the whole house and a new can of whipped cream."

Mark smiled at that thought and pushed the accelerator a little harder. "So, we can start in the kitchen and make our way to the bedroom."

"Tonight, we can start in any room you choose," she whispered in his ear and nibbled his lobe.

"In that case, we can start on the patio."

"What is your obsession with having sex outside?"

Mark was turning on their street. "Simple. Because I'm not supposed to. Remember that night you gave me a blowjob at the park? That was the best blowjob of my whole life."

Lexie laughed at Mark because he used his little boy voice. "So, all that work I've put in since that night isn't working?"

"Wait, I didn't say that. I just said the ambiance of being outside at a public park and us getting busted just made it a bit more exciting," he quickly said. "So…about the patio?"

"What if we set up the tent?"

"Nah, I'm thinking a blanket, in the yard and the neighbors peeking over the fence to see what the noise is," he said pulling her as close as he could with the console in between them as the garage door lowered.

"You know I'm such a prude," she blushed.

"Yeap, I know," he grinned. "But that adds to the fun of it."

Lexie didn't think too long, "Okay. You get the blankets and I'll get the can of whipped cream."

The envelope, please

Brie liked not having to clean up after the party. She looked around for Chris and he was nowhere to be found. She checked his office and he wasn't there. Brie was going to call him, but when she got into the bedroom to retrieve her phone, she heard the shower going. She walked into the closet and removed her dress and put on the robe that Chris bought her for nights she stayed there. She also grabbed the matching night gown.

She was too late. The shower turned off and she sat at the edge of the bed to remove her jewelry. Chris came out with a towel wrapped around his waist and not completely dry. He sat on the other side of the bed. Brie felt nervous. She didn't know if the fight was over or if now that they were alone he would bring it up again. The silence was killing her. Chris had a few drinks but she didn't think enough for him to be inebriated.

Brie broke the silence. "I hope the kids had fun. I know we did."

"I'm sure they did," he said with no real feeling in his voice.

"Are you still upset with me?" Brie needed to know. "From earlier?"

"No. I thought we go past that earlier," he said stretching. "I do have something that I'd like to talk to you about."

Brie's stomach flopped. "What is it?"

Chris leaned over to pull a white envelope out of his nightstand's drawer and motioned for Brie to sit next to him. "I want to give you this. I think you did a remarkable job tonight. Lexie was bragging about some database you created. Craig and Nancy mentioned they want to hire you for their next event. I see something promising. I have faith in you, so I want to invest in you. Help you get this dream off the ground."

He handed her the envelope and she opened it. Brie pulled out a check for $15,000. Her mouth gapped, "What is this for?"

"An initial investment into you getting your business started. If you need to take a class on starting a business, let me know. We offer them at the school and I can get you in and if I need to I'll pay for it."

"That's a lot of money. How am I going to pay you back," she asked with her hand shaking holding a check that large with her name on it.

"Don't worry about that part. Like I said, it's an investment. We'll come up with something later if we need to," Chris advised.

"Wow, thank you Chris. I really don't know what to say. Thank you," Brie jumped up to hug Chris.

"What time are you picking up the kids tomorrow?"

"After breakfast. Maybe about 11," she answered walking towards the dresser to lay the check, now tucked back into the envelope, down.

Brie was now standing in front of Chris. She leaned in to kiss him and then dropped her robe. The voice in her head asked if she was doing this for the money, or did she just want to have sex. She told herself they would have had sex anyways. He tugged at her waist wanting her to kneel in front of him. She instead continued to kiss him and grabbed his shaft with her hand. She had to be in charge. She couldn't feel like she was doing this for $15,000. Chris stopped tugging and laid back. He gave her control. It was to his pleasure.

Don't close that door

Maya lined all the kids up after breakfast to take them for a walk. Phaedra had slept in but emerged just before her daughter was walking out the door. She gave Maya a kiss on the cheek and patted the other four on top of their heads. Ron was standing in front of the coffee pot still yawning. Phaedra debated if she should go straight to her meditation room or speak to him. She decided on the later.

"Sleep well?" She asked stepping into her kitchen.

"After a cold shower I did," he smiled.

Phaedra giggled and poured herself a cup of coffee. "I'm surprised you are awake. We were out late."

"I heard Maya in the kitchen this morning so I checked to see if she needed help. She's pretty good with kids. I should have a talk with her about finishing college before starting a family."

"She's a smart kid," Phaedra reminded him.

"But we are her parents and we both are promiscuous and I don't want her out there having a bunch of kids with different men," he shared his concerns.

"You're a good dad, Ron. I don't think Maya will run amuck. And by the way, I keep my sex life separate from my home life," she told him. "Besides, I'd be more concerned about Caleb then Maya. Caleb is the sneaky one. I have a feeling he is not a virgin, but he won't tell me."

It had been a while since Phaedra drank coffee. She was making faces trying to get it down. Ron noticed and filled her tea kettle and put it on the stove. His small gestures had not gone unnoticed by her. She did wonder how long they would last.

"I am curious if he picked up those traits from his mother or his father," he teased.

"Both," Phaedra answered. "But please, talk to her. Better to have the talk too many times than not have the talk at all."

"What did last night mean?"

Phaedra got up from the table and poured the coffee down the drain. She got a tea bag and a cup before responding. "Why mess up a good thing? We make better friends, don't you agree?"

"I do agree. Maybe that is where we went wrong, we weren't friends first. Maybe we did it backwards," he offered.

"No, we did it right. It just wasn't meant to be. Again, why mess up a good thing?"

"Why do you keep shutting down the idea of a second chance?"

"Because I'm smart enough to know that you don't go back," she told him as she sat back down with her tea in hand.

"I don't see it as going backwards. I see it as second chances. I wasn't ready to be married but I didn't want to lose you and asking you to sit around and wait for me was not reasonable," Ron explained. "But now, we are both single and maybe that is not an accident."

"No, it's a coincidence. Ron, you don't really think you and I could be together again?" Phaedra asked realizing just how serious he was. "Are you dying or something else you are not telling me and just need money or an alibi?"

"Why can't you just believe I never stopped loving you? I'm not dying, I don't owe anyone any money, I don't have anyone after me, and if I did I would not put you or our children in harm's way. My Life is in order. I am near the kids because I want to be, and the only thing I'm missing is someone to love me."

Phaedra shook her head at him, "Maybe you staying here was a mistake."

Phaedra stood up to walk away and Ron grabbed her by the arm to stop her. "Phaedra, wait. It has nothing to do with me staying here. It's been all these years of seeing you when we pickup and drop off the kids. I'm just now brave enough to say something because...well, because."

Ron moved his hand down her arm until he was holding her hand. "Just don't close that door. That's all I'm asking. I don't expect you to all of a sudden to be ready to fall head-over-heels for me, but I'm asking you to remember the guy you wanted to spend the rest of your life with and not the asshole that I became."

Phaedra stayed silent inhaling the woodsy scent of his cologne. Ron kissed her on the forehead and headed for his room. Phaedra heard Maya and her army coming inside the front door so she went to go meet them.

"Did you guys have fun?" Phaedra asked as they were standing in the foyer removing their shoes.

"Yessss," they sung in unison.

"I had fun also," Lexie announced walking into the still open front door.

Phaedra hugged her as she entered. Lexie was still not used to Phaedra willingly touching her. "Hi. I bet you did with Anton out of the house."

Lexie blushed giving herself away. "We enjoyed our alone time."

"Where's Brie?" Phaedra asked.

"I called her, she is on her way," Lexie told her.

"Good. Follow me," Phaedra grabbed Lexie's arm and pulled her to her bedroom and closed the door. "I'm a wreck! I'm not supposed to be a wreck. I'm well put together. You and Brie are the ones that are all fucked up."

Lexie was offended for a moment. Just long enough to consider the source. "What happened?"

"So," Phaedra decided to sit down. "So, I get rid of George because I don't want to be the other woman. I need to call RJ, but I feel so guilty and I'm scared George might have him killed."

"Wait, what?" Lexie stopped her.

"Girl, we are talking about me right now. I'll tell you that story later," Phaedra explained. "Now Ron comes in with his feelings talking about how he still loves me and doesn't want me to close that door. And to top if off, there is this other person and they turned me down last night. Me!"

"I think you are officially certified crazy," Lexie joked but Phaedra did not share in the humor of the situation. "Okay, okay. I'm sorry. But Phaedra, step back for a second and ask yourself if this is really making you out of whack or is it an illusion of being out of whack?"

"Shut the hell up Lexie," Phaedra told her and then threw a pillow at her.

"I'm serious. When I first met you, you were juggling six guys. This is only four. Two you have pretty much gotten rid of. Every guy you go out with wants to marry you after the first date. Hell, after the first conversation. My point is, you never had an issue with men. You're scared! And what I think is scaring you is you are feeling."

Phaedra fell back on her bed. She already knew that. She knew she was going through a shift. She knew that she liked having Ron around, that she loved George and she missed RJ. Phaedra rolled over and screamed into her pillow.

Lexie sat next to her and rubbed her back. "It's okay. Even women like you succumb to love."

Phaedra rolled over on her back, "Maya is only 13 years old. I can't have a man in my house. I can't date. I just wanted to have fun and by the time she graduated I would be ready to find me an 80 year old billionaire with a foot in the grave."

"You are seriously warped," Lexie said trying to push Phaedra off of the unmade bed.

They heard a tap at the door and Brie poked her head in. "Good morning, ladies."

"I bet it was," Lexie teased

"How are you going to just take my line?" Phaedra asked hitting her with another pillow. "You here to pick up your litter?"

Brie sucked her teeth at Phaedra, "My children just finished telling me how nice Auntie Phaedra is. I didn't think they were talking about you."

Phaedra laughed her fake laugh, "They had a good time last night and this morning."

"I'm glad. I worried for nothing," Brie said. "I just saw Ron leave. Did he have fun?"

"Yeah, he did."

"He is really good looking. I can see Maya in him. Isn't it weird how our boys take on our looks and our daughters take on their father's looks," Brie observed.

"He's single if you want me to give him your number," Phaedra teased.

"I'm not though," Brie smiled. "Speaking of that, I have some news."

"Great! Tell us," Lexie said.

"Last night after everyone left, Chris told me how impressed he was with the work I did and he wanted to make an investment in my getting a business started. He gave me a check for $15,000!" Brie started jumping up and down as she said the amount and Lexie joined her.

Phaedra smiled at Brie and laughed at the two looking like school girls. "Way to go Brie. Lexie and Chris are correct. You've got a talent. Suppressing it is denying all of us your creative spirit."

"You really think so, Phae," Brie asked looking for an honest answer.

"Well, obviously. You saw how well last night went and all the compliments. Everyone can't be wrong. You have to know you are amazing. Annoying but amazing," Phaedra confirmed.

You just couldn't give a compliment could you?" Lexie teased her.

"No, no, it was just too much to ask of me," Phaedra said pretending to be dramatic.

Another knock came on the door, then some little knocks toward the bottom of it. Maya peeped in and then four little faces with her. "Hey, they were looking for their moms."

"We are coming out," Lexie told them but Anton was already in and hugging his mother's leg.

Phaedra started scooting everyone out when Maya whispered, "Where did dad go?"

"I have no idea. He didn't say anything to me," Phaedra informed her. "Why, were you guys going somewhere?"

"No...well yes. We were going shopping," she told her mother.

"Oh, why the secret?" Phaedra probed.

Maya grinned wide, "I can't tell you. We are just going shopping."

"Okay, I won't be nosey. However, if you need me to write my sizes down, just let me know." Phaedra winked at her. The two walked out arm and arm to join the rest of the group. The kids were gathering up their stuff.

"Have you told them yet?" Lexie asked Brie referring to them staying with Chris for the holiday season.

"Not yet. I'll tell them once we get home," Brie whispered back.

"What are we whispering about?" Phaedra asked after approaching the two.

"I was asking her about her and the kids staying with Chris. She hasn't told them yet," Lexie explained.

"Oh, I forgot you were playing house this week," Phaedra elbowed her. "You must be working that California King."

Brie giggled, "For a big guy, he's got some energy."

The three laughed and the kids came running in. They all thanked Maya and Brie and Lexie paid her. As they were leaving, Ron was coming in and Maya asked if they were still leaving. He told her yes and to go get ready.

He smiled at Phaedra and went to walk past her before she stopped him. "Ron, I'm...I'm not closing the door. I'm just not sure what I want. That's all. I'm going through something now and I just don't know how to process it yet."

"This George guy, he meant that much to you?" Ron asked stepping closer to her.

"Yes, I guess he did," she told him thinking she should step because now he was breathing her air.

"So, why did you break up with him?" Ron asked holding her arm.

Phaedra's heart was beating a little faster. "It wasn't going any further. Plus, it's hard to date seriously when you have a 13 year old daughter who went from a training bra to a B cup over night. I don't really want men here and it's not like I'm going to bring in a stepdad."

Ron leaned in and planted his lips on hers. Phaedra first hesitated, then surrendered. Maya came around the corner and gasped when she saw her parents. Phaedra stepped back, embarrassed. She forgot Maya was home. Her daughter was smiling at them both.

"You guys have fun," she said jogged to her room not looking Maya's direction.

Mom

Marriage was becoming more realistic to Lexie. It was mid-January and she was down to less than four months to become Mrs. Mark Leonardi. It scared her at the same time she was excited. Anton had put in a request to have his name changed. He wanted Mark to his daddy. She was actually comfortable with the idea because it would allow her to hide the fact that Anton was from another relationship. A dead beat father. It was on her list of things to talk to Mark about, but right now her agenda was the house.

They found a two-story, four bedroom, two car garage, office, den, and large backyard on the Intercoastal. It was crowded, but she convinced Mark he would love it. Now she had to figure out how to combine their furniture. How to combine their décor? How to get Mark to get rid of all of his stuff and keep only hers? Moving day was a week away and she hadn't completed inventory. She had the house, the wedding, her handful of clients, her speaking engagements, the blog and her friends and family. Lexie was ready for another escape. She was looking to act up so someone would put her in time-out. It was all happening and she wasn't in a financial position for an assistant.

Lexie needed to enlist help. "Hey Mom," she said into the phone.

"Good morning, Lexie. How are you?"

"Going crazy. I'm not sure how to get organized. I've got so much on my plate right now, and they all feel like they have top priority."

Little did she know that this is the call her mom had been waiting for. Lexie usually went to everyone but her mom for help and advise until it became overwhelming. "What's on your list?" Carol asked.

"Right now I'm trying to figure out the house. What goes to the new house and what doesn't. I'm at the townhouse trying to figure out what matches with Mark's décor, but my mind is on that presentation I have to give at the shelter for battered women. Then of course the wedding stuff. It's always wedding stuff," Lexie explained.

"Lexie, what's on Mark's list?" Her mother asked.

"Writing checks," Lexie laughed. "He's also doing most of the packing in both houses. I just keep getting in his way because I don't know what to keep and what to discard. Truth be told, I'd like to chunk it all and head to Ethan Allen."

"Alexis, sometime I wonder if you were part of a royal family in another past life. You've always had the mentality of someone with more money than what you have," her mom said shaking her head. "Why don't I come over and help you figure it out. In the meantime, work on your presentation. Those women deserve your best."

"Thank you, mom," Lexie cheered.

"You are welcome Lexie. I'll see you soon."

Lexie felt some relief. There was always a little tension when she had to deal with her mother. She kept her defenses up, but she needed her. She'd never stop needing her.

Lexie did as she was instructed. She put the clipboard down with the inventory list she printed and headed to her office. She connected her tablet to the keyboard and worked on her speech. She had to think of some Phaedraisms to throw in to motivate the women. Lexie was happy to have been invited. Her business was barely a few months old, but one of the women that worked at the shelter worked with Lexie years prior.

Phaedra always told her that no matter what you do in life always give back. Despite her bad girl persona, Phaedra was a good person. She helped out at food banks and donated money to other various charities. Lexie thought that maybe after the wedding, she could come back and volunteer at the shelter. It would be something to add to her list, right after she scratched a few things off of it.

The Parable

The new year had just begun and Brie was feeling closer to her goals. She had lined up a few parties that would keep her busy for the next couple of months. That was all she could take on while still working full-time. She was giving up her paycheck and benefits for a hope that everything would work out. That still scared her.

Chris loved her, this she knew, however, she was still living in her apartment. She and the kids only spent the one week with him and they went home after Christmas. Brie was hoping they would be invited back on a permanent basis. So far, not even on a temporary basis. The kids loved the house and the yard and were respectful of his things. Brie coached them well before they got there. She wanted to ask if there was something wrong, but she didn't dare. She was still holding back afraid of running him off if she said the wrong thing.

Seeing Brie deep in thought at her desk, Kenny did his favorite thing. He walked up behind her and startled her. "You must not be living right," he told her.

"You are like the sibling that I never wanted," she told him.

"Oh, come on. You love me. You know you do," he joked twisting her chair back and forth.

Brie sucked her teeth and rolled her eyes. He sat on the corner of her desk when he saw she was not busy. "Let me guess, you are thinking about Chris."

"No," she lied. "I'm thinking about my party planning gig. Did I tell you that I have three clients already? Four if you count Lexie."

"I'm always impressed when you do stuff just around here, and that Christmas party, wow! So why are you still here working this j-o-b?"

"That's what I was thinking about. I mean, four clients is not enough to quit my job and lose my benefits."

"I think differently," Kenny told her. "I think people look at a job as security, but the current economy tells us different."

"What would you do if you lost your job here?"

"Probably go full-time with my art. Maybe even go back to school and get a second degree in something like Graphic Design and sell t-shirts out the trunk of my car. I'd hustle. Do what I gotta do."

"I'm not good at hustling. It wouldn't be enough to survive on," Brie complained.

"It's however you see it. Me, I'd sell some stuff if I needed to. Hell, if things don't pick up soon, I might need to do that anyway," Kenny whispered. "I get paid to do something that I love. I draw for a living. The only difference is my side hustles are my choices. What I do here powers Stowett's battery. My dream is to power my own. So, I choose to see this as temporary."

"I've always wanted to know that feeling. Getting up and choosing what you want to do and not always being told what to do," Brie confessed. "I mean, I would still be servicing, but on my own terms. I don't have to do anything that I don't want to."

"You look like you just stepped into a fantasy world," Kenny pointed out.

"I did. You know, Chris gave me that money and I haven't done much with it except print up business cards."

"There's a parable in the Bible," Kenny started.

"You've read the Bible?" Brie teased him.

"Ha, ha," he smirked. "Do you want to hear the story or not?"

Brie cracked herself up, "Yes, I do. I'm sorry. I'm listening now."

"Anyways," he began again. "In this parable, a master goes away and he leaves a treasure with three of his slaves. Two of them invest their treasure, and the third hides his and keeps it safe. When the master returns, the two that invest their treasure are rewarded because they made his money grow. The third, who put his faith in safety of a paycheck with benefits, was punished. His treasure was taken away. What I'm saying Brie is that you have all these people that believe in you, but it does you no good if you don't believe in yourself. Don't lose your treasure playing it safe. No one ever going that route was successful. No one!"

Kenny kissed her on her forehead and headed back to his office. Brie took a minute to meditate on what he said. She reached for the phone to call Lexie because she wanted to know what to do. Brie put the phone down. "Damn," she said to herself.

"Ellie?" Brie interrupted her boss who was talking to another co-worker.

"Yes, Brie? What is wrong?" Ellie asked noticing Brie holding her stomach.

"I think I need to leave. Actually, I know I do. My stomach is turning flips."

"Go sweetie. I'll take care of the front desk. Are you going to make it home?" Ellie was concerned.

"Yeah, I will. Thank you," Brie said quickly walking towards her desk to grab her purse and keys. Again she said, "Thank you."

"Feel better. I'll call you later to check up on you," Ellie promised.

Brie got to her car and started to cry. She felt like a thousand butterflies gathered in her stomach and went to war. Kenny's story scared her. It meant stepping out of her comfort zone. Putting herself on front-street. The more she thought about it, the more her stomach hurt. She needed to go home and hide. Brie started her car and wanted to floor it out of the parking lot, but there was not enough room. She turned onto Southside Blvd. and it was crowded as usual. It felt like it was moving slower than it should be. Her stomach pains were becoming unbearable.

Traffic inched along and there were no shortcuts. Brie was looking for a button she could push that would turn her car into a flying car so she could bypass the traffic jam. Unfortunately, it hadn't been invented yet. Now her back was hurting. She noticed she was near Phaedra's office. She took a chance that she would be there. The tension in her neck was getting stronger and she didn't feel she could drive anymore.

Brie pulled her G6 into the parking lot and saw Phaedra's SUV. She parked next to it and tried to compose herself and walked into the building. She walked straight to Michelle's desk who told her to go in, Phaedra was not busy. Brie took five steps into the office and collapsed on the floor.

What the hell

Phaedra was on the phone with Ms. Wilson, a client that she had worked with for several years now. She had five rental properties and was looking to buy a sixth. Phaedra heard the voices outside her door and looked up briefly to see Brie walking into her office. She looked back down to continue her conversation, then she heard the thud. It startled her. Phaedra looked up to see Brie on the ground. Phaedra ran to her dropping the phone receiver and screaming for Michelle to call 9-1-1. She grabbed the pillow off of a chair to elevate Brie's head. She was breathing, just not conscious. Phaedra checked to see if there was a physical sign to why Brie passed out. There was none she could see.

Michelle came running into her office, "They are on their way. Is she hot? Has she been sick?"

"No, she's not hot and as far as I know she has not been sick. Oh, my goodness, Ms. Wilson, I left her on the phone. Can you check on her, please. If she hung up please call her back and explain. Just let her know I will call her back first chance I get."

Michelle did just that while Phaedra tried to make Brie comfortable. One of the other women brought her a cool washcloth for Brie's head. Phaedra stood up and grabbed her phone so she could call Lexie. She wondered how to get hold of Chris. Then she thought about the kids at school. She had no idea what school they went to. After all these years, she had no idea who to call in case of an emergency for Brie. This was the wrong time to come to that realization.

"Lexie, Brie just passed out. I don't know what is wrong with her. She is just laying here on the floor," Phaedra told her trying not to panic.

"What was she doing when she passed out?" Lexie asked panicking for both of them.

"She just walked in my office. I don't know what she was doing before," Phaedra turned to Michelle to ask her, "Did Brie say anything before she passed out?"

"No, she just asked if you were here. She looked normal as far as I could tell," she answered.

"No, Michelle didn't see anything out of the ordinary wrong with her. I hear the sirens," Phaedra reported. "Michelle, can you go to the front so you can direct them. Lexie, I don't know who to call. I don't know Chris' number. I also don't know the pass code for her phone to see who she has listed as her ICE. I don't even know when her kid's birthdays are to guess the code."

"Breathe, Phaedra. Her code is 0921, first day of fall. Her favorite day of the year," Lexie advised. "Call Kenny and find out from him if she was complaining about anything this morning. Afterwards, call Chris and let him know what hospital they take her to, but don't hang up with me because I need to know also. Let Chris know I will pick up the kids from school and Chonda from day care."

Phaedra laid her phone down and unlocked Brie's phone. She scrolled through the contacts and pressed on Kenny's name.

Kenny answered immediately, "Hey faker because you needed a day off."

"Kenny, it's Phaedra. She wasn't faking. She passed out on my office floor and she is not waking up. I'm waiting on the paramedics," Phaedra explained.

"What!" Kenny sat up quickly at his desk.

"What did she say was wrong with her?" Phaedra asked with urgency. The paramedics were coming through her door. Phaedra moved out of the way. Now there were a few more onlooker peeking towards her office. Michelle was telling the manager what happened.

"I'm going to ask Ellie, she didn't say anything to me,"

Kenny explained running down the hall to the front desk where Ellie was sitting at Brie's desk. "Ellie, I have Brie's friend Phaedra on the phone. Brie passed out before she made it home. The paramedics are there and she need to know what did Brie say was wrong with her?"

"Hello," Ellie said taking the phone from Kenny.

"Hi, this is Phaedra. Did Brie say anything to you?"

"Her stomach was bothering her. She was holding it when she came and let me know she needed to go home."

"Her stomach, her boss said she was complaining about her stomach," Phaedra relayed to the paramedic that was checking Brie's vitals.

"Phaedra, where are they taking her?" Ellie asked.

"Memorial. I've got to go. I'm going to follow them. Phaedra disconnected the call and grabbed both hers and Brie's purses. She walked behind the gurney and then jumped in her vehicle to follow the ambulance. The traffic had cleared so the trip was quick.

Lexie had tried to call Phaedra back because Phaedra never go back on the phone. Phaedra didn't answer. She did not want to drive at that speed and talk at the same time or they would be sending a second ambulance.

Phaedra parked and ran through the emergency room doors. An administrator stopped her to get Brie's information as they took her to a curtained room. The woman was asking her questions she had no answer to. Brie was the annoying unpopular girl that she allowed to hang out with her. She didn't know much about Brie except the basics. She knew how many kids she had and their names, that she grew up in South Carolina and that she worked as an administrative assistant. Phaedra was clueless about a person she had hung out with for several years now.

She called Chris because she hoped he would know Brie's family history, or at least know fall was her favorite season. It went to voicemail. She left a message that Brie was at the emergency room. Then she sent him a text from Brie's phone, 'This is Phaedra. Brie is at Memorial Hospital in the emergency room. I don't know what is wrong with her.'

Phaedra started wishing someone else would show up. Instead the doctor came out to meet her. "She's awake. We are still running test but you can go see her now." Phaedra was escorted to Brie's bed. She looked worried when she saw the needles in her arm. "What happened?"

"I don't know. Kenny and I were talking, and then my stomach started to hurt really bad, then my back. Then I felt all this tension in my neck and my temples started throbbing. Traffic was thick so I detoured to your office. Next thing I know I woke up here."

Phaedra frowned her eyebrows at Brie. "What were you and Kenny talking about?"

"He was telling me about a parable in the Bible, the one about the slave who hid the treasure instead investing it."

"I'm familiar with the story, "she told her now folding her arms.

"Anyways. I started thinking about what he said and quitting my job and how I haven't even spent $15,000 that Chris gave me. Why?" Brie asked her.

Phaedra shook her head and huffed, "Bitch, you had an anxiety attack. You scared me to death over an anxiety attack! Do you know how worried I was over your stupid ass?"

Phaedra's voice had gone up a little, then tears welled up in her eyes. Phaedra walked over and hugged Brie. "I'm going to kill you the first chance I get. I'm going to beat the shit out of you, then I'm going to kill you."

Brie was taken aback. Phaedra wasn't usually the emotional type. "I'm sorry. I thought I could make it home."

Phaedra stood up and wiped her eyes. "You know why I don't like you?"

This Phaedra Brie knew well. "I figured it was because I was competition."

Phaedra let out a loud laugh. "No Brie. Far from that. It's because you have no self esteem. You look to everyone else to tell you what to do instead of making your own decisions. You don't stand up for yourself without permission."

Brie looked away. Not what she wanted to hear while laying in a hospital bed with an IV drip connected to her arm. "Well, thank you for sharing."

"I know I just bruised your ego, but I'm not talking to your ego right now. I'm talking to your heart. I say it because I wish you would change. I wish you could see what everyone else sees. Kenny told you that parable because he also knows you need to change." Phaedra pulled up a chair and sat down next to her bed. Brie was still looking away. "Brie, if a man gave you $20, you were content with it. If a man took you out, you were content with that too. You don't know how much more you are worth. You offer up what's between your legs, then you try to offer up you and wonder why no one stays around to love you. Now, you have a man who not only wants you, but sees potential in you and what you are able to become that he has willingly put money on your ability to be more than what you are and you are still asking for permission to change."

Brie began to cry and wanted to tell Phaedra to get out. She wanted to make her go away, but that would mean bringing attention to herself and that was something she did not need at this time.

"Again Brie, know I'm talking to your heart, not your ego. This is not meant to hurt you. Your ego is going to try and block this out but I hope your heart hears everything that I say," Phaedra continued. "Just like in the parable, you are going to lose your treasure, and I'm not talking about the money. I'm talking about Chris. You are treating him as if he is temporary because that is what everything in your life has been. You can't bury this one in the backyard and keep him safe. The same way he is willing to invest in you, you have to do the same. Stop presenting him with something he can have sex with. Instead, present yourself as the woman he knows you are. Take that money and use it to your advantage. Be open to receive what he is giving you, because he is building something long term. Brie, don't throw your treasure away because you think everything is temporary."

Brie took a deep breath and dried her eyes. She sat the bed up, "I don't know how to be another way, Phaedra."

Phaedra reached for Brie's hand, "Yes you do. You just have to decide to do it. You decide, not anyone else. You decide," she said pointing her finger a little hard at her. "That feeling that you got in your stomach, that was fear. He's a bitch ass motha fucka. It sends lots of dreams to their graves. You have to tell his ass off, or he will control you. Brie, the only thing stopping you is you. Your body protected itself and laid you out on the floor because the war between your desires and fear was too much for it to handle."

Brie laughed at the analogy. "That actually makes sense. That is what it felt like, a war. You really think I've got what it takes?"

"I'm not making any decisions for you. You ask Brie that question because only Brie's answer matters," Phaedra told her. "By the way, why is the first day of Fall your favorite day?"

"Before my grandfather passes, he used to pack us up in the car with a picnic basket and drive up I-95N until we got to Virginia just to look at the trees changing. Even if it was on a school day, he thought it was that important. The trees weren't exactly changing yet so my grandmother thought it was stupid. He told me it was his way of saying goodbye. The leaves would be going through their process but there was hope because they would leave room for the new."

Phaedra gave her a wide smile. "See, you've been surrounded by philosophers your whole life. He was showing you change was good. Off with timid Brie and make room for brave Brie."

"So, does this mean you like me now?"

"No," Phaedra winked.

"She's lying," Lexie said startling both of them.

Lexie walked towards Brie and hugged her tight. Phaedra let her know that it was only an anxiety attack. Lexie had heard the conversation from the point when Phaedra sat down. Brie asked that they keep it between them. She was embarrassed and was hoping no one else would find out. They agreed after teasing her.

Brie's phone rung and Phaedra fished it out of her pocket. It was Chris so she handed it over to her. Lexie and Phaedra stepped outside the curtain so she could talk privately to him.

"Glad the Universe brought her to you. You are the only one that could have given her that message," Lexie whispered.

Phaedra smiled at her not wanting to agree. "I'm going to go call Michelle and let her know Brie's okay. She's text me three times now. Kenny also."

"Okay, sweetie. You gonna be alright?"

"Yeah, of course," Phaedra promised. She stepped out of Lexie's sight. Phaedra cried. She didn't know why, but she cried.

What are you doing now

"Mark, I need your approval on this list," Lexie yelled out.

"Approval for what? What list? What are you doing now?" Mark complained.

"The list for the movers," she yelled at him shaking the paper in his face.

Mark just looked at her for a minute without saying anything or taking the paper. Lexie laid it down on the counter when she realized he wasn't budging. "You need to take five, he told her.

"There is so much to do and you act as if there isn't," she complained.

"Lexie, I have driven to Goodwill several times and also packed and help clean two houses," he defended himself. "Babe, I get it, you are stressed about this. But I'm going to need you to stop taking it out on your ally."

Lexie started to stomp off but stopped herself. "Okay, I'm just saying I need you to look and sign. I don't want you to say I threw out something important to you."

"Just my football trophy from high school," he winked.

"That, I did throw away," she smiled.

Mark chuckled at her then confirmed she was joking. "Come on, we are in this together. We get moved, we get married and we live happily ever after."

"That would be nice," she told him.

"You didn't sound confident when you said that," he pointed out.

"I am. I'm just ready for it all to be done. The moving and the setting up the house. It's never any fun. I'm hoping we stay in the house for the next 50years."

Mark grinned and pulled her into his arms resting his chin on the top of her head. "I'm holding you to that statement the first time I hear the sentence I want a bigger house or I'm sick of this house. I'm going to play this recording."

"I'm going to deny it," she teased. Lexie took a deep breath, "Thank you, Mark."

"For what?"

"For being a great guy. That means the world to me," she told him.

"Just know that no one will love you more than I do," he told her.

Mark released his grip and picked the list up she wanted him to look at. Lexie sat down on one of the bar stools to make sure he didn't put it down and walk off. Mark stayed on task, or at least gave the perception that he was on task.

"Is Brie feeling better?" He asked after passing the list back to her.

"Yes, she took the remainder of the week off," she answered. "Is everything okay on this?"

"Yeah, looks good to me. Movers will be here in a couple of days. Everything is labeled. We are good and ready to go," Mark told her.

"Are you sad?"

"A little," he said. "But I'm excited and looking forward to our new life. Oh, by the way, Ana asked about you. She is going to be in town next week and was hoping you guys could meet for lunch. I take it you don't answer her calls. She feels like you blame her."

"I've just been trying to do other things. Does she know about my consulting business? I'm not breaking any contract rules."

"Yeah, she knows, but Lexie you are way past your six months. You have no obligations any longer."

"You are correct. If she calls I will go. If not, I'll see her at the wedding. I don't blame her. I just, I don't know."

"Don't fret about it, Lex. Ana is not your best friend. Besides, she's trying to hold onto her job right now. They want all of us to cover more territory without traveling. I told them I don't mind, but that won't work for new business," Mark told her.

"So you are going to have to do more traveling?"

"Not as much. I've done more video chats then anything."

"So you could possibly be traveling more?" Lexie wanted to clarify.

"Possibly, but just to Orlando. Orlando does not require me to stay overnight. And I don't see me having to go to Atlanta for a long time," he answered. "I will be here to help with the move and the wedding. I think you've been around your mom too much lately. You are about to crack."

"I guess I just need to pull up a bed right next to Brie's," she asked him with her hands on her hip and her eyes rolled.

"No, and I say that because Brie's not crazy. You, however my love, are on the verge of the nut house," Mark laughed.

Lexie grabbed an orange out of the fruit bowl and aimed for Mark's head. He ducked, laughing harder. Lexie walked away and Mark walked behind her yelling "but, baby," being ignored. Then the bedroom door slammed in his face.

WWW.SBA.COM

Brie had not returned to work for the last couple of days. She had not told Chris the truth about it being an anxiety attack. Only that all test came back negative. That first night he stayed at her place and slept on the couch. He had called to check on her several times and offered to bring dinner for her and the kids. She accepted his offer and was enjoying the care and attention she was receiving.

Deena had not gone to daycare and was sitting down reading a book to her doll that Chris' mom had given her. Brie sat down at her computer and pulled up www.sba.com. She felt her stomach flip as she pushed the enter key. She stared at the homepage for a minute before she started clicking around on different links.

"I can do this," she told herself. Brie started reading all the services they offered. She got up and headed for the closet with school/office supplies and pulled out a white legal pad. She sat back down in front of the computer and started taking notes.

"Mommy, what are you doing?" Deena asked now standing next to her.

"Educating myself on how to start a business," she explained.

"You don't have a job anymore?"

"Honey, I still have a job. I just want to work for myself. I feel like I will do better working for myself. No ceiling on how much money I can make," Brie explained as she clicked around the website.

"If you don't have a job then we don't have any place to live like before," Deena reminded her.

The light bulb went off hitting Brie like a freight train. She realized her source of fear was coming from reliving her past. Deena's comment resurfaced buried memories of being homeless twice after losing jobs.

One she was fired from and the other was a layoff. She knew what life without a paycheck would do to her and her family. She couldn't survive and that was not a road she wanted to travel again. Right now things were tight and there was no money for extras. She made $34,000 a year, decent but still considered under the poverty line for a family of four. Stressfully, she could juggle tight. She did get some government assistance with food and day care. That was a secret she kept from Chris and her friends.

Brie did not like reliving the pain of sleeping in a car, living in a shelter and the financial hell she went through. She was just staring at the computer when she decided to abandon this dream and get up. She turned to get out of her chair and Deena was standing there still waiting on an answer to her question. Brie felt a panic attack coming on and quickly tried to get her composer. She did not want to pass out in front of her young daughter. She was not as strong as she pretended to be and she was not sure she could conquer her fear. But there Deena stood, looking in her mother eyes for a promise that she could take care of her and Brie was being slow to answer.

Brie took a deep breath and started, "Deena, if mommy...". Brie paused and then nudged Deena back so she could get up.

"Mommy, what's wrong?"

"Nothing, honey," Brie told her as she headed for the refrigerator. She stood there with the door open not really wanting anything.

"You are not supposed to hold the door open," Deena told her after following her to the kitchen.

"I know honey. Would you like some ice cream?" Brie noticed the worried look in Deena's eyes.

"Okay," she answered with no enthusiasm for her favorite treat.

Brie fixed them both a bowl of strawberry ice cream. They sat on the red couch and Brie decided to be brave. "Deena, honey, Mommy wants a better life. We are surviving, but I want better than just surviving. I want to be able to buy new clothes, go places, travel on vacation, and just have a really good life."

"Like going to Disney World and Universal?"

"Yes, honey," Brie smiled at her.

"Can we get a big house like Aunt Phaedra's?"

"That would be nice, wouldn't it? Everybody would have their own rooms."

"I want my own room," the little girl announced.

"Then, my sweet Ms. Deena, I am asking you, your sister and brother to have some faith in me," Brie said feeling a little more confident. "I've got to have some faith in myself also. I think...I mean, I know I can do this and be successful at it. Our lives will be better for it. I'll even hire you to be my little assistant."

Deena smiled at the thought of that. "Okay, but I don't come cheap."

Brie laughed at Deena and they finished their ice cream. The worry in both of their eyes was gone. When they finished, Brie went back to her computer and started taking more notes. She sat there and worked on her business plan. She spotted a link to make an appointment with a counselor. She did it immediately before she talked herself out of it.

Later that afternoon Lexie called to check on Brie. Brie let her know she was doing better and bragged about how attentive Chris had been. Then Brie told her about working on her business plan. "The process was scary, but I kept working."

"I'm proud of you. I used SBA to get my consulting business started. I still meet with the guy that helped me. I know it is scary but it is so worth it. Just think about the lesson you will give your kids."

"I am. I just have so many ideas and need to figure out how to do it all," Brie told her excited about getting it off the ground.

"Just don't forget my wedding," Lexie teased.

"My top priority. Oh, and speaking of that, I did follow up about the garland you wanted on the bride's table. I'm stopping by tomorrow to view what Alex, the florist owner, came up with," Brie assured her.

"Great. And what about Chris' co-worker? Is his wife still going to have you plan her party?"

Yes. Believe it or not, I've already met with her. Well, it was over the phone. It was weird because she is the first person outside my circle that I am working with. She's planning a huge birthday bash for her husband and she's got the bank to pull it off."

"That will be your real experience. I know you will do great," Lexie cheered.

"Thanks, but as Phaedra said, it only matters if I know I will do great," Brie sighed.

"You don't sound convincing. Put some authority behind that. You can't repeat Phaedraisms half heartedly. They don't get released to the Universe correctly," Lexie explained.

Brie laughed. "You are correct. I know I will do great!"

"That's what I'm talking 'bout," Lexie clapped.

Brie laughed because she felt silly, but she also felt better. "I'm not going to lie. I always ask myself what would Phaedra do, and I know she would have a plan and be set to execute it. Do you think I'm ready to quit my job? Wait, no, don't answer that. I'm going to stop leaning on others to make my decisions for me."

"See, you already started," Lexie smiled.

"I know. But, to tell you the truth, Lexie, the whole reason I get scared to decide for myself is because look where all my decisions have landed me. I'm still renting an apartment because I don't have any money in saving except what Chris just gave me. And I am horrible at budgeting so I'm living paycheck to paycheck. If I lose my job, the kids and I are going to be homeless again. I have no sense of business..."

"Okay. Brie. Stop!" Lexie interrupted. "This is where you count your blessings, sweetie. Stop focusing on what's missing. Remember, that is what my whole trip to the lake was about. I couldn't see pass the problems and I made excuses for them all."

Brie sighed, "You are right. I just don't know how to do that yet."

"You practice until you get it right. Trust me, Phaedra does not wake up every morning well put together," Lexie suggested.

"That's good to know. Sometimes I just want to throw water on her just to see her messy and disorganized," Brie joked.

"If you decide to, make sure you are wearing sneakers so you can run like hell," Lexie laughed.

"And have my car keys in hand," she laughed with her. "Well, I gotta go get ready to pick up my other two. Chris is stopping by with dinner, but won't be here until seven."

"Okay, well, enjoy dinner with all of your babies. I'll talk with you later," Lexie told her and disconnected.

Brie again found herself thinking of her past and future. She thought about what both Lexie and Phaedra have said in the past few days. Brie admired them both because they were where she trying to go. "I got this," Brie told herself this time with confidence. She walked back to her computer and printed out her business plan. She looked at Deena with a wide grin. "We got this!"

Their tears met where their lips touched

Phaedra had an appointment scheduled for a potential buyer to view a house that was going up on the market. When she arrived the landscapers were working in the front yard. She waived at them as she passed. She walked through inspecting every corner and making sure the tan carpet had been cleaned, the white paint job was done correctly, and the silver door knobs had all been replaced. She also lit apple cinnamon candles and placed them strategically in the kitchen. She was ready to show all the little gems that made it special.

Phaedra wanted to check the backyard hoping that the landscapers had already completed it. She stepped out on the patio and was startled by the figure sitting in the lawn chair with their back to her. At first, she assumed it was one of the workers taking a break away from his boss. Then Phaedra noticed the bottle of Crown Royal. "Can I help you," she called out nervously.

"Yes you can. Why don't you come over here and join me?" The familiar voice answered.

Phaedra wanted to be surprised but she wasn't. She stayed on the steps and asked, "George, what are you doing here?"

"I'm your 2 p.m. appointment. My wife couldn't make it, so it's just you and I," he told her getting up out of the brown chair being careful not to spill his drink. "You didn't wear the Christmas present I bought you?"

"The ring is beautiful. I just didn't understand such an eccentric gift since we broke up." Phaedra was trying not to smile at the site of seeing him.

"Oh, I didn't know we broke up. I thought we were just taking a break because your ex-husband showed up and it confused you. Or maybe you just wanted to be able to test the waters without any guilt." George pulled Phaedra's arm making her walk down the step and pulled her in for a hug.

Phaedra didn't resist. She was happy to be in his arms no matter how much the voice in her head was telling her no. "Who are you buying this house for?"

George laughed, not letting her go. "I'm not buying this house. I'm just browsing the real estate agent."

"I hate customers like you," she said pushing him back and walking into the house. "We did break up, since you weren't paying attention. It had nothing to do with my ex-husband or anyone else."

Phaedra walked to the kitchen and started blowing out the candles. George put his drink down on the counter and reached out for her again. This time she moved away. He stepped closer. Phaedra's expression went from smiling to impatient. George didn't step back. He matched her stance. Her heart rate began to increase when she realized no noise coming from the front yard.

"Are you crazy?" She asked him.

"Not at all," he said raising his eyebrows.

"I'm not playing this game with you," she tried to threaten but he was not phased. "What is it that you want from me?"

"All I asked you for was to give me some time."

"We had this talk. We can't do this," she huffed throwing her hands in the air.

"Then you need to look me in my eye and tell me you can walk away from this." The alcohol on his breath was strong, but he was in control.

Phaedra walked out of the kitchen distracting herself from her feelings. She looked out the window asking, "Where the hell is the crew?"

"I paid them to leave us alone for an hour," George informed her.

"How do they not know you might be some kind of rapist or murderer? I know who's getting fired tomorrow," she said starting to pace.

"Do I look like a rapist?"

"Like a rapist has a certain look," she sucked her teeth.

"Phaedra, what the fuck are you talking about?"

Phaedra stopped pacing and calmed herself down giving herself a minute to meditate. After inhaling through her nose and exhaling through her mouth, she confessed, "I can't look you in the eye and break up. I love you too much. I'm vulnerable around you. But, I know the man you are and you will do what makes me happy because you know I'm right. Even if you don't agree, you know I'm right."

Now George was the one pacing. "I can't Phaedra. I can't just say okay and walk away. You said it. You love me. Why would I just...bow out? That ring was a symbol of my commitment to you."

"Then answer me this one question, and if you answer honestly, it will decide this relationship. But, you have to be honest. Promise me you will be honest," she told him putting her hands on his chest to stop him from walking in the circular pattern he created in the carpet. George looked her in her eyes as she whispered, "Promise me."

"I promise," he smiled rubbing his finger across her check.

"Are you willing to destroy what we had, both of our families and your reputation to hold on to air?"

George stepped back and moped towards the counter and downed the rest of his drink. Phaedra did not leave her spot. She just watched him as he hurt. She watched his ego shed its outer shell. She saw his face soften. She saw the tears form. She watched the man she fell in love with emerge. That was the man she moved towards.

"I'll have to cancel all of your accounts," he said choking on the words.

"I know," she responded putting her hand on his shoulder. She wanted to console him but knew that would make things worse.

"Do you love him also?" George asked through the tears.

"I'm not in love with anyone else. I'm not seeing anyone else. If you are referring to my ex, we are just friends who are raising two kids together," she assured him.

George finally turned to face her. He lifted her chin and put his lips to hers. She kissed him knowing it would be the last time. Phaedra and George's tears met where their lips touched. She held his face a minute longer wishing there was another way. George couldn't stand there any longer. He walked out closing the door behind him. Phaedra felt her heart drop. She slumped to the floor and cried one last time for love lost.

Being a productive member of society is so rewarding

I demand a girl's night out! Let's go to Friday's! was the text Lexie had sent to Brie and Phaedra. It had been weeks since it was just the three of them, not counting the emergency room visit. Brie was feeling better and Phaedra was withdrawing. It was time for liquor and laughter. The two of them must have been feeling the same because they both responded with a definite yes.

Lexie had arrived early so she could finish up notes on a potential client. They usually sat at the bar but she grabbed a booth. The bar tender assured her he had showered that morning feeling rejected. Lexie smiled at him and held up her tablet and told him she had work to do. Lexie ordered a water, sat down and powered up her tablet. Twenty minutes later Phaedra walked in heading straight for the bar. Before she could get all the way on the stool, the bar tender pointed towards Lexie at the booth she was working at. Phaedra smiled and ordered a drink then walked Lexie's way.

Lexie was on the phone so she just waved. Phaedra sat across from her and stared impatiently trying to rush her off the phone. Lexie held her index finger up telling her one minute. Phaedra started making faces. Lexie was trying not to laugh because she was on the phone with a client. Finally, Lexie kicked her from under the table.

"What is wrong with you?" Lexie playfully scolded as she hung up.

Phaedra was making sad faces then laughed. "Bout damn time. This is girl's night. No work allowed."

"Work is officially done," Lexie told her putting her tablet away. "If feels so good to say that. Being a productive member of society is so rewarding. Even if it doesn't make me rich, it makes me happy. I'm supplying a need and that means something."

"I slept with Ron!" Phaedra blurted.

Lexie almost spilled her drink on herself. "You what? You bitch. All that talk about an ex is an ex for a reason and your skanky ass caved."

Phaedra laughed at Lexie. "I know, but George came by on Wednesday..."

Lexie's voice went up an octave. "Wait, what? I thought he was out of the picture."

"He is, well, now he is. He showed up at an open house. Scared the shit out of me. I called AmEx this morning and my card has been cancelled. He sent me a text letting me know this is the last house payment he will be making. I told him not to make it, but he said it was on autopay and his secretary couldn't cancel this one. It was so hard to walk away from him, but I put on my big girl panties and did it."

"Then pulled them off and rode Ron," Lexie added.

"You know what, peanut gallery?" Phaedra laughed. "So anyways, I've been sad all week. Ron was dropping Caleb off after football practice. Caleb went and jumped in the shower and Maya was at a friend's house. We were laughing, that led to kissing, then..."

"You slipped and accidentally fell on top of him," Lexie laughed again at her own joke.

"Will you shut the hell up," Phaedra laughed too throwing a piece of ice at her.

"So was it like you remember?" She asked.

"Actually better. Someone taught him something over the years," Phaedra answered. "It was just nice to be with someone I was familiar with. I thought about how many guys I've slept with and got depressed. But girl, I'm not going to lie, I needed some dick. It's been a minute."

"Okay, but Phae, you know you're playing with that man's feelings. He wants to get back with you," Lexie reminded her.

"You are such a downer. Let me order you another drink," she said waiving for the waitress.

"I'm just saying," Lexie sang. "You know you."

"That's just it. I don't anymore. Things keep changing in my life. Everything I used to like no longer makes me happy.He just asked me to keep the option open. We'd eaten a few meals together but no physical contact until last night."

"So, you might be ready to settle down?" Lexie asked her.

"Well, let's not get to far ahead. One step at a time," Phaedra told her sipping on her frozen margarita.

"I can keep hoping," Lexie smiled.

"Here comes Brie," Phaedra announced. "Why do you want everybody coupled up when you just got coupled up yourself?"

"Because I'm doing it so everyone should want to do it. Everyone should want to be like me," Lexie teased. "Hi Brie!"

"Why are y'all at a booth?" Brie asked.

"I had some work to finish. Why are the two of you bent out of shape because we are at a booth?"

"Brie hunched her shoulders, "Cause we always sit at the bar."

"Well, tonight, we are going to do something different," Lexie said. "Change is good. Even Phaedra is going through a change. She's going to settle down."

"Really now?" Brie said with a big grin. "And what magic man was able to contain all this?"

"First, I'm not settling down. I'm just dipping my toes in the water," Phaedra explained.

"But look at the timing, Phae. Ron shows up when you finally walk away from George," Lexie pointed out. "Tell me the Universe didn't shift that on purpose."

"You and Ron? I knew it! I knew he would get that ass and RJ, George and anybody else would be out the picture," Brie said dancing in her seat. "I'm right, aren't I?"

Phaedra just stared while the two high five one another. "Second off, an ex is an ex for a reason."

"Give it up, Phae. You still love that man. He is the father of your children and you built up a wall all these years to protect your heart," Brie told her.

"And that shift you've been talking about, remember it started right before Ron got here. So, you asked for love thinking it was an impossible wish. It didn't show up where you were expecting but instead from what was already in your heart," Lexie added.

"Preach, my sister," Brie cheered her on.

They both looked at Phaedra for a response. Phaedra simply asked, "Does anyone want an appetizer?"

"Oh, come on sensei, you know I'm right. I learned all that from you," Lexie contested.

"I thought we were getting together to have fun. This is the last time I ever tell you who I sleep with." Phaedra picked up the menu and ignored them.

"So he did get that ass," Brie laughed.

"You need to worry about who's tapping your ass and not mine," Phaedra snapped.

Now both Lexie and Brie were laughing. Brie asked, "When did this happen?"

"Last night, since you must know." Phaedra was still trying to playoff her emotions.

"Are you guys, like official now?" Brie continued to inquire.

"Brie, this is not high school. We are two adults who happen to have once been married to each other, that are now just enjoying each other's company."

"Don't forget to tell her about the part of being with someone familiar," Lexie told her.

"Will you shut the hell up," Phaedra rolled her eyes at Lexie.

"Phaedra, honey, you can't play this one off. Say what you need to say to convince yourself, but I'm with Lexie. The timing is more than a coincidence."

"I'm ordering loaded potatoes. Anyone want anything?" Phaedra said once again ignoring them.

Lexie chimed in telling her, "I want wings. I know I don't usually eat them in public, but I don't care today."

"Why not?" Brie asked.

"Because we are at a booth and fewer people can see me lick my fingers and smack my lips," she answered.

"Now we know why we are at a booth," Phaedra said to Brie. "So how is are feeling, Brie? Anxiety settled?"

"Much better," she answered. "I never told Chris the truth, or my job, but I have made progress. I am getting a tax ID and created an actual business plan. Chris offered before that if I wanted to take an entrepreneurial class at the Community College he would pay for it. So, I signed up for a class that starts in two weeks."

"Why don't you use SBA? They offer a lot of help and mentors," Phaedra advised.

"I am. I have an appointment Tuesday at 3:30 to meet with someone to look over my business plan and get information on budgeting."

"I'm glad to hear that. You seem so much happier. Like you found your purpose. Making your own decisions," Phaedra winked her.

"Yes, making my own decisions," she smiled raising her glass of water while her gold bracelets jingled as they clashed.

The waitress brought their food to the table and the ladies ordered another round of drinks from her. Lexie updated them both on the move and how her client list was growing. She gave Brie the number to a couple of web designer. Phaedra also offered to leave Brie's card with home buyers at the close and suggest they call her for their house warming parties.

It wasn't all business. They talked about the kids and of course their men. They teased each other about their love lives. Lexie was content. She had her two closes friends and she had her girl's night out that she had been missing. Mark noticed the difference as when she got home.

"Good time?" He asked.

"Yes, a very good time," she answered giving him a hello kiss.

"I'm glad. My ears were burning earlier. Were you talking about me?"

"No, not that I remember," she said looking at him confused.

"Yeah, right," Mark smiled.

Lexie laughed at him. "Okay, okay. Maybe you came up once or twice."

"Yeah, okay. I'll take that. Just like to know I'm being thought about," he told her.

Lexie stepped closer and grabbed on his gray tank top to pull him to her lips and kissed him with more passion then earlier. "You are. All the time."

Maybe we should have a talk

Brie and the kids were heading over to Chris's to spend the day. He invited another family over that had two kids close to Ike and Chonda's age. She assumed, again, that he was trying before he buys. He would be testing to see how the family thing fit him. She did worry that if it didn't her heart would not be the only one broken. She was trying not to live in a mindset of worse-case scenario. Instead she packed up her crew, the girls with their dolls and Ike with his portable game and his football, and they headed for Chris's wealthy neighborhood humming the theme song to *The Jeffersons*.

Chris had left the door unlocked so she wouldn't have to ring the doorbell. When she and the kids arrived, he was in his office. She told them to keep it down in case he was working. They made their way to the kitchen and were greeted by the house keeper and a tray of cookies. Brie headed to his office and knocked lightly. Chris yelled for her to come in.

"How are you feeling?" Chris asked as she walked towards him.

"I'm good. The girls and I had a great time last night," she told him.

"Good. Sorry I didn't call you back last night. I guess the guys and I had a good time too, I lost track of time."

Brie smiled a cautious smile at him, "I'm glad. Where did you guys go?"

Chris smirked at her, "Sure you want to know? My mother always said don't ask questions you don't want to know the answer to."

Brie felt uneasy. "Um, yes. Now I'm really curious."

Chris laughed, "I'm just teasing, Brie. We just went out for drinks. We joked about the strip club. Jay said his woman would not approve and Paul said his wife would put him on the couch."

"And you? Were you worried?" She asked with her arms now folded across her chest.

"No, not really. You've never mentioned it bothered you," he answered to get a reaction.

"Well then, let me mention it now. It would bother me. Why would you need to go to see women strip for you when I'm right here?" She asked.

Chris grinned a huge smile and raised his eye brows. "So, that means tonight I'm getting dinner and a show?"

"Would you like a show after dinner?" She asked realizing she just got reeled into that one.

"I just asked didn't I? He unfolded her arms and pulled her into his lap.

"What about the kids?"

"They can find their own show," he said. "Brie, they have their own rooms. It's not like they can hear us."

"I didn't think we were spending the night," she said coyly.

"Why not? It's the weekend. The Andersons will be here all day. Why would you drive all the way home after that?"

"You didn't invite us to stay. I didn't want to assume anything."

"I didn't know you needed an invitation, so I guess we both assumed," he said disappointed. "If I say hey you and the kids come over, then pack a bag. Or, go shopping and have stuff here like tooth brushes, pajamas and clothes. Whatever you need."

"I can run home real quick," she suggested.

"Shopping center is closer. Just get whatever you need, plus several outfits each. Here's my card," he said pulling his wallet out of his front pocket. "You might want to stop to the ATM first so you don't have any problems. My pin is 2112. Just take out $500. Do you think that will be enough?"

"I can work with that," she said accepting the card. "Strip club might have been cheaper."

"Not necessarily," he slipped then laughed. "I'd rather have you than some woman at a strip club."

"That didn't clean it up," she said walking away.

Chris followed her to the kitchen where the kids were seated at the island with their glasses of milk and an almost empty tray of homemade chocolate chip cookies. "Hi Chris," they spoke in unison. Chonda was the only one to jump off the bar stool and greet him with a hug.

"How is everyone this morning?" Again, they spoke in unison this time singing good.

"I'm heading to the store so finish your snack and come on," Brie told the 3 of them.

"They can stay if they want. Whatever is easiest," Chris told her as he sat down with the kids and picked up a couple of the cookies.

Ike and Chonda asked to stay, but Deena jumped off of her bar stool to stand at her mother's side. "Well, Deena and I will go to the store. What are you two going to do?"

"Chris, I brought my football with me. Do you want to play with me?" Ike asked.

"I would love to," Chris told him rubbing the top of Ike's head.

"I've got my book and my doll. I'm all set," Chonda announced confidently.

"Okay, we will be back in a little while." Brie looked at Chris to make sure he knew what he was getting into.

"I got this," he said as confidently as Chonda had made her statement.

Brie kissed both kids on the cheek and reached for Deena's hand. Deena waived good-bye to her brother and sister and walked with her mother to the door. Chris excused himself and met Brie at the car. He knelt down to get a hug from Deena and then picked her up to buckle her into her car seat. He kissed her on her forehead and told her to be good for her mother.

"They will be okay. It's not as if we are strangers," he said addressing the concern in her face.

Brie hadn't got into the car yet. "Chris," she whispered," I don't want them getting hurt. This is pretend for you but it's real for them."

Chris was surprised and his face showed his hurt. "Brielle, who is pretending? You think I'm being nice to your kids just for fun?"

"Well, no. I'm just protective of the day you decide this doesn't work for you." After she heard herself out loud, she was wishing she had articulated that better.

"I'm sorry to hear that. Since you don't know, I love you and the three of them. I do this because I want them to get to know me. I enjoy our time together. Maybe instead of a show, we should have a talk."

"I didn't mean that like it sounded. I'm just saying..."

"Don't worry about it. We'll talk tonight after the kids go to sleep. You can tell me what you meant when Deena is not looking in our mouths," he suggested. "Kiss me."

Brie did just that and was blinking to hold her tears back. "My mouth always gets me in trouble.

Chris did not want to have this conversation in front of Deena, but he also did not want Brie to leave upset. "Brie, I get it. What I don't get is all of the assuming you do, like assuming one day I'm going to wake up and not want you anymore. Please know that I am investing all of my time and energy into you and them because this makes me happy. Please don't cry. Deena is still not exactly ready to cozy up to me even after all these months. If she thinks I made her mother cry, she never will be. I'll have to bribe that one with her very own island to get her on my side."

Brie laughed because she understood. "Okay. You three have fun." She kissed him again and slid into her car and dug out her sunglasses. She tried to dry her eyes so Deena would not see them and put on the glasses to hide them.

It didn't work. Deena asked her as they were pulling off, "What's wrong, Mommy. Why are you sad?"

"I'm not sad, honey. I'm just so in love with Chris. These are tears of happiness," she answered.

I was civilized when you cheated on me

"Hey, what are you doing?" Ron asked Phaedra when she answered the phone.

"Working. What else would I be doing on a Saturday?"

"What time are you wrapping things up?" He clarified.

"About 3:30, but then I have some errands to run. Why, Ron?" She asked impatiently.

"I was going to invite you over for dinner if you did not have plans."

"Ron, I know the other night happened but don't read too much into it. I think we were both feeling vulnerable and it wasn't an open invitation for us to hook up on a regular basis," she explained.

"Still the same old Phaedra."

"What is that supposed to mean?"

"You know what it means. Everyone is disposable to you," he yelled and disconnected the call.

Phaedra threw her hands up in the air and a few people looked her direction. "Are you kidding me?" She yelled for Michelle who peeked up from the kitchen. "I'm sorry, I have to run for a minute. Family emergency."

"Okay, I can handle things until one of the other agents get here," Michelle promised.

"Thank you so much. I am sorry to leave you like this," Phaedra said walking out the front door excusing herself. She jumped into her SUV and accelerated to Ron's. When she got there he was outside washing his car.

Ron looked up shocked and scared to see her. "What are you doing here?"

Phaedra jumped out of the SUV, heels and all, and yelled as loud as she could, "I'll tell you what I'm doing here. Who the hell are you to tell me about being disposable."

Ron, trying to hold face since other neighbors were outside, grabbed Phaedra by her arm telling her to lower her voice. She refused. He dragged her into the garage picking her up by her waist with her hitting and screaming at him. Ron put her down and before he could take a step for the garage door opener to close it, Phaedra turned around and slapped him.

"Will you act like a civilized human being," he yelled rubbing the sting on his right cheek.

"No I won't! I was civilized when you cheated on me. I was civilized when you cheated on me, again. I'm through being fuckin' civilized!"

Ron walked back towards her from closing the garage door with his head down. "I've apologized for that over and over."

"When Ron? I don't remember a fucking apology. I only remember my heart hurting. I only remember the humiliation when I went by your job and was greeted by the bitch you were sleeping with. I remember the humiliation when you had a kid outside of our marriage. I remember my family being pulled apart while I tried to hold my head up and pretend I was okay. I only remember being put in a position to raise two kids on my own. But what I don't remember was a mother fuckin' apology." Uncomfortable tears began to flow as she finally stopped fighting them. She wanted to slap him again but held it back.

Ron reached out to hold her but Phaedra slapped his hand away. "Don't touch me," she threatened. "Now you show up and expect me to just drop everything and let you hurt me again? You sorry ass mother fucka'. You sorry...ass!"

"Phae, please," he said reaching for her again.

"Don't say my name and don't fucking touch me," she said taking a step back and folding her arms.

"Then allow me to say it now. I am sorry. I am so sorry. I didn't mean to ruin both of our lives or our children's. I wish I didn't put you through that," he started.

"Too late. That does not fix it, Ron. That doesn't fix shit, you lying, cheating, bastard, son of a bitch. Why should I believe or trust you now? I married you because I thought you loved me. I thought I would be enough."

"I did Phaedra. I still do. I want to make it right. I want to prove to you how much I love you," he told her. "I want our family back. I want us back. I want to finish what we started. I want the forever we started out promising each other."

"I'm not the one that broke the promise, Ron!"

"Tell me what to do. I'll do whatever it takes. I don't want to lose you again," he begged reaching for her one more time.

"Why did you move to Jacksonville, Ron? Why? The truth this time."

Ron lowered his head and sighed. He stepped back and leaned against the cabinet in the garage and crossed his arms and legs for balance. "When I woke up in the hospital after my second surgery, you were the first person I thought of. I kept wishing you were there. Truth is, for years I have wanted to try and work things out with you again, but my pride would never allow me. I wanted my family back. I was by myself in that hospital bed because there was nobody in Miami that I wanted to comfort me. I just wanted you, Casey and Maya. Phaedra, believe me when I say I am not that guy anymore. I will never do to you what I did then."

"I never should have kissed you. An ex is an ex for a reason," Phaedra told him.

They still stood a yard apart from each other in the two garage. Phaedra stopped screaming at him so he felt he could step closer to her. He reached up and wiped the tears from her eyes, then he pulled her closer to him. Phaedra put her head in his chest and sobbed. He repeated he was sorry several more times. They heard the door to the house close causing them both to jump. Maya had been looking and calling for them.

"Mom, what's wrong?" Maya asked dropping her bag and running towards her parents when she saw they both were crying.

Phaedra took her daughter in her arms and Ron took them both in his arms. "Nothing Maya. Just finally getting around to telling your father off."

Maya stepped back surprised. "What do you mean?"

Ron, frightened by what answer might come out of Phaedra's mouth spoke up quickly, "The divorce, honey. She's finally getting around to telling me how she felt about me asking her for a divorce."

"I thought the two of you were going to work it out?" Maya asked them.

"No promises, Maya. We've been apart for a long time. This can't be fixed overnight," Phaedra explained.

"We have to sort through our mess first. That's not always easy when you are adults," Ron added.

"Not when you are kids either," Maya told him. "I'm just glad that we do things as a family now. I'm going to go put my stuff away." Maya kissed them both and went back into the house leaving them alone again.

"Look, maybe sleeping together made thing a little more confusing but I'm not going to apologize or wish it didn't happen," Ron told Phaedra.

Phaedra smiled, but then got serious again. "I'm not sorry about that either, but I still hate you."

"I deserve to be hated. I am going to prove to you that I'm worth a second chance. I'll do whatever it takes. We can go to therapy or whatever."

"Lexie said I sent a prayer up to the Universe for love and it sent me what was in my heart. It sounds nice because it sounds like something from a movie. I'm realistic, Ron."

"But you kept that door open. We went out, we are getting to know each other again, we are being parents together," he defended. "My only concern is the kid's expectations. Especially Maya's."

"Really, because my only concern is your wandering dick."

Ron shook his head. "Not only am I going to earn your forgiveness, but convince you to forget the past also."

"Good luck with that," Phaedra told him rolling her eyes. "I didn't know Maya was spending the night."

"That make two of us," he answered. "She didn't mention anything to me."

"Well, then let's go be parents and find out what our young Maya is up to."

"Wait, are we okay?"

"I don't know yet. Let's take this one moment at a time," she insisted.

"I can do that," Ron agreed grabbing her hand.

Phaedra pulled it away. "Good, because you know an ex is an ex for a reason."

"How many times are you going to say that?"

"Until you convince me otherwise."

Ron smiled knowing that at least there was hope. He opened the door for her and then followed her in.

It's going to take the three of us

"I'm supposed to have a conversation with you and I'm not sure how to approach you with it," Lexie told Mark while they were sitting up in bed.

"Just say it," he told her. "Wait, you aren't calling off the wedding are you?"

"Heck no!" Lexie said looking at him squarely. "Never. You are stuck with me."

"Okay, then, what's up?"

Lexie had her head on Mark's chest and her hand under his shirt playing in his hair. "Have you considered manscaping?"

"You no longer like my hairy chest?"

"I do," she said unconvincingly. "I'm just saying."

"I'm full blooded Italian. You can manscape all you want but Mother Nature will win the war."

Lexie laughed, "It just gets caught in my teeth sometimes."

"Have you considered removing your teeth?" Mark joked. "Is that what you really wanted to talk to me about?"

"No," she confessed.

"So what is it you want to ask?" Mark pushed.

"It's about Anton."

"What about him?"

"He wants to know if you will be his father," she blurted out before she lost her nerve again. Lexie sat up fearing rejection as she clarified her statement. "He wants your last name."

Mark looked at her surprised. "Really?" he wasn't sure how to answer. The thought never crossed his mind.

"You don't have to. I can tell him how important his name is," she said giving him an out.

"I just never expected him to want that. Technically, I am his dad. Did you talk to his father about it?"

"No, I haven't. I don't think the sperm donor cares. Look, Mark, don't make an immediate decision. Doesn't matter, we are still a family."

"It's not that, Lexie. This is obviously important to him. Yeah, I should take time to think about it," he said with guilt. "Are you disappointed that I didn't immediately say yes?"

"No, Mark. It's not one to be taken lightly. I prefer you think about it first. I don't want you to make a decision that you will regret later," she said trying to convince herself more so than him.

Mark's heart was racing and his palms were starting to sweat. "You know I love Anton, so it's not that."

"I know Mark. Give yourself a few days to think about it and then we will talk," she said patting him on the shoulder. "Speaking of Anton, I need to wake him up or he'll be up all night. Are we still meeting Jose and his family at Joe's for dinner?"

"Yes, we still are," Mark answered getting out of bed along with Lexie. "I'll wake him up."

Mark kissed her and headed towards Anton's room. Lexie sat back down on the bed and was feeling rejected. She wanted to hate him. Lexie was ready to pack the house and move back home. "I'm over-reacting", she told herself. She got up and headed for the kitchen. She heard the two of them coming down the stairs. Anton was on Mark's back, half sleep but smiling.

"Hey, hey sleepy head," Lexie greeted raising up on her toes to kiss him.

"Hi, Mommy," he said yawning.

"Do you want a snack before dinner?"

"No, I'm not hungry," he told her.

"I wouldn't mind a snack," Mark said.

"Get it your damn self," Lexie said in her head. "Sure, what would you like?"

"Whatever you were going to fix Anton. Maybe I can get him to eat it with me," Mark told her.

"Sure, honey," she said as sweetly as she could.

Mark stared at her for a minute and then Anton interrupted his trance. "Mark, I'm really not hungry."

"Well, we are going out to eat and you know how long it takes for them to get our food to us. I just figured if you ate a little then you won't be grumpy later," Mark explained and then started to tickle him.

Lexie was enjoying listening to Anton cracking up while she was cutting up an apple for him. Her heart was hurting but she loved the sound of the two of them playing together. She knew Mark loved Anton and would never treat him differently than his own. And if Mark chose not to give Anton his name, it would be for a good reason. It still did not stop her from hurting.

Mark and Anton sat down at the kitchen table and Anton took an apple wedge off the plate she put on the table. Mark picked up a pretzel and gave Anton a smile of approval. Lexie smiled at Mark but he saw it as more of a smirk. She sat down and grabbed an apple wedge also and Mark pulled out a board game for them to pass the time before they had to leave.

Lexie knew that Mark knew that she was disappointed. She didn't want that to affect his decision. She truly wanted him to give it some honest thought. She couldn't handle another man not wanting her child. Now she was regretting having asked him. Having put them both in this position. What would she do if he said no, even if it was a good reason. A shadow was forming over her future. She wished they had discussed this before they bought the house, sent out the wedding invitations and put the deposit on their honeymoon Now Lexie had to ask herself if she could handle no.

"Lexie," Mark yelled bringing her back to the kitchen. "Are you okay?"

"Yeah, sorry. Running through my to do list in my head. Is it my turn?" She told him putting on her happy mask.

"Yes, Mommy," Anton answered her. "Mommy, I'm winning. I have two more left to get home."

"Good job, Anton," she sang. "But Mommy is still going to try to beat you."

"You can try," he laughed.

The three played for an hour, which was just long enough before it was time to get ready. Anton won one game, Lexie won the other. Lexie ushered him off to wash his face and hands and get his shoes. As always he obeyed. Before Lexie could disappear into her room, Mark grabbed her hand and put his arms around her and his chin on her head. After holding a fake smile for the past hour, she didn't think she could continue with just the two of them.

"Hey, talk to me," he told her.

"I'm fine, Mark. What do you want to talk about?"

"Lex, don't be mad. I just want to make sure before I say yes, I'm doing the right thing. It's not that I don't love Anton. I think it scared me," Mark tried to explain.

"I know Mark. I'm the one that said take your time. I'm not mad."

"Are you disappointed?"

"No. I know it won't change our family. Just a little scared that if you do say no," she explained.

Mark squeezed her a little tighter. "I can understand that. If it's any consolation, I'm scared also."

"Of what?"

"Because I have to deal with Carlos. He has a say in this. As a man, he is going to react one of two ways. He is going to be offended because he will have to admit he is a dead beat son of a bitch, or he will have no guilt at all and say okay and I will have to tell him he is a dead beat son of a bitch and want to put my foot in his ass. Either way, this convo has to happen."

"I don't understand," Lexie started pulling back from him. "Why do you have to speak with Carlos?"

"Because he is Anton's father. He might not act like it, but he is. One day down the line, he might even decide to be Anton's father. In the meantime, as much as you might not like it, this decision involves the three of us."

She knew he was right, no matter how much she didn't want him to be. She didn't want him to have a talk with Carlos. Lexie's dream was Carlos would fall off the face of the earth and nobody would give a damn. At least not anyone in her household.

"Are you okay?" Mark asked.

Before she could answer Anton came down the stairs. "I'm ready Mommy!"

"Good job. Let me grab my shoes and we can leave." Lexie grabbed her purse off of the couch and turned to Mark and nodded and smiled. She slipped into her black flats by the door and they headed out. Lexie noticed Anton's buttons were uneven so she knelt down to fix it before he got into the car.

"I love you, Mommy," he said and reached over to hug her.

Lexie put a real smile on her face. "I love you too, sweetie. Now jump in."

Look, Mommy. Purple towels!

Chris's friends came for lunch and ended up staying for dinner. By the time they left, Brie was exhausted. Deena was curled up asleep on the floor in the Florida room and Chonda was sleepy creeping towards grumpy. The two had been playing all day with the little girl that had come over. Chris picked up Deena and took her up the stairs. Brie pulled Chonda along so she could take a shower. Ike was off in his own world with his eyes glued to his game.

"But, Mommy, I'm not tired," Chonda complained.

"You still need to get into the shower. And look, you have new pajamas. Ms. Sarah has washed them and laid them out for you," Brie told her.

"Do I get to take them home?"

"No, we are going to leave them here so that when we stay over you have something to sleep in."

Chonda huffed and headed for the shower. Chris kissed the top of her head as she passed him. "Deena is tucked, but she is fully dressed."

"Thank you. I'll put her in her pj's. She was so looking forward to wearing them. They have her favorite princess on them and they have footies."

"Maybe I should get me a pair," Chris smiled. "I'll be downstairs. Probably in my office."

Brie kissed him and then he walked out the bedroom. Brie picked up Deena's little pajamas and uncovered her tightly tucked daughter. Deena grumbled because she was being moved again. She didn't cooperate as Brie was trying to pull her shirt over her head. They tussled as Deena whined, but Brie was successful at getting her out of her clothes and into the light green pajamas.

As Brie picked up Deena's clothes, she noticed the purple shag rug. Then she looked around the guest bedroom and realized it was redecorated as a little girls rooms. The comforter was pink with large blue, green and purple circles. There was a vanity with a mirror that she had not paid attention to earlier when she brought the bags up. This had been done since the holidays.

She recalled his words from earlier when he told her he was not investing his time and energy for nothing. Now she wanted to know why. She was as nervous as earlier to talk to him. Brie peeked into the bathroom and told Chonda not to take too long. The shower curtain matched the comforter and there was a purple rug in front of the tub and one in front of the sink.

"Look, Mommy. Purple towels!" Chonda shouted from behind the curtain. She noticed the change also.

"I see. It is very pretty," Brie told her. "I'm heading down to check on your brother."

"Okay, I'll be out in a minute," Chonda promised.

Brie decided to stop and look in the room the Ike slept in. His comforter was a football theme with a navy blue back ground and a red border. The bed was on a red shag rug and in the seating area a football shaped rug with two navy blue bean bag chairs. A poster of Ike's favorite football player was on the wall. The same theme was in the bathroom.

Brie skipped down the stairs and towards his office. She tapped lightly on the door. No answer. She looked in and he wasn't there. She walked over to the bedroom, he wasn't there either. Now she headed to his favorite room in the house, the Florida room. He wasn't there either. "It's a damn shame you have to call people on their cell phone to find them in the house," she complained about the mansion size house.

Chris and Ike were playing a video game in the media room. Some kind of car racing game. When she peeked in they were laughing and teasing one another. Brie decided not to interrupt. The moment was priceless for her. She backed out and went to the bedroom. She'd wait for Chris to come to bed. Brie wanted to work on the birthday party she was planning for a client. Chonda had knocked on the door with her doll in one arm and a book in the other. Brie put her work down and the two climbed into the huge bed together.

When Chris came into the room, he woke up Brie shaking her lightly. "I'm going to carry Chonda up to bed."

"Oh, wow. I fell asleep?"

"Yes, you both did," Chris said picking Chonda up like a sack of potatoes.

Brie got up and opened the door for him, not that he needed her too. She walked back to the chaise lounge where she had her laptop and journal and put them away. She straightened things up before he came back down. She didn't know why, but she always felt guilty if it looked like she and the kids were there. It didn't take long for him to return. She was sitting on the bench at the end of the bed waiting when he walked in. "Did Ike go to bed?"

"I told him to get his shower. I don't know if he is in bed yet or not. Do you want me to check on him?"

"No, that's okay. It's been a full day. I'm sure he will be out soon if he isn't yet," she answered. "I noticed you decorated the two bedrooms."

"I asked Sarah for help. I was going to ask you, but then you got sick. I ordered it and Sarah set it up. It wasn't much. Just something I wanted to do for them. You can finish it or change it if they don't like it."

"It's beautiful. Thank you. I love the thought you put into it."

"Did the girls like it?"

"Chonda did. Deena was sleep and I haven't talked with Ike. I'm so sorry I didn't notice it earlier when I went up there."

"Ike told me he liked the room. That kid loves football. Why doesn't he play?"

Brie hated telling Chris when she could not afford something, but it was the truth. She never had the money for cleats and football pads, or the $250 registration fee to sign him up. Instead she said, "With my schedule, it wasn't going to be easy to pick him up."

"We could have arranged something," he told her. "He told me he played when he was younger but after Deena you have not been able to afford to do a lot of things."

Brie looked away when she was called out on her lie. Being the poorest person in your circle was the worst position. "That too."

Chris was aware that Brie was not comfortable talking about money. Anytime he mentioned the cost of something or gave her money, she stiffened. "You know if you or the kids need something, all you have to do is ask?"

"I know," she smiled. "I'm going to go shower."

"Wait, Brie," he said before she could stand all the way up. Chris sat down on the bench next to her and put her hand on his. "What is it that I'm doing wrong?"

"Who says you are doing anything wrong?"

"You still don't feel comfortable with me. If you need anything, money or otherwise, you will not mention it to me. It's like you want me to initiate everything."

In a low voice, Brie admitted, "I don't know how to ask for anything. I don't want to come off like a gold digger."

"Baby, if I thought you were a gold digger, do you think I would be with you? Besides, I'm the one that offers."

"Chris, what did you mean when you said that you were investing time and energy in us?" She finally asked.

"Just that. I enjoy our time together. Now I look forward to the weekends."

"I guess I'm asking what is your agenda. What do you get out of all of this?"

"I have the same agenda as everyone else. I want someone to love me for me. Someone to build a future with. What man does not want a good woman by his side that makes him look and feel good?"

"Is that what I do for you? Do you see me as a good woman?"

"You don't see your value?"

Brie looked away again. "I hate being honest with you. When I'm honest I feel like I'm going to lose you."

"Being honest with me isn't going to break us up. It's when you are not honest I get frustrated," Chris explained turning her head back towards him.

"Chris, I'm not good at this part. I can get the guy, but I'm not good at keeping the guy," she started. "I'm so scared that if you get to know me, you won't want to be with me. I don't want to come off like I need a man to take care of me."

"Really? Because, I need someone to take care of me. My entire manhood is about having someone to take care of and someone that will take care of me. If I'm not needed, what's the point?"

"But, I thought men wanted women who were independent and had their own and didn't need any help?"

Chris gave a light chuckle. "Your first mistake was you assumed that men knew what they wanted. Brie, if you are independent and don't need me, again, what is the point of being in a relationship?"

"I told you I wasn't good at this part."

"Then, how about this. Why don't you ask me what it is that I want? This way you don't have to assume anything anymore," he suggested.

Brie smiled, "Chris, what do you want in a relationship?"

"I want a woman who is comfortable in her skin. A woman who has a good heart and takes care of not only herself, but her family and friends. A woman that I can hold a real conversation with. A woman that is just as comfortable at the Opera as she is at a Frankie Beverly and Maze concert. A woman with goals for her and her family. Now, your turn."

"My turn?" She asked surprised. "You mean, what do I want in a man?"

"Yes, Brie. There had to be a reason you were attracted to me."

Brie had never thought about what she wanted. Her only goal was always to just find a man that she would make happy enough that he would stay with her. "Well, I want a man that make me feel like a woman. A man that puts me first because I'm worth being put first. A man with a sense of humor. Someone who believes in family and the family unit. Someone who works hard and is great role model for the community." Brie was finding it easier to describe Chris because he really was everything she wants. "I want a man that wants to build something real."

"Then allow me to be that guy. Let me be the one that puts you first and build something real with you. Stop being shy with me. If you need or want something, be bold and ask for it. I don't have a problem asking you for anything that I want."

"Alright, then. I can do that. But, right now, I have what I need. I'm working on the party planning business and doing what I need to get prepared so I can quit my job and build my own thing."

"So, you need money to quit your job?" Chris asked smiling at her.

"No, I need to get other stuff together first."

"Promise you will let me know if you need money so you can quit your job."

Brie stiffened again. "I promise. I'm nervously promising, but I promise."

"I'm good with that," Chris winked. "Now, back to what I want."

"Oh, and what's that?" Brie was relieved they were done talking seriously.

Chris picked up his iPad and asked, "My private strip show. What kind of music would you like me to choose?"

Brie went back to being nervous, but she did say she would dance for him. "How about something with a techno beat."

"I can find that. Too bad I don't have a pole in my room."

"Why, so you can watch me bust my behind? A pole takes skills."

Chris leaned closer to her ear and whispered, "My birthday is in March. You can take some lessons and make it a happy birthday."

Brie blushed, "Really now? That might be a fun idea. Even I would get a happy on your birthday."

Chris turned on the music and leaned back on his footboard. Brie wished she had had a drink to ease the feeling of looking like a fool. Despite the butterflies, she danced for her man.

Surrender

Phaedra had been standing in the same aisle at the grocery store for 25 minutes. She didn't know what she wanted for dinner. She only knew she didn't want any more chicken. That seem to be the only thing that Ron knew how to cook or wanted to cook. It had been a week since that Saturday in the garage. She was supposed to be treading lightly, but each night she was either at his house or he was at hers.

She knew Ron was all in and as far as he was concerned they were a couple again. Phaedra wasn't though. "I'm still figuring this out," she told Lexie when she asked. Lexie reminded her that she had warned her. Phaedra did things on her own terms, and anyone that didn't know that didn't know Phaedra. After a week, she was ready for a break. At least for tonight. Ron and the kids were going to the movies and she was heading home to enjoy some alone time.

Phaedra was looking over all the different salads and bypassing anything with chicken. The young man behind the counter had been watching her and smiling wide. She looked up once in a while and smiled back cautiously so he would not take it as an invite. It was a sign that she needed to pick something and move on. Phaedra reached for a kale salad.

Phaedra's next stop was to grab a pint of frozen yogurt and a pack of her favorite cookies. "Dinner and dessert," Phaedra said to herself while standing in line. "I remember when that used to include some good sex in between."

"I guess coming to your place for dinner is out of the question," said the voice coming from over her shoulder.

Phaedra was startled hoping he didn't hear her comment. Phaedra slowly turned around and smiled and the handsome man behind her. "Dinner for one tonight."

"Leonard. Leonard Maxwell," he introduced himself.

"Phaedra Escobar ," she extended her hand for a proper greeting.

"Nice to meet you, Phaedra. Why is someone as beautiful as you eating alone?"

Phaedra liked his wide smile. His teeth were so straight and white. His bottom lip was fuller than the top lip and naturally lined. His eyebrows were thick and wild and his eyes a dark brown. He was a little lighter complexion than she normally paid attention to, but the dark brown eyes kept her mesmerized.

"Ladies choice. The kids are off with their dad and I'm going to relax," she explained.

By now Phaedra was having her three items rung up. Leonard reached over with his card and paid for her items. "I can at least buy your dinner."

"How kind of you," she said not impressed.

"I'd prefer to buy you a real dinner, at a restaurant. Your choice," he proposed.

"Do you always pick up women at the grocery store?"

"No. But in my defense I've never met someone as beautiful as you at the grocery store," he said flashing his wide smile.

Phaedra picked up her bag and thanked him for her dinner. She smiled at the cashier and headed for the exit. Phaedra was opening her door when Leonard walked up. "You aren't a stalker are you?"

He laughed. "Not at all. I was hoping maybe I can call you sometime. Or if you are more comfortable, I could give you my number."

Phaedra ripped off a piece of the brown bag her groceries were in and wrote her cell number on it. "Just don't call tonight. I really want to put my feet up tonight."

"I can respect that. Enjoy your evening Ms. Escobar. Maybe we can get together tomorrow night. I'll call you tomorrow afternoon if that's okay."

"That works for me. I get off tomorrow at four and I don't have any plans."

"Great! I look forward to speaking with you then," he said opening her door for her as she climbed into her vehicle.

"Same here," she smiled.

As Phaedra pulled away her first thought was Ron, then her kids. She was not sure why, or at least not wanting to admit why. She had that strange feeling in her belly that this was wrong. That she would let her kids down. She had to remind herself that she and Ron were not an item, however, she smiled when she thought of the past week. Two nights she had come home to Ron and the kids cooking in the kitchen. The laughter that emanated from the kitchen was better than the smell of the marinara sauce in the pot. The other nights she and the kids went to his house and were greeted by his smile, his hugs, and of course, chicken.

When she pulled up in the garage she was reciting her mantra to herself, "An ex is an ex for a reason." She walked into her empty home working on convincing herself not to confuse the relationship. They were just friends. However, it wasn't easy being around him when she was so horny. "Why should I feel guilty about betrayal when he was the one that ruined our marriage?" She asked herself. It was easier for her to remember the hurt than to allow the love in.

Phaedra sat the bag on the kitchen table. She was about to walk away when she remembered the frozen yogurt and pulled it out to put it in the freezer. Phaedra walked into her room and came out of her work clothes. She laid the off white suit on her bed and got into the shower. Phaedra's plan was to spend the evening with no agenda. She squeezed out the last of her papaya and Aragon oil bath wash and washed the day down the drain.

Once she got out, she picked up her cell phone to check it. There were two text. One from Maya and one from Lexie.

'Hi Mom, hope you enjoy your alone time. Love you.'

'Hey Chica, haven't talked to you today. Hope everything is good.'

Phaedra slipped into a baggy pair of pink and white striped pajama pants and a tight, plain, white t-shirt. She headed back to the kitchen and pulled her salad out of the bag. She grabbed a bowl out of the cabinet and poured her salad into it. She shook salt and pepper on it and cut a lemon in half and squeezed the juice over it. Phaedra finally sat down to eat. After the first bite, she called Lexie.

"Hey, sweetie. How are you?" Lexie answered.

"I'm good as always. You sound happy."

"I am. I am only three months away from being Mrs. Mark Leonardi What are you up to tonight?"

"Not. A. Thing," Phaedra sang. "And I like it like that. The kids are with Ron and I'm going to put on some jazz music and eat cookies in peace."

"Sounds like such a lovely evening. So why do you sound a little depressed?"

Phaedra sighed. "I'm not depressed. Just got other things on my mind. I met a guy at the grocery store today. Dark brown eyes, beautiful lips, nice abs. You'd think I'd be excited about it, but I'm not. What the hell is wrong with me?"

"I keep telling you that you are going through a shift. I don't know why you refuse to listen to me," Lexie was shaking her head.

With a mouthful of food, Phaedra asked, "And what exactly am I shifting into?"

Lexie laughed, "You want love just like the rest of us."

"Humph," Phaedra responded. "Whatever."

"So, tell me more about this guy you met."

"Like I said, he was sexy. Light complexion, spoke very well, nice guy." Phaedra was having to think hard to even remember what Leonard looked like.

"What does he do for a living? Did you find out what kind of car he drives?"

"Don't really know. I just know his name is Leonard Maxwell," Phaedra said wondering why the probing.

"Because the Phaedra I know would have had the full history on some guy she just met if she was interested."

"I feel so confused right now. Why do I feel like I am cheating on my family? Why Lexie? Why?"

"I would say it's because you love the family being back together again. You might still hate Ron for what he did, but having your family as one is important to you. Like I said, you put out a cry to the Universe for love and it delivered what was in your heart."

Phaedra stuffed a fork full of kale in her mouth and then said, "What about an ex is an ex for a reason. Ron cheated on me several times, had a child with another woman and I'm supposed to lay down and pretend it didn't happen?"

"Your whole family has paid for that. It's time to move past that and heal."

"Easy for you to say. Mark never cheated on you. Mark is the perfect guy," Phaedra said with bitterness.

"You know that's not true."

"I know. I'm just mad. I don't like not knowing what to do about a decision I have to make."

"I get that Phae. It's scary to give someone a second chance. Mark's done it a hundred times with me. You are scared. That is expected. You still love him but you are not satisfied that his only punishment was losing you and the kids. You think there should be more. Am I getting anywhere close?"

"No, you are not. I'm none of those things you just mentioned," Phaedra fussed.

"Bull. Shit," Lexie laughed. She heard Phaedra laughed with her. "And what the hell are you crunching on in my ear?"

"I'm crunching a yellow bell pepper. I'm eating a kale salad. It has yellow and orange bell peppers, with juicy grape tomatoes, sliced radishes and what looks like jicama but has no taste to it."

"Where is the meat?"

"Didn't want any. Saving my calories for yogurt and cookies. Besides, I had a piece of salmon at lunch."

"I would feel better about myself if you gained like 20 lbs," Lexie gripped.

Phaedra laughed, "Bitch please. That's not happening."

"I tried," Lexie joked. "So, how long before you are ready to admit you want just one man and you are done dating all of the others for sex?"

"Wow, just put it out there like that," Phaedra said and then smacked in her ear. "I don't know, Lexie. I really don't know. I supposed when I'm ready, I will call Brie and tell her."

"Whatever!" Lexie yelled and laughed. "Call Brie. Let me know how that goes."

"How is Brie doing?"

"She's good. I went to the flower shop with her and she showed them her database and bartered a 15% discount for her customers," Lexie bragged. "I think we are watching a little business woman bloom after all."

"I'm actually happy for her. I told her to give me some business cards and I can give them to home buyers who want to plan a house warming party."

"Why would they need a professional party planner for a house warming party?"

Phaedra shook her head at the question. "Because I told them it was a really good idea. They will believe me because I'm the woman that just put them in their dream house."

"You the boss!" Lexie joked feeling the ridiculousness of her question. "Well, go finish enjoying your alone time. Mr. Leonard is not sneaking over later is he?"

"Isn't that the whole point I made to you earlier? My guilt? Of course he is not. That's it, I'm firing you as a friend."

"I was listening. I'm just double checking. You know sometimes you leave part of a story out. And as a friend, about tomorrow night, I say don't go."

"That's your advice? Don't go? What if I'm hungry?" Phaedra teased.

"Have Ron make you a salad," Lexie laughed.

"Get off my phone, Lexie! I'm through with you."

Lexie laughed even harder. "Good night Phae. Love you."

"Good night silly child," Phaedra said and disconnected.

"How the hell do you love someone you hate?" Phaedra asked herself. "I should have just stayed with RJ. No, wait, he was trying to grow a pair. Never mind." Lexie shuffled the vegetables around in her bowl and took a few more bites. She scrapped the remainder in the trash and put her bowl in the dishwasher. She pulled out the frozen yogurt and scooped half of it into an ice cream cone shaped ceramic bowl. She grabbed her bag of cookies and headed for the TV.

She had to admit that she did want her family back together. She hated the process she was going to have to go through to get past the feelings of anger because of betrayal. She was feeling, and she hated every part of that. Her phone startled her when the text alert chimed. She sat down on her couch and grabbed her remote before getting comfortable. She crossed her legs and opened her bag of cookies and sat them next to her. Phaedra checked her text. It was Caleb.

'Mom, wish you were with us. Love you.'

Phaedra smiled and sent back, 'Hope you are having fun. See you tomorrow. Love you.'

She gave a big sigh as she sent it to her son. This was sort of a sign, she thought. Phaedra stomach began to hurt as it tightened. The numbness to emotions was fading. She could feel the pain of longing. She sat her bowl of yogurt down on the wooden tray on her ottoman.

"What the hell is wrong with you?" She asked herself. "I'm acting like a little girl." Phaedra stood up and began to pace back and forth in the living room. "I didn't ask for this shit. I'd know if I asked for it. My life was fine. I had a millionaire boyfriend and a 20 something boyfriend. You really expect me to give that up for some deadbeat husband that didn't give a shit about me? I can pick up this phone right now and call both of them and they both would be at the door. I'm that damn good. I'm that, that damn good."

Phaedra's stomach was getting tighter. The tears were started to well up in her eyes. "Do you hear me?" She yelled out to the heavens. "I'm Phaedra Escobar! I'm that damn good!"

Phaedra knelt down on the floor wiping the tears from her face. "I don't want to walk this path. I don't want the pain that comes with walking down this path. In case you forgot, it hurts too much. How do I not surrender when I know you have never steered me wrong? How do I resist when I know you have always shown me the right way and lead me to my needs? How? How do I love somebody I want to hate?"

Phaedra got silent during her prayer and meditated for a minute. She heard the text notification again. Phaedra got up and walked over to pick her phone up off of the ottoman. It was from Ron.

'Remember this song? It was playing over the speakers just now so I thought of you.' He had linked a video to the song *Adore* by Prince.

She did remember it. It was playing on the radio when Ron was dropping her off after a dinner date. It was the first time he told her he loved her. They had been going out for a month and she wanted to go home with him after that, but she resisted. She waited another couple of weeks before she slept with him the first time. It had always been love at first sight, but hard for a girl that wasn't sure if she knew what love was. Ron made her happy back then. Even if she wasn't sure how to return the love, she did her best with him.

Phaedra sighed one more time, then whispered to her Creator, "I surrender."

Are you proud of anything I do

The month of February had rolled in colder than usual. Lexie had been complaining about her dry skin to her mother, but she wasn't really listening. They were going over the seating chart. Sitting at the kitchen table with the layout spread over the table, Carol was somewhere else other than that table.

"Mom, are you listening?" Lexie asked for the second time.

"Yes, I hear you. You were saying your skin felt like sand paper."

"You just seem to have other things on your mind," Lexie pointed out.

"I guess it just dawned on me I will never do this with your sister."

"The laws have changed, Mom. Not that I see Roni as the marrying type." Lexie felt dejected once again falling to her sister's shadow.

"Alexia, I just don't know why she chose to be gay," Carol complained.

"I don't think anybody chooses to be gay. We like what we like."

Carol's eyes looked away from Lexie as she regained her composure. "Did you know? I mean growing up, did she ever confide in you?"

"No, Mom. She didn't have to. I also assumed that is why she moved South," Lexie said now being the one to regain her composure. "I know you would rather being doing this with Roni since she is your favorite, but I am grateful you are helping me."

Carol giggled at her daughter and then sipped her hot green tea. "I don not have a favorite. I gave birth to two daughters. There are things I favor about Veronica, but there are also things I favor about you."

"I just always thought Roni was your favorite, and I was dad's."

"No, Alexia. That is something you will learn when you have more children. Father nor mother have favorites."

"Oh, please don't tell me that. My whole self-esteem was built around being dad's favorite."

Carol looked at Lexie curious. "I'm sorry to be the one to tell you, but you have two parents that love you and are very proud of the woman you are. Mistakes and all my beautiful. Your dad did find it easier to talk to you then he did Veronica. He used to say that you always made him laugh. I loved hearing him laugh."

The two reminisced for a moment to themselves before Lexie broke the silence. "Mom, can a man truly love a child that is not his own?"

"I think so. Especially a man like Mark. He is a protector. Your house will probably be the neighborhood kid's house. Mark will be everyone's dad. Whether he adopts Anton or not, he will never treat him any differently," she promised.

"I wish I was going to this meeting with him and Carlos. Or, at least be a fly on the wall. I shouldn't say this out loud , but part of me wishes Mark would just walk in and punch him one good time."

"That is immature of you. You are better than that. Mark is going out of his way to have this sit down with Carlos. He feels this is the right thing. That's a man showing you he cares and loves your child as much as he loves you. I'm proud of him for that."

"What about me, Mom? Are you proud of anything that I do?" She pouted.

Carol had a huge smile come across her face watching Lexie revert back to the little girl that used to scream "watch me, Mommy, watch me." She told her,"Of course I am. You make goals and you achieve them. You have a drive like it's nobody's business. Not only are you smart and beautiful, but you are capable of setting the world on fire with both of those qualities. You look after your friends and you love hard. You are a great mother. But most of all, you are my daughter. Why wouldn't I be proud of you?"

Lexie slouched in her chair. "I don't know. I guess I feel like I do everything wrong."

Carol snapped her fingers so Lexie would sit up then walked over and hugged her. "Don't be so hard on yourself. Life happens. We learn our lessons, we hopefully improve. There is nothing wrong with that as long as we are growing. That is what makes the difference."

Lexie squeezed her mother a little tighter and held onto her a little longer. "Thank you, Mom."

"So, let's get back to this seating chart. The last thing you need is your Uncle Ray sitting next to your friend Phaedra. Aunt Clarice will be reaching across to strangle her," she joked sitting back down.

Lexie laughed so she could hold in the tears. "A double homicide suicide at my reception. That wouldn't go over so well."

"Don't really see Clarice committing suicide, but I do see her getting a plea deal of insanity. The woman has always been a little off."

"Be a waste to have to spend all of Uncle Ray's millions on a lawyer. I'd be out of the will just because it was my wedding and my friend."

"And what makes you think you are in their will?" She asked surprised.

"Look at me. I'm adorable. I'm the sweet niece that always remembers to call them on their birthdays and anniversary. I am so in their will."

Her mom laughed at her. "If you say so."

Lexie laughed with her. She had her mother's attention again. Lexie sipped on her tea and picked up her pen. With a smile on her face, the two went back to work on the chart.

Making a decision

The phone call had gone to voicemail again and Brie was feeling anxious. She had called Phaedra twice in the last 30 minutes and there was no answer, nor had she called back. Brie had acquired two more clients, she was working like a dog at work and still had to give the kids and Chris her attention. She was looking exhausted and feeling overwhelmed. Late nights staying up trying to work on her own company and working late at her job was catching up with her.

"What would Phaedra do?" She asked herself. "She'd tell me to make a damn decision, that's what she would do. Then I'd tell her that I'm too scared to make a decision. Then she would tell me that's my problem and call me a stupid bitch."

Brie was standing in front of her bathroom mirror. She noticed the darkness under her eyes. They were looking sunken. She was still tired and wanted to go back to bed for another few hours. She stayed up until one in the morning putting a proposal together for another faculty wife who wanted to have a Welcome Spring dinner party. She thought of the perfect flower arrangements and a spread that was light but filling. It would include a grilled pork tenderloin with spring vegetables such as asparagus, carrots, rhubarb, and new potatoes. Dessert would be chocolate covered apricots. Her plan was laid out well making her proposal perfect. Her only complaint was she wanted to do it during the daylight hours.

Brie reached for her phone again. She'd try Phaedra one more time before she woke the kids for school. As she went to press the number, instead she found herself calling Chris, because that's what Phaedra would actually do. He did offer and it was time for her to stop being scared to ask for what she wanted. She heard the phone hit the ground and could hear him fumbling for it. The sleepy voice said hello.

"Good morning, Chris. We need to talk," Brie greeted.

"What's wrong? Kids okay?" He was still trying to sit up in his bed.

"Kids are fine, but I'm not."

"Baby, what's wrong?" He was too tired for a guessing game.

"I don't want to talk over the phone. Can we meet for lunch today?"

"Are you breaking up with me?" He said joking.

Sarcastically she answered, "Maybe."

Chris laughed, now awake. "Well, in that case, why don't I swing by this morning so I can convince you otherwise."

"You know I'm not breaking up with you, but can we to talk?"

"Okay, I'm on my way. Give me a minute to brush my teeth and wash my face. You'll have to overlook the stubble."

"Lunch would be fine Chris. You don't have to come over now," she pleaded.

"I don't want to wait for lunch. I want to see you now."

"Okay then. I'll see you when you get here," she said in a huff.

"Great, now I've got to untwist these bantu knots, put on makeup and attempt to get dressed. All he has to do is brush his teeth, wash his face and put on a pair of jeans," she fussed. Brie was now frustrated. She had only slept for five hours, if that much.

It was time to get the kids up. She would start with Ike because he needed to sit for 10 minutes in the bathroom just to wake up. That would give her time to do her face before she woke up Chonda. Ike did his usual moaning but headed for the bathroom. Brie headed for hers to wash her face and put on her makeup.

"Here I tried to be more assertive, but instead I made my morning more hectic," she complained while scrubbing her face. "Phaedra would have made it work. And why has she not called me back?"

Brie had woken up the girls, finished her makeup and did her hair. The doorbell rang while she was combing Chonda's hair. She asked Ike to answer it while she checked her faced again. She heard Ike and Chris high five one another. Chonda jumped out of her chair when she heard Chris's voice.

"Good morning," he greeted as he bent over to kiss her.

"Good morning. How are you?"

"Just curious," he smiled.

"Chris, we have oatmeal for breakfast. Do you want some?" Chonda volunteered.

"Will you please sit down. I still have to get dressed young lady," Brie told Chonda.

Chris smiled, "Thank you for the offer, Chonda. Go ahead and let your mother finish your hair."

"Yes, sir," she pouted but sat down as she was told.

"Mom, I'm heading out. Did you sign my permission slip?" Ike asked her.

"Oh, sweetie, I forgot. I think I left it on the coffee table."

Ike ran to the living room to get the paper off the coffee table but it wasn't there. Brie jumped up to see if she took it to her room. She wanted to scream at someone or something but Chris was there. She didn't see it and Ike had to get going.

"Honey, I will find it and bring it to school, or if I don't find it, I will get one from the school," she promised and hugged him.

"Okay, but please don't forget. All of my friends are going," he told her. Love you, Mom. Bye Chris, Chonda and Deena.

When the door closed, Brie felt guilty. "I can't believe I waited for the last minute and misplaced it."

"I'm sure it is here somewhere," Chris tried to encourage her.

"That's just it, Chris. It is somewhere and I don't know where. I'm getting unorganized, I'm tired, and I have dark circles under my eyes."

"Hey, slow down. Why don't you finish helping the girls get dressed, we can drive them to school and then you can tell me about it."

Brie sighed, and then sighed again. "Okay, fine. Did you want some oatmeal?"

"No, I'm good. I figured we would have time to stop and grab some breakfast," he advised.

For Brie, that meant one more thing she was going to have to add to her list of things to do. "We'll see."

Both girls were ready and Brie went to her room to get dressed. She had laid out a navy blue wrap dress with pink flowers and white piping. She was putting it on when Chris came through the door.

He walked up behind her and wrapped his arms around her. "Why are you stressing out?"

"I told you, I'm unorganized."

"What can I do to help?" He was now kissing on her neck causing her loosen up.

Brie pulled his arms open and turned around to face him. "Business is going well. I could do even better. I just can't work my 40 plus hours a week and take it to the next level. I'm ready to quit my job. That may require me asking you for a financial assistance. I'm not saying I will need it, but if I do, will you be there?"

He lifted her chin and kissed her. "I will be there if you need me. For whatever you need me for."

"Thank you. It would help to not have to worry if I will have the money to pay the rent while I'm building." She finally felt the tension rising off of her shoulders.

"Then why don't you and the kids move in and you only have to worry about the business. Get it up and going full-time, you'll have Sarah there to worry about the cleaning and cooking, and you will be able to stay organized."

Brie slightly tilted her head to make sure she heard him correctly. "The kids and I, move in with you?"

"Yes," he confirmed.

Brie had been waiting to hear those words since the first time she walked into Chris's house. Now he was standing in front her pushing his hands into his dark indigo jeans, and she was hesitating to answer him. "Oh, my..." was her only response. After a deep inhale, she finally said, "I want to so bad to say yes, but it is a big decision. Are you going to recant if I ask you to give me some time?"

However disappointed he was, he kept his face emotionless. "I understand. I am willing to wait."

Brie couldn't believe she asked for time, but with so much going on with her right now, she did not want to make another mistake. At first all she could do was stare at him. "I love you," she said as she kissed him.

"Why don't you finish buttoning your dress. We don't want the girls to be late," Chris suggested as he allowed a slim grin across his stubbled face. He turned to walk out of the door to allow her to finish getting ready.

"Chris!" She called just before he closed the door. "Yes."

"Are you sure?" He asked, this time showing teeth when he smiled.

"I am. Just scared," she laughed.

Chris walked back into the room and wrapping one arm around her waist and the left arm to the back of her head pulling her close and kissing her with his full mouth open pressing hard against her. "What do you have to be scared of?" He asked as she caught her breath.

Brie blushed with his starring in her eyes. "You know me. I'm going through all the what if's in my head."

Chonda knocked on the door and yelled, "I'm going to be tardy."

"Wow, that's new. Usually she's trying to get out of going to school," she told Chris. "Okay, honey. We are coming."

"I'll wait in the living room with the girls while you get finished." Chris leaned in and kissed her again.

Brie finished her top buttons and tied the strap on her dress. She reached for her navy closed toe heels and slid into them both. She checked the mirror one more time and wiped the lipstick off that had smeared around her mouth. She fluffed her hair once more and walked out of her room.

"We are ready, Mommy," Deena announced.

"I'm glad baby girl," Brie answered picking up Deena kissing all over her cheeks. "Where is Chris?"

"He's moving car seats from your car to his," Deena reported.

Brie thought he would be heading home since they had talked. She grabbed her purse and Deena's backpack, then zipped Chonda's jacket. The three headed out the door with Brie locking it behind her.

"Double check that I put those in correctly," Chris asked her.

Brie did just that and then the girls climbed up into their individual seats. Once Brie and Chris were buckled in she finally asked him, "Are you going to take me to work?"

"Yes, I was. I was going to pick you up also."

"Oh, okay. Well, remember, I have to go to Ike's school also to sign the field trip form. I'm sending my boss a text to let her know I will be late."

"Then we have time," he told her.

Brie didn't disagree. She was going with the flow today. She was visioning in her head giving her two weeks' notice, gathering boxes and moving in with the man she was in love with. Better than that, she was moving in with a man that loved her. A man that showed her something in herself that she hadn't believed in. Brie saw her dreams coming true.

Why are you here?

Lexie and Phaedra had met at a coffee shop that morning. "So, what happened?" Lexie asked in reference to Leonard.

"He called, we spoke for a minute or two. He asked about us going to dinner and I said I couldn't. I told him I wanted to but I needed to figure out this relationship that I'm currently pursuing and didn't need to make it any more complicated than it already was," Phaedra explained.

"You okay?" Lexie asked pouring raw sugar into her large cup of dark coffee.

"Of course. Turns out he is a doctor at Memorial. Some kind of surgeon. I just need to stand still and listen. I am curious to find out what this is between Ron and I."

"I'm glad. I only say that because I think it is great that the two of you are trying to put back together something so special. And Ron taking responsibility for his part," Lexie toasted her coffee to Phaedra's chai tea.

Phaedra looked at Lexie crossed. "I think you are seriously deprived of oxygen."

"Oh, come on, it is so romantic."

"Between you and Mya, I don't know who is more excited," Phaedra laughed. "So, Brie has called me five times this morning."

"Is she okay?" Lexie asked with a mouth full of a bite of an everything bagel.

"Yeah, she is fine."

"What was up with her?"

"I'm sure she needed to make a decision about something and was scared to make it on her own."

"You didn't talk to her?"

"Of course not. Lexie, Brie is a big girl and she needs to act like one."

"But you could of at least talked to her. Maybe it was an emergency." Lexie started feeling for her phone in her purse.

"If it were an emergency she would have called you," Phaedra reminded her.

Lexie did not see a message or text from Brie. "Either way, Phae, you still should of answered."

Phaedra pushed on Lexie's phone to stop her from calling Bire. "I plan on calling her back. I'm giving her time to make up her own mind. Lexie, if we keep telling Brie how to live her life, she is always going to call on us to make her decisions for her. Do you really still want to be raising Brie 20 years from now? Hell, Anton will be grown and out of the house making decisions and Brie will be calling you asking, should I get paper or plastic?"

Lexie cracked up, "Now who is lacking oxygen?"

"You know I'm right. I've got to go. I have a 9 o'clock appointment at my office."

"Okay. Glad we had a chance to get together. We'll have to plan a girl's spa day."

"That I can look forward to," Phaedra said and hugged her goodbye.

Phaedra was sitting at her desk by 8:45 and was booting up her computer. While she waited she checked her schedule on her phone. Since she had a few minutes she called Brie.

"Hey, Phaedra!" Brie answered.

"Did you make a decision on your own?"

"I did. Is that why you didn't answer me?"

"Yes," Phaedra confirmed. "So I gave you enough time?"

"Yes. I decided I'm giving my two weeks' notice today and Chris asked me to move in with him so I said yes," she proudly announced.

"Wow! I'm impressed. You made two major life decision all before 8 a.m. What brought this on?"

"Dark circles under my eyes," Brie jokes. "Let me call you back. I'm at Ike's school."

"Congratulations. I'll talk with you later."

"Thanks. Bye."

Michelle tapped on Phaedra's office door and let her know that her appointment arrived. Phaedra told her one minute and pulled out her mirror to check her hair and makeup. She reapplied the cherry shade of lipstick she was wearing and then smoothed her light gray slacks and tucked the rayon cream colored shirt. She told herself she looked good and walked out to meet the woman that insisted on a morning appointment with her.

Phaedra stepped into the waiting room with her usual wide smile and extended hand to greet her client, but stopped in her tracks. To her dismay in a dark teal pencil skirt and a lighter, long sleeved, teal, silk button down blouse stood George's wife, Diane, who extended her hand to greet Phaedra.

"Mrs. Austin! What a delight to see you," Phaedra said trying not to look nervous.

"You also, dear. And it is Diane. No need to be so formal," she said smiling back at Phaedra.

"Can I offer you something to drink?"

"No, dear. Michelle took very good care of me. She made sure I was comfortable," Diane answered impatiently.

"Good. Please, this way to my office." Phaedra with her palm up, directed Diane toward the door she had just come from. "So, how can I assist you? Are you in the market for a new home? You were pretty vague over the phone."

"No, Phaedra, I'm not, but I think you know that already," she said sitting down crossing her leg and balancing her cream colored platform heels on the tip of her toe.

Phaedra sat down behind her desk and nervously asked, "Then why are you here?"

"I'm here about George. You have made my life a living hell for the last few months."

Phaedra slowly asked, "How did I make your life a living hell?

"Oh, come on Phaedra, don't play coy with me. I know you are the woman George was having an affair with. You broke it off with him, I'm guessing right before Christmas, and he's been moping around miserable making me miserable."

Phaedra started off defensive but Diane quickly stopped her letting her know she was not there for a fight. "Then what is it that you want?"

"To ask you to take him back," she said. "Now he is around the house and he won't leave me alone."

Phaedra's facial expression went from nervous to confused. "You are kidding me right?"

"No, I'm not. I know you think I sound crazy, but he obviously loves you. You made him happy for the last couple of years."

Phaedra wasn't sure how to respond. She wasn't sure if Diane was fishing for information or if she really knew that she and George had been seeing each other for that long. "Shouldn't that be your job as his wife?"

"Oh, please, Phaedra. I'm being straight with you, so be straight with me. I've known my husband was having an affair. I also know that you weren't his first. I'm pinpointing it started about two to two and a half years ago. And you made it very obvious when you showed up at the restaurant that you are in love with him also."

"Look, whatever relationship your husband and I might, or might not of had is nonexistence. You coming in here asking me to get with him is very puzzling. I would think if anything you would be upset to find out he is cheating."

"Then, allow me to explain." Diane sat up taller in her chair and overlapped her hands on her knee. "Look, Phaedra, I am a dutiful wife. I take care of George, but that part of our marriage, neither one of us are really interested in each other anymore. I am not going to divorce him. I am however, extending you an olive branch here. He took care of you financially, you weren't in want for anything. You can have all of that back, continue to pretend that I don't know, and then all three of us get what we want."

Phaedra remembered saying similar words before the restaurant incident. Her agenda was different now. "I can't help you with that. Besides, I would be upset if I found out my husband was having an affair. Actually, I was, so excuse me for looking at you like you are crazy. This is just asinine."

"So, you are going to sit here and deny you and George were having an affair?"

"I'm not having that conversation," Phaedra snapped.

"You sit there as if I don't have proof and could give you an ultimatum." Diane leaning back in the chair again.

Phaedra leaned back in her chair also. "You want to black mail me into fucking your man because you don't want to. Am I hearing you correctly?"

Diane read Phaedra's eyes for minute before she answered her. "You have a nice gig going here Phaedra. I'm sure you don't want home buyers or the people you work with to know what extra curricular activities you participate in. Even without proof, a seed planted can grow in all sorts of directions."

Phaedra smiled. "You are some kind of crazy aren't you. So, allow me to explain how that is going to go. My assistant? Affair. My manager? Affair, with Todd who works in the back office. Then there is Theresa, the Spanish lady you passed. She is happily married with two kids, a dog and a beautiful house right on Jax beach. She actually like women and has a girlfriend stashed away in Orange Park. And if I gave a good guess, you Mrs. Diane Austin, affair. My point is, everyone has a secret. Plant whatever seed you want. It won't grow. Don't try to come in her hoping to throw shit on my wall thinking it will stick."

Diane was trying to think as quickly as Phaedra, but did not have another threat to come back with. She underestimated how much in love with George Phaedra was. "I see I should have done my homework on you. You are not the usual dumb lay he prefers. Phaedra, you slept with my husband and I don't think I'm going to let that just slide. So while the two of us are threatening to sling poo, only one of us will survive, and Sweetheart, it won't be you."

Diane stood up, picking up her cream colored clutch and her keys off of Phaedra's desk. Phaedra stood up also and lifted her cell phone and took a picture of Diane. "Just in case George ask when I spoke to you, I'll have a date and time stamp. Instead of playing this game, maybe you should just have sex with your husband and make both of you happy."

"You have a good day, Phaedra Escobar." Diane gave her a fake smirk and walked out of her office.

Phaedra sat back down and pulled out a burner phone. She made a call. The person only answered, "Yeah."

"Meet me at eight."

They both disconnected and Phaedra threw the phone back in the zipped compartment of her purse. She would put an end to this before it got started.

Whoa, wait. What?

"Whoa, wait, I have to sit down," Lexie said walking to her couch in response to Brie's news. "You did what?"

"You heard me correctly. I gave my two weeks' notice. Remember Chris said he would help me financially if I wanted to quit and work on the event planning business full time? Well, I decide to say yes to his offer."

"So, is that what you were calling Phaedra about this morning?"

"Yes, well, to ask her how to confidently ask Chris, but that heifer wouldn't even pick up the phone. Then called me talking about 'did you make a decision on your own'. What if it had been an emergency?"

"If it were an emergency you would have called me and she knows that. But, Brie, she is right. You are going to have to learn to rely on your gut to start making some decisions. You can't expect us to keep directing you. I mean, what are you going to do, stop in the middle of a conversation and tell Chris you gotta get back with him so you can consult one of us?"

Brie sighed. "I did that this morning. I made a decision."

Lexie laughed at her because she was whining. "Well, I'm proud of you. What other decisions did you make today other than what to eat for breakfast?"

"Well, smartass," Brie snapped causing Lexie to laugh even more. "Chris asked the kids and I to move in with him."

Lexie stopped laughing and gasped. "Are you serious? I would have beat your ass if you needed to consult anyone to make that choice. What did you say?"

"I said yes," she smiled. "At first I said let me think about it, then I immediately said yes. I know, stupid right?"

"I would never call you stupid, and you shouldn't either. I do understand not trying to jump to quick. I'm happy for you though."

"I am happy also. Ellie was in here with mixed emotions. She was happy for me accomplishing my goals but sad to be losing me."

"How about the kids? What did they say?"

"I haven't told them. He asked me while everyone was getting dressed. Then drove the girls to school and me to work."

"Who the hell is ringing my doorbell like a crazy person?" Lexie asked stomping towards the front door.

"Maybe Mark left his key," Brie suggested.

"He comes through the garage." Lexie swung the door open.

"That crazy bitch showed up at my job!" Phaedra pushed her way through the front door.

"Which crazy bitch are we talking about?" Lexie asked.

Brie laughed, "How many are there?"

"George's wife was my 9 o'clock appointment," Phaedra announced.

Both women yelled, "What?"

Lexie added, "...the fuck?"

"Oh, that is not the crazy part. She showed up to tell me to get back with her husband because now she has to fuck him."

"Whoa, wait. What?" Lexie stuttered.

"Exactly. She said she knew we were having an affair and my breaking up with him was making her life inconvenient. Who does that kind of shit?"

"A woman who has her own thing on the side. That's what you are actually making inconvenient for her," Lexie said.

"Oh, I haven't gotten to the craziest part," Phaedra said.

"It can't get any crazier," Brie said over the speaker phone.

"It did Brie. When I told her no, she tried to black mail me. This bitch has lost her mind." Phaedra was pacing back and forth with her hand on her forehead. "this crazy ass woman got my head hurting. I wish I was still with RJ. I need something to smoke."

"Wait, she black mailed you for not sleeping with George? That is ass backward," Brie said.

"Exactly! I'm sorry, if I have to suck my husband's dick then she has to suck her husband's dick. It should be a written rule. You have to suck your own husband's dick before you are allowed to suck anybody else's dick," Phaedra joked.

"You are stupid," Lexie said holding her stomach laughing.

"Now you know for sure she has something on the side that she is hiding. Find her side piece and you can black mail her right back," Lexie told her.

"So what did you tell her Phaedra?" Brie asked.

"I told her to get the hell out of my office. I let her know that if she wants to play that game be prepared. She was trying to figure out if she should take me serious or not. We'll see."

"She will learn the hard way. Well, I gotta go act like I still work here for another two weeks. I will have to catch up with you two later," Brie said.

"Phaedra, did Brie tell you she is quitting her job?" Lexie asked before Brie could hang up.

"Girl, I don't remember anything that happened before nine this morning," Phaedra said waiving her hands.

"I did. We talked briefly before the appointment," Brie reminded her.

Okay, then sweetie, I'll talk to you later," Lexie said.

"Okay, love you both," Brie said and hung up.

Lexie sat her phone down on the coffee table and sat back down on the couch. "So, Phae, what are you going to do about this situation?"

"It's being taken care of," Phaedra said calmly.

"What does that mean?" Lexie asked cautiously.

"It is what it is, Lexie. I'm done for the day. I need a drink and it's not even noon."

"It's noon somewhere," Lexie said heading to the bar.

"I hate it when things go awry. When people don't just play their roles. Dutiful wife my ass.," Phaedra rolled her eyes.

"News flash, sweetie. You don't control the outcome. You gotta let the crazies be themselves," Lexie said jokingly but was serious.

"News flash, yes I do. And you do realize that we can be lumped up in the category of crazies because of the messed up stuff we do sometime."

"First, my mama tells me I'm not my dad's favorite, now you are telling me I fall in the same category as the crazies. I think I'm losing my identity," Lexie clowned sipping on the glass of merlot she poured.

Phaedra threw back her second shot of bourbon and curled her lip up at Lexie. "You need to get out of the house a little bit more. Working from home is making you coo-coo. It's not for everybody you know."

"I do miss going to the office. I miss being around people. But enough about me. Back to you. How is this situation making you feel?"

"Who are you? Lexie Freud now?" Phaedra laughed at her but saw Lexie was serious. "I hate feeling. You of all people know that. I just want to be.

I don't want everyone else's energy. Besides, everyone should be on my time."

"And now that things have gone awry, how are you going to put your world back in place?"

"I already told you," Phaedra started and took another shot of the warm liquor. "She is being taken care of. My dark side will handle her."

"Well, Phae, your dark side is scary. Don't make this worse. Right now it's a minor detail. Don't restart the cold war." Lexie picked up the crystal rectangular shaped decanter after she saw Phaedra pour a fourth shot and put it back on the bar.

"I won't, under one condition. She doesn't show up anywhere near my family," Phaedra promised feeling the effects of the fourth shot. Her head was feeling light and her arms were feeling numb.

"She has too much to lose to act that ignorant."

"I hope so for her sakes." Phaedra tucked a gray square toss pillow under her head as she laid down on the couch.

Lexie pulled the throw off the arm of the couch and covered Phaedra up. She left out to let her friend sleep off her anger.

Business woman to business woman

"Look at Ms. Boss Lady!" Kenny said smiling from ear to ear. "Got that look going today. So high. Touch the sky. Game face. On!"

"Will you sit your silly behind down somewhere," Brie said blushing and laughing.

"Feels good, doesn't it?" He asked sitting down on the corner of her desk.

"Yes, it does. Like I'm unstoppable."

"You are! Your destiny is in your hands. The sky is the limit for you."

"You sound like a billboard," Brie told him.

"I am in advertising" Kenny smiled. "So what are your plans?"

"Well, I have five clients right now. I've gone around to a few different florist and bakeries to see who is the best. I want to also interview a few independent chefs and check out some caterers to add to my database. I also want to meet with the local magazines and see what kind of advertising budget I need and what expo's are coming up."

"Sounds like you have a long to do list. I'm impressed that you have been able to do so much in such a short time."

"The list is not as bad as it sounds. I am having so much fun doing it. When I sit up at night I'm in a good mood," Brie explained.

"Then you, my dear, have found your calling," Kenny announced.

Ellie had walked up and joined the conversation. "I know she is going to do a super job. Every lunch, party and event she has put together around here has been beyond words."

Brie blushed again fighting the uncomfortable feeling of being praised. "Thank you. And you know if you need me, I'm willing to plan any event you have."

"I thank you, but Brie, I am confident that you will be too busy," Ellie said hugging her.

"I'm proud of her. I'm going to ask my girlfriend to marry me just so Brie can plan the wedding," Kenny said folding his arms and pushing up his chest.

"Really! Kenny, that is exciting," Ellie cheered.

"Well, I'm not going to actually go through with it. You know, just give Brie some business. Help her out."

Ellie's face turned bright red and her smile straightened. She punched him in shoulder and told him, "You are fired, Kenny. Go pack up." Ellie walked back to her office shaking her head at him.

Kenny laughed a low laugh. "So, Brie. I need a job. You gonna help a brother out?"

Brie punched the other arm. "Nope."

"You just gonna leave a black man in the unemployment line like that?"

"Fired Kenny," Brie answered but then couldn't help but laugh. "You are an ass."

Throughout the day, Brie's co-workers one by one heard the news and congratulated her. Ellie had offered to take her to lunch. She looked over Brie's business plan while they ate and talked. Brie picked Ellie's brain for inexpensive ways to advertise and who to talk to at the local magazines. Ellie had always shown Brie kindness, but today was different. This time the conversation was on an equal level. Business woman to business woman. Brie sat up straighter and was more attentive. They agreed to meet once a month for the next 12 months as a mentorship. Brie was grateful.

When Chris came to pick her up, Brie was walking on water. Her smile was wider, her head was higher. "Good day?" He asked noticing.

"Yes. Yes, it was." She leaned over in the truck to kiss him. "How about you?"

Chris smiled to match hers taking credit for the way she was feeling. "I had a good day also."

They were pulling out of the parking lot and Brie pulled down the mirror to check her hair. "I just realized the kids will have to change schools. I don't think that will be easy for them."

"They just have a few more months left in the school year. We can both share the responsibility of getting them to school," he suggested.

"And we probably need to discuss some rules with the kids," she added uncomfortably.

"Definitely," he agreed. "Especially discipline expectations."

That was the one thing that made her stomach drop. Chonda's father was the last guy that Brie lived with. He was verbally and physically abusive the her and Ike. In her heart, she knew Chris was not like that, but it did not stop her from worrying.

"I don't want to come off like they are my kids so don't touch them," Brie told him.

"That sounds like a however is going to follow."

"Not really. I'm just scared of someone else spanking my kids. I will do it with love. Other people will do it with anger."

"I understand your thinking. Maybe it will help you to know that I don't believe in corporal punishment. My parents never spanked me. My mother was all about taking away privileges," Chris explained.

"Did you get locked in a room or tied to a chair?"

Chris chuckled, "Heavens no. I got sent to my room and couldn't play with my toys or watch TV."

Brie laughed at herself. "Sorry, I didn't mean to sound crazy. Something I saw on the news the other night."

"Brie, I love you and the three of them. I would never do anything to harm any of you. I won't beat them, molest, curse them or any other thing that would cause them or you to hate me. My only intent is love," he promised.

"I can handle that. Being loved would be a nice change for once," she whispered holding in her tears.

"I told you, I just want to the man that takes care of you."

"Can we go out to dinner tonight? We can tell that kids then."

"That sounds like a plan. Where would you like to go?"

"How about we allow them to choose, except no fast food. The more stories I read the less I want it."

"Good, because I don't think it is healthy for them." Chris smiled because he was making suggestions for the kids already. "And since we are on the subject of the kids, I was going to talk to you about them attending private school next school year."

"Private school?"

"Yes. I think they will get a better education which will give them an opportunity to pick any college they want. Plus, it would give you an opportunity to build relationships with people that you will most likely be working with in the future."

"I never considered it," Brie hunched.

"I can talk to some of my colleagues at work who have kids to find out which are the better ones," he offered.

They continued their conversation about the kid's education and also about what activities they would sign them up for. Brie was starting to understand what the phrase under privilege meant. Her kids did not have much because she didn't have the money for extras. There days off of school were usually spent at home watching TV, not camps, piano lessons or sports. Chris was wanting to give them just that. The opportunity to be able to do and be whatever they wanted. She put the smile back on her face that she was wearing when he picked her up. They arrived at the daycare to pick up Deena and they both got out of the car. Chris held her hand as they walked in. Brie, still walking on air.

So, what happened

Mark was meeting with Carlos this evening and Lexie was impatiently waiting for him to call or text. After she and Anton had eaten dinner, she had him go take his bath. She was sitting on the couch flipping through a magazine daydreaming about Mark coming home with bruised, swollen knuckles. Then she remembered her mother calling her immature, so she stopped smiling about the fantasy.

An hour had gone by and Anton was dressed and ready for bed. Lexie put him in front of TV and told him he could watch a show for 30 minutes and then they would read a book. When Anton's show was off, Lexie looked at her phone and still nothing from Mark. Anton grabbed a book off the shelf. It was the one about the spotted elephant. She walked him upstairs to his room and tucked him into bed. She climbed up next to him and they read the book together. She made the funny heavy voice when she read the parts of the elephant. Anton laughed. When they were done, she kissed him good night and turned off his light. Still, no Mark.

Lexie went to her room and began to pace back and forth between the dresser and the bed. Finally, she heard the garage door opening. She ran towards the kitchen to be there when he walked through the door. He hadn't come in yet. She sat down in the chair at the kitchen table. He still had not come in. She got up and opened the door to the garage. Mark was still sitting in the car gathering his things.

"So, what happened? I thought you would have called by now," she asked opening the car door.

"I had to get my thoughts together on the drive over," he said trying to get out of the car with his jacket and his laptop bag.

"So, what happened," she asked again impatiently.

"Lexie, can I get in the house first?" Mark was trying to get past her to get in the door.

"I'm sorry," she said turning to walk back in the house. "You look very frustrated."

Mark laid his bag and keys down on the counter. "I am. Carlos is a piece of work."

"I appreciate you doing this. I know it wasn't easy."

Mark grabbed a beer out of the refrigerator and Lexie passed him the bottle opener. He sat down at the kitchen table and Lexie sat across from him starring in his mouth waiting for him to speak. Mark put the beer down after a couple of swallows. "He is not willing to relinquish his rights to Anton. He doesn't want to be a part of Anton's life, right now, he says. He has a new family and does not want to complicate things. I asked him if his new family knew about Anton. He wouldn't answer me."

Lexie's eyes saddened. "I'm not surprised. I'm sure they don't know about Anton. Carlos has never been one to offer the full truth about himself. But that does not make any sense that he would want to hold onto his rights."

"It does. It's a pride thing. It's okay to suck, but it's another thing to actually put it on paper admitting to it. That would give Anton leverage to come back with proof that he gave him up. This way, he can just keep giving excuses."

Lexie shook her head. "I really hate that man."

"Well, you aren't hurting him by hating him. Look, Lexie, I know we don't need the money. It can just go into an account for Anton so when he graduated from college he will have a nice chunk of change." Mark reached over and grabbed her hand across the table. "I told Carlos we will see him in court. His days of not being financially responsible are over. Hating him is not hurting him, but suing him for child support will make him have to acknowledge his responsibilities."

"He'll just start getting paid under the table."

"But he will have to tell his wife and he will have to be accountable."

"Carlos is not the accountable type."

"No wonder he's got a million excuses. You make up just as many excuses for him as he makes for himself." Mark was becoming even more frustrated. "What attracted you to this guy?"

Lexie put her head down and wiped the tears forming. "Mark, there is something that I never told you. Something I never told anyone except my big mouth sister. Carlos was married when we were together. I watched his first wife fight for alimony and child support and not get it. I guess that is why I never bothered."

"He was married?"

"Yes. Not my proudest moment. He told me they were separated and he was filing for divorce. I believed him. I was one of those dumb women that people write about in books and movies. The one foolish enough to want to believe that the man you are in love with is telling you the truth. Even when I realized that it was all lies, I pretended it wasn't. My ego was bruised and I was trying to save face." She paused and looked in his green eyes waiting for a response. There was none. "I wanted the fantasy. I wanted him. I was already in and I paid dearly for my sin. My son is paying for my sin."

"So you are going to sit here and keep paying for a mistake you made? You are smarter than that."

Lexie didn't know how to answer. "I...I don't know. I just want Carlos far gone."

"And how fair is that to Anton?"

"What is not fair is forcing Anton to spend time with a man that does not acknowledge him."

"I'm not asking you to force Anton to spend time with him. I'm asking you to force Carlos to pay. This was not your sin alone."

"I'm done talking about this," Lexie said pushing back from the table.

"No we aren't," Mark said his voice dropping an octave.

Lexie scooted her chair back up to the table. "What's the point?" She asked.

"The point is you are taking your feelings for this man and using them as an excuse that you are protecting Anton."

"I'm protecting my son from a man that abandoned him. I don't know what that feels like. I don't know what it will do to him. I just don't want him to have to feel like he was not worth loving. I don't want him to feel rejected."

"He may feel like that Lexie, ha may not. It sounds to me like you are the one feeling abandoned and rejected."

"That hurt Mark!" Lexie stood up pushing the chair back with her legs. You are an asshole." Lexie walked away and headed back to their bedroom. She locked the door and laid on the bed curled up in the fetal position. "Why can't I have a happy ending?" She asked herself.

Mark knocked on the door but Lexie wouldn't open it. He sent her a text but the alert was going off from the kitchen. "Lexie, I wasn't trying to hurt you," he said through the door. He went and got his laptop and headed for the office the two of them shared. There was a couch for him to sleep on in there.

I threw away a few things

Those two weeks had gone by quickly and Brie was at home doing laundry. She had been thinking about what she would pack and take with her and what would get donated or trashed while she was folding her clothes. She knew the furniture was not going. She could probably sell it. Chris had already purchased furniture for what would be Deena's room. She was feeling like a queen moving into a palace and was giddy about the whole thing. For once, she told herself, she was the lucky one. She was learning to stop waiting for others to tell her what her worth was.

Brie had several boxes set up in the living room. Deena was being Mommy's little helper throwing unwanted, and some wanted, items away. She was looking forward to the big house, as she called it.

"Mommy, why do you need your stuff? Why don't we just take our clothes like we always do? Or if we just come over, Chris will just buy us all new stuff."

"Because, I like my stuff. Plus, I want it to be as much our house as it is his house."

"I'm just saying his stuff is way cooler, Mommy."

"Thanks, Deena. Thanks," Brie said shaking her head at the little girl. "Why don't you go see what of your stuff you are going to throw away."

"I just have my toys, Mommy. I'm going to have my own room so all my toys will fit in it and then I can get more toys, too," she planned.

"Well, we will see. First, we get settled in, then you can earn some new toys."

Deena sighed the way she always heard Chonda sigh. "Okay, but do I have to throw away all my toys?"

"No, honey. Only the ones that you don't play with anymore. Now, scoot," Brie said taping her daughter playfully on the butt.

Brie stood up and surveyed her stuff in the living room. She had already packed her pictures of them that were in frames. She wasn't sure where Chris would allow her to put them. Her lamps were the only expensive thing in the room. A tax season splurge. The base was hammered silver with a round bottom. The shade was white with red emerald shaped beads across the bottom. She couldn't give those up.

Deena appeared with doll in tow. "Mommy, I'm done."

"I don't' think you are done."

"I threw away a few things," she promised.

"If you say so. Get one of those boxes and I will tape it for you so you can start packing your stuff."

Deena did as she was told and brought her mom the flattened box. While Brie was tapping the box together, she heard a sniffle. She looked down at her four-year-old and saw she was crying. Brie put the tape down and sat on the couch. She picked up Deena and sat her in her lap.

"What's the matter?" Brie asked rocking her back and forth.

"I'm going to miss my friends," Deena answered wiping her face and sniffing harder.

"I promise you will make new ones. You will like this new life."

"Why can't we keep our old life?"

"Our old life is filled with worry, struggle and not being able to afford anything," Brie explained. "I want to give this life up for a better life. I want a great life, Deena. I want to be able to provide my children a great life."

"Do you love Chris?"

"I really do, honey. He makes me smile and he loves the three of you."
Brie gave her daughter a wide smile and kissed her watery eyes.

"I love Chris also, Mommy. He's nice. I don't think he will throw us out."

"What are you talking about?"

"On TV the man threw the woman out when he didn't like her no more."

"You and your sister are not allowed to watch Lifetime," Brie fussed and
laughed at the same time. She ticked her daughter and blew raspberries
on her belly.

"Chonda likes the station, not me," Deena giggled.

"Umm, hmm. I'm going to have to block some channels on your TV's, Ms.
Lady."

"Are we going to be with Chris forever?"

"I hope so, honey. I really hope so," Brie told her. "Now, go fill this box so
we can start our new life."

"Okay, Mommy," Deena agreed dragging the box to her room.

A gift of control

"I have something for you," Phaedra told Ron as she entered his house.

"Yeah, what is it?" He asked closing the door behind her.

Phaedra pulled out a small box wrapped in shiny and matte gray wrapping paper topped with a black bow. "A gift."

"Wow, and it's not even my birthday. What did I do to deserve this?"

"Just open it," she told him.

Ron unwrapped the small rectangular box and pulled out a small curved purple and pink object. "What the hell is this?" He asked examining it.

"This is a toy," she said smiling and raising her eyebrows. "This piece goes in my panties and this book is the code for you to download the app. Whenever you want to, you can open the app and you get to control the vibration of this toy."

Ron smiled very huge. "So, I can make this vibrate while it's in your panties."

"Yes. If I'm at work and I cross your mind, you just press a button. Or if I'm at home and you are here, again, press the button."

"What if I press this so called button and you are with a buyer? I guess my real question is, do I need to call you first?" He asked stepping closer taking the device out of her hand.

"That would take the fun out of it. You get to have control," she whispered.

Ron rubbed his hand up the back of her neck and tightened his grip in her hair pulling her head back enough to kiss her. Phaedra almost lost her balance but he put his other arm around her back. He lifted her in his arms and carried her to couch. "It's not like you to release control," he said pressing his forehead to hers as he laid her down.

"No, it's not, but if I want something different, I have to take chances. I'll take it back if you abuse it or hurt me. If I love you this time Ron, you have to be true."

"I can be a man of my word this time. I just want a forever with you."

"Then tell me there is not something you are leaving out. Tell me there is not something that you are forgetting to tell me," She begged.

"Phaedra, I promise there is nothing I'm hiding. Everything I've told you these last few months are true. I wanted my wife back. I wanted my family back. Why can't you believe this man can wake-up one day and regret all the bad decisions he made?"

"Because I'm realistic and I always think people have a hidden agenda because I usually have one."

"Yeah? So, what's yours?" He asked.

"It was originally curiosity. Then to hurt you the way you hurt me. Then I realized that I had already done that. Then, I just didn't want to play that game anymore. I saw the smiles on my children's faces. I saw the smile on my own face," she confessed.

Phaedra lifted up on her knees and leaned in to kiss Ron pushing him on his back. He followed her lead and laid down on the gray plush sectional. Again, he went for her hair as she maneuvered to put each of her legs on each side of him. She could feel Ron's reaction in his pants. She pulled his belt loose and went for his zipper only to discover he was wearing button fly.

"Why do you wear these things?" She complained.

"Don't get mad when you have to work a little harder for what you want," he teased.

Phaedra finally got the four buttons undone and reached in to massage him. Just as she sat up to pull her shirt over her head, she heard the key in the front door. They both looked at each other jumping up. Ron buttoned his pants and Phaedra smoothed her hair.

"Dad, are you home?" Caleb called out.

"In the living room," Ron answered.

"Damn!" Phaedra laughed.

Ron laughed with her.

"Hey, Mom. Where you guys...talking?" Caleb smirked.

"Yeah, we were just talking," Phaedra smiled. "Where is your sister?"

"At home. I think she is doing her homework."

"What's up?" Ron asked.

"The dance is this weekend. You said you'd take me to the mall," Caleb reminded him.

"Oh, yeah, I did. Okay, let me get my keys and log off from work," Ron told him leaving the room.

Caleb sat down next to his mother on the couch. "So, when are we going to live in one house?"

"Don't rush it. I don't want to make any mistakes this time," Phaedra told him laying her head on his shoulders.

"I told one of my teachers my parents were dating. She thought that was cool and said not many kids of divorced parents get to see their parents get back together. I guess Maya and I are lucky."

"Count your blessings and always be grateful for the small things," she told him playing in his curly hair.

"I will," he promised and kissed her cheek. "I'm going to make myself a sandwich. You want one?"

"No thank you. I'm heading home."

They both got up and headed for the kitchen. Phaedra grabbed her toy and the book off the counter hoping Caleb wasn't paying attention. Ron walked in with sneakers in one hand and keys in the other. He asked Caleb to make him a sandwich while he walked Phaedra to the car. Caleb was happy to see the two of them together.

"You guys have fun," Phaedra said passing the instruction book for her device to him."

"Maybe we can pick up where we left off later," Ron said kissing her goodbye.

"Maybe," she told him. Phaedra lifted the new toy and said, "Buzz me later.

Ron grinned. "I will do that."

Phaedra climbed into the SUV and pulled away. She felt happy and this time did not block herself from feeling. This one man was satisfying all of her needs.

I love you

"I'm going to go stay with my buddy Jason for a while," Mark announced to Lexie.

The tension had increased since the night Mark talked with Carlos. Lexie stopped wanting him to touch her. She snapped at him any time he tried to talk to her. Mark needed a break. This was the first time she had looked at him, but with fear in her eyes.

"You are leaving me?" She asked.

"I thought we finally pushed pass the part where you shut me out when you are hurting. I'm tired of being your enemy."

Lexie sat on the couch and began to cry. "You hurt me and now you are leaving me?"

Mark sat down on the end cushion leaving some distance between them. "You have rejected my every attempt to talk about this. I don't even know how I hurt you. I want to get through this but I don't know what else to do, Lex."

"Just go, Mark. If that is what you need to do, then just go," she yelled.

Mark sighed. He didn't want to leave and he didn't want to stay. "Will you talk to me now?"

Lexie curled up on the couch pulling her feet up so she didn't touch him. "What do you want me to say?"

"I want you to tell me what is wrong."

"So, you can fix it? That's what you do, you fix things."

"I'd like us to have a conversation where you talk to me and not growl at me," he told her.

"Why do you get to make all the rules?" She asked.

"I don't. I'm asking you to talk to me," Mark begged.

"Just go Mark. If you need to run away, then go. Anton and I don't need you."

"That's not fair, Lexie. All you have ever done is run away." Mark stood up and walked to the room. His suit case was already packed. He rolled it out and picked up his keys. Mark knelt down in front of the couch and kissed the top of her head. "I love you," he said and walked out.

When Lexie heard the garage door open she felt a lump in her throat. The pit of her stomach fell out. She rolled off the couch and fell onto the floor. Her world had just ended. Lexie screamed into the rug and pounded on the floor with her fist. She had just run Mark off again.

Lexie woke up the next morning still in the same spot. The doorbell had startled her before she was completely conscious. She ran for it hoping it was Mark. It was Brie.

"Girl, what happened to you? You look like a semi-truck hit you head on in the face," Brie informed her. Lexie walked to the couch without saying a word. Brie had bagels and coffee in her hand and placed them down on the coffee table. "Honey, what is wrong?"

"Mark...Mark," she couldn't say the words and cried uncontrollably.

Brie pulled Lexie's head down on her chest and patted her back. She could only think the worse because Lexie never told anyone that she had been fighting with him. "It's okay. What happened to Mark?"

"Brie, Mark left me," she finally said.

"Oh, no," Brie gasped. "We will get through this. I promise we will. Tell me what happened."

"He hates me. Brie, he hates me and it's my fault. It's my fault Brie." Lexie's crying was getting harder and harder and her words were not comprehensible.

"Mark could never hate you."

"He moved out, Brie...he moved out," she continued to sob between each word.

Brie began to rock Lexie a little more as she pat her back a little harder. Brie lifted Lexie's head and tried to smooth down her bob styled hair. "Why don't we get you in the shower and get some coffee in you. Then you can tell me what happened and we will try and figure this out together."

"What is there to figure out? He's gone," Lexie told her laying back on the couch.

"Mark wouldn't leave you forever. You guys just have to work this out. You always do."

"Not this time Brie. It's over this time," Lexie said putting her face into the pillow. "Nobody love me. Nobody ever stays in my life. I'm not worth it."

"Lexie, you are being unreasonable. You know we all love you."

"Not this time, Brie. Not this time," she said shaking her head no. "I run everybody off." Lexie laid back down and curled up into a ball.

The front door closed causing Brie to be startled. Carol was calling out for her daughter. "Alexia!"

"We are in here, Ms. Carol," Brie answered.

Carol walked in and saw Lexie laying there rocking back and forth. "Did she call you?" She asked Brie.

"No, ma'am. I was coming over this morning anyways. We were doing some planning stuff," she said cautiously not wanting to say the word wedding.

"Brie, do you mind if I speak with my daughter alone?"

"No, ma'am. Not at all. I brought her breakfast if you can get her to eat later," she said pointing to the brown bag on the coffee table. "I'll check on her later."

"Thank you so much," Carol said and walked her to the door. Carol locked the door behind Brie and walked back and sat down on the couch with Lexie. She pulled her up and put her daughter's head on her lap. "Mark called me this morning. He was crying also. He asked me to check on you. He is worried."

"What for? He is the one that left," Lexie told her as she wiped her runny nose on her mother's taupe slacks.

"Alexia, tell me what happened."

"He hurt me," she said sniffing snot back up her nose.

"And how did he do that?"

"He was mean to me," she wiped her eyes.

Carol was patient with her. "What did he say that was mean?"

"He said Carlos didn't reject Anton. It was me that Carlos didn't want. I'm the reason that Anton's father doesn't want him," she answered and started the convulsing crying again.

Carol attempted to smooth down the wiry hair that was all over Lexie's head. "There, there, Alexia. I can see where a comment like that would hurt. Can I ask where Mark would have insight on that kind of information? Were those Carlos's words?"

Lexie sat up and looked at her mother. She used her shirt to wipe her tears and snot leaving white lines on her face. Her eyes were swollen and her hair was still standing up all over the place. "I don't know why he said it."

Carol knew that this was Lexie's interpretation. She picked up the cup of coffee and made Lexie drink some. "I think you should get in the shower, wash your face, and then put on some clean clothes. Then we are going to church. It's been a long time since you have been there. So, let's stand up," she told her pulling her up off the couch.

Lexie resisted, but stood up anyway. "Mom, church can't fix anything."

"No, you are right. Church can't fix anything."

"So, why are you dragging me there?"

"Because prayer makes all things possible. I have stood back as you have talked to the Universe, meditated to Buddha, and journaled all day long. Now let's try talking to the Spirit that created you. It just might work, especially when things fall apart, you might find an answer."

"I don't have to go to church to talk to my Heavenly Father. I can do that from here," she whined.

"True also, but we aren't going to church so that you can pray. We are going so others can pray with and for you. So, go. Go shower. Now."

Lexie followed orders and headed for her shower with the cup of coffee in her hand. Church was the last place she was interested in going. Not that she stopped believing in God, but the building and the people became a turn off. However, being the obedient daughter she is, Lexie was going to church today.

She turned on the hot water as hot as she could take it. She needed to feel something. Lexie needed to wash away two weeks of sadness. She had run Mark off because she felt like she had been forced to confess to her own shame. Now she was in this big house by herself. Anton was with her sister. Mark was with a friend. She was in her own self-inflicted hell. Lexie let the hot water run down her head and race over her body. "What if he doesn't come back this time?" She asked herself. "What if I really fucked up this time?"

Her mother knocked on the bathroom door, "Alexia, I'm going to find you something to wear."

Lexie heard her but didn't answer back. She picked up her shower gel and inhaled the citrus scent. It didn't wake her up like on the commercial, but the scent made her smile. Her mother knocked on the door again to check on her. She announced she was laying the clothes on the bed and was going to cook some breakfast. Lexie yelled out okay.

She wanted to stay in the shower all day but she turned the water off because it was turning warm. She grabbed her towel and starred in the mirror wondering what she was going to do with the wet moppy hair on her head. She walked out and saw the outfit her mother laid on her bed. It was her floral print lavender sheath dress. She paired a short beige cardigan with it to match the flowers and her neutral colored Steve Madden pumps. Lexie shook her head no and swapped the dress out with a black sheath dress that matched her mood. She wasn't feeling flowers and pastels.

Lexie dried her hair and pinned it back in a bun. She got dressed and walked to the kitchen and sat down at the table. She could smell the butter and onions that her mother was seasoning the shrimp with. That meant the other pot had grits. Lexie was starving because she hadn't eaten much in the last couple of weeks being a martyr to her pain.

"Do you feel any better?" Carol asked stirring the food in the pan.

"Yes, a little. My eyes look awful."

"Well, you've always been an ugly crier," her mother laughed.

"I suppose that is why I try not to cry too much."

"Holding it in is worse. You are going to stress yourself out trying to pretend you are holding it all together."

Lexie didn't want to talk anymore. She just wanted to eat. "Is that shrimp and grits?"

"Yes. Your favorite breakfast. I figured you would like something that would cheer you up."

"It does. Thank you. When did Mark call you?" She had been wanting to ask since her mother told her.

"This morning. He told me he was at his friend's house since last night. He said the two of you had not been doing well for a while now and he felt he had to leave," she explained as she fixed a plate for Lexie. Carol sat the plate down in front of Lexie along with a glass of apple juice. She wiped her hands on the Mark's blue grill master apron that was protecting her wine colored blouse from splatters.

Lexie took a fork full of grits and stabbed one piece of shrimp and put it in her mouth. She savored the flavors of the butter and pepper from the shrimp and each grain of the grits. She chewed until the one piece of shrimp was just minced meat. She took another bite before she decided she should speak up for herself not knowing what Mark might have told her mother. "I run everybody off. Nobody ever wants to take the time to put up with me."

"You are feeling sorry for yourself. Alexia, Mark has fought for you for over two years. Even he will have his limits. My question is why do you feel the need to keep testing it?"

"I don't! He was being unreasonable," she pouted and then realized she was acting childish. She put her fork down and then put her head down. "Actually I was the one being unreasonable. I didn't like the fact that he went and spoke with Carlos and I didn't like the news he came back with. He said a few things that were true and they hurt. Carlos is just one of those chapters I want to move past. Never to deal with it again. Now I'm marrying Mark, and then there is Anton and it's like I'm dealing with stuff I wasn't prepared for. I just wanted everything to work out."

Carol laid her hands on her lap and in a soft voice told Lexie, "What makes a strong marriage is putting all the dirt out there front and center and then getting on the floor wrestling through it until you are both covered in each other's filth. Then no one can judge because you have a mutual trust. You love each other despite the imperfections."

Lexie laughed because she was visioning her parents mud wrestling. "What if some of that dirt is a big secret?"

"All the dirt is a secret. Better to get it out now then to wait. Cheaper than a divorce lawyer." Carol cracked a smile and put her hand on Lexie's shoulder. "Alexia, your biggest problem is that you don't want anyone to know that you ever made a mistake."

"Mistakes are frowned upon, Mom," Lexie reminded her.

Carol sighed because she knew that comment was aimed at her. "Do you want your relationship with Mark to work or do you want to sit around for the rest of your life wallowing in the shadows of your memories?"

"I want Mark back. I don't want to know life without him," Lexie told her as her eyes began to water.

"Do you know where this friend lives?"

"Yes, ma'am, but Mom, you aren't suggesting that I go knocking on Jason's door are you?"

"Do you want Mark to come home?"

"Yes, ma'am."

"Then put your pride aside and go tell him that," she encouraged. Carol sat back and took another breath. "Alexia, your father packed his bags once."

"Really? Dad?" Lexie sat up and wiped the water in her eyes away with her napkin.

"Yes, your dad. He and I were arguing every day. If he said the sun was shining, I'd argue him down that it was raining while standing outside baking in the hot Florida sun's rays. We just hit a point after three years of marriage where I was sick of looking at him and he was sick of my prudent ways." Carol put her hand over mouth and then laughed when she heard herself say it out loud. "Believe it or not, it all started over something as simple as buying a couch."

Lexie laughed also. It was the first time she had related to her. "You guys didn't have the same taste?"

"Far from it. Your father was country and cheap," she said shaking her head. "He kept looking at the price tags and I was looking at style and value. He wanted this cheap ugly wood furniture with orange and brown plaid cushions. Didn't even care if it matched. Just knew how much he was not going to spend. We looked for a solid two months. We were both frustrated. At that point, we hated each other and we still didn't have any new furniture."

"How did you fix it?"

"See, that's the thing, Alexia. You don't fix it. You work on it. It will always have some cracks. It will never be perfect, and neither will you."

Lexie understood that part. "I just don't remember Dad complaining. He was laid back about things. It's like he provided the money and smiled at whatever you bought."

"Richard complained, but he also appreciated my talents. I came home and started pulling all of my clothes out of the closet and the dresser drawers and put them on the bed. Laid that big red hard plastic suit case out and then he freaked out. He asked me where was I going to go. I reminded that man that I had a mother and a father that would take me back in a heartbeat so putting up with his foolishness was not mandatory.

Do you know that fool hearted father of yours asked me if I needed cab fare?" Carol laughed remembering that day when she looked at her husband in shock.

Lexie laughed with her. "What did you do?"

"I slapped him as hard as I possibly could. He picked up his keys and he left out the door." She got a little more serious telling the rest of her story. "For two days he didn't come home. The third morning I woke up and went to his job. He was angry with me and had a right to be. I grabbed his face with both of my hands and kissed him as hard as I could and told him I loved him. I don't know if he was more upset about me showing up at his job or for making him cry. Whatever the reason was, I begged him to come home and we work this out. He did that night. We slung mud laying it all out about what got on each other's nerves. He cried, I cried and by the morning we had a plan. I was given permission to shop for furniture without him and he would not complain as long as I stayed within his budget. I honored that and always honored it. I furnished and decorated that house and your father was so proud when his friends came over and bragged about how beautiful it was. I was willing to do it his way and he was willing to give me room to do my thing."

"Wow, hard to believe Roni and I almost weren't here. But Mom, Mark and I are not arguing about furniture."

"That's not the point of the story. It doesn't matter what the argument is about." Carol scooted her chair closer to Lexie's. It's about fighting to hold onto something you truly want. I loved Richard. Still do. There was no other man on this earth I could have loved more. He was mine and I would have moved heaven and hell to have him. He called my bluff and walked out. I knew I could find another man, but I didn't want another man. I sat on my bed that night and imagined another woman loving on my man. That wasn't about to happen either."

She reached for Lexie's face, "You have two years invested in Mark. You have fought and refined to get here. Are you really going to allow your feeling for Carlos to prevent the man that wants to build a life with you, that loves you, that wants the role of father for your son, stand in the way of your happily ever after?"

"I don't have feelings for Carlos!"

"Yes you do. You feel like you don't measure up because Carlos for whatever reason gave you up. You are not going to be happy because of how he left you feeling. Alexia, don't keep making Mark responsible for what happened between you and Carlos. You are treating Mark like a paper doll. You have taken Carlos and folded the little flaps over Mark's shoulders and trying to get the same results so you can say I told you so. Stop trying to prove you are not lovable. Nobody wins."

Lexie understood what her mother was saying. She realized that her love life was really based on her feeling of not being good enough. A label she wore by choice. "Maybe I will take Roni's advice and find a good therapist."

"In the meantime?" Her mother asked.

"I know you want me to go to church, but I have to go find Mark," Lexie told her getting up from the table and leaving her half eaten plate of shrimp and grits.

"I'm good with you not going. I'll have the congregation say a prayer for you." Carol stood up and hugged Lexie. It was just as surprising as getting hugs from Phaedra. "I'll clean up the kitchen. You go."

"Thank you, Mommy," she said grabbing her keys and purse. Lexie went out the door and started her BMW while waiting for the garage door to open. She pulled out hoping she remembered which apartment was Jason's.

I've been dreaming this vision for a long time

When Brie pulled up in the driveway, Chris and the kids were outside. He was putting up a basketball hoop and Ike and Chonda were giving him directions. That was their version of helping. Chris had moved his little red sports car to the unattached garage that was caddy corner to the house to make room for Brie's car. That is where he was hanging up the goal. Deena was sitting in the front yard playing with a little girl that lived a couple of houses down. The two were playing with their dolls near the flower bed where Chris could keep his eye on them.

"You are back early," Chris said as Brie walked over to see what everybody was doing.

"Yeah. Trouble in paradise," she explained giving him a hello kiss when he came down the ladder.

Her kids greeted her and Deena brought her new friend, Susie, over to introduce her. Brie felt a tug on her heart when it dawned on her she was home. She was in suburbia heaven with a family that now included a father figure. A basketball goal was going up over the garage door, the kids had a yard to play in and she was the owner of her own business. She was in the middle of a déjà vu' moment because she had had this vision so many times before.

Brie turned towards Chris and gave him a bear hug and a sloppy kiss to the background music of four kids going "Eeewww." She didn't care.

"What was that for?" Chris asked.

"Just because I love you. Have the kids eaten?"

"Yes. Sarah also just gave them a snack. They shouldn't be hungry," he told her.

"Nope, were not," Chonda volunteered for all of them.

"Mom, do you think my friends Brian and De'Sean can spend the night next weekend?" Ike asked.

"Let's get settled first. Then we will talk about it."

"Yes, ma'am," Ike said. "Chris, is it ready?"

"Almost my man. Let me screw in the last side and then you and I will play a game of 21." Chris climbed back up the ladder to finish his task at hand.

"Cool," Ike smiled watching him as he went up.

"You guys have fun. I'm going to go put my stuff away and change clothes," Brie said.

"Is everything going to be okay?" Chris asked her.

"Yeah, well no. I don't know. I hope it will be," she carried on. "Mark left Lexie, but it's not their first break up, so I hope they will work it out."

"I'm sorry to hear that. I hope they work it out too. They seem pretty happy."

"They will. I'll pray for them. Lexie is like the rock in our little group. I used to want to be just like her," Brie said with sadness.

"Used to? What changed?" Chris put the drill down on the ladder and gave her his full attention. Ike started bouncing the ball around when he realized this was going to take longer than he hoped.

Brie walked back closer to him. "I discovered it was okay to be me. Lexie had the great job, parents, a nice car, she was a homeowner. I love the way she dresses, her confidence and she had Mark. What we had in common when we met was that we were both single mothers dealing with exes that were out of the picture. She and I just clicked. Then it's like one thing after another for her. Her father died, she got laid off of her job that she had for 12 years and now Mark has walked out on her."

"But how did she handle all of the tragedy?"

"Well, you never recover from the death of a parent. She describes it as good days and bad days. The job, you saw how resilient she was with that. It took her a minute but when she opened up, she turned it around. My admiration was how well she was prepared financially. She didn't have to lose the roof over her head and go on welfare. She didn't have to rely on Mark either. Sure, she was nervous because money was going out and nothing was coming in, but since I've known her she has had her stuff together. I wanted to be more like that."

"That is how I see you. You are well organized and you have the kids organized. You set daily goals and you achieve them. You make sure everyone is taken care of."

"But, I didn't achieve anything. I'm an administrative assistant with three kids and not even making 40 thousand a year. I'm considered to be on the poverty line. I rent an apartment and my car is five years old with payments a little more than what I can actually afford," she told him.

"No, that is not who you are," he started as he came back down the ladder. "You are Brielle Jackson, business owner, mother of three wonderful kids, the love of Chris Hollingsworth's life, very smart, capable of programming databases, a great friend to Lexie and Phaedra and all around good hearted person," he told her taking her hand into his. "You are choosing the wrong labels to attach to yourself."

Brie smiled and put her head on his chest. "Thank you. Thank you for all of this."

"I better finish putting up this goal. Ike is giving me that impatient stare. You going to be okay?"

"Yeah. I figured I'd give Lexie a call later. I left her with her mom."

"Speaking of moms, mine is planning to fly through here next week. She said she'd let me know what day, but she is thinking it will be Saturday."

"Okay. Is it just the for the day?"

"Yeah. She coming for a meal and then probably heading out."

"Good," Brie thought in her head. "I look forward to seeing her again."

"Really?" Chris laughed.

"There are children listening," she said raising her eyebrows. She smiled at him and headed back for the garage and got her bag out of her car and went into the house.

Sarah greeted her and asked her if she needed anything. Brie told her no. It was going to take some time getting used to having a maid in the house. She liked Sarah. Sarah was kind and loved the kids. They gave her a reason to bake more cookies. Brie also like the fact that Sarah was 62 years old and plump and no chance that Chris would be sneaking off with the maid.

Brie stood in the closet where her clothes now hung. She hadn't moved everything in yet. Just a few boxes. But there were clothes, finally hanging and put away in this closet as she once imagined. Chris on one side, hers on the other side. She grabbed a pair of jeans and pulled out a long sleeve navy blue t-shirt. Lexie had been her only appointment for the day so she could get casual. She made it a point not to schedule anyone on a Saturday.

Chonda knocked on the bedroom door while Brie was getting dressed. "Mom, can I come in?"

"Yes, Chonda," she called out from the closet.

"Mom, when are we going furniture shopping?"

Brie laughed at how immediately her kids adjusted to their new found tax bracket. "I was thinking next weekend, but I'm not sure now because Chris's mom is coming in town."

"Oh, I was hoping soon. I can't wait to have my dream room."

Brie was sitting on her bed and invited Chonda to sit next to her. "I know you are ready to get everything you want, but let Mommy get settled. I promise we will get the furniture you like, the comforter you want and pictures on your wall. We will make it really nice for you. I promise. Just be sure to tell Chris thank you."

"I will, Mom. I'm just excited," Chonda said.

"Me too, Chonda. I never thought I'd be somewhere like this."

"Are you and Chris going to get married?"

"I hope so, honey. I hope we are happy enough that he wants to make this forever."

"Are you going to have kids?"

"No. He doesn't want any and three is enough for me," she said hugging on her.

"So, Deena and I will be his daughters?"

"I guess so," Brie said still squeezing her in her arms.

"I'm going to be a good daughter."

"You already are," Brie smiled releasing her.

"Are you going to redecorate this room?"

"Yes. I would like to make it a little brighter. It's too masculine."

"What does masculine mean?"

"Manly. These browns and golds are very manly."

"I hope I meet some friends around here. The houses are so far apart. It's not like I can go outside and somebody will show up," Chonda told her.

"Well, I was talking to Chris and maybe we can finally get you those piano lessons you wanted. You'll meet kids your own age there."

"Actually, Mom, I want to take karate instead of piano."

"Well, how about both? We have options now. We no longer live in an either-or world."

"What is either-or?"

"Either...or," Brie wasn't sure how to clarify it. "It means we can choose more than one thing."

"I wouldn't mind doing both. Or something else I might like. What else can I do?"

"I'm not sure, Chonda, but you have a lot of questions and I just got home."

"Okay," Chonda sang. "Well, can I help you do something?"

"Yes you can. I need to find some center piece pictures for a birthday party. You can help me do that."

"Cool," Chonda told her. "I'm going to go put my stuff away."

"Okay. Meet you in the kitchen," Brie told her kissing her forehead.

Chonda jumped up to run to her room but bumped into Chris falling backwards. Chris helped her up and told her to slow down. She apologized and waited until she hit the stairs to start running again.

"Why is Chonda in such a hurry?" Chris asked Brie as he walked into the bedroom.

"I don't know. She was putting her stuff away so she can help me with my work."

Chris pulled her into his arms and hugged and kissed her. "No kids around so I can kiss you like I want to."

She smiled as she stood on her tip-toes to kiss him again. "Are you and Ike still playing basketball?"

"Yes. He already needed a bathroom break. I guess it did take me a while to put the hoop up," he smiled.

"Thank you for making us a family. I mean, I know we aren't like a real family, but my kids are so excited that you do things with them."

"There you go again, talking yourself right out of what you want," Chris pointed out. "I'd say we were a family. Unlike you, the kids jumped right in and called it home."

Both Chonda and Ike got to the bottom of the stairs and yelled, "I'm ready."

"I'll take the little boy, you take the little girl," Chris said.

"Cool," Brie said mocking Chonda. "Hey, how about a movie later?"

"Sounds like a good family day plan. Come up with where we can go for dinner after," Chris suggested smiling.

"Saturdays are family days," Chonda said following her mother to the kitchen.

He was right. She was the only one hesitating. Monday's agenda, finish unpacking. She was home.

Busted

Phaedra had been meditating in Ron's living room when she heard him coming out of his room. He was trying to be quiet, but it wasn't working. Ron walked heavy without trying. Then he bumped into the door way turning too soon. She laughed at him.

"Sorry, I was trying not to disturb you," he said rubbing his forehead.

"It's okay. I'm used to mediating in a room full of screaming kids and not be phased."

"Oh, but me hurting myself takes you right out of your trans to laugh?"

Phaedra had gotten up and walked over to him and checked his forehead. "No. My prayer time was more about me thinking than listening. I had some questions to ask and I'll listen for the answer later."

"What questions do you need answered? Maybe I can help."

"Probably not, since you were most of my questions."

"Me?" Ron was getting himself a bottle of water out of the fridge.

"Yes, you. I'm not surrendering to this relationship without praying about it."

"Do you do that with all of your relationships?" He asked then taking a sip of the cold water.

"Not all."

"How about with George?"

Phaedra was not expecting that name to come up. "Why are you asking about him?"

Ron smirked. "Just curious."

"I know you better than that. You don't just ask questions. So why your curiosity with George?"

"You seem defensive. Why?"

Phaedra walked out of the kitchen and headed for the bedroom. She slipped her jeans on and pulled off Ron's Miami Dolphin shirt and reached for her own.

Ron grabbed her arm to stop her tantrum. "Why are you leaving?"

"Because I don't like games. Let go of my arm please," Phaedra demanded.

"Why don't you sit down and stop acting up."

Phaedra snatched her arm back and put her shirt on. "I'm going home."

"I said sit down, Phaedra." Ron's tone was as heavy as his walk now. His eyes were squinting. Phaedra complied and sat down on the edge of the bed. Ron picked up a manila envelope and threw it on the bed next to her. She recognized it as the envelope with her information on Diana Austin.

"You are snooping through my stuff?" She yelled.

"You sound like Maya."

"Why do you have this?"

"The question is why do you? If you broke it off with this man, why do you need that?" Phaedra didn't answer him. "Well, let me ask you a different question. Why are you running around playing high and mighty and making me beg for forgiveness every time you feel the need to throw guilt down my throat so that you can be in control when you yourself are sleeping with a married man? You lied to me Phaedra."

"I lied about what, Ron? I never even told you his name so how can I lie if I never said anything?"

"You act like you are doing me some favor by forgiving me and I'm not the only cheater in the relationship."

"I am no longer with him. I have not cheated on you."

"So why the blackmail pictures? Why on his wife?"

Phaedra looked away from him so he walked to her side and sat down face to face. She crossed her legs and her arms attempting to turn away again. He stopped her. "Look, our relationship started the moment we decided to make this work. It has nothing to do with these pictures or my relationship with George. I told you I was committed to this. I was committed to us."

"Yeah, I heard all of that. Why a married man? And don't give me the psychology mumbo jumbo about how I ruined you because I destroyed our marriage so you decided to destroy someone else's. Why do you need these pictures?"

"That is none of your business." Phaedra attempted to get up but Ron sat her back down.

"I'm going to give you two choices. You can answer me, or I go find the woman in these pictures and ask her what is going on."

Phaedra knew he was serious and decided it was just easier to tell him what was going on. "She was going to tell you."

"Tell me what?"

"Tell you that I was sleeping with her husband. She wanted me to start dating George again so she wouldn't have to sleep with him. If I didn't she would tell my family, my friends, my co-workers and my customers that I was sleeping with her husband. She threatened to try and ruin my reputation," Phaedra explained. "I knew if she wanted to blackmail me into sleeping with him, then she had something to hide herself."

"Did you find what you were looking for?"

"Yes, you saw the pictures."

Ron shook his head and stood up. "Have you given them to her yet?"

"No, why? And don't tell me to take the high road. This woman came to my office and threatened me."

"You were sleeping with her husband. She had a right to do that."

"She needs a distraction. She's cheating on her husband."

"And now that I know, what's your agenda, Phaedra? Who are you protecting your secret from now?" Ron's voice was getting louder and more frustrated.

"My children," she whispered.

Ron sighed. "Give me the pictures."

"Why?"

"I'm going to say this for the last time. If you ever bring it up in my face again I'm going to take my kids and leave you here to sulk in your mess all by yourself." Phaedra stood in defensive mode. "I am sorry I cheated and I caused our family to split apart. I will never do anything like that again. And if you say you forgive me, you are going to have to forget it also. You never get to bring it up again."

"How are you going to take my children from me?"

"Because you were supposed to be the better parent. Not set the same damn example!" He yelled. "And this bullshit with you and the silly wife, is over."

Phaedra wanted to yell back but the words wouldn't come to her. She picked up the envelope and pulled out the pictures. The man in the picture was younger, maybe early 30's. Not very handsome, but he had nice lips. His shoulders were broad and his pecs were overworked, out of proportion with the rest of him. Diane looked happy with him. Satisfied.

The same look Phaedra had after being with RJ. That feeling of the dick was good and the itch was being scratched.

"You never told me why you want these," she said still holding onto the pictures.

"Because two women scorned are going to mess up two families and I'm trying to put mine back together. And doesn't seem like either of you thought of what it will do to your kids for this information to get out on either of you."

"And what are you going to do with them," she asked again.

"Phaedra, I met Diane," Ron said. Her eyes got big. "She introduced herself to me when I was at the grocery store a couple of days ago. I guess the both of you are running around being little information gatherers. Hand me the pictures unless you think getting even with Diane is more important than us."

Phaedra stuck the pictures back in the envelope and passed them to Ron. "So, you already knew."

"It took me a minute to put all the pieces together once I saw the pictures. You see, Diane introduced herself as a friend of yours but I knew that wasn't true because she didn't know my name and you've never mentioned hers. Then there is the car. You were so adamant about me not riding in it I figured it was from a boyfriend. I asked Caleb and he told me it had been a birthday gift but he never met the guy. And then there is that ring you are so defensive about. Anyway, I started assuming all of it must be related."

"So, what now? You have the pictures, the ring is put away. Are you going to ban me from the car?"

"No wife of mine is driving around in a car another man bought her," he huffed.

"Your wife," Phaedra chuckled.

"Yes, my wife." Ron pulled out a small black box and opened it. He followed up on his ego's conscious and bought her a bigger ring. It was an emerald cut diamond with smaller emeralds on each side of it. Phaedra's birth stone.

"Aren't we moving too fast?" She cupped her hands around the box starring in awe.

"We've already gone through the get to know you stage. What is the point of dragging this on?"

"Because we need to get to know each other all over again."

"Phaedra, you already know me. What's left?"

"I don't know," she shrugged. "I was comfortable taking baby steps. I get to have sex with you and then go home."

"And how long do you think that would have lasted? You know? Before I said forget this and went and found someone that was not looking for a fuck buddy."

"I'm used to running things, Ron. Everyone bends to my will. So it would have lasted as long as I wanted it to."

"Well, you don't have that power over me. I'm not your boy toy. I'm the man you have to choose to wake up to every morning, the one who will be there raising your children with you, the one growing old with you. I'm the one that is going to bring you soup when you are sick. If you just need a fuck buddy, go take Diane up on her offer." Ron closed the box and put it back on the dresser.

"Oh, so," she started and then stopped. Phaedra remembered she couldn't bring up the cheating because now he knew she was not as innocent as she pretended to be. "You are right."

"About what?" He asked surprised.

"Everything. I don't have to be in control any more. I finally get to rest. Someone else gets to make the decisions. I have a man that can take care of me and I can bring him around my kids." As soon as Phaedra said that, her head felt immediately clear. "That's the prayer that got answered! Damn, Lexie was correct. I was praying for something subconsciously and didn't realize it." At this point she was thinking out loud.

"What are you talking about?" Ron asked with his eyebrows lowering.

"Nothing. Nothing at all," Phaedra said grabbing his face and kissing him. "I've got to run home."

"Why?"

"Because I finally understand my shift. I get it now. Everything I believe, I preach, I practice, I get it now. It makes perfect sense. I Love you."

Ron was confused but accepted Phaedra's light bulb moment was something she needed to figure out. He watched as she tucked her shirt and then straightened the covers. She always hates a messy bed. "Is that mine or not?" She asked pointing to the box he put back on his dresser.

"Depends. What are your intentions?"

"I've already told you that I was committed to this relationship."

"You also said I was just good for sleeping with."

"That was me being, well, me." Phaedra held her left hand up and wiggled her fingers at him.

Ron smiled and pulled the ring out and slipped it on the appropriate finger. She smiled looking at it and then kissed him again. "Let's go to lunch today. The whole family."

"Sure. Are we telling the kids?" He asked following her to the garage.

"Of course. I don't think I can hide this from Maya. I'm with Caleb, this going back and forth from house to house is getting old."

"You are the one that made me buy this house."

"How about we put them both on the market and buy something together?" She suggested after she climbed into her vehicle.

"Or, we can stay where you live since the kids are already established there. Why make them move?"

"Because if you don't want me driving a car another man bought, then I know you don't want to live in a house that that same man had been making payments on for the last two and a half years." She smiled and blew him a kiss. She closed her car door and Ron hit the garage button. "You don't get to run things Ron. I'm still the queen," she said to herself as she backed out.

Should I put on my naughty nurse uniform

Lexie pulled into the apartment complex hoping her memory would be jarred once she saw the layout. It wasn't, so she wasn't positive which one was Jason's. She instead drove around hoping to see Mark's car. The candy red Cadillac stood out. Not only was it parked where she could see it, but Mark was standing by it.

She took a deep breath and pulled into the parking spot next to him. He stood up from wiping his tires. He didn't move away, but instead leaned back against the car crossing his legs. Lexie walked around her car towards him wearing her large framed black sunglasses to hide her puffy eyes. She wanted to run to his arms but feared rejection. That made her want to cry again, but she didn't. She needed Mark to hear her.

"I'm sorry I push you away when I feel like my imperfections are going to be found out. I'm so scared of you not loving me that I try to be this person that I am not. I don't know why I am like that, but I'm willing to go to therapy to figure it out."

Mark pushed off the car with his hip and stepped closer to her. "Lex, no man will ever love you as much as I do."

"I know, but even you can only take so much. I didn't want you to know about Carlos and me which is why I didn't want to bring up the whole Anton thing. But I knew if I didn't bring it up, he eventually would. When you said you needed to talk to Carlos, I got scared you were going to judge me."

"Judge you for what? Lexie, all I want is to build a life with you. I'm the one that is always being rejected," he said rubbing his temples. "I never judged you for anything. I never would have. I'm willing to do whatever it takes. I'll go to therapy with you if you want."

"No, Mark. I just want you to come home," she said and she could no longer hold in the tears.

Mark embraced her and Lexie laid her head on his shoulders. "You have to stop pushing me away when you are trying to hide pieces of your past. I don't care about your past. I care about us. I care about our future."

Lexie pulled the glassed off and wiped the tears from her cheek. "I'm sorry. I really am sorry."

Mark pulled her hands down and looked into what of her brown eyes he could see. He smiled at her. "I think I have food poisoning."

Lexie smiled back at him. "Why do you think that?"

"Jason can't cook. He mixed leftovers together last night that have probably been sitting in his fridge for too long. My stomach has been hurting all night."

"I'll stop and pick up some medicine and some ginger ale."

"I like it when you take care of me."

"Should I put on my naughty nurse uniform?"

Mark blushed. "No, save that for when I don't think I'm going to throw up on you for real."

Lexie laughed. "Then go get your stuff and come home."

Mark agreed and told her he would be there soon. She kissed him and turned to walk off but he grabbed her hand. "Lex, I just want you to know I'm imperfect also."

She smiled, "I know."

Mark laughed. "Wow. But, is it okay if we be imperfect together? No fun being the only one in the relationship making mistakes."

"I can do that. I can be imperfect," she promised.

"Good." He kissed her once more and told her he would get his stuff and head home.

Lexie pulled off and took a deep breath then called Brie on her Bluetooth to tell her that the wedding wasn't off. Lexie did as she said and stopped to pick up the pink stuff and a two-liter ginger ale. Maybe she would put on the nurse's uniform. It couldn't hurt.

You can have both

Brie hung up with Lexie and then within a few minutes received a text from Phaedra. It was a picture of her left hand wearing her ring. Brie text congratulations to her. After 10 minutes, Phaedra was calling.

"I don't believe all I get is a one-word text from you and nothing from Lexie," Phaedra complained.

"You haven't talked with Lexie?" Brie asked concerned.

"No, why?" Now Phaedra was worried.

"I was giving the two of you time to talk, then I was going to call you, but if Lexie hasn't called," Brie was saying.

"Brie! What's going on?" Phaedra was impatient.

"Mark walked out last night."

"What! Are you fucking kidding me?"

"I went by this morning and she looked a hot mess. She had been crying all night. Her mom showed up not long after me. Mark had called her and asked if she would check on Lexie.

"So, what happened then?"

"The two of them got in a fight, but I didn't get the details because her mom asked me if I would leave so she could talk with Lexie alone."

"Wow. So did they break up? Is the wedding off?"

"No. She called me back to say they worked it out."

"You, little...Brie...Dammit! Start off with they are fine now but this is what happened," Phaedra shouted. "You took me down the roller coaster and back up and left out the important part."

"I'm sorry," Brie told her wanting to giggle. "I was starting from the beginning.

"You were mighty damn slow with the beginning."

"Well, good news is, whatever pushed him out the door, he is back home."

"That's good. I'm sure Lexie is what pushed him out," Phaedra said shaking her head.

"So, who put a ring on it?"

"Ron. Who else?"

"Whatever. You know I've got a list to pick from," Brie said rolling her eyes. "Are you going to marry him?"

"Yes, I am. Why you ask like that?"

"This isn't the first time a guy has asked you to marry him. Usually you announce it, you stay excited for a week or two, then you change your mind," Brie reminded her. "I hope you get to the alter with this one. I like Ron. He's a good guy. And he has the bank account to support you."

Phaedra sighed because Brie was right. "I like him, too. Well, I love him. And it's not about the bank account, but it does help. We want the same things. We both want to raise our kids and then grow old together. If I tell the truth, he is truly the only man I have ever wanted."

"You sound happy. I'm glad to hear it."

"Thank you."

"Are we planning a wedding?"

"Hell, no. Been there, done that. However, we can plan a party," Phaedra told her.

"Good. Then I am your go to girl. Always will be," Brie smiled.

"Don't go getting sentimental."

"Why? You know the three of us are stuck together. Men have come and gone, but nothing beats friendship."

"A fat juicy dick beats friendship."

"Whatever, Phaedra," Brie laughed.

Phaedra laughed also. "I hear you and I kind of like having both. We should be able to have a man we can depend on and loves us more than the air they breathe, and also friends whom we love. Yeap, I can see having both."

"We started off as three single moms, and now look. Not single any more."

"Are you going to hold onto this one and not let him walk all over you?"

"I don't let anyone walk all over me," Brie answered in a high pitch squeal.

"If you say so. But, I am glad you found love with big man."

Brie sucked her teeth. "Why does he have to be big man?"

"Because I know it drives you crazy," Phaedra laughed.

"I would like to plan a dinner at my house. A celebration of sorts," Brie announced.

"Sure. When?"

"In two weeks. Instead of girl's night out, it will be family night out. You, Ron, Maya, Caleb, Lexie, Mark and Anton."

"Do we still get to escape to a corner of the house and have girl talk?"

"Of course. Wouldn't be a night without it."

"Good. And by the way, I'm proud of you. You went after something you truly wanted and didn't quit before getting it."

"Coming from you, that is pretty big. Thank you."

"You're welcome Brielle Jackson. Bliss is a beautiful thing."

"It sure is. I learned a lot watching you."

"Well, you didn't learn everything, but at least you learned the important stuff."

"I learned the lessons that were mine. I'll take that."

Phaedra smiled thinking about how far Brie had come. "Let me know when. I'm going to see if I can hunt down Lexie. Talk with you later."

Brie disconnected and smiled. A compliment from Phaedra was a big deal for her. It had taken years to build, but she and Phaedra were finally friends. No longer two people that hung out because they both knew Lexie. She liked the way things had turned around for her. Brie had her man, her children, and both of her friends. She also had her business, her clients and the support of many. Bliss did feel good. She never wanted to go back to the other life. Brie was genuinely happy.

We should talk

Ron had been holding onto the pictures all week. He was glad that Phaedra hadn't asked him any questions. He needed to know she trusted him. He needed to know she would stick to their agreement. Ron found Diane's schedule and knew where she would be today. He had been sitting outside of the restaurant when she was leaving. His car was parked next to hers. He got out as she approached.

"Mrs. Austin," he called.

She recognized him and was curious so she walked over to him. "Diane. How are you?"

"I'm well, and you?"

"I'm good. What do I owe this surprise visit to?"

"We should talk." Ron told her.

"Is that all we are going to do?"

Ron smiled, "Yeah."

"I have to admit, I'm disappointed. Phaedra does have good taste in her men. I won't lie, I've imagined you in the most inappropriate ways."

"Get in the car," he told her.

Diane dropped her keys in her Coach bag and got in the passenger side of Ron's Audi. "Where are we going?"

"Nowhere. Like I said, we need to talk. This game my wife and you are playing is over. Here," he said passing her the envelope.

Diane pulled the pictures out and her heart and mouth dropped. "You had me followed?"

"No, I didn't. You see, you and Phaedra are both cunning. While you were telling her secrets, she was digging up yours. I'm not going to allow you or her to ruin the lives of any of our children over this petty bullshit."

"So you stopped her from doing me in. Thank you, Ron. She really doesn't deserve a man like you," she said putting her hands on Ron's thighs.

Ron removed the hand. "You come anywhere near my family and your husband will find out you like it in the back door with Matumbo here. Nobody wins here. You can consider your threat with Phaedra sleeping with your husband not happening. And, I'm sure as hell not sleeping with you."

"Why? Am I not pretty enough for you?"

"Diane, take your pictures. You have your hands full already. I'm happy where I'm at."

"I don't think it's fair," she pouted.

"You are sleeping with another man. You've got your revenge. I'm asking you to leave my family out of it."

"So, you are just going to forgive her? Just like that?"

"I wasn't with her, but yes. I'm going to look beyond it. I'm moving on. I think you should do the same."

"What do I have to do to get all these pictures from you? I have money."

"Do I look like I'm hurting for money? When I trust that you have taken my advice, I'll destroy them," he offered.

"And how long will that take?"

"Don't worry about," he told her and then leaned over her and opened the car door. "Just go enjoy the rest of your life."

Diane stuffed her pictures into her bag and turned to get out of the car. Ron saw her conspicuously drop something on his floor. When she closed the door, she smiled and waved goodbye to him. Ron leaned down and picked up the lipstick that was planted there to get even. He shook his head. His first thought was to stop by the post office and mail it to George. Ron realized he was stooping to Diane and Phaedra's level. Instead, he downed his window and threw the lipstick out the window, then pulled off.

The teacher had a new student

Phaedra was at the office finishing up paperwork for a house she just sold. She had convinced the new homeowners to contact Brie to plan their house warming party. It was her first million dollar sale for the year. It usually didn't take her that long to sell at that price, but she promised herself she wouldn't use the phrase 'it's the economy'. She was tired of hearing everyone blaming the economy.

After a sale, her ritual was to light some sage and sit back and say her mantra. "Good things come to me naturally. I attract things in my life that will take me to my goals. I am the best in my business and will always be the best in my business."

Phaedra repeated it 49 more times. She did this whether the sale was $50,000 or a million dollars. Phaedra has always been the top selling agent at her firm, but was no longer satisfied with that. Her goals were becoming complacent. She needed to move up to a next level. She knew what she wanted just not sure what she needed to get there. The shift she was experiencing was pulling her. Both of her friends were now business owners which made her question why she was someone else's employee. It didn't make since to sit around and make somebody else rich.

She loved the freedom she had being an employee, but at the same time hated asking permission to do things she wanted to do. Phaedra was comfortable and that was a problem. It meant she wasn't reaching high enough. Phaedra needed to get out on her own. It was something she would have to pray about. She was meeting with Ron to sign over the T-bird to a seller Ron found. The car that George bought for her and she had made love to RJ on. Ron had threatened to roll it to the curve and put a free sign on it with the keys in the ignition. Instead, they found a dealer that wanted to purchase it at a really good price.

However, there was no intent in keeping the money. They found a charity they would donate it to. Phaedra accepted he was an alpha male so she got out of his way. He asked her about moving back to South Florida, but Phaedra said no. The kids had built lives here and this is where her friends were. So the compromise was to find land and build a home. They were moving forward. The only thing left was to pick a date to go to the Justice of Peace and elope then plan a party. Caleb and Maya were excited. So were Brie and Lexie.

Michelle knocked on Phaedra's door and entered. "Phaedra, your mail."

"Oh, thank you," she said reaching for it and placing it on the desk.

"You're welcome. Now that you are remarrying your husband, are you going to quit your job?"

"No. Why would I quit my job?"

"Because Ron has more than enough to take care of you."

"True, but sitting around eating bon-bons all day is not my style," Phaedra told her shaking her head.

"I think I could learn to do nothing all day."

"Then we need to find your purpose in life. I don't think it is being a person who does nothing."

"I'm just saying, it would be nice," Michelle shrugged.

"It would grow old," Phaedra disagreed. "Anyways, Ron should be here soon. I'm going off with him for a minute and then I'm meeting the Jefferson's in Clay county."

"Okay. Do you need any help out there?"

"No," Phaedra answered then realized Michelle was also looking to move to the next level in her life. "But you know where I could use some help? Do you feel like driving to Riverside?"

"Sure!" Michelle perked up.

Phaedra passed Michelle a file with an address, picture and key code in it. "I need to have a walk through on this one, but I won't have time. Would you like to do it?"

"I would love to," Michelle said taking the file and skimming it. There was a check list included in it with everything that she would be looking for on the property.

"Take some pictures and then make appointment with the landscapers and painters. We'll also need to contact Frank and have him do his inspection so if there are any repairs that need to be made."

Michelle took notes and exclaimed, "I can get all of this done."

"Great. Call me if you run into any problems or have any questions."

"Thank you, Phaedra!"

"I appreciate you asking for more responsibility. It would be a great help for me."

"Do you think I would be good at real estate? You know, selling it?"

"Doesn't matter what I think. Only matters what you believe," Phaedra smiled. The teacher had a new student.

I wanted the façade of a real family

"An interior decorator?" Lexie asked Brie.

"Yes. And said it right snobby too," Brie laughed telling Lexie about a conversation with Chris's mom.

"Well, you are now living in an area where that would be the norm. When in rich Rome, do as rich Rome does," Lexie reminded her.

"Lexie, I'm perfectly capable of decorating my kid's bedrooms," Brie told her sitting in Lexie's kitchen.

"Okay, but think of it this way, sweetie. You might be capable, but financially you leave it to someone else. Also, think about your time. You are getting a business off the ground. So you need to put it in someone else's hands."

Brie let out a deep sigh. "I just think it's silly."

Lexie laughed shaking her head. "Okay, let me paint this from another angle that you might understand." Now she put her hand on her hip and rocked her head back and forth. "Most of your clients can plan their own parties, but they call you."

Brie picked up her cell phone and opened her search engine. "Do I just put in interior decorators Jacksonville?"

Lexie laughed at her, "Yeah. Or better yet, ask around and get a reference."

Brie started laughing, I just feel guilty spending his money, even with his permission."

"Well, you shouldn't because he is asking you to. And his mom was just coaching you on how to. And Brie, girl, you have to think about this. If his mom is coming in telling you how and what to do, imagine the conversation he must be having with her."

"You mean, he is probably telling her I suck and don't know what I'm doing?" Brie grasped.

"No, girl!" Lexie just shook her head. "He is probably telling her how he wants this long term."

"You think so? Because I hope so. By the time Deena graduates we will still be young and could travel the world."

"Yes, Sweetie, I think so."

Brie smiled and felt relief that someone from the outside could see positive in her future. "So, how are things with you and Mark?"

"They are good. We took my mother's advice and talked about the whole Carlos thing. I'm content and ready to move pass Carlos."

"I never knew you hadn't moved passed him. I thought you relinquished that hold years ago?"

"I did to, but, I guess I didn't."

"Do you still love him?"

"Carlos?" Lexie said almost spilling her tea. "No. I can honestly say I don't. You know what else I can honestly say for the first time?"

"What's that?"

"That if he walked through that door and said he wanted me back, I could actually say no."

"You would have said yes before?" Brie asked surprised.

"Yeah, but for the wrong reasons. It would have been because I wanted us to look like a real family. I wanted the façade of a happy family. Don't you ever get jealous of women who have kids from the same man?"

"Well, yeah, but...I don't know. I'm just saying that if I had all my kids with Ike's dad, I don't know," Brie fumbled.

"Well, it doesn't matter. Besides what would be the point of being with someone that makes you miserable just because you are trying to give a false perception of yourself because you give a damn what other's think of you."

Brie knew that Lexie cared way too much about what others thought, but she didn't say anything. "Does that mean you think Phaedra is a fool for getting back with Ron?"

"No, not at all. She is happy and don't think he will make the same mistake," Lexie told her.

"I hope not. If he does, you do realize we will be accessories to the murder."

Lexie let out a loud chuckle. "Maybe we won't get caught if we leave pieces of the body in all three of our houses."

"That's how we get caught, Lexie. You don't know how to hide a body correctly. Someone else will have to be in charge of that."

"I'm sorry, planning a murder is not my specialty. Obviously you can plan parties and crimes."

Brie laughed with her. "Phaedra and I will handle the body, you can be in charge of going to the hardware store and purchasing cement."

"You look too serious saying that. I'm getting scared," Lexie continued to laugh.

"I better get going. I'm sitting here as if I have nothing to do today, not to mention I have my own dinner party this Saturday."

"I am so looking forward to it."

"Good, because Chris would like me to plan one and invite his friends next month," Brie said with a smile.

"I'm sorry, I think Chris is wifing you up. He done got a whiff of Brielle Jackson and don't want to let that go."

"We'll see. Maybe next year this time we will be planning my wedding," Brie said and high fived Lexie.

"I am definitely looking forward to that happening."

"Oh, did I tell you the florist I went to for your wedding gave my name and number to a young lady and she called me about doing her wedding?"

"Congratulations. You are picking up clients left and right."

"And one of Phaedra's home buyers called me about doing a house warming party for them. I'm considering hiring a temporary person to help me out."

"Your business just got started and you are already hiring an employee. I am proud."

"Just a temp. Just to do some minor things for me," she said trying to play it low key.

"Hey, it's growth. Don't sell yourself short."

"I won't. Love you," Brie said hugging Lexie. "I will see you Saturday."

"Love you too. I will be the first one there," Lexie smiled.

Lexie closed the front door after Brie pulled off and headed for her office. She had to finish getting her latest blog up and had an appointment with a client in an hour. The phone call would be to prepare them for an interview they had coming up in two days. She still needed to open the email that had pictures of what they were wearing.

She was also experiencing growth in her business. She was maintaining eight clients at a time and had coached a total of 15 people so far into new jobs. She was fortunate that as one found a job, a new person called to take their place. She liked this so much better than her 12 years at Grover and Hudson Computer Group. She was getting calls to come and speak to different groups. She had volunteered for a presentation at the technology high school to discuss job hunting skills with Juniors and Seniors.

Lexie's days allowed her to do her work, pick up Anton after school since Mark dropped him off in the morning and have dinner ready on days she wanted to cook. She was feeling useful and that was making her happy. Lexie saw that she had asked for this life and she openly received what was coming her way.

Brie was enjoying the moment

Brie and Sarah were sitting down at the table double checking her list for Saturday's dinner. She had checked her list several times because she wanted to always impress Chris and Sarah understood that. It would be casual. The menu would include halibut, fresh greens, rutabaga and squash. There was a new independent bakery she wanted to try out so she ordered a carrot cake. The bar was always stocked and she found a couple of punch recipes for the kids. The florist would be there Saturday morning to set up arrangements.Brie was feeling confident everything would go right.

"I'll pick up the ingredients for the punch, Ms. Brie," Sarah told her in her heavy voice.

"Thank you. Do you think I should have gifts?"

"Party favors? Not for this, no ma'am," Sarah offered.

"Okay. Thank you for your help," Brie told her grabbing her iPad and leaving out of the kitchen.

Brie stopped and stared at the living room. She liked the colors and the sea motif. She wanted to add something that said she lived there too. She snapped a picture of the living room with her iPad and made a note to stop by a custom decorator store to have some pillows made.

She walked around the rest of the downstairs to see where else she could add her touch. The media room was always occupied by Chris and Ike. Then there was his office. It was definitely hands off. The dining room was formal and stuffy. She thought about stripping the golden hues and going with something toned down. The family room could be made more kid friendly. Not that anyone really went in there because there was the Florida room. Chris's, and now everybody else's, favorite room in the house.

The Florida room is where everything seems to happen. The kids played there, watched TV there and it was their gateway outside. Brie didn't want to touch it, except for the few pictures of the kids she put up. Walking through the house, Brie felt at home. It was hers to do what she wanted. Chris and his mother were making that clear.

"Lexie was probably right," she said to herself. "This isn't a try before you buy. Chris has something else in mind, and it's not going to take him years to figure it out."

Brie pulled out her phone and sent Chris a simple text. 'I love you.' Within a minute, he sent her one back telling her the same. Brie had what Phaedra was talking about. She had both. She wasn't as much worried about decorating the house with stuff as she was about filling it with love and good memories. Brie pulled up YouTube and searched for Luther Vandross's song, *A House is not a Home*. As the song played, she felt a lift off of her shoulders. Chris loved her as long as she was herself and for once, Brie was happy being just herself.

"What are you doing, Mommy?" Deena asked walking into the room after waking up from her nap.

"I'm dancing," Brie said with a smile as wide as her face. She picked Deena up in her arms and twirled around the living room with her laughing.

"Can we dance to one of my songs?" She asked laughing with her mom.

"We can dance to whatever you would like to dance to Deena." Brie passed her iPad to her daughter and watched her search for a different song to play. It made her happy to watch Deena. Life was good and Brie was enjoying the moment. She was enjoying happiness and letting go of the fear of losing it.

Gratitude

Phaedra had been looking for some property as Ron suggested. The kids were excited about moving but she let them know it would be over the summer after they got out of school. Ron wanted to make up for the last six years, but Phaedra kept reminding him that he couldn't. Phaedra was looking forward and she was confident that eventually he would figure it out sooner or later. The kids were better off, and so was she.

Now that the little silver T-bird was gone, Ron was a little more comfortable at her house. She never confessed to him that it was the dream car she had obsessed about since she was a child. He wanted to buy her a replacement, but she always declined. She had her experience with her dream car, and though it was provided by another man, she would always treasure it. Ron would have to be responsible for his own ego.

For the first time, Phaedra was content. The naysayers told her she was out of her mind if she was giving Ron another chance. She blocked their vibes. Phaedra lived by her gut, and if her gut told her not to do it, then she would have told him to go to hell and gave him the cab fare to get there. Instead, she woke up each morning and said thank you. Sometimes it was at his house. Sometimes it was at her house. However, each morning it was together.

Phaedra had been concentrating so hard on her search that she jumped when her phone vibrated on her desk. "Hey, Lexie," she answered.

"Caller ID took the fun out of being surprised who was calling you."

"That is why it was invented. People got tired of being surprised."

"I guess so. So, were you busy?" Lexie asked.

"I've got a minute. What's up?"

"I wanted to get Brie a gift."

"It's not her birthday."

"I know. We shouldn't have to wait for her birthday to buy a gift," Lexie said.

"Wait. First you said you wanted to buy her a gift, now it's we. How did you wanting to do something turn into us doing something?"

"Because it should be from both us. She has accomplished a lot, including moving in with Chris and adjusting to a new life."

"You make it sound like moving from a rinky dink apartment to a multimillion dollar house was a strain on her," Phaedra said being condescending. "What are we getting her?"

"Can we give with joy?"

"That was joy."

"A charm bracelet," Lexie suggested.

"Why a charm bracelet? That sounds like an odd gift."

"So she can mark all of the stuff from this year. I was thinking a heart, a house, something that would represent a business, and maybe all three kids' birthstones to remind her why she is doing what she is doing."

"That does sound like a nice gesture," Phaedra had to agree. "How are we going to get all of that by tomorrow night?"

"Yeah, I was going to see if you wanted to go to the store tonight or tomorrow afternoon."

"Tonight would be better. I promised Maya we would do a spa day together. She wants the works. A massage, mani-pedi and her hair done. I'm raising a little diva."

"That sounds fun though. I can't wait to have a daughter."

"You and Mark are planning on having kids?"

"Yes. We finally agreed on two because he was trying to fill the house," Lexie laughed.

"Well, don't want a girl too bad because then you will end up with a house full of boys trying for a girl."

"That would be bad. Besides, I don't care what I have. I'm stopping at two."

"So, whatever happened with the Carlos fiasco?"

"I'm suing him for child support. He offered to give up rights after that but I told him no. Anton is his responsibility and it was way past time he started paying. He wasn't happy, and I didn't care."

"Wait, you talked to Carlos?"

"Yeap. My heart was in my stomach the whole time. I was scared but I did it anyways," Lexie explained.

"You go girl. I don't know why you were scared of that stupid little man in the first place."

"He always intimidated me. I could never make him happy when we were together."

"None of that matters now, Lexie," Phaedra said to stop Lexie from traveling back in time. "You have Mark and he loves your crazy ass."

Lexie laughed. "He does, doesn't he. I can't believe we will be married soon. Til death do us part."

"You got that right, because if either one of you try to get out of this marriage, I will shoot both of you. You guys have drug me through some highs and lows breaking up, getting back together, breaking up again. Oh my goodness. Stay the fuck together. You belong with one another."

"The good thing is all that breaking up-getting back together made us stronger,"Lexie said.

"I just ask please give birth to a boy with those pretty green eyes."

"I hope so, but hey, my brown eyes are pretty also."

"Whatever helps you sleep through the night," Phaedra said laughing at her own comment.

"Whatever!" Lexie had to laugh also.

"So, 6:30 a good time? We can grab something to eat, too."

"Sounds good. We are eating something light?"

"Don't I always?" Phaedra reminded her.

"Very true. I will see you then. Love ya."

"Love you too, Lexie." Phaedra disconnected. "A charm bracelet. That is a sweet idea," she told herself.

Phaedra was grateful that life moved forward. It was the ups and the downs that had brought them closer. It took her until 40, but she had women in her life she could call friends. For that, she was the happiest.

Wedding day

It was the morning of her wedding day and Lexie was unusually calm. She spent the night at her mom's house after going out with Phaedra and Brie. Lexie didn't get drunk. She kept it together. Her goal was to get through this day. She was ready to be married and into the daily routine of everyday life. Her mother had told her she was already doing just that since they lived together, but Lexie disagreed. It was going to be different now. The signed piece of paper was going to make the routine different as far as she was concerned.

"So, what all needs to be done this morning?" Roni asked her.

"Let's start with breakfast," Lexie suggested as they stood in the bathroom brushing their teeth.

"What time is your hair appointment?"

"At 10:30. That's like in two hours. Plenty of time."

Roni, with a mouthful of toothpaste, stopped brushing her teeth and reminded Lexie, "Okay, but you know you. It will be 10 and you will be running around like a crazy person."

"No I won't," Lexie told her as she rinsed her mouth. "I'm getting my hair done, then getting my makeup done, and then putting on my dress. Then, I will walk down the aisle, say I do, sign my piece of paper, party, eat, make love, then jump on a plane to Rome. I got this big sis."

The two headed down the stairs to the kitchen and grabbed bowls for cereal. Lexie sliced up a banana in hers and Roni dropped blue berries into hers. Lexie laid a napkin across her pink satin pajama pants and sat at the table texting Mark. Roni grabbed her tablet and pulled up a business blog to read. All you could hear at the table was crunching as the two sat in silence.

Carol had been leaning in the doorway watching her girls. She spoke after enjoying the scene. "You two look like teenagers sitting here. I thought about yelling no electronics at the table."

"Morning, Mom," they both greeted.

"Good morning, ladies." Carol poured herself a cup of coffee and joined them at the table. "I'm proud of you Lexie."

Lexie sat up straight. "Really? Why?"

"Because 18 months ago you didn't know what to do with yourself. I was worried about you. However, you kept going. Kept pushing yourself. You kicked and screamed the whole time, but you never stopped until you accomplished your goal. I'm proud of your resilience."

Lexie smiled. She wanted to cry. She hadn't thought of the journey that took her from being laid off to now having her own consulting business, more time with her son, buying a new home with Mark, and today becoming his wife. "Thank you, Mom. It means a lot coming from you," she said.

The three sat at the table for a while talking while Lexie and Roni finished their cereal. Lexie washed her bowl when she was done and headed for the shower. When she got out, she checked her phone. She had two text from Brie. One to let her know that she was at the church working on the decorations and the next to let her know the florist was going to be on time. Phaedra had also sent her a text. It was five lines of happy faces. She sat on the edge of the bed wrapped in the white terry cloth towel texting them both back. Roni walked in the room and gathered her things so she could take her shower.

"Are you going to announce anything crazy today?" Lexie asked her.

"I hadn't planned on it. Why, would you like me to?"

"Don't be sarcastic," Lexie told her. "I just want to know that when you and Phaedra see each other, no one is going to be weird about it."

Roni was stunned. "She told you?"

"No, but you just did."

"Wow, and I'm a trained professional to not volunteer information."

"Yeah, but I'm a trained professional in Phaedra and Roni. I suspected by the way she is always asking cautiously if you are in town. I want to be mad. I've even cussed both of you out in my head. But, then I realized, why bother. You are both grown, you are both whoe-ish, and she is not the first friend of mine you have slept with."

"Well, I'm glad you only cussed me out in your head. Are you upset that it was at your house?" Roni asked grinning.

"At my house!" Lexie yelled. She shook her head. "I'm not going to let you mess up my day. Wait, the guest room right?"

Roni smiled and walked into the bathroom without answering. Lexie shook her head again and then grabbed the lotion. Lexie got dressed in a pair of faded blue jeans and Mark's marathon t-shirt that he received running the Gate River Run marathon two years prior. Lexie headed back down the stairs and went into the half bath to wash her face and brushed her hair back into a ponytail. She checked on her mom and let her know she was ready. Lexie sat on the couch and waited for the two of them. She laughed, because she realized she was the first to be finish. Lexie stayed calm, awaiting her spotlight moment.

Brie continued to update Lexie until it was time for her to get dressed. She had sent Lexie a few pictures so she could see the progress. Brie was impressed at the masterpiece being created. Eggplant, lilac and silver were placed strategically throughout the sanctuary. She even had them cover the red carpet with a silver gray rug that ran down the aisle and up the stairs. Brie had large eggplant bows tied on the end of each walnut brown pew. There were light purple color hydrangeas and eggplant colored calla lilies in small silver vases making a border leading up the stairs. She was confident for choosing the right people since she would have to leave before it was completed.

It was time to leave and head to Phaedra's house. She left instructions for her assistant. She took one more picture of the front and sent it to Lexie with a caption, 'Looks good. Just needs you and Mark". Lexie text her back to tell her it was beautiful.

Phaedra and Maya were coming back from the beauty salon. She was ready to put on her dress and shoes when she saw the text from Brie saying she was 20 minutes away 10 minutes ago. Ron and Caleb were in the den watching ESPN and arguing about baseball teams. Phaedra yelled at them to go get dressed. She went to her room to do the same.

Phaedra was standing in her closet when Ron entered the room. She was wearing an eggplant colored chiffon dress. It was a knee length, chiffon dress with a strapless, sweetheart neckline. She wasn't crazy about the A-line style of the dress because it hid her best assets. She didn't complain, much, since it wasn't her wedding. "Can you zip me?" she asked him.

Ron was already dressed in his black suit with a gray shirt and a purple paisley tie. He walked over to zip her up and whispered, "You were a beautiful bride."

Phaedra blushed with her smile. "Which time," she asked.

"Both," he answered. "I can't wait to mess your hair up later."

"As long as it's later. A matter of fact, step back. Don't even breathe on me."

Ron laughed. "I might could pin it back up."

"Whatever," she said rolling her eyes. "Brie called. She should be here any minute."

"I'm going to find a snack. You know it takes forever for them to take pictures before we get to eat."

Phaedra leaned in to kiss him. "Okay. Listen for the door."

Just as she said it, the doorbell rang. Ron left out to let Brie in. He directed her to their bedroom. Brie walked in the room with her dress draped over her arm. "Hey, it's me."

"Hi, come on in," Phaedra told her still in the closet. She was putting on her jewelry.

"You look beautiful," Brie told her.

"I love your hair. Turn around," Phaedra said to Brie.

Brie turned to show Phaedra the up do. She had lightened her hair. It was now a chestnut brown. She had a large twist coming up the back and around to the front, zig zagging into a bun on the top. "Thank you. I feel like I slept sitting up all night so it wouldn't mess up."

"Why didn't you wait and have it done this morning?" Phaedra asked.

"Because, as Brielle Jackson, planning architect and owner of Creative Event Planning, I worked this morning. I was at the church at 7:30," she explained.

Brie went into the bathroom and first applied her makeup and then slipped into the lilac chiffon dress. Since she was a double D in the chest, her neckline was square and she had straps that hooked behind her neck. She appreciated the A-line because it cinched her waist and flared out around her hips. "I'm glad this is one of those dresses I can wear after the wedding," Brie called out.

"You won't be able to."

"Why not?" She asked coming out of the bathroom.

"Because I'll be there making fun of you," Phaedra smiled.

"You were one of the mean girls in high school, weren't you?"

Phaedra laughed. "Actually, I was, but I was quiet and sneaky with mine."

"I can see that."

"You were the happy cheerleader, weren't you?"

"Not at all. I stayed in the shadows and blended in. I was on the pep squad though."

"That doesn't surprise me. Glad to be a witness to your light finally shining."

"Thanks. It's nice to feel proud of something I've accomplished. So, have you talked to Lexie?"

"Yeah, but only for a few minutes. I was heading to the salon. She said she was going to hold her breath until she said I do."

"That girl better breathe. This day is going to be fine. No worries."

The two finished getting dressed. Brie switched purses using one of Phaedra's that was a hammered silver evening clutch. It matched her jewelry, including her charm bracelet. They came out of the room and Ron complimented them both. He and the kids would meet them at the church. He didn't have to be there for another 30 or 40 minutes. Phaedra would ride with Brie in her new ruby red Lincoln Navigator that Chris bought her for her birthday.

Phaedra kissed Ron and yelled goodbye to the kids. When they got into the SUV, Phaedra and Brie took a selfie and sent a text to Lexie which read 'we are on our way'. Lexie was relieved because she was tired of talking to Roni. She was ready to cut up with her girls. Lexie was sitting in a chair in the dressing room in just her under garments and the slip for her dress staring in a mirror. In a couple of hours, she would be Mrs. Mark Alexander Leonardi. She still held her breath.

"Penny for your thoughts," Roni said passing her a cold bottle of water.

"My fees are as high as $60 an hour. Penny won't get you a syllable."

"That would be a dollar a minute, barely two cents a second, and you said as high as which means there is a cheaper rate."

"Do you ever just talk? Like a normal conversation?"

"No. Just be thankful I don't charge you my rates," Roni smiled.

"God doesn't like bragging," Lexie told her sticking her tongue out at her. "Truthfully, I'm not really thinking. I'm kinda just waiting. If I just get to tomorrow, I'll be okay."

"Then you'll miss out on all the wonderment of today."

"Whoa, you just sounded human," Lexie smiled and stood up to hug her sister. "Thank you for being by my side today."

"I give you a hard time, but I do have your back. I'm also uncomfortable hugging you while you are in your underwear," Roni said pushing Lexie off of her and laughing.

Lexie picked up the decorative lace pillow that she was sitting on and threw it at Roni. It was nice to finally loosen up. Plus, Roni was right. She didn't want to miss any moments of today.

I'll be the good looking guy at that end of the aisle

Brie and Phaedra had arrived at the church and went in different directions. Brie headed for the sanctuary to check on everything with her assistant. Phaedra headed to the back to check on Lexie.

"Are you going down the aisle like that?" Phaedra asked.

"I think I am sexy enough to pull this off," Lexie teased.

"It would give the church something to talk about."

"Trust me, Sister Simmons would have me skinned alive before I reached the door," Lexie said laughing. "You look beautiful.

"Thank you. Brie looks alright," Phaedra cracked herself up.

"You can't be mean today."

"I know. Just don't tell her that. I don't need her thinking I like her."

"She already knows you do. You can't hide it anymore. I don't know if Ron hit that back wall or what, but whatever it was he released something. You have been different."

Phaedra blushed for the second time that day, which was unusual for her. In her coyness, she could only respond with, "Whatever."

Brie walked in with Roni causing Phaedra to stop smiling and get a little more serious. She said hello and Roni nodded. Roni complimented on how nice she looked and congratulated her on her recent nuptials.

Lexie and Brie hugged and Brie asked, "Are you ready to put on your dress."

"No, I still have an hour. I don't want anything to get on it."

"Have you talked to Anton?" Brie asked her.

"Yes. Mark sent me a picture of him in his little gray suit," Lexie told her as she pulled up the picture in her phone. "Isn't he too cute? He is more excited than Mark and I combined."

"He is adorable. I love his smile. Glad you did this before those front teeth start to come out. He is picture ready," Brie told her.

The four talked and joked. As the minutes ticked by, Lexie's stomach became more and more queasy. Her mom brought her some ginger tea to help her to get calm. Lexie sat back and sipped the tea as her mom talked to her friends. She was grateful to be surrounded by the most important people in her life. This day did make her miss her dad. She closed her eyes and she could feel his presence. His love was surrounding her.

Lexie heard her text alert again. She picked up her phone and notified her little group, "Hey. I got a text from Mark's sister. She is outside and doesn't know where to go."

"I'll get her," Brie volunteered.

Carol turned and put her hand on Lexie's shoulder. "It's time to put on the dress."

Lexie exhaled and then smiled at her mother. "Okay." She stood up and Roni and her mother helped her step into the all lace white dress. There were a hundred satin buttons down the back that they worked on together. The top part of the dress fit tight hugging her hour glass shape and the bottom mermaid tailed out higher in the front. They got her buttoned, her straps on straight and her slip adjusted. Phaedra put the pearl drop necklace that once belonged to Lexie's grandmother around her neck.

Lexie stood in the mirror and adjusted her pinned up curls. She was amazed at what she saw. There she stood in a place she thought was unattainable for her. She was the bride. "I'm going to have everything I want."

"You've always been capable," her mother reminded her.

Her text alert went off again. This time it was Mark. He was at the church. 'I'll be the good looking guy standing at the end of the aisle.' Lexie smiled wide. She text him back, 'On my way'.

Lexie passed her phone to her mom so she could put it in her purse. She checked her makeup, smiled and checked her teeth. Lexie turned to her sister and three bride's maids and said, "Okay, ladies, let's go have a wedding."

The End

Made in the USA
Lexington, KY
20 September 2019